Scandal Becomes Her

Scandal Becomes Her

SHIRLEE BUSBEE

ZEBRA BOOKS
KENSINGTON PUBLISHING CORP.
www.kensingtonbooks.com

ZEBRA BOOKS are published by

Kensington Publishing Corp.
850 Third Avenue
New York, NY 10022

Copyright © 2007 by Shirlee Busbee

All Kensington titles, imprints, and distributed lines are available at special quantity discounts for bulk purchases for sales promotion, premiums, fund-raising, educational, or institutional use.

Special book excerpts or customized printings can also be created to fit specific needs. For details, write or phone the office of the Kensington Special Sales Manager: Attn. Special Sales Department. Kensington Publishing Corp., 850 Third Avenue, New York, NY 10022. Phone: 1-800-221-2647.

Zebra and the Z logo Reg. U.S. Pat. & TM Off.

ISBN-13: 978-0-8217-8024-4
ISBN-10: 0-8217-8024-7

First Printing: July 2007
10 9 8 7 6 5 4 3 2 1

Printed in the United States of America

To my brother,
BILL EGAN, who has waited for far too long
for his book. There are
brothers,
and then there are brothers—
I'm lucky and proud *to have you for mine.*
You've done OK, kid.

And, of course,
HOWARD, my husband,
who shares the adventure
with me—and boy,
do we have some adventures!

Chapter 1

The nightmare came shrieking out of the depths of dreamless sleep. One second Nell was lost in quiet slumber, the next the nightmare had her in its taloned grip. Thrashing amongst the covers of the bed, she fought to escape the ugly images that were flashing through her brain, but it was useless—as she knew from other terrible nights.

As had happened before, she was a helpless spectator to the vicious acts that followed. The setting was the same: a dark place that must have been in some half-forgotten dungeon hidden away under the foundations of an ancient ancestral home. The walls and floor were of massive, hand-hewn, smoke-stained gray stones . . . the wavering light from the candles revealing instruments of torture from an earlier, more savage age in England—instruments that *he* used when the mood suited him.

The victim tonight, as in other times, was a woman, young and comely and fearful. Her blue eyes were huge and full of stark terror, terror that seemed to please her tormentor. The candlelight always fell upon the faces of the women, the man remaining in the shadows, his face and form never fully revealed, yet every act he perpetuated on the young woman's shrinking flesh was horribly clear to Nell. And in the end, after he had done his worst and taken the corpse and carelessly tossed it down the old sluice hole in the dungeon, the light would fade and Nell would finally manage to claw her way up out of the realms of the nightmare.

Tonight was no different. Released from the appalling images, a scream rising in her throat, Nell jerked upright, her sea green eyes bright with unshed tears and remembered horror. Throttling back the scream she glanced around, relief pouring through her as she realized that it had, indeed, been only a nightmare. That she was safely in her father's London townhouse, the faint shapes of the furniture of her bedroom taking shape from the glow of the waning fire on the hearth and the soft dawn light that slipped into the room from behind the heavy velvet drapes. From outside her windows came the familiar London clatter, the sounds of horses' hooves on the cobbled streets and the clang of the wheels of the carts, wagons and carriages that the animals pulled. In the distance she could hear the cries of the street vendors already hawking their various wares—brooms, milk, vegetables and flowers.

A shudder went through her. Ah, God, she thought, burying her face in her trembling hands, will the nightmares never stop? The infrequency of them was the only thing that kept her from going mad—no one, she was convinced, could remain sane if compelled to view such violence night after night.

She took a deep breath and pushed back a strand of heavy tawny hair that had fallen onto her breast. Leaning over, she groped for the pitcher of water her maid had set on the rose marble table near her bed. Her fingers found it and the small glass next to it, and pouring herself a drink, she gulped it greedily.

Feeling better, she sat on the side of her bed and stared into the gloom that greeted her, trying to get her thoughts in order, trying to take comfort from the knowledge that *she* was safe . . . unlike the poor creature in her nightmare. With an effort she wrenched her thoughts away from that track. After all, she reminded herself, it had only been a nightmare. A horrible one, but not real.

Eleanor "Nell" Anslowe had never been troubled with nightmares in her childhood. No bad dreams had ever disturbed her sleep until after the tragic accident that had nearly killed her when she was nineteen.

It was odd, she mused, how wonderful her life had been before the tragedy and how very much it had changed in the months that had followed her brush with death. The spring of that awful year had seen her triumphant London Season and her engagement to the heir of a dukedom.

Nell's lips twisted. Having just celebrated her twenty-ninth birthday in September, as she looked back at that time a decade ago, it seemed incredible that she had ever been the carefree, confident girl who had become engaged to the catch of the Season, the eldest son of the Duke of Bethune. When Aubrey Fowlkes, Marquise Giffard, the heir to his father's dukedom, had declared that he intended to marry the daughter of a mere baronet, albeit a *very* wealthy one, there had been much gossip about the match in that spring of 1794. And there had been even more, Nell thought with a snort, when the engagement had ended, that same year. The same year that she had suffered the horrific fall from her horse that had brought her near death and had left her with a leg that had never healed properly—to this day, she still walked with a limp, mostly when she was tired.

Getting up from the bed, Nell walked over to one of the tall windows that overlooked the garden at the side of the house. Pulling aside the rose-hued drapery, she pushed open the tall double doors that led to a small balcony. Stepping out onto it, she glanced down at the stone terrace below and the sculpted beds and shrubs that surrounded it, the mauve light of dawn fading, and the pink and gold flush of the sun beginning to touch the tallest rosebushes. It was going to be a lovely October day—the same sort of crisp, sunny October day on which she had taken that fateful ride that had changed her life forever.

She had arisen early that morning ten years ago at Meadowlea, the family estate near the Dorset coast, and had hurried to the stables. Heedless of her exasperated father's admonishments not to ride alone along the cliffs, she had brushed aside the services of the groom, and once her favorite mount, Firefly—a sassy little chestnut mare—had been saddled, she had galloped away from the house and manicured grounds. Both she and the mare had been eager to be out in the brilliant sunshine and as they raced on their way, the cool morning air had whipped roses into Nell's cheeks and made her eyes gleam with pleasure.

It was never clear what had caused the accident and Nell, once she regained her senses, never remembered. Apparently her horse had stumbled or reared and they had both plunged over the ragged edge of a cliff. The only thing that had kept Nell from death that day was a small ledge where she had landed, some thirty feet down the otherwise sheer face of the cliffs. Firefly had died on the sea-swept rocks far below.

Nell had not been missed for hours and by the time she was found, dusk had begun to fall. In the flickering light of a lantern, one of the searcher's keen eyes had noticed the torn-up ground near the edge of the cliff and had thought to glance over the side. His shout had brought the others. It had taken hours to bring her up from her slim perch above the sea and, blessedly, she had remained unconscious. Not even when she was finally brought home and the physician had attended to her, setting the broken bones in her leg and arm, did she stir. It was feared in those first days, as she lay like one dead, that she would never recover.

Of course, Lord Giffard was notified immediately. And, she thought sourly, to give him credit, he had come immediately and remained at Meadowlea for the long fortnight afterward while they all waited for her to wake, wondering if she ever would.

For several days after she became aware of her surroundings, she was confused and there was talk that the fall had left her addled. With such a bleak outlook, no one was very surprised when her father, Sir Edward, informed Giffard and the duke that he would understand if they wanted the engagement to end. Giffard had leaped at the chance—after all, his wife would one day be a duchess and the maimed, mumbling creature who lay in bed upstairs at Meadowlea was not the wife he'd had in mind when he had proposed. That November, the engagement was discreetly ended, just five short months after it had been announced.

Nell's recovery had been slow but by the following spring her confusion had vanished, her arm had healed without incident and she was able to limp about the grounds of Meadowlea with the aid of an ivory-knobbed cane. In time the only effects of the near-fatal brush with death that remained were her limp and the nightmares.

Much of what had occurred during her recovery she did not remember. All that was clear in her mind from that time was the nightmare that had haunted her senseless state. The first one that drifted repeatedly through her brain had been different from the ones that wrecked her sleep these days. The victim had been a man, a gentleman, she thought, and the setting had been in a wooded copse. But the ending had been the same: ugly death at the hands of a shadowy figure. Only in later nightmares had women become the prey and the dungeon the favored site for brutality and murder.

As her recovery progressed, Nell had hoped that the nightmare would fade, that it was just some odd remnant connected with her fall. She had been elated that first summer when the nightmare finally stopped. Into autumn and winter she enjoyed month after month of deep, undisturbed sleep. Certain that she had finally put the tragedy and its aftermath behind her, she had been thrilled. Until the nightmare, in its present form, had come storming back to haunt her nights.

Sighing, she turned away from the view of the garden and walked over to poke at the faint embers on the hearth. Like her intermittent limp, the nightmares seemed to have become a permanent part of her. Not, she thought gratefully, that they afflicted her as frequently as her limp. Sometimes an entire year would pass before she was visited with the nightmare, and after each one she would pray that it would be the last. But, of course, it never was. It always came back, with the only changes over time the faces of the women and the degree of savagery. Tonight, she realized with a chill, was the third time this year that she had suffered through the awful thing.

The third time this year. Her breath caught. The knowledge she had been avoiding since she had awakened slammed into her: the nightmares were increasing, the faces of the women changing with horrifying regularity. Worse, in tonight's nightmare, she had the feeling that she had seen the young woman before, that she knew her.

Leaving the fire, Nell picked up her robe from a nearby chair and shrugged into it. She really was going mad, she decided, if she thought that she had recognized tonight's victim. It was pure nonsense. Ugly and appalling to be sure, but it was not real. And if she was foolish enough to think she recognized the woman, well, that was merely a coincidence. It had been, she told herself fiercely, only a bloody nightmare!

Marching into her dressing room that adjoined the bedroom, she poured water from a violet-patterned china urn into its matching bowl. Scrubbing her face and washing her teeth, she forced her mind away from those troubling thoughts. Today was going to be busy; the household was returning to Meadowlea for the winter within the week and there was much to be done.

When Nell reached the morning room she wasn't surprised, despite the early hour, to find her father there ahead of her.

Dropping a kiss onto his balding pate as she passed where he was sitting at the table, she wandered over to the mahogany sideboard positioned against one wall. Selecting a piece of toast and some kippers from the various food displayed there, after pouring herself a cup of coffee, she joined her father at the table.

At nine and sixty, except for his baldhead, Sir Edward was still a handsome man. His daughter had inherited his eyes and his tall, slim build, but her tawny hair and fairy features had come from her mother, Anne—along with the teasing laughter that often lurked in those gold-lashed sea green eyes.

There was no laughter in those eyes this morning and noting the purple shadows under them, Sir Edward stared at her keenly and asked, "Another nightmare, my dear?"

Nell made a face and nodded. "But nothing for you to worry about. I managed to sleep most of the night before it occurred."

Sir Edward frowned, "Shall I send a note around for the physician to call?"

"Absolutely not! He will dose me with some vile concoction, look wise and then charge you an exorbitant fee." She grinned at him. "I merely had a nightmare, Papa, nothing for you to worry over."

Having from time to time in the past been awakened by her screams when the nightmares had been unbearable, Sir Edward had his doubts, but he did not press the issue. Nell could be stubborn. He smiled. A trait she had also inherited from her mother.

For a moment, his expression was sad. His wife had died fourteen years ago, and while he had learned to live without her gentle presence, there were times that he still missed her like the very devil—especially when he was worried about Nell. Anne would have known what to do. A girl needed her mother's guidance.

The opening of the door to the room broke into his thoughts. Catching sight of his son, he smiled and said, "You are up early, my boy. Something important on your agenda today?"

Robert grimaced and, helping himself to a thick slice of ham and some coddled eggs from the sideboard, he said over his shoulder, "I promised Andrew that I would go with him today to look at some bloody horse he is certain will beat Lord Epson's gray. The animal is somewhere in the country and nothing would do but that I agree that we leave London no later than eight o'clock this morning. I must have been mad."

At two and thirty, Robert was the heir and the eldest of Sir Edward's three sons. He resembled his father to a fair degree—tall and rangy, the same color eyes and the same stubborn chin and hard-edged jaw. His tawny hair, Robert thanked providence frequently, he had inherited from his mother, grateful that it was still thick and *there*.

Normally, Robert would not have been staying at the family townhouse. His own rooms were on Jermyn Street but, having closed up the place when he had left for Meadowlea in July, only the necessity of driving home the new high-perch phaeton he had ordered from the London carriage builder had brought him back to town. His brother Andrew had offered to drive the new vehicle home for him, but Robert would have none of it. As he had told his father when he had arrived on Thursday, "I appreciated his offer, don't think I didn't, but I'd as lief let a blind man drive it home as that jingled-brained brother of mine. Drew would be ditched before he had driven ten miles." Sir Edward privately agreed. Drew was known to be reckless.

Casting a glance at his sister as he tackled his breakfast, Robert asked, "Did he tell you about this horse he is so set on buying?"

Nell nodded as she took a sip of her coffee. "Indeed he did. I have been having its praises sung in my ear this past fortnight."

"Do you think there is any chance the animal has even half the potential that Drew claims?"

She shook her head, a twinkle leaping to her eyes. "I saw the creature the first day the owner brought him to town. The stallion is a lovely bay and beautiful to look at, but has no substance or stamina—the usual pretty face that always takes Drew's eye."

Robert groaned. "Oh, lud, I knew it would be the case. I'd hoped that he had learned his lesson from that last bonesetter he bought."

"Give the boy credit," Sir Edward muttered. "He can't help it if he doesn't have the eye for horses that you and Nell have."

"Boy?" Nell burst out laughing. "Papa, have you forgotten that both Andrew and Henry are thirty years old? Neither one of them is a 'boy' any longer."

The subjects of the conversation entered the room just then and it was obvious at a glance that they were twins; Andrew a mere half inch taller and ten minutes older than his brother, Henry. Few people, except those who knew them well, could tell them apart, both having the same aquiline nose and firm jaw and their mother's golden-brown eyes and tawny hair. Shorter than Robert, they stood just over six feet, but had the same slim build as the rest of the family.

Andrew, a major in the cavalry, was serving with Colonel Arthur Wellesley in India. Having been severely wounded during the last days of the war against the Mahrattas, he had been in England for several months recovering. He was due to rejoin Wellesley just after the first of the year. Henry, too was a major, but being less dashing than his twin had elected to serve in an infantry regiment. He had seen his share of battle in Europe, but to his chagrin, he was presently assigned to the Horse Guards in London. Only the resumption of the war with Napoleon the previous year gave him hope that he would soon leave his desk duties behind and once again be in the thick of things on the continent.

"Ah ha," Andrew remarked, a grin slashing across his face, "you are awake. I had a small wager with Henry that we would have to wake you."

"You lose," Robert said, as he pushed away from the table and rose to his feet. "I am ready. Let us go view this incredible horse you have found."

Over Andrew's shoulder, Henry made a face and shook his head. "Waste of time," he mouthed silently to Robert.

Robert shrugged and turning away, took his leave from Sir Edward and Nell. The room was quiet for a moment after the three men had left.

"And what," Sir Edward asked, "do you plan to do today, my dear?"

"Nothing as exciting as buying a horse," Nell replied with a smile. "If we are to leave on Monday as planned, I must make final plans with Mrs. Fields and Chatham. Are you going to leave a few servants here? Or is everyone coming to Meadowlea with us?"

"I can think of no good reason to leave anyone behind, can you?"

"Housebreakers?"

Sir Edward shook his head. "We will take all the silver and plate with us, and except for the furniture there will be little else to steal."

The twinkle in her eye became pronounced. "The wine cellar?"

He smiled. "Secured behind a stout door and barred and locked. Chatham assures me that my wines will be safe."

"Very well then, I shall get busy," she said, rising to her feet. "Far be it for me to argue with Chatham."

As she passed her father, he reached out and caught one of her hands. Surprised, she glanced at him. "What is it?"

Quietly he asked, "Have you enjoyed yourself, Nell? I know this is the first time you have come with me to London in many years. Has it been very bad?" His expression troubled, he added, "Was it difficult seeing Bethune and that wife of his?"

"Bethune?" she inquired in astonishment. "Oh, Papa, I got over him a long time ago—it has been ten years, after all." Seeing that he was not quite convinced, she kissed his head and murmured, "Papa, it is all right. My heart is not broken, even if I thought it was once upon a time." She grinned. "And as for that wife of his—he got precisely what he deserved. He should not have been so quick to throw me over."

"If I had not been so quick to offer him his freedom, then instead of locking yourself away in the country and acting as my hostess, you would have been a duchess, a leader of society," he said, watching her carefully.

Nell wrinkled her nose. "And utterly bored and miserable. I am glad you offered him his freedom—and that he took it. If he cared so little for me that he could so quickly rid himself of me, I am much better without him." She patted his arm. "Papa, I have told you time and again, I am very happy with my life. I like the country. I know that I could come with you to London whenever I want—I *chose* to stay at Meadowlea." When he would have protested, she put a finger against his lips. "And, no, I do not stay there because I fear running into Bethune and his wife, or anybody else, for that matter." Her face softened. "It happened a decade ago, I am sure that few people even remember that I was engaged to him. I do not repine over it and you should not, either." She grinned at him. "Unless of course it is *you* who hungers for a great title for your daughter."

"Don't be ridiculous! You know that my first concern is for you to be happy. A title be damned." He looked wistful. "Although I will confess that I was proud of the grand match you had made. But title or no, I would like to see all of my children married and with their own families." He sighed. "I will be honest, Nell, it baffles me that none of you has married. Robert is my heir—he should be married and have a quiver full of children by now. I would like to dandle a grandchild or two on my knee before I die. As for the twins . . . I would have thought by now that at least one of them would have married."

Nell could think of nothing to say. Her own spinsterhood she took for granted. In the beginning, she had realized that even with her fortune, there were few men who wanted a crippled wife. It didn't matter these days that her limp was nowhere as obvious as it had been during the first few years after her fall, the stigma was still there. And then there was the fact that, for awhile at least, it had been common knowledge in the ton that she had been a bit, well, strange for a time after she had regained consciousness. No gentleman of breeding wanted a wife who might become a resident of Bedlam, the home for the insane. Her eyes hardened. She had Bethune to thank for that bit of lingering gossip. He had wanted to make certain that no blame ever fell in his direction for the ending of the engagement and so he and his family had made certain that her mental state was touted about as being far worse than it had actually been. Supercilious swine.

Touched by her father's concerns, she sank down onto a chair near Sir Edward. Leaning forward, she said earnestly, "Papa, you know that I do not wish to marry. We've discussed it many times—and, no, it is not because I am heartbroken over Bethune. I simply have not met any gentleman who rouses my interest." She smiled. "With my fortune, there is not the necessity for me to marry. Even when you are gone, which I pray will not be for years and years yet, I am well provided for. You do not need to worry about me."

"But it is unnatural for you to remain unmarried," he muttered. "You are a beautiful young woman and, as you just said, you are wealthy, and while we may not have a great title, our ancestry is as proud and grand as any in England."

Nell dropped her gaze and, her expression demure, she drawled, "Well, there is Lord Tynedale . . ."

Sir Edward sucked in a breath, aghast. "That scoundrel! He has gambled and whored away his entire fortune. It is common gossip that he owes so much money that, peer or not, he stands a good chance of being thrown into debtor's prison." He shook his finger at her. "Everyone knows that he is desperate and hanging out for a rich wife. I heard it from Lord Vinton that he actually tried to kidnap the Arnett heiress. Said her father caught up with them before any harm was done. You be careful around him. If you don't watch your step, you might find yourself in the same position." He shook his finger harder at her, saying fiercely, "I ain't blind, you know. I've seen him sniffing around you this past month. Probably thinks that your fortune will do him nicely. You mark my words, gel, he'll beggar you pulling himself from the River Tick." His fire fading, he asked anxiously, "Surely, you would not consider such a match?"

Nell raised a pair of laughing eyes. "Papa! As if I would! Of course I would not consider throwing myself away on such a fellow. I am aware of his reputation—even the gossip about the Arnett heiress—and I assure you that I am very careful around him. If I were to marry, it would not be to a poor creature like Tynedale."

Sir Edward relaxed, a smile curving his mouth. "You should not tease your dear old papa that way, my dear," he scolded. "You could send me off to meet my maker sooner than any one of us would like."

Nell snorted. Rising to her feet, she kissed his baldpate again and made for the door, tossing over her shoulder, "Papa, you worry too much about us. Robert will marry one of these days and I am sure that the twins will not be far behind him. You shall dandle those grandchildren you long for before too many more years pass. You wait and see."

Across town, a few hours later, in the grand London house of the Earls of Wyndham, a similar conversation took place. The present Lord Wyndham, the tenth, having endured one unhappy marriage for the sake of his title and his family, was not about to undertake another. No matter how many tears and scenes were staged by his young stepmother.

Looking across the scattered remains of their breakfast into her tear-filled eyes, Lord Wyndham murmured, "Now let me see if I understand you correctly. You want me to marry your godchild, because if I were to die, your godchild, presumably having presented me with an heir, would ensure that your future was secure?"

The Countess Wyndham, looking far too young to be his

stepmother, stared back resentfully. She was a lovely little thing, possessed of speaking velvet-brown eyes and enchanting dusky ringlets that framed an equally enchanting face. She was also, at five and thirty, three years younger than her stepson.

"I don't see," she muttered, "why you have to take that tone with me. Is my position so hard to understand? If you die without an heir, your cousin Charles will step, no, leap, into your boots. You know that he will toss me and my poor, darling child out onto the streets."

"I thought that you liked Charles," Lord Wyndham replied innocently, amusement glimmering in his eyes.

"I do like Charles well enough," she admitted. "He can be very amusing, but he is a rake and wild to a fault. And his women! You know very well that if Charles inherits that he won't want Elizabeth and me underfoot. You know that he'll toss us out onto the streets."

Lord Wyndham grinned. "Yes, he would most likely toss you out onto the streets—out onto the streets where you and Elizabeth will pick yourselves up and order your carriage brought round to drive you to the Dower House at Wyndham."

Her dainty fingers tightened on her teacup. "Yes, it is true that we could live there . . . buried in the country, in a house that has sat empty for decades and is in need of repair. It is also true that your dear, sainted father settled a handsome sum on me when we married." She leaned forward. "But don't you see, Julian, it isn't just about money. You must remember it may not be Charles who inherits—don't forget that he barely escaped with his life this past summer when his yacht sank and there was that terrible accident with his horses just last month. With his reckless ways Charles may die before you and it may be Raoul who inherits."

She looked pensive. "I like Sofia Weston, but you have to admit that Raoul's mother is a strong-minded woman. If Raoul were to inherit, she would see to it that he wasted little time in marrying, and you can be sure that it will be to some little mouse that Mrs. Weston can keep under her thumb. Mrs. Weston will be the Countess Wyndham in all but name—not my sweet-natured godchild, Georgette. If Charles or Raoul inherit, I shall probably never be allowed to step foot in these halls again."

She buried her nose in a scrap of lace. "These same halls," she said in muffled tones, "that your dear, *dear* father first brought me to as a bride five years ago. How different things would be if something did happen to you, and you were married to Georgette! *She* would see to it that I would always be welcome. And Elizabeth, too. If she doesn't run away and marry that awful Captain Carver." She peeped over the top her handkerchief. "You know the one, the captain in the cavalry, who goes around looking romantic and dashing with his arm in a black sling. Why, I don't even believe he needs it. He is, no doubt, wearing it just to impress my dear child."

Julian sighed. Following Diana's thinking always exasperated his supply of patience, but this morning her thoughts seemed even more disjointed and confused than usual. He glanced at her curvaceous little form and delicate features and he could understand, at least partially, why she had so captivated his father. Of course, he thought dryly, that was the basic difference between him and his father: he would have enjoyed a discreet affair with the young widow, not married her. He sighed again. Not that he blamed his father. His mother had died some twenty years ago and his father had been alone, except for the occasional ladybird, for some twelve years before the taking little widow Diana Forest had caught his eye.

Polite society had been stunned when the ninth Earl of Wyndham had suddenly married the impecunious widow of a lieutenant in the infantry. Not only was she poor, and younger than his only child, but she came with a child herself, her twelve-year-old daughter, Elizabeth.

But the odd marriage had worked and, Julian reminded

himself, Diana had made his father happy. Very. His father had adored her and he had doted on Elizabeth, going so far as to settle a nice tidy sum on his young stepdaughter so that she was not penniless. It was too bad that he had died within two years of his marriage, three years ago, leaving his son with the care of a young stepmother and stepsister. Not that Elizabeth gave him any trouble. Sunny-natured and accommodating, Elizabeth adored him and he had a decided soft spot for his sister by marriage. Of course, he had one for Diana, too—when she wasn't trying his patience.

Recognizing from past experience that Diana had finally come to the crux of her conversation, he asked neutrally, "Do you want me to talk to someone at the Horse Guards about this, uh, Captain Carver? Perhaps the captain can be assigned another post. Say, in Calcutta?"

Diana's eyes opened wide. "Could you do that?"

He smiled, his harsh-featured face suddenly very attractive. "Yes, I could do that—if it pleases you."

She looked uncertain. "Well, I don't think that Calcutta would be very healthy for a man who was wounded, do you? I would feel dreadful if something terrible happened to him. Couldn't you just have your friends at the Horse Guards see that he is kept very busy—too busy to dangle after my daughter?" She paused, struck by a new worry. "Oh, dear, that might not be wise. Suppose it was discovered that you are keeping them apart. Why, they might be compelled to do something rash." In a voice full of horror, she breathed, "Oh, Julian, you don't think that Elizabeth would consent to a runaway match, do you? She is so innocent, of such a sweet, easy-going nature that there is no telling what this man might convince her to do."

His patience at an end, Julian rose to his feet. He needed to escape before *he* did something rash. Bowing in her direction, he said, "Do not worry, Diana. I shall take care of it." Dryly he added, "As I always do."

Chapter 2

Since it was Saturday, and he doubted that he would find his friend Colonel Stanton at the Horse Guards, Julian put off the chore of settling Captain Carver's fate. The problem could wait until the beginning of the week. But Diana was not so convinced and to head off the incipient hysterics he could see brewing, before he left the house that afternoon to follow his own pursuits, he wrote to Stanton, requesting a private meeting on Monday afternoon. He was not worried about the situation and he doubted that Elizabeth would throw her cap over the windmill for a mere captain—no matter how dashing. Elizabeth had a good head on her slender shoulders. His mouth twisted. Unlike her mother.

The woman was quite mad, Julian decided several hours later as he strolled down St. James Street toward Boodle's. Quite mad if she thought he would ever make another marriage based solely on pleasing his family. His lips thinned. His marriage to Catherine had taught him the folly of that!

Catherine had been an heiress, the only child of the Duke of Bellamy and she had been very beautiful. His father had been pleased at the match—Julian had been twenty-nine at the time and to his father's despair, he had not shown the slightest interest in marriage. "Think of the title," Lord Wyndham had exhorted him on many an occasion. "When I am gone, and you stick your spoon in the wall, I want *your* son, not Daniel's—fine boy that he is—to be the one stepping into your shoes. You need to marry, boy, and present me with grandchildren. It is your duty." His father had winked at him. "Pleasant one, too."

When the alluring Lady Catherine had crossed his path a few months later, to please his father, Julian had offered for her. Their wedding had been the most anticipated social affair of the Season of 1795. As he and his new bride had driven away from the reception, Lord Wyndham had fairly rubbed his hands together in glee at the thought of the grandchildren that were sure to be soon forthcoming from the union.

Except, he had thought wrong, Julian recalled grimly. Catherine was not eager for children and Julian discovered almost immediately that behind that beautiful face lived a spoiled and petulant child. Before many months had passed they were openly sniping with each other, and before they were married a year, except for necessity, were seldom seen in each other's company. Neither one of them had been happy, he admitted, and Catherine had probably found him as boring, insipid and infuriating as he had found her. But they had hobbled along together for a few years, like many other couples in their position, and might still be yoked together if Catherine, pregnant and hating every moment of it, had not been killed in a carriage accident. Julian sighed at the memory.

Despite the fact that the marriage had been a mistake, he had never wished Catherine dead and her sudden death had stunned him. He had felt both guilt and grief and it had been years before he could think of her and the unborn child without an anguished pang. It had all happened over six years ago, but Julian would not have been honest if he had not admitted to himself that with every passing year his determination never to marry again had grown. Let Charles or Raoul step into my shoes, he thought sourly, I'll be damned if I tie myself to another woman simply to oblige the family!

He was scowling by the time he walked into Boodle's. Unaware of the fierce expression on his face, he was startled when his friend Mr. Talcott accosted him in the grand salon and demanded, "By Jove, but don't you look glimflashy this evening! And with hunting season just started!" He studied Julian's face. "I'll wager that stepmother of yours has put you out of sorts." Talcott's usually merry blue eyes became thoughtful. "She's a taking little thing, won't deny it, but think she'd drive me mad."

Julian laughed, his dark mood vanishing. Clapping Talcott on the back, he said, "Very astute of you. Now come join me in a drink, and tell me that you have decided to accept my invitation to stay at Wyndham Hall."

They had just started to leave the grand salon when Julian caught sight of a slim blond man. His expression grim, he asked, "Since when has Boodle's started letting any ragtag bobtail join its ranks?"

Talcott looked startled, then, following Julian's gaze, he stiffened. "Tynedale! He is pushing his luck, isn't he? Surely not even he would dare—" Catching sight of the burly man who stood to Tynedale's left, he muttered, "Well, that explains it—he must have prevailed upon Braithwaite to sponsor him."

Julian started forward, but Talcott grabbed his shoulder and jerked him into a nearby small alcove. "Don't be a fool!" he hissed. "You've already fought one duel with him—and won. Leave it be. Challenging him again is not going to bring young Daniel back."

Julian's gaze never left Tynedale's handsome form. "He killed him," he snarled, "as surely as he had held the pistol to the boy's head himself. You know it."

"I agree," Talcott said quietly. "Tynedale ruined Daniel, but Daniel is not the first green 'un to fall into the hands of an unscrupulous scoundrel like Tynedale and lose his fortune at the gaming table. Nor is he the first to kill himself rather than face what he had done—and he will not be the last."

Julian glared at his friend, his expression one of anguished fury. "I remember the day when Daniel was born and his father asked me if I would be willing to be Daniel's guardian if something ever happened to him." He sighed. "We were both half-drunk, celebrating his son's birth and neither one of us ever thought that the need would arise. Why should it? John was only twenty-two and I wasn't even of age—not yet eighteen. Who could have guessed?" Julian looked down, his thoughts far away. "Who could have guessed," he said in a low tone, "that my cousin would be murdered when his son was not quite eleven years old? That I would actually become Daniel's guardian?" One hand clenched into a formidable fist. "John trusted me to keep his son safe, not only from a rakehell like his own brother but safely away from any other danger that might cross the boy's path." His voice bitter he added, "I was so busy making certain that his uncle Charles did not corrupt Daniel that I failed to protect him from the likes of Tynedale."

"Daniel was not," Talcott said bluntly, "your ward when Tynedale fleeced him and he killed himself." His voice urgent, he added, "I know that you loved Daniel's father, I know that John was your favorite cousin and I know that you were shattered when he was killed. But none of it was your fault! Not John's murder, or Daniel's suicide. My God, man! You weren't even in England when Tynedale got his hooks into the boy. You were off playing spy for Whitehall." His fingers tightened on Julian's shoulder. "You have nothing to blame yourself for—let it go." When Julian appeared unmoved, Talcott said quietly, "You bested him in the duel this spring and scarred that pretty face of his—and do not forget, you have the means to ruin him . . . Won't that be revenge enough?"

Julian suddenly smiled, like a big predator in anticipation of an easy kill. "How kind of you to remind me. For a moment just now, I had forgotten that." He studied Tynedale. "I suspect that he has learned by this time that I am the holder of all his vowels. He must be rather desperate, wondering when I shall demand payment—and he knows that I shall allow him no extensions." Julian looked thoughtful. "I had thought that I could take pleasure in watching him twist in the wind before demanding payment, but I find that I have changed my mind. I shall call upon him tomorrow." He smiled again, not a nice smile. "Come," he said, "let us forget about Tynedale for the evening. I find myself in need of a drink. Shall we go?"

Ordinarily Nell's evening would have consisted of an early dinner with Sir Edward and then quiet hours spent reading in the library. During her rare trips to London, she tended to visit bookstores and museums and had never cared much for the giddy round of balls, soirees and such. But since she had reluctantly accepted an invitation to one of the last balls of the Little Season at Lord and Lady Ellingsons's, her evening that night did not follow routine.

The Ellingsons were old friends of her father's, one of the reasons she had consented to attend—that, and his kindly badgering—and he happily escorted her to the ball.

Once Sir Edward had seen her settled amongst several female friends, and Lord Ellingson had completed his most pressing duties as host, the two men had toddled off to the card room. It was several hours later when Sir Edward finally ambled out to the main room looking for Nell.

It took him awhile to find her—she was half-hidden in a quiet corner, deep in conversation with a golden-haired gentleman. Recognizing Lord Tynedale, he frowned. What the devil was that fellow doing here? Then he remembered: Tynedale was related to Lady Ellingson. Lord Ellingson had complained to him often enough of having to entertain the bounder just to keep his wife in charity with him. She doted on him. Most women did.

Eyeing the exquisite form attired in a dark blue formfitting jacket and black knee breeches, his linen starched and glistening white, Sir Edward had to give him credit for his appearance. With thick, curly blond hair and femininely lashed blue eyes, he made a handsome sight. His features were aristocratic, from the chiseled nose to the sculpted jaw, and he possessed a winning smile and a practiced grace. Despite the clear signs of dissipation on his face and a narrow scar across one cheek, considering all his charms, it wasn't surprising that women tended to be taken in by his manner and even thought the scar rather dashing. On the point of marching to his daughter's side and routing a man he plainly labeled a loose-fish, Sir Edward recalled this morning's conversation and hesitated. Nell wouldn't thank him for acting the outraged father. Besides, he thought to himself, she was quite capable of ringing a peal over Tynedale all on her own.

Out of the corner of her eye Nell had seen her father come out of the card room and she was conscious of a feeling of relief. Tynedale had been annoyingly attentive since he had arrived a short while ago and he hovered over her like a bee around a sweet blossom. She was as susceptible to the notice of a handsome man as the next woman was, but aware that it was her fortune and not herself that aroused his interest, she had been trying to keep him at arm's length, to no avail. He was either, she decided, very dense, very desperate or impervious to insults.

Meeting Tynedale's limpid blue eyes she murmured, "Ah, there is my father. I am sure that he is ready to leave—I know I am. I shall be glad to retire and rest."

"Must you go?" He flashed her a warm look. "I am afraid that the evening will become quite flat without your charming presence to enliven it," Tynedale said, a winning expression on his handsome face.

Nell smiled at him sweetly. "Really? When there are at least two other heiresses in the offing?"

His eyes hardened. "Why must you think that my only interest in you is your fortune? Hasn't it occurred to you that amongst all the chattering giddy females here tonight that you, and you alone, are the one who has captured my regard?"

She tapped a painted silk fan to her lips. "Oh, you're absolutely right! How could I have thought any differently? Silly me. After all, I am only suspected of being half-mad, known to be a cripple and as near to being an ape-leader as possible." She looked pensive. "Of course, I *do* have a rather vulgar fortune." She grinned at his expression and added, "Naturally that must put me high on your list of possible brides."

Fist clenched at his side, the scar flaming an angry red across his cheek, he muttered, "This isn't the moment or the setting I would have chosen to approach the subject, but we could do well together, you and I. There is no denying that I could use your fortune . . . and you could use a husband. I may not have a feather to fly with at present, but your fortune would change all that." Tynedale leaned forward, urgency in his voice. "You should consider the possibility—it would be a good bargain for you when all is said and done. Remember, I do have an old and valued title."

"Thank you, no." Insulted and annoyed, she said bluntly, "Since this conversation is already unseemly I will leave you with this comment: I would much prefer being considered an antidote than married to you."

She turned her back on him, only to be swung around by his hand on her arm. Bending his face to hers, he growled, "You will come to regret those words." He hesitated. "You must understand me: I have received unfortunate news and my need is great—I am a desperate man." His voice took on a threatening note. "And desperate men have been known to take desperate measures. Be warned that I am not to be trifled with."

"Take your hand off me," Nell snapped, outraged. Her eyes glittering with indignation, she said, "I will give you a little advice, my lord: I am leaving London on Monday. Who knows when I will next return to the city, but when I do, keep away from me. I do not wish for your company!"

He let go her arm, a nasty smile on his face. "We'll see about that." He bowed. "Until we meet again."

Deigning a reply she swept away, the skirts of her cream- and gold-spangled gown fluttering behind her.

Sir Edward turned at her approach and his gaze narrowed at the expression on her face. He glanced over to where Tynedale stood.

"Should I be issuing a challenge to that puppy?" he asked as he took her arm.

Nell looked startled. "Oh, good heavens, no! Do not give him another thought." She grinned impishly. "I promise you I shall not." She pinched his cheek. "Do not worry, Papa. I will confess that he was brazen enough to suggest a match between us—I think his creditors must be dunning him. Do not let it upset you. I assure you that I gave him a decided set-down, he will not trouble us again."

Sir Edward was affronted. "Suggested a match, did he? Without a word to me? Insolent bounder! How dare he? I shall have a word with him."

Nell grabbed his arm. "Papa! No, do not. I beg you. Re-call, if you will, that I am not an innocent miss dazzled by my first trip to London. I am quite capable of repulsing the at-tentions of a contemptible creature such as he is. *Please* do not let us waste another second of our time on him."

He gave her a searching glance and, satisfied by what he saw in her face he nodded, and beyond a bit of grumbling about the effrontery of certain fellows said no more on the subject.

As Sir Edward escorted her down the steps of the Ellingson residence and into their coach, Nell discovered that it was raining. She had noted the heavy clouds late that afternoon, but she had hoped that they had been merely threatening and would blow over.

Damp from the dash to the carriage and listening to the pounding rain on the carriage top, Nell pulled her velvet cloak closer around her and grimaced. If it was a big storm and lingered, by the time they left on Monday, the roads were going to be atrocious.

A bolt of lightning crackled across the night sky and she flinched. Oh, bother. It was probably, she decided, going to be a long, wet, muddy and, no doubt, harrowing journey home.

A few moments later Nell and Sir Edward were home and rushing inside to escape the rain. After bidding her father a fond good night, Nell hurried up the stairs to her rooms, eager to get out of her finery and crawl into bed.

Twenty minutes later, she was cozily abed, having shed her ball gown and slipped gratefully into a nightgown of soft cambric. Sleep came at once.

At first, she slept dreamlessly, but then, gradually she became uncomfortable, her breathing heavy, her limbs feeling trapped. She moaned in her sleep and twisted in the bed, seeking to escape the invisible bonds that held her. Another nightmare, she thought, as she fought her way up through the layers of sleep.

A particularly nasty one, too, the sensation of smothering, of drowning in blackness almost overpowering. Still half-asleep, she struggled to escape the oppressive blackness, but her hands tangled in the same enveloping darkness of her dream.

Feeling herself sliding across the bed her eyes snapped open and to her horror she discovered that she *was* trapped—in a smothering mass of heavy fabric—and being swiftly hauled out of her bed. Panicked, she writhed and thrashed, her fingers clawing against the cloth that engulfed her in its folds.

"Be still!" hissed a voice she recognized immediately.

"*Tynedale!*" she gasped. "Are you mad? My father will kill you for this—if I don't first!"

He gave an excited little laugh. "I will take my chances. Once you are my wife, I think that your father will change his mind."

"But *I* will not!" she swore and increased her struggle to escape.

The breath was knocked from her as she was lifted and suddenly flung over his shoulder. Keeping one arm clamped across her buttocks, he strode across the room.

Wide-awake now, Nell's brain raced. There was only one way he could have gained entry to the house: from her balcony and in through the unlocked glass doors. But how had he known in which room she slept? A chill slid down her spine. He must have spied on her, followed her home tonight from the Ellingson ball. He would have guessed her father would not retire immediately, but that she probably would. She had as good as told him that she would. Anger poured through her. All he had to do was watch the upper floor and observe in which room the candles were soon blown out. Blast him! And how lucky for him, she thought grimly, that hers was one of the few that possessed a balcony. Her heart sank. It appeared from both sounds and movement that he was taking her out the same way he had entered.

Knowing that every second counted, aware that once he had her away from the house and her father's protection, that all was lost, she dragged in a deep breath and screamed.

His nerves razor-edged, Tynedale jumped at the sound. Cursing he half-fell, half-climbed over the balcony rail. "Bitch! Do that again," he snarled, as they started the perilous journey down to the ground, "and I shall throttle you."

Nell squeezed her eyes shut, suddenly terrified as she felt them swaying wildly in the air. He must have used a rope, she thought. Attached it somehow to the balcony and climbed up it. And now, dear God! We are going down it!

Frightened by the knowledge that if Tynedale's grip on her or the rope slipped she would go crashing to the stone terrace below, Nell remained frozen as he made the descent. The instant she felt his feet thud against the ground, she screamed again, kicking and twisting wildly on his shoulder.

"I warned you," he growled.

His grip shifted and she slid upright. The next instant there was a blinding explosion in her head and the world went dark.

But Nell's screams had not gone unheard. Above the sounds of the storm, Robert barely heard the first scream. But he had heard something and, about to enter the house, he stopped at the door and listened. He had just decided he was imagining things when a faint sound came to him again. The wind and rain and the bulk of the house distorted the sound, yet Robert was convinced that he had heard something. A kitten? A dog howling?

Frowning, he entered the house. Sir Edward was just crossing the black-and-white-marble-tiled floor of the main hall and he smiled in his direction.

"Drew buy the horse?" he inquired with a lifted brow.

Robert laughed. "It was a near thing, but Henry and I convinced him that it would not be wise." The frown returned. "Have you heard anything strange tonight?" he asked.

"Strange? No. Just the usual shrieks and creaks of the storm. Why?"

"I thought I heard something . . ." He shrugged. "It is probably nothing, but I think I'll take a look around before I seek my bed."

Finding nothing amiss, Robert was feeling rather foolish several minutes later when he tapped on Nell's door. He was not alarmed when she did not answer; Sir Edward had mentioned that she had retired just as soon as they had returned home. She was, no doubt, asleep. Robert smiled. Nell was known to sleep like the dead and even with a storm howling outside it was unlikely that anything short of a lightning bolt next to her bed would disturb her. His smile faded. A lightning bolt or one of those damn nightmares.

He stood there, undecided whether to intrude upon her, but prompted by some instinct, he tapped again and hearing no reply, opened the door and entered. Crossing the sitting room, a small candle held in his hand, he peered into her bedchamber, the bed and furniture outlined by the light of the dancing fire on the hearth. A sudden flash of lightning jerked his gaze to the double doors.

He noticed two things simultaneously: Nell's bed was empty and the glass doors to her balcony were thrown wide. Calling her name, in three swift strides he covered the distance to the balcony. It was empty. Only the storm howled back in answer to his next frantic cry of her name.

A terrible feeling came over him as he remembered those nights when she had awakened the entire household with her screams from the nightmares that haunted her. In the grip of who-knew-what horrors, had she stumbled to the balcony and fallen? Standing in the rain-lashed darkness, his heart frozen in his breast, he forced himself to peer over the short railing to the ground below. Relief swept through him when the flickering flame of his candle showed him that Nell's body was not lying crumpled on the stone terrace beneath the balcony.

His relief was short-lived. If Nell was not in her bed, then where was she? A quick search of her rooms did not reveal her presence. He called her name again and again, his voice more urgent each time he called out, but only the sounds of the storm met his ears. Uneasiness growing by the second, he raced downstairs. Finding his father pouring himself a brandy in the library, he demanded, "Are you certain Nell went to bed?"

"Said she was," Sir Edward replied, surprised by Robert's interest in his sister's whereabouts. "Did you look in on her?"

"Yes—and she is not there. I cannot find her anywhere. I've looked." Robert bit his lip. "The doors to her balcony were thrown wide."

Alarm on his pleasant features, Sir Edward put down his

brandy and swept past his son. With Robert on his heels, Sir Edward hurried to Nell's rooms.

The wind and rain were pouring in through the doors that Robert in his anxiety had left open. Paying it no heed, both men quickly lit several candles.

Nell's room was ablaze with light and in that bright light both men stared in mounting fear at the muddy boot prints that marred the surface of the cream and rose carpet that covered the floor. Muddy prints that led from the balcony to the bed and away again . . .

"I knew it! I knew he was up to no good. It is that bastard Tynedale!" Sir Edward burst out, his face a mixture of horror and fury. "He has abducted her! And is probably at this very moment on his way to Gretna Green. We must stop them."

"Wait!" Robert said, when Sir Edward would have run from the room. "I know it looks suspicious, but how do you know that it is Tynedale that took her? I agree that it appears that someone has taken Nell, but we must completely search the house first. We will feel perfect fools if there is a simple explanation for this."

Looking at him as if he had lost his wits, Sir Edward snapped, "You rouse the servants and have them look. I am ringing for the coach and sending a note around to the twins—we may need their help. We must not delay."

Drew and Henry, full of anxious questions, arrived shortly. Upon hearing what was feared, outraged and hungry for Tynedale's blood, they were impatient to set off in pursuit. The search of the household was completed and beyond a scrap of delicate material caught on one of the bushes leading away from the house, there was no sign of Nell.

Within moments of finding the scrap of material, Sir Edward and Robert were in the family coach and rattling over the London streets. Drew and Henry, swathed in greatcoats, their heads bent against the storm, had chosen to ride astride and their horses splashed alongside of the swaying coach.

Until the coach was clear of London, Sir Edward and Robert sat grim-faced and tight-lipped, neither inclined to talk. Finally leaving the city behind them, Sir Edward tapped on the roof and sticking his head out the window, yelled to his coachman, "Spring 'em!"

The driver cracked his whip and the horses leaped forward. The coach, flanked by the twins, rocked and lurched through the night, the blackness lit now and then by the silvery flashes of lightning.

Tynedale possessed nothing so luxurious as a coach—his had been sold weeks ago to pay off his most pressing debts. He was driving his curricle and even with the top up, he and Nell were pelted with rain as he urged the pair of rented horses on to greater speed. He didn't believe that anyone had heard Nell's cries, but he was taking no chances. Besides, he had to have her safely hidden away by daylight. He had known from the beginning that Gretna Green on the Scottish border was not feasible—and the first place the family would look for her. He smiled tightly. There were other ways to bring about a hasty wedding . . . Once he had compromised her, he was confident that their marriage would follow immediately. All he had to do was get through the next twenty-four hours and all his problems would be solved.

Tynedale glanced over at Nell sitting next to him. She held herself rigid, one hand wrapped around the leather strap to steady her swaying body, her eyes fixed on the galloping horses in front of her. Wrapped from head to toe in the concealing folds of his cloak it was unlikely that anyone—anyone fool enough to be out on a night like this—would recognize her. The blackness of the night would have shielded them, anyway, and the storm was a stroke of luck.

He would have preferred to have planned the abduction more carefully and he certainly would not have chosen a curricle in which to make his escape, but the news that Nell was leaving London on Monday had left him with no time to make other plans. That and the news that Wyndham had bought up all his vowels. Bloody stiff-necked bastard! Wasn't it enough that Wyndham had beaten him in that duel earlier this year and scarred him for life? It wasn't his fault that Wyndham's ward had been weak and unwilling to face the loss of his fortune. "Play or pay" was his motto and if the boy couldn't stand the nonsense, then he shouldn't have played . . . Tynedale smiled. Especially since the dice were loaded. It was a pity what had happened and he'd admit that if he had known that the boy would take such final and drastic action, that he might not have *completely* ruined him. But his own needs had come first and he had needed the Weston fortune to bring himself about. And I should have followed my first instincts, he thought grimly, and with the Weston fortune at my fingertips, put my own affairs in order. He sighed for the lost chance. But once a gambler, always a gambler, and he had been convinced that his luck had finally turned. With an ill-gotten fortune to back him, he was positive that he could recoup all of his former losses. If one fortune was nice, two would be even nicer. With that thought guiding him he had continued his reckless gaming and whoring. It wasn't until he had discovered himself once again on the verge of ruin a few months ago that he had begun to cast around for a way out of his difficulties. Marriage to an heiress seemed the only answer.

He glanced again at Nell's set face. Yes. Marriage to an heiress was the simplest solution. And Eleanor Anslowe suited him. She knew the ways of the world and having reached her majority, her fortune was hers to command—his, once they were married. Sir Edward might puff and rail, but there was nothing that he would be able to do. Once Nell was married to him, all his worries would be over.

Her courage waning with every mile that took them farther from London, Nell stared out into the night. She was exhausted. Fright had taken its toll and her leg was aching unbearably. But she was not beaten and she was not going to make Tynedale's task easy for him. She had a fair idea what he had planned and she knew, with a sinking feeling, that she would not be able to prevent him from raping her. She swore to herself that even if he succeeded in his evil plans and she had to hide her face in shame for the rest of her life, she was *not* going to marry him! She took a deep breath. She would get away from him. Somehow.

Since it was unlikely her screams had been heard or that she would be missed until the morning, her escape was going to have to be of her own devising. She looked out at the rain-drenched countryside revealed in the flashes of lightning. She had no idea how far they had traveled from London and in the darkness everything looked different, anyway. She doubted that Tynedale was going to stop soon, but she determined that when he did finally pull the horses to a halt that it would be then that her best chance for escape would present itself. And if there were other people around so much the better. She wasn't a bit averse to revealing his perfidy.

Nell's chance came sooner than she expected. A jagged bolt of lightning streaked across the night sky and struck the ground less than fifty feet in front of the racing horses. The very ground seemed to shake and the carriage shuddered. The gigantic flash was followed by a boom of thunder that sounded like the end of the world was at hand. The horses screamed and reared and fought Tynedale's nervous jerk on the reins. One horse slid on the muddy road and became tangled in the traces; the other was plunging and rearing, fighting to escape. Tynedale could not regain control and the curricle was dragged off the slick road. As the vehicle lurched drunkenly into a ditch at the side of the road, the nearside horse broke free and galloped off into the darkness.

Nell was almost thrown from the curricle by the accident, but she managed to stay inside the vehicle. Tynedale was not so lucky. The jolt and plunging of the curricle pitched him into the ditch.

Cursing, he climbed to his feet. Clutching his shoulder, he

surveyed the damage. In the midst of one of the worst storms he'd ever seen, one horse was gone, the vehicle was mired in a muddy ditch and if he wasn't much mistaken he had broken his collarbone. The night could not get much worse.

But it could. Nell hesitated not a moment. The instant the curricle came to a rest, ignoring her throbbing leg, she scrambled down from the vehicle and stumbled for the protection of the trees that edged this section of the road. She heard Tynedale's shout behind her but the sound only added wings to her flying feet.

The trees enveloped her and she gave fervent thanks for the night and the storm. Heedless of the branches that whipped at her and the debris that tangled around her feet she plunged forward, deeper and deeper into the concealing forest. Tynedale's cloak impeded her progress, but she dared not throw it aside—her white nightgown would be a beacon for him—if he was following. She stopped once, listening intently, but beyond the furious howl of the storm, she heard nothing but the frantic beating of her heart and her own labored breathing. She smiled suddenly. She had no idea where she was; she was cold and sodden and frightened, but, by God, she had gotten away from him!

Chapter 3

Nell stood under the branches of an oak tree for several more moments, catching her breath and planning her next step. The fury of the storm had not abated and she was aware of the danger of lingering beneath the tallest object in the area.

Pulling the cloak up over her head to shield herself from the worst of the rain, she left her shelter and began the arduous task of finding her way out of the rain-slick forest. It was not easy; she fell to her knees many times, sliding on the slippery branches and brush beneath her bare feet. The rain and the lightning and the booming crash of thunder overhead did not help matters. Nor did the utter blackness of the night and the wind that howled through the treetops.

Time was suspended and Nell lost all sense of direction. Now and then as she fought her way through the darkness, she had the eerie feeling that she was trudging in circles and she feared that she would walk right into Tynedale's arms. Her first burst of euphoria at having escaped from him had vanished long ago, and as the minutes played out and she grew wetter and more exhausted and her leg began to ache and drag, she almost hoped that she *would* stumble into him. Almost.

Thunder rolled overhead and a second later, right in front of her, a bolt of lightning slashed through the darkness. The strike was so close Nell was knocked to the ground. Several minutes later, dazed and shaken but unhurt, she scrambled to her feet. More importantly, in that blinding flash of light her disbelieving eyes had spied a cottage or hut a few hundred yards in front of her.

Hope surging through her, she half-stumbled, half-ran toward the promise of shelter. Another blaze of lightning revealed that she had not been mistaken and, her breathing ragged and labored, she fought her way to the small building that sat in the open, a few yards from the forest.

It was indeed a cottage and relief poured through her. She was safe! Help was at hand. But with a sinking heart she became aware that there was no welcoming candlelight flickering in the tiny windows and no sign or sound of human habitation. Suppressing a sob, she sagged against the wooden doorjamb, disappointment knifing through her as she realized that the dwelling was abandoned and deserted.

But at least the place offered shelter and, gathering the last of her strength, she pushed open the door. The door gave way easily and another streak of lightning revealed that there was nothing to steal or pilfer beyond a scarred table, three or four rickety chairs and a bed of rushes against the wall.

Despite the rubble on the floor, leaves, branches and the worthless debris left behind by its previous inhabitants, the interior looked like a palace to Nell as she stepped inside and out of the bruising storm. Relying on the lightning bursts, she explored her domain on unsteady feet.

The place was small, consisting of just two rooms, the one she had first entered and one other. There was a rough stone fireplace and some old faggots resting on the hearth, but they did her little good—she had no way of starting a fire.

Having completed her survey, she dragged herself back to one of the dirty windows and looked outside. She glimpsed a wide, muddy expanse of road through the rain and lightning and guessed that she had stumbled upon an abandoned toll keeper's cottage. Travelers would once have had to pay a toll to travel this portion of the road, but no longer, and hadn't for some time, if the condition of the cottage was anything to judge.

At the moment none of that mattered to Nell, she was simply grateful to be out of the storm and free of Tynedale. Feeling battered and exhausted, too worn out to think beyond the next second, she wrapped her damp cloak around her slim form and somewhat gingerly made herself comfortable on the bed of old rushes.

Her back against the wall, her legs curled beneath her, she sat watching the lightning as it danced and dazzled in the darkness. She shivered from the cold, her torn and bruised feet were throbbing, and she was conscious of a great weariness stealing over her. At least the intensity of the storm was lessening, she thought drowsily, the crash and boom of the thunder just a faint growl in the distance, the lightning no longer so terrifyingly near.

A huge yawn overtook her and she blinked sleepily. Tynedale was still a danger to her, but she was beaten. She could run no farther and it was possible, indeed likely, that she had given him the slip. Her mouth twisted. Of course, it was also possible that the road in front of the cottage was the Great Road North that Tynedale had taken from London and that at any moment he would come driving up to the front door of the cottage. She yawned again. She didn't give a damn. She had run her race and could not run any longer. Her head dipped and a second later her body followed. She slept sprawled on the rushes, her small frame concealed by the heavy folds of the cloak.

Cursing the storm, his stepmother and particularly his stepsister, Julian urged his horse forward. Of all the devilish inconvenient, inconsiderate things to have happened! He still didn't quite believe that he was out in the black of night, far from London in the wee hours of the morning, riding along in the midst of one of the most powerful storms he had seen in many a year. Blast Elizabeth! If she was going to make a runaway match with Carver, why the hell couldn't she have chosen less inclement weather?

The wind tore at his cloak, and rain blew down on him while the lightning and thunder made his horse shy and dance crookedly down the road. He didn't blame the horse— he was miserable, too. And wet. And tired. The jagged streaks of lightning exploding across the black sky did not help the situation, the bay stallion snorting and half-rearing at each strike. It was a thoroughly unpleasant ride.

At this hour, Julian thought bitterly, he should have been at home, warm and asleep in his own bed, and he would have been if Diana hadn't fallen on his neck the instant he had returned home. As he tried to disentangle himself from Diana's stranglehold, he became aware that his spacious hall seemed awash with people. Meeting Julian's eyes, Dibble, his butler, had sniffed and declared that he knew nothing of the affair. Elizabeth's maid suddenly left off wringing her hands and wailed that she had only been obeying Miss Elizabeth's orders by not delivering Elizabeth's note to Lady Wyndham sooner. Clinging to him, Diana had shoved the tear-damp note under his nose, sobbing that he must save her baby. Now.

Ignoring the note that Diana seemed insistent upon thrusting up his nose, Julian pushed it aside and taking Diana by the arm, escorted her into the morning room and got the tale out of her. It seemed that Miss Forest, chaperoned by Lady Milliard, Julian's great-aunt, had not yet returned from the Ellingsons's ball. The hour was not late and Lady Wyndham, having attended a social function of her own, had only returned home a short while ago. She had not been alarmed by Elizabeth's absence until Elizabeth's maid delivered to her, not ten minutes previously, a note stating that she was running away with Captain Carver.

Julian was disinclined to set out in pursuit. His ride home in the sedan chair he had hailed upon leaving Boodle's had already acquainted him with the fact that there was a wicked storm moving through the area. And if Elizabeth was damn silly enough to throw away her future on Carver, let her! But Diana's sobs and pleadings finally overcame his common sense and convinced him that it was his *duty* to stop such an imprudent match.

Grumbling and muttering, he ordered his horse brought round and changed his clothes. Within a matter of minutes, a broad-brimmed hat pulled across his forehead and swathed in a many-caped greatcoat, he was riding hell-bent for leather out of London. As the weather did its best to make his ride a nightmare, and he doggedly pressed forward, his thoughts were not kind toward his stepsister. In fact, he rather thought that he would beat Elizabeth soundly and throttle young Carver when he caught up with them.

The weather continued to worsen and he considered seeking shelter until the bulk of the storm passed, but the need for haste was imperative if he was to overtake Elizabeth and her gallant. The weather and the condition of the road, which was slowly turning into a slick, muddy slop, made for treacherous going and Julian cursed again the fate that had sent him out on a night like this. His only comfort was the knowledge that Carver and Elizabeth were somewhere out there ahead of him in the storm and he bloody-well hoped that they were having as uncomfortable a time of it as he was.

He smiled grimly from beneath the brim of his drenched beaver hat and thought about how this thankless task seemed a fitting end to an evening that had gone sour from the moment he had laid eyes on Tynedale, at Boodle's. Oh, the time had passed pleasantly enough, but even when he had appeared at his most relaxed and urbane, his mind had been on Tynedale and his nephew's senseless death. The anniversary of Daniel's suicide was just over a month away and he suspected that he would be able to face it with far more equanimity if Tynedale had been brought to justice.

But before he could seal Tynedale's fate, he thought wearily, he had to catch his erring stepsister and rescue her, whether she wished for rescue or not, from the dashing Captain Carver.

Catching sight of a vehicle resting drunkenly half-in, half-out of a ditch, his pulse quickened. Could luck be on his side? Had the lovers been thwarted by the storm?

Pulling his horse to a stop, Julian stared down at the curricle, disgust on his face. Only a damn silly fool, and a lovesick one at that, would have chosen a curricle in which to make a runaway match—and on a night like this. He studied the scene in the flashes of lightning. The pair of horses that had been pulling the curricle were gone and so were the inhabitants of the vehicle.

The sky lit by an incandescent arrow of lightning, he looked down the road and smiled. He would have them now. Knowing Elizabeth, he thought it unlikely that she would relish riding astride through a raging storm. They had probably holed up at the nearest house or tavern—and that, he concluded, was the first reasonable decision they had made tonight.

It was a desolate stretch of road that he was riding along and after he had ridden another few miles, his confidence began to flag. He did not think that he missed any signs of habitation, but in the dark and the rain it was possible.

A blinding flash of lightning sent his horse screaming and rearing up in the air. Dancing on two hind feet the stallion could not find purchase on the slippery road and despite Julian's effort to control him, horse and rider went over backward.

Instinctively Julian kicked free of the stirrups and dived to the right. The last thing he wanted was for the stallion to come down on him. Both he and the horse landed hard and Julian winced at the pain that bunched in his shoulder as he hit the muddy ground. Horse and man immediately scrambled to their feet and ignoring his painful shoulder, Julian lunged for the dangling reins. The stallion shied and spun on his heels and Julian watched in furious dismay as the horse disappeared into the darkness.

Slapping his ruined hat against his leather breeches, Julian swore. Bloody hell! It had only needed this.

All thoughts of Elizabeth vanished. Finding shelter and seeing how badly he had hurt his shoulder were now his first priorities. Knowing that he had passed the last sign of habitation miles back, there was nothing to be gained from following after the horse. Resigned to a miserable walk, he set off in the opposite direction taken by his fleeing mount.

If he had thought he had been miserable previously, he had not realized how much *more* miserable he could become, but he soon learned. The mud dragged at his boots, the wind buffeted him unmercifully and the rain was incessant. Never mind the idea of being struck by a falling tree or lightning— by the time he had fought his way two miles away from where he had parted company with his horse he almost welcomed it.

He had just begun to consider seeking shelter in the forest when he realized that he recognized the area—particularly that half-dead, gnarled oak tree at the edge of the road. Unless he was mistaken, there was an abandoned toll keeper's cottage just a short distance ahead. Bending his head and shoulders into the wind, he plowed forward. Finally making it around a bend in the road, his persistence was rewarded; through the blowing rain, he glimpsed the building he sought.

He sprinted the last few yards and sank against the door. Pushing the door open, he entered the dark, musty-scented cottage. Bliss flooded him. It didn't matter that the cottage was only one level above a hovel, all that mattered was that he was no longer at the mercy of the elements. He shut the door behind him and with it the storm and its fury.

Picking his way across the littered floor, guided by the angry brilliance of the lightning outside, he reached one of the chairs and sat down in front of the cold hearth. He sat there for several minutes, letting the quiet of the cottage, after the brute force of the storm, wash over him.

Chilled and shivering, he forced himself to move. A fire was his first priority. The old faggots were aged and dry and since he carried his tinderbox in one of the pockets of his greatcoat, as well as a brace of pistols, shortly he had a meager fire flickering on the smoke-stained hearth. The faggots would not last long and he ruthlessly sacrificed one of the chairs to keep the fire going.

His immediate need taken care of, he took an all-encompassing glance around the room, noting for future reference the bed of rushes and the crumpled rags upon it. When necessary, the rushes could be used to keep the fire burning, and the table and the rest of the chairs, for that matter, he thought grimly—they were certainly otherwise useless.

He took off his soaked greatcoat and using one of those chairs arranged the heavy garment off to one side of the fire. His hips resting against the table he pulled off his boots and stockings, aware that they were ruined. He shrugged and checked for the knife hidden in his right boot. Carrying the knife was a practice begun after one of his errands on the continent for the Duke of Roxbury, one from which he had almost not returned. Finding the knife, he carelessly slipped it into the waist of his breeches and placed his boots, the stockings draped over them, near the chair holding his greatcoat.

Seated in one of the remaining chairs, he stretched his long legs out toward the fire, wriggling his bare toes in sybarite pleasure as the heat from the fire toasted them.

Checking his shoulder he was pleased to discover whatever he'd done when he fell was minor and would heal on its own. He sighed in contentment, pulling at his rumpled cravat. The cravat undone, he tossed it on the table and absently loosened his fine linen shirt.

All I need now, he thought drowsily, is a mutton pie, a bottle of port and a willing wench. He smiled; his head drooped and sleep took him.

*   *   *

Nell's father and brothers did not find sleep so easily. Having left London well ahead of Julian, they had come upon the tipped curricle some time before he had, and after a cursory inspection of the abandoned vehicle, had pressed onward. There was nothing to identify the curricle as having been owned by Tynedale—it could easily have belonged to some other unfortunate soul. On the off chance that it had been the vehicle used to spirit Nell away, they were alert for any sign of wandering pedestrians as they rode through the pounding storm. The abandoned toll house they passed by; with no sign of life to betray its presence, they overlooked it in the rain and darkness.

Sir Edward and his sons traveled swiftly, anxiety and fury mingling in their collective breasts. Sir Edward's main thoughts were for the safe return of his daughter; those of his sons were of a more savage nature. Once they finally overtook Tynedale, and there was no doubt that they would, Tynedale would be lucky indeed if he lived to see another sunrise.

At every inn or tavern, and even the few houses nestled near the road that they came upon, they halted long enough to satisfy themselves that Tynedale had not stopped and taken refuge within. As the hours passed they grew weary and more discouraged and the confidence of the twins began to lag. Having ridden astride they had suffered the most from the vicious strength of the storm and when a shabby little tavern appeared on their right in the early hours of the morning, they were more than willing to stop.

The tavern was set well back from the road, almost hidden by a copse of shaggy trees, and if not for the winking yellow light coming from one of the windows, they would have ridden on by. A few bony horses were tied to the hitching rail, their backs hunched against the storm.

Leaving their horses to the care of the Anslowe coachman and the grubby ostler who had stumbled out of the tavern at the sound of their arrival, the four men entered the building.

The tavern did not look to be the sort that catered to the gentry, but they were too discouraged and exhausted to care very much that the place was more likely the haunt of local highwaymen and suchlike than of gentlemen like themselves. All they wanted was a place to warm themselves by the fire and to partake of a drink of hot punch and perhaps swallow some sustenance.

The arrival of four gentlemen caused a stir, and after some furtive observation, a few of the inhabitants disappeared out the back door. The others watched the gentry with curiosity.

Sir Edward had begun to remove his greatcoat when he caught sight of the man seated at a scarred oak table near the fire.

"*Tynedale!*" he roared, striding across the room. His three sons having spotted their quarry almost simultaneously were fast on their father's heels, their expressions murderous.

At the sound of his name, Tynedale glanced up from his contemplation of the tankard in front of him. He blanched and leapt to his feet. His gaze darted about for a way of escape, but there was none, the Anslowe men crowding him back into the darkened corner. The other inhabitants watched with interest, but no one moved to intervene.

Robert's hand was at Tynedale's throat, his face dark with fury. "Where is she?" he snarled. He shook Tynedale like a dog with a rat. "Speak! If you wish to live another second, tell us what you have done with her."

Tynedale gargled some reply. Despite the icy cast to his eyes, Sir Edward said to his son with deceptive mildness, "My boy, perhaps if you loosen your grip just a trifle . . ."

Reluctantly Robert did so, his fingers relaxing fractionally.

Tynedale gasped for breath and his eyes everywhere but on the faces of the men in front of him, he muttered, "Have you gone mad? Why did you attack me?"

Robert's teeth were bared as he growled, "You know very well why we are here. Damn you! Where is she?"

Recovering somewhat, Tynedale said, "I can see that you

are laboring under great duress and for that reason, I shall not hold you accountable for your action." Tynedale lifted his chin. "I am afraid," he said, "that I have no idea what you are talking about. And as for a female . . . I am traveling alone—you may have seen my ditched curricle several miles back." He nodded in the direction of the tavern keeper, a brawny fellow who stood behind a long counter watching the exchange. "If you do not believe that I am alone, ask him. He will tell you I arrived here an hour or more ago and that no one else—male or female—was with me."

Robert's hand tightened and Tynedale's fingers clawed at the choking hold. "What have you done with her? Tell me or I will throttle you where you stand."

"Er, excuse me, sir," said the tavern owner in a diffident tone. "We don't have many gentry stopping here and I do not mean to intrude into the business of my betters, but I can assure you that what the gentleman said is true: he arrived alone."

Not content with the tavern keeper's word, Sir Edward insisted upon a thorough search of the place. It did not take long and revealed no sign of Nell. Even an inspection of the ramshackle building that passed for a stable at the rear of the tavern turned up no clue as to Nell's whereabouts.

Tynedale vehemently protested his innocence despite dire threats from Robert and the twins. As the minutes passed, Sir Edward began to have doubts. Perhaps he had been wrong. Nell had been snatched from her room, of that he was certain, and Tynedale seemed the likely culprit. But was it possible that he had been mistaken? Dread filled him. Had his darling daughter been spirited away by some nefarious fellow with something uglier than a runaway marriage on his mind? Was she, perhaps, even still in London, having been whisked away to some den of iniquity, to be forced into whoring? He shuddered. It was not unheard of for comely females to find themselves in such a position, but for it to have happened to someone of Nell's station seemed impossible and Sir Edward could not believe that she had suffered such a fate. The fact remained, however, that someone had snatched Nell. With Tynedale eliminated, he could only wonder whom. And for what reason?

They could get nothing more out of Tynedale and eventually, with many a black look, removed themselves to a small table as far away from him as possible to discuss the situation. At a loss to know what to do next, it was decided that Sir Edward and Robert would return to London, watchful for any sign of Nell along the way. They were agreed to not abandon the suspicion that Tynedale had been the one to steal Nell. Because of that, and the impracticality of attempting a covert action with the coach, Drew and Henry would pretend to leave with them, but they would secret themselves nearby and watch and follow Tynedale. It was possible that he had hidden Nell somewhere nearby. And if he had . . .

It was the ache in her leg that woke Nell. As she struggled upright, daylight was seeping into the cottage, but it was cold and gray and a glance out the window revealed that the day would be the same. The worst of the storm seemed to have passed—a steady rain was falling but nothing like the downpour of the previous night. And Tynedale had not found her. With her back once again against the wall, she stretched and rubbed her eyes, disoriented from the events of the previous night.

The room felt warmer and Nell wrestled out of Tynedale's cloak and pushed it aside. She looked down at her nightgown and made a face. Even protected by the cloak, it was ripped and torn in places and splattered with mud and who knew what other disgusting substances.

A sound—a snort? a cough?—alerted her to the fact that she was not alone. Heart banging in her chest, she rose unsteadily to her feet. Her gaze fell upon the greatcoat and boots a second before she spied the dark head of the man who slept in a chair in front of the dying fire.

She gasped and shrank back, terror flooding through her. Tynedale had been bad enough, but to be at the mercy of a stranger, possibly a robber, a murderer or a highwayman was far worse. At least Tynedale had not frightened her. Not really.

Her gasp had been soft, but it had been enough and in one lithe movement the black-haired man surged to his feet. He spun around to face her, a silver-bladed knife appearing in one of his hands.

Nell's eyes dominated her face, the tawny hair hanging in tousled glory around her slim shoulders. Helplessly she stared at the tall man who confronted her, thinking she had never seen such a dark, dangerous face in her life. His eyes were a bright, glittering green beneath the scowling black brows; his black hair was untidy and tumbled across his wide forehead. The word dangerous came again to her as she stared at him.

She would not have called him handsome, but there was something about those granite-hewed features that made Nell think that, in other circumstances, she might have found him attractive. His nose was certainly handsome, straight and haughty, and those hooded jade green eyes with their thick lashes were mesmerizing. His mouth was wide and well shaped, the upper lip thin and the bottom one full. As she stared, his lips lost their grim line and a smile appeared. A very, *very* appealing smile.

"Forgive me," he said in a cultured voice for such a rough-looking fellow. "I did not mean to startle you." Before Nell's astonished gaze, the knife disappeared and he added, "I did not realize that anyone lived here."

"Oh, I don't—" she caught herself and cursing her impetuous tongue, looked away from him.

Over his first shock at finding himself not the sole inhabitant of the cottage, Julian frowned as he studied the slender creature in front of him. He cast a considering glance around the room, his frown increasing. The place was a hovel, a mere shell, and revealed none of the usual effects found in even the poorest of homes. And the girl . . . No, he decided, not a girl, a woman, young to be sure, but past the first blush of youth. The woman did not belong here. The lace at the throat and cuffs of her tattered nightgown was too fine and that face . . . Instinct shouted that all was not as it seemed.

The sight of that fairy-fashioned face left him reeling, as if a fist had slammed into his belly. He was breathless and dizzy at the same time. The sensation had been so powerful, so unexpected, that it was a wonder that he had recovered quickly from the jolt she had given him. Unsettled, as much because of the effect she had had upon him as a strong feeling that there was something very wrong about this situation, his gaze narrowed as he stared at her.

Her eyes were downcast and she was chewing uneasily on her bottom lip. A bottom lip that Julian found himself fascinated with, the strong desire to replace her teeth with his own sweeping through him. That lip would be warm and so very sweet . . . His gaze swept down her slender form, his loins suddenly pulsating with a decidedly inappropriate reaction. Cursing the unruly member that swelled in his breeches and annoyed at his wandering thoughts, he pushed aside the unexpected and unwelcome notion of dalliance and considered the situation.

She did not belong here, of that he was convinced. There was something about her . . . Her night attire spoke of wealth—at least at one time—and aside from their effect on him, her features had an aristocratic cast to them. The skin was too pale and fine to have suffered the effects of poor food and the unsanitary conditions that many of the common folk endured. And there was nothing common about her. She was no tavern slattern, or hulking farm maid, nor an apple-cheeked milkmaid. There was something about her, an air, an impression of gentle breeding, that puzzled him. Her form was dainty and appealing; the flowing tawny hair gleamed with good health, and no lice that he could see.

He shrugged. Nothing would be gained by simply staring at her, although he found it, to his unease, vastly enjoyable.

"You don't—?" he asked gently, picking up the thread of conversation.

Confused, Nell stared up at him. It took her a moment to realize that he was referring to her earlier exclamation. She quickly gathered her thoughts, deciding to stick to as close to the truth as possible.

"This isn't my home—I do not live here," she said carefully. "You may have passed my curricle a few miles back. The horses spooked during the storm and broke free of the traces. There was nothing for it but for me to remain here, while m-m-my driver went to find help." Left unexplained was why she had been out on such a foul night in the first place and only garbed in her nightgown.

"I see."

"I hope you do," she added, looking down her delightful little nose at him. Boldly she demanded, "And you? How is it that you are here?"

He smiled that singularly attractive smile. To Nell's dismay, her knees turned to mush.

"I, too," he admitted, "am the victim of the storm. My horse bolted and I sought shelter here. I did not realize that you had already taken possession."

She nodded regally. "Well, these things happen. Now if you will give me a few moments privacy, I shall gather my things and be on my way."

"Will you not even give me your name?" he asked, with an upward flick of his brow.

"N-n-no, that is not necessary. We are strangers. Let us leave it at that."

"I think not. Allow me to introduce myself." He bowed. "I am Julian Weston," giving his family name, "and at your service should you need it."

She looked uncertain, thinking that he must be one of those gentlemanly highwaymen often mentioned in the newspaper. "Thank you," she responded shyly. "But it will not be necessary. M-m-my driver will be along any moment. You may be on your way."

In the distance the sound of an approaching vehicle gave credence to her words, but Julian paid no attention. He knew that he should turn away from her, but he could not. She was a mystery to be solved and heaven knew that curiosity had gotten him into more than one quagmire in his life.

Fascinated against his will, all his instincts telling him to turn his back on her, Julian looked her up and down, noting with a smile the pink toes peeping from beneath the bedraggled hem of her nightgown. He found those dirty little digits charming and deciding that he was quite mad, he forced his gaze upward. His eyes landed on the small, high bosom and he could not look away, the most lascivious urges flashing through his mind. He jerked his gaze away and swallowed. Lud! Had he been *that* long without a woman?

Keeping his eyes averted from her troublesome form, he muttered, "It would be ungentlemanly for me to leave you alone in this place."

Nell nearly stamped her foot. "I assure you that I shall be perfectly safe."

"Will you?" he asked, his gaze fixed on her mouth. "Will you, indeed? Shall I show you precisely how dangerous your position is?"

Her eyes widened as he reached for her. She leaped backward, but that blasted leg of hers buckled as his hands closed round her shoulders. She fell, dragging him to the floor with her.

They landed in a heap, Julian on top of her. His warm weight crushed her to the floor and, panicked, Nell struck him. "Let me go!" she gasped. "You are no gentleman to treat me so! My father will have your hide if you dare touch me."

Julian smiled down at her, the feel of her slender body beneath him the most delicious sensation he had ever experienced. Rape, however, had never appealed to him and two things were apparent: she was an innocent and wanted none of him. But that mouth was an overwhelming temptation and he coaxed, "One kiss, poppet. Just one."

"Never! Let me go you beast!" Nell put a great deal of outrage in her voice. It was difficult. This stranger, felon or highwayman, was the most devastatingly appealing man she had ever met, but pride alone, and a strong dose of common sense, demanded that she extricate herself from this invidious situation immediately. Sharply she said, "I insist that you let me go. Now."

"I would, if I were you," said Sir Edward, from behind him, "do as the lady requests. Otherwise, I shall be compelled to shoot you in the back—like the piece of offal you are."

"And if he were to miss," drawled Robert, at his father's side, "I should not. If you wish to live, unhand her this instant."

Chapter 4

Julian had been in hazardous positions before, but none that had left him feeling so silly. He rolled off the young woman on the floor and onto his back, considering and discarding hasty plans to escape with his life—and possibly his dignity intact. Finding himself facing two narrow-eyed gentlemen, the pistol in the younger man's hand aimed at his heart, he threw any concerns about dignity to the winds and concentrated on saving his life. He did not recognize the two men who stared so menacingly at him, but he did recognize them as belonging to the gentlemanly class. He sighed. He really would throttle Elizabeth when he finally got his hands on her. If she had not taken it into her mind to run away with her dashing captain, none of this would have happened. Julian was fair—it wasn't his stepsister's fault that he had been found rolling around on the floor with a young woman who was obviously *not* the sort to enjoy a stolen kiss, but it *was* because of Elizabeth that he was here at all. And if he managed to avoid being shot this morning, he had every intention of letting her know in just what a devil of a fix she had landed him.

Gazing at the two men before him, he considered using his knife, but he hesitated. The two men probably had good reason for looking so outraged and lethal and he suspected their attitude was brought on by something more than his, uh, friendly tussle with the wench lying next to him. Despite their looks and the pistols, he sensed that he wasn't about to be shot—at least not at this moment. So who were they and what was their connection to his companion?

The answer came from the fascinating creature herself. Scrambling awkwardly to her feet, the drag of her left leg very noticeable, she half-stumbled, half-fell into the older man's arms. A sob broke from her as he clasped her to his bosom. "Oh, Papa!" she cried. "You found me! I so hoped that you would."

Julian's lips twisted. Oh, lud! He had certainly plunged himself into a tangle this time. The fetching little baggage was the gentleman's daughter. His position became even more invidious—even the most indulgent parent would not look kindly upon finding the daughter of the house lolling about on the floor with an unmarried gentleman. He frowned. *Any* man, for that matter. But what the devil, he wondered with a frown, had she been doing here alone and garbed in nothing more than a nightgown? It appeared that her lack of proper attire was just another mystery connected to the young woman and, of course, he had always been intrigued by mysteries . . .

The two men forgot about Julian as they reassured themselves that the woman was unhurt. Since they were not paying attention to him, he sat up. The younger man recalled instantly to his presence flashed him a glance and said, "Do not move, you black-hearted villain! How dare you lay a hand on my sister!"

Well, that was a relief, Julian thought, he had been a trifle worried that the younger man had been a husband—and husbands, in his opinion, were very unreliable when it came to their wives . . . especially wives found in the arms of other men.

The younger man stared at him puzzled. "Do I know you?" he asked. "You look familiar to me—have I seen you before? Perhaps in London?"

"He says his name is Weston," said the young woman, turning in her father's arms to stare at Julian with troubled eyes.

"*Weston!*" exclaimed the younger man. "Are you related to Wyndham?"

Julian smiled wryly. "Despite my less than sartorial elegance at the moment and the pressing need for a bath and a barber, I am indeed related to Wyndham. I *am* Wyndham."

"Never say so!" exclaimed the older man. He studied Julian's face and despite Julian's unshaven cheeks and rumpled clothing and his resemblance more to a dangerous brigand than to the elegant Earl of Wyndham, Sir Edward realized he spoke the truth. "Yes, I recognize you now," Sir Edward said. "You have been pointed out to me. I have seen you about London." He looked bewildered, but politeness took over. Putting away his pistol, he motioned for Julian to rise and said stiffly, "I am Sir Edward Anslowe. This is my son, Robert, and my daughter, Miss Eleanor Anslowe."

Julian rose to his feet and bowed. "My pleasure—although I could have wished to meet you under more pleasant circumstances."

Frowning, Sir Edward looked from his daughter to Julian. "I do not understand any of this," he began slowly, "but what in blazes, man, was your reason for snatching my daughter from her very bed last night? Was it some infamous wager you made? I cannot believe that a gentleman of your stature would act so dishonorably and seek simply to ruin her." Looking even angrier and confused, he demanded, "If you fancied her, why did you not approach me? We are not as wealthy and powerful as your family, but our name is a proud one and my daughter is an heiress in her own right— surely you must have known that I would have approved your courtship."

Nell gasped and glanced horrified up at her father. "Papa, I have never laid eyes on the man before this morning! And he is not the person who t-t-took me away last night—that vile creature was Tynedale."

Julian stiffened. "What does Tynedale have to do with this affair?"

"I think a better question," said Robert, as he put away his pistol, "would be what do *you* have to do with Nell's abduction?"

Leaning his hips against the table, Julian crossed his arms over his chest and said, "I had nothing to do with, er, Nell's abduction. It is an unfortunate set of events that has brought us together." He glanced at Sir Edward. "My presence here is by accident—my horse bolted during the storm last night and left afoot I remembered this place and sought refuge. I had no idea that anyone else was here."

Sir Edward cast an uneasy look down at Nell. "If it was Tynedale who snatched you last night, how is it that we found you alone this morning with Lord Wyndham? And in a most compromising position?"

Forgetful for the moment of his own precarious position, Julian watched the volatile emotions that rushed across Miss Anslowe's face. She shot Julian a burning look. "It is not *my* fault that you found us in such an awkward situation!"

Julian smiled sunnily at her, thinking that she really was a taking little thing with those fairy features and tumbled tawny hair. Which was just as well, he decided dryly, since he had a very strong notion where this was going. He sighed. He had sworn never to marry again, but fate seemed to have other ideas. At the moment, he didn't see any honorable way out of the circumstances *except* marriage. And there was the mention of Tynedale. He was not a stupid man and he had already put together much of what must have happened last night. Tynedale had been the abductor, but the clever wench had escaped from him and found her way to the abandoned toll house. That the young lady was an heiress explained much; Tynedale had planned a runaway marriage. Julian eyed Nell, noting again the high bosom and slender form only partially hidden beneath her thin garment. And if he knew Tynedale, and he did, Tynedale's interest had not been just in her fortune. She was a fetching armful, and if he could deprive his enemy of her, well, putting his head into the parson's mousetrap was a small cost to pay.

Nell gritted her teeth at Julian's smile. Turning her back on his aggravating presence, she spoke to her father and brother. After assuring them that she had escaped from Tynedale with her virtue intact she finished by relating the sequence of events that had brought her to the toll house. "I slept so soundly that I never heard him"—she flashed Julian a dark look—"enter the building. My first indication that anyone else was here with me was when I awoke this morning."

Sir Edward rubbed his chin, looking unhappily from Julian to Nell. Julian knew what was on his mind.

Sighing, he straightened his shoulders and said, "Sir Edward, I understand your predicament and though none of this is anyone's fault, except Tynedale's, I am prepared to do the honorable thing and marry your daughter."

"Marry you!" Nell hooted, green eyes derisive. "I think not, my lord! Why I don't even know you." Her gaze narrowed. "And from what little I have learned of you, I don't like you—you are the last man in England that I would marry!

"Er, I'm afraid that you don't have much choice in the matter," Sir Edward muttered.

"What do you mean?" she demanded, glancing from one set face to the other.

"Nell," Robert explained, "you were alone through the night with him. It doesn't matter that, uh, nothing happened between you. The point is that you were with him in an intimate setting with no chaperon. If it is discovered you will be ruined."

Nell's chin went up. "I don't care! I will not marry him. My reputation is my own and I don't give a fig what some filthy minded people may think."

"But I do care," said Julian silkily. "I do not want it bandied about that I seduce and ruin young women. Nor would I deliberately bring shame and scandal upon my family—even if you would."

Nell's fists clenched at her sides. "I would do nothing to dishonor my family—even," she said between her teeth, "if it meant I had to marry you. But do not forget that no one else knows what happened." She glanced nervously from one grim male face to the other. "And as long as we do not speak of it, no one need know."

"What about Tynedale?" Julian taunted. "He'll know."

"He knows that I escaped, but he doesn't know about this place or you!"

Robert and Sir Edward exchanged a glance. "We will see to Tynedale," Sir Edward said. "While his abduction failed, he must be brought to account."

"And how," asked Julian, "will you do that? You cannot bring him before the magistrate—not if you want tonight's events to remain secret. And if you chose a duel to settle the matter, that act would give rise to speculation as to its cause. Sooner or later the reason for it would come out. And, consider if you will, Tynedale might not be above blackmail."

"Blackmail, but how?" asked Nell. "Of course he could threaten to tell that he abducted me, but what would be the point? And if he did reveal what happened, he would face rejection and scorn. He would not dare."

"Can you be so certain?" Julian inquired with a lift of his brow. "He is a desperate man—and vindictive. He might not care about the consequences."

"Hmmm, you are right, we cannot run the risk that he would not try his hand at extorting money from us," agreed Sir Edward, nodding. He sighed. "And we would certainly pay to keep him quiet."

"Oh, this is utter nonsense!" declared Nell. "We could remain here all day and come to no conclusion." She looked at her father. "Papa, I am very tired. I am chilled to the bone, dirty and hungry. Please, may we just go home and put this dreadful experience behind us?"

The sound of an approaching vehicle caused them all to freeze. They listened intently as the sound of horses' hooves and the jingle of a harness grew near. A moment later the vehicle slowed and Nell held her breath, half-hidden behind her father. Please, she prayed, let them travel onward.

Her prayer was not answered. A male voice called out, "Hallo, the house! Sir Edward, are you there?"

Sir Edward looked undecided as he glanced at the others. "It is Humphries—he must have recognized my carriage parked outside."

"Not," Julian asked in hollow accents, "the Lord Humphries who is married to Lady Humphries?"

A strident female voice was heard. "Of course he is there. Are you blind? That's his coach, his crest is upon the door and that is his coachman, Travers, as you very well know. I wonder what Sir Edward is doing here? Help me down so that we may investigate."

Sir Edward cast a look at Julian and smiled grimly. "The very same. And I see by your expression that his lady's reputation as the greatest gossip in London is known to you." He sighed. "I am afraid that this changes things, my lord."

Julian shrugged. "I already offered to marry your daughter, sir. Lady Humphries's arrival does not affect that."

"I am not," Nell hissed, "going to marry you."

"You don't have any choice," Julian replied, an unwarranted feeling of satisfaction building within him.

The next instant, an elegantly attired gentleman and a small, equally splendidly dressed woman entered the room.

"Ah, there you are, my friend," said Lord Humphries, his kind blue eyes alighting on Sir Edward. He glanced around, a frown puckering his forehead. "Is something wrong?"

Lady Humphries spied Nell and taking in her bedraggled

appearance, she smiled brightly. Here was scandal, as sure as she was born. Her birdlike gaze fell upon Julian and her eyes widened. Wyndham! Now this was most interesting, indeed.

Flicking aside the skirts of her russet and fawn traveling gown, she marched up to Nell and questioned, "Why Nell, dear, whatever has happened to you? You look ghastly. And Julian! My boy, what is going on?"

While Nell stared at her in dumb horror, Julian stepped into the breech. "I take exception to your words, Lady Humphries," Julian murmured, as he bowed and kissed Lady Humphries's outstretched hand. "You are speaking to my bride-to-be, you know," adding with the charming smile for which he was famous, "and I will not have you casting aspersions on her undeniable beauty."

Even against Lady Humphries that smile had its usual effect and she smiled girlishly—despite having celebrated her seventieth birthday the previous month. "Your bride-to-be!" she exclaimed. "Oh, the hearts that will be broken over this announcement." She looked around. "But tell me, why are you all here?"

Her question paralyzed the Anslowes. But still holding Lady Humphries's hand, Julian said smoothly, "An accident. The storm, you know. Sir Edward had given me permission to pay my addresses to his daughter and I thought a ride in the countryside to a private little meadow I know of would be an appropriate place to lay my heart before Miss Anslowe." He smiled conspiratorially at Lady Humphries. "My instincts were correct and having received the answer I longed for, we were on our way back to London when we were over taken by the storm . . . a, uh, wheel came off my rig, leaving us stranded, and we were forced to seek shelter here." He waved an encompassing hand toward the silent Anslowe family. "Fortunately, before there could be any hint of impropriety, knowing we were in an open carriage and that we would be caught unprepared by the storm, Sir Edward and Robert arrived. The storm was at its height and we, er, decided it would be unwise to travel back to London. We spent the night here, together. We were just preparing to leave when you arrived."

"I see," murmured Lady Humphries. She knew very well that she was being fed a Banbury story. There was a great deal that was being left unsaid, but short of calling Wyndham a bald-faced liar, she saw no way of learning more. What she did know, however, was fascinating enough. Why, once it was learned, and she would make certain that it was learned, that she had come upon the newly engaged couple under such extraordinary circumstances, she would be the most sought-out person in England this winter. Everyone would want to hear the story from her lips—and she was certainly eager to tell it.

Smiling at the quartet, she murmured, "Well, if there is nothing that we can do for you, we shall be on our way." She looked arch. "I will look forward to reading your announcement in the *Times*."

With all the enthusiasm of a condemned prisoner approaching the gallows, Nell watched Lord and Lady Humphries depart. Her gaze fell upon Julian's enigmatic features and she grimaced. She was engaged. To *him!*

As the Humphries's coach rumbled away, Julian glanced at Sir Edward and said, "I believe the presence of Lord and Lady Humphries settles the matter, sir. As of this moment, your daughter and I are officially engaged—you can be certain that Lady Humphries will be spreading the word amongst the ton. I would suggest that we leave for London immediately—before we have any more visitors. You may leave it to me to insert the notice in the *Times*."

Sir Edward concurred, and shortly the four of them were in the Anslowe coach and headed for London. Except for planning the details of the coming nuptials, and it was decided, despite Nell's objections, that the marriage should take place speedily, there was scant conversation among the quartet—particularly between the newly betrothed couple. As the coach rattled and bumped its way over the rough road, beyond terse replies to any question sent her way, Nell contented herself with glaring at Julian, and Julian passed the time by wondering if he hadn't gone mad.

After Catherine's death, he had determined never to marry again and in the intervening years, he had seen nothing to change his mind. And yet here he was contemplating that very act. It was true that it had been thrust upon him and that there had been no other honorable choice, but he was discovering that the notion of marriage to Eleanor Anslowe did not fill him with quite the distaste and resentment he should have felt. He must be mad, indeed, he finally decided. Why else was he viewing this turn of events with such cheerful acceptance?

His cheerfulness fled the instant he was let down from the Anslowe coach and prepared to mount the steps to his townhouse. He paused, staring at the disappearing coach, the events that had been set into motion last night flooding back. His stepmother would be inside, no doubt frantically waiting for news of her daughter. He made a face. Regrettably, he had nothing to tell her about Elizabeth and he was confident that the announcement of his impending wedding was not going to be met with resounding acclamation. Quite the reverse. Lady Wyndham might yearn for him to marry, but it was clear that she already had his bride picked out—a bride who would be biddable and bow to her stepmama-in-law in all things. He doubted that Miss Anslowe would be a young woman who would meet with his stepmother's approval. He grinned. No, definitely not. Miss Anslowe's intelligent eyes and sharp tongue made it clear that she was not a meek and malleable creature who could be easily manipulated by his stepmother—or anyone else, for that matter. He shook his head. His domestic life was certainly going to be very, *very* lively during the coming weeks. Uncertain whether to laugh or curse, he mounted the steps and entered the house.

Julian had expected to be met by a hand-wringing Lady Wyndham and he was astonished that the first person who rushed up to meet him was Elizabeth. The heavy front door had barely shut behind him before Elizabeth, her brown eyes full of anxiety, the skirts of her primrose muslin gown billowing out behind her, catapulted into the grand foyer.

Relief washed over her features as she ran up to him and flung her arms around him. "Oh, Julian!" she breathed, her expression contrite as she hugged him. "I am so sorry, so very sorry, that mother sent you off on such a sleeveless errand! When I returned last night from Ranelagh Gardens—" She stopped at the look on his face. She smiled wryly. "Yes, that is where I went last night instead of the Ellingsons's ball. It was to Ranelagh Gardens that Captain Carver escorted me, not Gretna Green! Even without a storm in the offing, I knew that we would be late and that Mama would not approve of either the lateness or the place—even if dear Millie was with us, and so I left her a note so she would not worry." She sighed. "I never dreamed that she would think that I would be so foolish as to run away with Captain Carver or that you would allow her to bully you into coming after me." She dimpled. "I am flattered that you would do so and I thank you very much for being so kind." Her eyes danced. "You should have known better, however—as you have told me often enough, I am much too expensive for the likes of a mere captain." She tried to look demur but failed miserably.

Julian burst out laughing. "Baggage! I spent a most miserable night because of you, but I am glad to see that my estimation of you was correct."

She grinned at him. Taking his arm and pulling him toward the front saloon, she said, "I imagine you are longing for your bed and bath, but come in and tell Mama that all is well. She has been terrified that you will be in a raging temper when you discover that your gallant actions were all for naught." Glancing up at him, she asked, "Was the weather very bad? And are you very angry with Mama?"

He wasn't and that startled Julian most of all. He would have assumed that his reaction upon discovering that there

had been no reason at all for his journey through the storm—
a journey that had led to his subsequent engagement to a
young lady who obviously did not like him—would have
been one of fury. He discovered instead that he was not at all
angry with Lady Wyndham, in fact, he had a notion that he
should thank her. And again it occurred to him to wonder if
he had gone mad.

Patting Elizabeth's hand where it lay on his arm he murmured, "Nay, I am not angry with your mother. And, yes, the
storm was very bad."

Elizabeth stopped and stared up at him. "I must say, Julian, that you are taking this rather well. I would be furious
to have spent the night riding through a storm, only to have
discovered that there was no need for it. I am so glad that
Flint caught up with you with mother's message to return
home. I'd hate to think of you still riding madly toward Scotland." At Julian's start of surprise, she said, "Surely you didn't
think that we would let you continue on your journey without trying to send word to you that it was no longer necessary? Just as soon as I returned home last night and had
calmed Mother, we sent him after you. You had almost three
hours head start on him and unless you stopped along the
way, we didn't think he would overtake you until late this
morning—if then." Suddenly realizing that Julian was home,
long before he should have been, she frowned. "Flint did find
you, didn't he?"

"Er, no. We can only hope that he will enjoy the Scottish
countryside—or did one of you think to give him alternative
orders, should his mission not be successful?"

"Of course! I am not a complete ninny. I told him that if he
had not managed to catch up with you by this morning that
he was to turn around and come home."

"Leaving me to continue onto Scotland?" he asked dryly.

"What else could we do? There was no reason for two of
you to be haring off all the way to Gretna Green. Besides, I

knew that if you found no trace of me by morning, that you would know further chase was futile and return home anyway." She glanced at him, a tentative smile curving her mouth. "So all is well that ends well?"

"From your perspective, yes."

Elizabeth frowned. "What do you mean?"

"Only that it was a most momentous night for me." He sighed. He had hoped to put off explanations until later in the day when he was more in command of his senses, but it seemed he could put paid to that plan. And a few more besides, he admitted wryly, thinking of Talcott's mention of the hunting season. "Come along, let us go find your mother. I have an announcement to make that will affect all of us."

At Julian's entrance, Lady Wyndham rose to her feet from the chair in which she had been sitting. Her cheeks pale, one hand pressed against her bosom, she exclaimed, "Oh, I know that you have every right to be furious with me, Julian, but please, please try to understand my feelings last night. I was an utter fool, but I was blinded by a mother's love for her only child. Surely you can understand?"

"It is all right, Mama, he is not angry with you," Elizabeth said quickly. Crossing to her mother's side, she urged her to return to her seat.

Lady Wyndham ignored her and, looking at Julian, said dramatically, "If you wish never to lay eyes on me again, I will not blame you." She glanced away and bit her lip. "We have no place to go, but if you cannot find it in your heart to forgive me, we shall remove ourselves from your sight this very afternoon."

"Oh, don't talk fustian, Diana," Julian begged. "I am in no mood for you to turn a simple misunderstanding into a playhouse tragedy. I am partly to blame—I should have read the bloody note. I'm sure that I would have put a different interpretation on Elizabeth's words and would not have gone tearing off into the teeth of a storm. We are both to blame for me spending a deucedly uncomfortable night. I forgive you. I am not angry with you. I understand your emotion. So I beg you, let us put it behind us."

"T-t-that's very h-h-handsome of you," Lady Wyndham stammered. A dazed expression on her face, she sank back down in her chair.

Elizabeth had taken the chair next to her mother. Holding Lady Wyndham's hand in hers, she asked, "What is it that you wanted to tell us? You said that you had an announcement to make."

The room suddenly felt stuffy and Julian was aware of a hollow feeling in his chest. Both women were staring expectantly at him and he cravenly considered postponing the moment. To what avail? he asked himself. There was no answer. He cleared his throat. "I am to be married," he said baldly. "To Eleanor Anslowe. On Wednesday next."

"*What?*" shrieked Lady Wyndham, jumping to her feet. "Surely my ears have deceived me? You could not possibly have said that you are going to be married and to-to-to Eleanor Anslowe."

"Married, Julian? You?" demanded Elizabeth, staring at him big-eyed. "I did not know you were contemplating marriage. And to Miss Anslowe? I didn't know that you had even met her."

"Oh, I have met her, all right," Julian admitted. "And it is true that until, er, very, *very* recently I had never considered marrying again." He glanced at Lady Wyndham's stunned features. He was not fond of lying, but he saw no reason for the ladies of his household to know the whole truth of his decision to marry. In fact, for the success of his marriage and Miss Anslowe's comfort, he could think of several very good reasons why they should not be told the truth. Yet, they had to be told something. Inspiration struck and he added, "Actually, it was your mother's idea."

"*My* idea?" Lady Wyndham exclaimed, her eyes nearly starting from her head. "Have you gone mad? It is true that I mentioned the possibility of marriage to you, but it was my godchild, Georgette, I put forth as a suitable bride, not a woman who has been on the shelf for years—and a cripple in the bargain."

"I would not," Julian said gently, but the expression in his jade green eyes gave Lady Wyndham pause, "refer to my bride-to-be as a 'cripple' again. She pleases me and that is all you have to know."

"Of course," Elizabeth said quickly. "You must forgive Mama—it is a shock."

"Yes, yes, a great shock," repeated Lady Wyndham, following her daughter's lead. Curiosity rampant in her voice, she asked, "But how did this come about? You have never given a clue to anyone that you were thinking of marriage again."

Julian had often thought that spying for the Duke of Roxbury had been dangerous. He had frequently been in situations where he had been forced to think on his feet if he wished to escape with his life, but he had never felt so exposed to sudden death as he did during the next half hour. The ladies had numerous questions and he fielded them as best as he was able. He stuck to the premise that he'd taken Lady Wyndham's words to heart that he should marry. And that at his age, he had not wanted a very young bride. He had met Miss Anslowe several times over the years, he said mendaciously, and had been much struck by her calm, good sense and, er, deportment. When Lady Wyndham protested, he trotted forth the indisputable facts that the Anslowes were an old and respected family and that Miss Anslowe was an heiress.

By the time he escaped the interrogation and fled to his rooms, the worst was behind him. Lady Wyndham was resigned; Elizabeth, who had met Miss Anslowe several times and had liked her, was intrigued and, from the gleam in her eyes, he suspected, suspicious of his glib story. But Lizzie was a good sort and she wasn't likely to throw a rub his way, he thought, as he sank into a tub of hot water. Besides, his story of meeting up with the Anslowes last night and of the four of them being stranded in the storm together at the abandoned toll house had been a brilliant stroke. It was true that it differed somewhat from the tale he had told the Humphries, but it held together, and he expected that there would be several versions of the story all over London in a matter of days. One more would not hurt anything and the main facts were the same: he and Nell were to be married and he and the Anslowes had been found together in the abandoned toll house.

Of course, Lady Wyndham and Elizabeth had to have an expanded version and he had gone on to explain how impressed he had been by Miss Anslowe's uncomplaining nature and nobility throughout the night. Lady Wyndham's words had come back to him and it had suddenly occurred to him that Miss Anslowe would make the perfect bride for him. Before he knew what had happened he had declared himself and been accepted. That story differed slightly as well, but it satisfied the ladies.

Slumped bonelessly in the deep copper tub Julian groaned pleasurably as the heated water gradually worked its magic on his exhausted body. Bliss. Sipping a goblet of warmed wine, tenderly handed him by his butler, Dibble, he decided that he might live after all. And perhaps, after a meal and a few hours of rest, he might be able to flesh out his original story. He shook his head as he recalled the tale he had spun out. Elizabeth might be suspicious, but she had thought it all very romantic and that, he thought with a grin, might be enough to keep her from asking more questions.

Despite the weariness that dragged at him, Julian was pleased with the outcome. He had gotten over the heavy ground as lightly as possible and he had stuck to the truth, or at least, the truth that would be ladled out for public consumption. The facts of his story melded well with what the Humphries had seen. There was going to be gossip and speculation aplenty, but no one could prove that he or the Anslowes were lying. Once he and Miss Anslowe were married no one would dare question the circumstances. His mouth tightened. Not unless they wished to face him on the dueling field. And he was very, very good when it came to duels.

His thoughts strayed to Tynedale. Tynedale must be livid that the heiress had slipped through his fingers. And he would be even more infuriated when he discovered into whose hands she had fallen. Julian smiled, but it did not reach his eyes. Thwarting Tynedale was reason enough to marry Miss Anslowe, but then there was his own unexpected fascination with her. With a jolt, it dawned on him that he would have offered to marry her even without the pleasure of causing Tynedale fury.

He frowned into his wine. He would have to be careful there. He would marry her, but surely, he would not be fool enough to commit the greatest folly of all and fall in love? With his own wife? Nay.

Chapter 5

"Papa, are you very sure that I must marry him?" Nell asked quietly.

It was midmorning on Tuesday and the pair of them were in the library where Sir Edward had retreated to read his newspaper and savor the news that it contained. The earl, he noted with approval, had not wasted a moment and had managed to insert the announcement of his impending marriage to Miss Eleanor Anslowe in time for today's edition.

"Eh? What's that, my dear?" Sir Edward asked, the pleased glow that Nell's future was settled apparent in his face.

Nell sighed. She hated disappointing her father, and her brothers, for that matter, and it was clear that they were all cock-a-whoop at the turn of events. Upon their arrival home, Sir Edward had dispatched a servant to find Drew and Harry to tell them to return at once to London. The twins had arrived back in London very late that evening, tired and dirty, but after a bath and a change of clothes, they'd joined their father, brother and sister for an impromptu celebration of Nell's good fortune that had lasted into the wee hours of Monday morning. The Anslowe men had been jovial and ignored Nell's glum countenance. But then, they would be happy as larks, Nell thought, *they* weren't being handed over to a stranger!

She had not slept well and it had been well past noon on

Monday before she left her bedroom. Not even the knowledge that her father had set a burly servant to guard the area beneath her window from any further intruders had calmed the turmoil in her breast. It was not intruders she feared but the future. And if she was truthful, she did not *fear* the Earl of Wyndham, she just didn't want to marry him.

Nell did not deny that she had found him attractive, overpoweringly so, and there was no pretending that he was not imposing—even, as he had been when she first laid eyes on him, with a night's growth of beard darkening his cheeks and his clothing stained and disheveled. Nor could she ignore the fact that as a prospective husband he met several of the criteria any sensible young lady, and certainly the young lady's family, would demand. He was well born, titled, in fact, and, to make matters worse, it was an old and venerated title. He was respected in the ton. And, he was rich. Very.

All of those things were important to her father and her brothers. Sir Edward was elated that she was making such a grand match, even if it had come about in an unorthodox fashion. She supposed, if she was fair, that she should be grateful that Lord Wyndham had proved to be honorable. And it wasn't, she admitted, that she had found him repulsive. Quite the contrary, if she was honest with herself, remembering the unexpected thrill she had felt when his hard body had pressed against hers and his mouth had hovered so near to hers.

But all that did not mean that she wanted to marry him. She had known better than to immediately tackle the issue with her father, nor had she wanted to bring up the subject when he and her brothers had been half-drunk with relief and gratification at the lucky outcome. *They* were ecstatic at the notion of their sister becoming the Countess of Wyndham.

Despite taking all of that into account, Nell was not comfortable with the idea of being handed over to the earl in such a hurly-burly fashion. Marriage was for life and it was the rest of *her* life that they were all so busy arranging. She was grateful to the earl, but there must be another way out of the situation other than marriage. With that in mind she had waited to seek out her father until after Robert had left the house this morning. Having found her father in the library, she wasted not a moment putting forth her question.

When Sir Edward looked blank, she repeated, "Must I marry him?"

"Well, of course you must! Besides the impropriety of what happened and the Humphries arriving at a dashed inconvenient time—it is in the *Times!*" He stared at her. "What is wrong with you, gel? The Earl of Wyndham! Why every matchmaking mama in England has been after him since his wife died. And to think that my daughter is the one who snaffles him right out from under their very noses."

"In the *Times?*" she squeaked, her heart dropping down to her toes. Snatching the proffered newspaper out of her father's hand, she read the small notice, any hopes of preventing the marriage fluttering away with every word of black print.

Features pale, she sank down into the oxblood leather chair next to Sir Edward. The newspaper slipped unheeded from her fingers.

" 'Tis a grand match, my dear. One that should make you happy," her father said gently. "It is the sort of match I have always hoped that you would make." He paused and sent her a keen look. "Nell, you know that your happiness is paramount to me, it always has been, and if I thought for one instant that Wyndham would make you an indifferent husband, scandal be damned! I would not countenance the match. But he is a fine man—we may not move in as high a circle of the ton, but your brothers and I are aware of his reputation. It is without stain. Friends we share in common with Wyndham have always spoken highly of him and I know of no reason that would make him unacceptable—even if we did not have a scandal to avoid."

Her father meant to help, Nell knew that, but all he did was cut the ground from beneath her feet. "But I don't know him," she muttered. "I don't love him." Accusingly she added, "You and mother loved each other and she wasn't a stranger. It isn't fair that you marry me off to someone I don't know—and don't love."

Sir Edward sighed. "My dear, your mother's and my marriage was arranged almost from the moment of our births. Neither of us had any say in it. She was an only child, as was I. Our parents were dear friends whose lands marched side by side and they yearned for a closer tie between the two families—and there is no denying that they wanted to unite our estates." When Nell would have interrupted, he held up a hand. "Yes, we grew up together, knowing that someday we would wed, but we were not in love with each other at the time of our wedding. We liked and respected each other and the union made our families happy—that was reason enough for us." A faraway expression in his eyes, he murmured, "Love came later, as our relationship deepened. Within months, nay, weeks of our wedding we could not imagine life without the other and we realized that our parents had known what they were about in arranging for us to wed—even if practical matters played a part in it. I have never regretted a day of my marriage to your mother. I miss her still."

Defeated, Nell stared at him, the feeling of being trapped increasing. She could offer no argument to refute his words. And she knew her father well enough to recognize that his mind was made up; she would find no help from him in escaping marriage to Wyndham.

Aware that he had dealt her a blow, Sir Edward reached over and placed a hand over hers. "Nell, it will not be as bad as you fear. Wyndham strikes me as a likeable, reasonable sort, and even if you do not love him, remember that love is not a requirement for marriage among our sort." He touched her cheek and smiled. "You may, you know, surprise yourself by falling in love with him."

Her stormy eyes met his. "But what if he never falls in love with me? What then?"

Sir Edward winced. "I cannot predict the future, my dear. Your marriage will be what you make of it." His eyes met hers. "And you can make it happy . . . or you can make it miserable. The choice is yours."

Julian had never linked the words love and marriage together before and as he contemplated his nuptials, the word love was not paramount in his mind. He was realistic about his marriage. And looking at it as a purely practical matter, he could see several advantages in marrying Miss Eleanor Anslowe.

In fact, when Lord Talcott arrived that morning demanding to know how in the devil the *Times* could have made such an outrageous mistake, once he had his friend calmed down, he ticked them off for him.

Quickly ushering his apoplectic friend to the rear of house, Julian had proceeded with care. Ordinarily, he would have laid the entire tale before Talcott. He trusted his friend and there were few, if any, secrets between them. But events were different this time, this time a lady's honor was involved, a lady who would become his wife, and it seemed to him that the fewer people who knew the truth the better. Adrian Talcott, who knew him intimately, might guess that a rig was being run, but Julian had no doubt that his friend would follow his lead—even if puzzled and eaten alive with curiosity. He quelled a flicker of guilt at not divulging the truth and, sticking to the bare bones of the story he had put forth already, it still took Julian several minutes to make Talcott understand that there had been no mistake: the *Times* had it correct. He was going to marry Eleanor Anslowe. On Wednesday next. Talcott was, of course, invited to the wedding.

"B-B-But you don't even know the chit! At least," Talcott added after a moment's hesitation, "I don't think you do. And marriage! You have sworn to me often enough in your cups, that marriage was a trap that would not catch you again."

His long legs crossed at the ankles, Julian slouched in a dark green mohair chair next to Talcott's, his long fingers steepled beneath his chin. His gaze was on the small fire crackling on the gray marble hearth in front of them and for a moment Talcott thought that he had not heard him. But a second later Julian murmured, "I know. And I will admit that another marriage was something that I had not thought to undertake—even if it meant that my bloody cousin Charles would inherit the title and all that goes with it, and which he would promptly gamble away."

Talcott grinned. "Well! I am happy to see that at least your opinion of him has not changed. The way you were going on about the wisdom of this marriage, I next expected you to start singing his praises."

"Hardly. But if you think about it, this marriage may be a very good thing. I *do* need an heir and a hostess of my own— I have estates that need a woman's hand and I have no inclination to oversee the running of my various households. Diana does well enough, but she is still a young woman, a beautiful one, and she could—in fact it is my most ardent desire—remarry, and then where would I be? Having my own wife would solve that problem before it arises."

When Talcott would have interrupted him, he raised a hand and added, "I know what you are going to say next: if I am set upon marriage, why not select a bride from a more recent crop of eligible damsels? Why choose a female not in the first blush of youth?" He rubbed his chin. "Quite honestly, the thought of shackling myself to any one of the flighty bits of muslin that are currently trotted out at Almack's makes me view with delight the notion of joining a monastery." Julian shook his head. "No. I've considered the situation from all angles and Miss Anslowe is the perfect candidate for me— perhaps the *only* candidate. Consider it, Adrian! She is young enough to give me a nursery full of offspring and yet old enough to know the ways of the world. She will not bedevil me by demanding that I dance attendance on her—or saddle me with someone else's brat. Her family's name and respectability are without parallel—and don't forget, she is an heiress. The more I consider it, the more convinced I am that marriage with her is wise."

"My ears must deceive me—surely this is not the same man who has been declaring for years that marriage is the worst fate to befall man?"

Julian grinned. "There will be compensations, you know—when she produces an heir, Charles will be blocked from inheriting and, remember, my wife will have to deal with Diana and all of her fits and starts. At least I shall be free of that."

"A poor reason to saddle yourself with a woman who has been considered on the shelf for years." Talcott looked morose. "And don't forget, there are those rumors about her."

Julian sent him a hooded glance. "What rumors?" he asked in a tone that made Talcott uneasy.

"Uh, well, you know that years ago she was engaged to Bethune?" At Julian's nod, he said, "It is common knowledge that she suffered an accident that left her crippled . . . But the reason Bethune was able to escape the engagement without being branded a blackguard is that there was talk that she was not, um, quite right in the head."

Julian pictured Nell as he had first seen her, dirty and bedraggled. She had not been, he would admit, a reassuring sight, but what he remembered most of that moment was the intelligence gleaming in those wary, sea green eyes. He smiled to himself, finding the memory endearing. But one thing had been clear in an instant: this was no madwoman. Not even, he thought, *half*-mad.

"You do realize," Julian asked softly, "that you are talking about the woman that I am to marry?"

Talcott swallowed, his precisely arranged cravat feeling as if it was choking him. He recognized the deceptive mildness of Julian's tone. Past experience had taught him that a prudent man treaded carefully when that particular note entered his friend's voice—either that or take the consequences . . . which were never pleasant.

Talcott cleared his throat. "Now, don't come the ugly with me—I am only repeating what has been said."

"Do not . . . not if you wish to remain my friend. I would suggest also, that for their own good, you promptly disabuse anyone else of that notion."

"Oh, of course. Absolutely."

Julian smiled at him, that warm, utterly charming smile that always disarmed its object. "I know you will. And I know that you will wish me happy."

"Naturally. Wouldn't do otherwise." Talcott fidgeted in his chair. "Thing is, Julian, it comes as a shock. Bound to be talk."

Julian rose to his feet and, picking up the poker, prodded the fire. "People have been talking and gossiping about me for years—what is one more round?"

Talcott sighed. "I know, but this time it is different. It ain't just that you are getting married, it is to whom you are getting married. And the suddenness of it is certain to cause a flurry amongst the old tabbies."

"And why should I care about that?"

"You might not . . . but what of your lady?"

Julian paused. He could stand the nonsense, but with an unsettling feeling of protectiveness, he was aware that he did not want the ton sinking their collective claws into Nell. "What do you suggest? I am going to marry her. And it will be on next Wednesday."

Talcott cleared his throat again. "Perhaps, if we were to, uh, put forth some sort of explanation?" He sent Julian a glance, trying to gauge his mood. Feeling his way, he said, "Lady Humphries will, of course, be busy spreading the news about how she found you and the Anslowes at the abandoned toll keeper's cottage." Talcott paused, making certain that he had Julian's full attention—and that the earl was not on the verge of calling him out. The expression on Julian's face was encouraging, so Talcott plunged on, "Knowing Lady Humphries, she will give out the worst reading of the situation. You need a, uh, clarification of the tale to dilute her tale—something that would satisfy, or at least divert, the more determined gossips."

"You have something in mind?" Julian asked with a quirk of his brow.

Settling back in the chair, Talcott considered the matter. Having concluded that, for whatever reasons, Julian was determined to marry Miss Anslowe, he threw himself into the fray. Now what, he wondered, would be a reason for Julian to have kept his courtship—if there had been a courtship, and he seriously doubted it—wrapped in such secrecy? A smile slid across his face as an idea occurred to him. "I suppose," he said, "that the most obvious reason for you to have kept your, er, growing passion for Miss Anslowe a secret is because you did not wish to distress Lady Wyndham by thrusting a stranger into the household."

Julian put away the poker and, amusement gleaming in his eyes, he said, "Yes, that sounds plausible. Diana enjoys being the Countess Wyndham—she will not be happy to claim the title dowager, not at her age."

"Er, yes. So that explains why you kept it a secret—you wanted Lady Diana to become used to the idea."

Julian nodded. "But why," he asked, the gleam in his eyes more pronounced, "did I decide to spring this, uh, growing passion, I believed you called it, on her now?"

Enjoying himself now, Talcott smiled. "Why, my dear fellow, after your unfortunate carriage accident, which left you in such close proximity with the alluring Miss Anslowe, you simply could not contain your passion any longer. You had to speak and the consequences be damned!"

Julian guffawed. "Of course. It will do all the old tabbies good to think of me snarled in the throes of love. They will look upon Miss Anslowe as the avenging goddess who brought me to heel."

"And has she?" Talcott asked slyly.

Thinking of Nell and the emotions she roused in his breast, Julian shook his head. "I cannot tell you—I do not know the answer to that question myself."

How very interesting, Talcott thought to himself. Could it be that Julian's heart had been well and truly snared?

Studying the shine of his boots, Talcott inquired, "Tell me, why the suddenness of your marriage? I mean, aside from your inability to control your growing passion for the lady? Why not wait and marry her in the spring? Why so precipitous?"

Julian thought back to the plans that had been put together so hastily during his ride back to London yesterday with the Anslowes. Lord and Lady Humphries finding them at the toll keeper's cottage had been unfortunate and it had seemed logical to arrange for a swift outcome. Julian had known that his engagement to *any* young woman would cause talk and speculation—not all of it kind. With Eleanor Anslowe named as his bride-to-be, the old stories about her and Bethune were bound to arise and add to the furor. Simply put: the longer the engagement, the more time he and Miss Anslowe would be at the center of a firestorm of gossip. And, of course, there was Tynedale's part in the whole affair. For a moment, Julian's mouth thinned. The Anslowes were unaware of his connection with Lord Tynedale and he had seen no reason to enlighten them. But Miss Anslowe's abduction by Tynedale had been another reason for a hurried marriage—with the lady safely married to him, not even Tynedale would dare hint of abduction gone wrong.

Julian sighed. It had seemed wise to get it all behind them as quickly as possible—the sooner they wed, the sooner the nine day's wonder surrounding their unexpected engagement would end. And there was a practical reason, too. In another week or two, except for a few stragglers, the majority of the ton would desert London until the spring. By marrying next Wednesday, there would be a respectable contingent to celebrate their nuptials—and spread the word. By the next Season his engagement and marriage to Miss Anslowe would be old gossip and soon forgotten.

Smiling wryly, Julian said, "There is nothing suspicious about the sudden marriage—I wish to spare my lady as much gossip as possible. It is far better that we stand the nonsense all at once, than to have it dragged out over the winter and into next spring."

Talcott could get no more out of him and had to be content. They took their leave of each other, Talcott promising to head immediately to Boodle's to begin lamenting Julian's fate. Julian made plans to call upon his bride-to-be.

Let into Sir Edward's fashionable townhouse by the family butler, Chatham, Julian was whisked into the study, where he found Sir Edward seated behind his desk.

As Julian approached Sir Edward rose from his chair and, a wide smile on his face, shook his hand. "Lord Wyndham. A pleasure. Please, please take a seat. Some refreshment?"

While the most pressing issues had already been decided upon, the business arrangements of the marriage, money, and settlements, had not been finalized. These matters were quickly handled by the two men, Julian agreeing to a generous settlement for his wife-to-be and Sir Edward laying out the extent of her fortune—a fortune that would be under Julian's control once they were wed.

Since Nell had little say in the matter she did not even know that her future bridegroom was in the house until a servant tapped on the door to her rooms and passed on her father's request that she join him and Lord Wyndham in the library.

For an instant she considered sending back a message that she was indisposed. But knowing that there was no escape, she took a swift look in the cheval glass, shook out the folds of her kerseymere gown and pinched roses into her cheeks. A critical glance at the curls that framed her face, the remainder of the tawny mass caught up in a braid at the back of her head, satisfied her that she bore little resemblance to the harridan the earl had first seen. Then, berating herself for caring what Lord Wyndham thought of her, she turned away from the glass and left the room.

Reaching the double doors to the library, she took a breath, stifled the urge to run and pulled open the door. Like a trim frigate with fighting canvass spread, she sailed into the room.

In the act of raising a glass of hock to his lips, Julian froze. Stunned, he stared at the lovely young woman who stalked across the length of the library and came to halt before him.

"My lord," she said, her manner stiff.

Julian made a polite reply, gathering his thoughts. He could hardly believe that this entrancing creature was the same female he had met just twenty-four hours ago. She was taller than he recalled, but the soft curves of the slender form beneath the sage green gown he remembered very well. Her sea green eyes still held the same wary expression and the strawberry-hued mouth was still just as tempting, but gone was the bedraggled urchin he had first spied. In her place stood a fashionable young woman who would have instantly elicited a demand for an introduction from him if their paths had crossed previously. Where in Hades, he thought, had she been hiding all this time?

"Thank you for joining us so promptly, my dear," said Sir Edward, reaching out a hand to bring his daughter to his side.

Nell started, hoping her face did not show the shock she felt at the sight of the gentleman standing next to her father. From their first encounter, she'd had a memory of a tall, raffish fellow, a man with a beard-shadowed face and hard eyes, a man who had made her think of a highwayman or ruffian, and she was having difficulty reconciling that memory with the elegant man before her. He was meticulously groomed, his thick dark hair waving near his temples, the clean cut of his jaw and lips no longer half-concealed beneath black stubble; the dark blue coat and nankeen breeches fit him superbly, the white cravat arranged by an expert hand. The effect was staggering. She was certain that she had met other men as attractive and urbane as the Earl of Wyndham, but at the moment, she could not remember one of them.

Dazedly she let her father pull her beside him, only half-aware of the warmth and comfort of his hand. Tearing her gaze from Lord Wyndham's face, she dropped her eyes to the floor, her thoughts careening.

Having observed the effect they had on each other, Sir Edward bit back a smile. A twinkle in his eyes, he patted Nell's shoulder and said, "I shall leave you two alone for a few minutes . . . I believe that Lord Wyndham wishes to speak privately with you."

With trepidation Nell watched her father leave the room. She did not like this at all. Not the fact that she was being rushed into marriage with a man she barely knew, nor the fact that she found that same man far too attractive for her own good. Resentfully she shot a look at him from between her gold lashes, her heart leaping when she discovered that he was watching her intently.

Her chin lifted. "What? Why are you staring at me so?"

He smiled and Nell blinked at the powerful charm in that simple expression. Oh, lud! she thought. Her wits must have fled completely if a mere smile from him could make her feel so bedazzled.

"Forgive me," Julian said, amusement in his voice. "I could not help myself—I did not expect you to, er, clean up so well. You are very beautiful—far more beautiful than I remembered."

Nell snorted, ignoring the spurt of pleasure his words gave her. "You do not have to court me, my lord," she muttered.

"My father has made it clear that we are to be married on Wednesday next and that nothing short of death will prevent it."

Sir Edward had hinted that his daughter was not happy with the situation, but Julian had not quite believed him. Without being vain, he knew he was, after all, quite a catch. Her words and manner, however, made it apparent that Sir Edward had not underestimated the fact that she was singularly *un*impressed by him—and his title and wealth. And to think, Julian mused, that instead of this angry-eyed little shrew, he could have found himself a sweet, docile young thing to marry—a fawning creature who would not have caused him a moment's distress. Fighting back a grin, his gaze swept up and down her form before returning to her face and lingering on the stubborn jaw and willful mouth. His new bride, he decided, was going to be a challenge . . . and a handful—if the defiant set of her head was anything to go by.

Aloud, he merely asked, "And would you prefer death to marriage with me?"

Nell's lips tightened. How ungentlemanly of him! She shot him a hostile glance. "Of course not—I am not a fool."

"Then don't act like one."

Nell started at the crisp tone. Some of her belligerence fading, but not much, she demanded, "What do you mean?"

"I mean, my dear, that we are in this together. Both of our lives have changed in a manner neither one of us could have imagined twenty-four hours ago. Do not forget that you are not the only one being forced into marriage with a stranger. We can either make the best of it, or we can spend our time making ourselves unhappy. The choice is ours. I, for one, do not intend to spend the rest of my life in misery."

"But aren't you angry at what happened? Doesn't it make you furious that you are compelled to marry a woman you hardly know?" Nell's lips trembled and she looked down at the floor. Honesty compelled her to add, "You will be marrying a woman who has been branded half-mad by society and, as you may have noticed, a woman who is also a cripple."

Julian tipped up her chin, his hand warm against her skin. His eyes gleaming with an emotion she could not name, he demanded softly, "Do you know that I nearly called out one of my best friends for referring to you in those terms?"

Nell's eyes widened and her heart banged painfully in her chest. "D-D-Did you?" she managed, her skin tingling where he touched it.

Julian nodded. "And if I was prepared to fight a duel with him, what should I do with you for daring to say the same thing about the woman I am going to marry, hmmm?"

Nell couldn't think. He was too close. She was too aware of his hand beneath her chin, too conscious of his wide-shouldered body and blatant masculinity, to do more than stare, her reaction to him evident.

Something clenched painfully within him at her wide-eyed expression and, giving into the whim that had been with him since they'd met at the toll keeper's cottage, his lips captured hers. Her mouth was soft and startled, the taste and texture of it beyond his imagination. He had known that he would enjoy kissing her, had known that her lips would be sweet and warm, but he could never have guessed at the fierce, powerful desire that would twist and knot within him the moment his mouth touched hers.

Nell gasped, her fingers clutching at his shoulders as his lips caught hers. His mouth was firm and knowing as it slid across hers, the roiling emotions it left in its wake like none she had ever experienced. Her blood raced and warmth bloomed within her, her entire body responding to the caress of his lips like a bud to the April sun. Instinctively she arched nearer, her mouth eager for him to continue the kiss.

The effect of her nearness on him was no less dramatic for Julian, but while he had never felt such explosive desire before, he recognized the signs . . . and the danger. If he did not bring a halt to this sweet dalliance now, within minutes, he would have that charming gown up around her waist and he would be securely notched between her legs. With an effort, he tore his lips from hers and set her away from him.

"That," he said in a thickened tone, "was not why your father left us alone together."

Fighting off the giddiness his kiss engendered, she asked with credible command, "Why did he leave us alone?"

"To allow me to formally ask for your hand." A faint smile lifted the corner of his mouth. "We both thought that you might like to receive a proper offer."

Her resentment returned and turning away from him, she said, "My lord, you are wasting your time. I will be honest: I do not wish to wed—you or any other man. And having you formally request my hand is not going to change my mind."

He turned her back to face him. "Are you so very certain that you don't wish to marry me? Do you find me so very distasteful?"

"I could name several gentlemen that I do not find distasteful," she hedged, "but that does not mean that I wish to marry them."

Julian grimaced. Aware of his worth and used to being much courted and petted by the opposite sex, he did not know whether to be amused or insulted by her refusal to fall in with his wishes. One thing he did know: he wanted her, and her rejection of him roused the hunter within him. Having her resist him was a novel occurrence for him. He could not remember a time when he had cast out his lures and a woman had made it so plain that his advances were not desired. He smiled, anticipation curling through him. He was going to have to work hard at wooing his reluctant bride . . . and he rather thought that he was going to enjoy it . . . immensely.

Chapter 6

The days after the scene in the library with Julian passed in a terrifying blur for Nell. The news of the engagement created the furor that the earl and Anslowe family had assumed it would. In the time before her wedding, at the few social functions she attended, Nell was stared at and pointed out as the future bride of the Earl of Wyndham. Conversation stopped when she entered a room and she was aware of the whispers that followed her. Of course, she knew they were speculating about the reasons behind the sudden wedding and she knew that all the old gossip about her and Bethune had been disinterred. With every passing moment Nell began to understand why the earl had been so adamant about a quick wedding. He was, damn him, correct: the sooner they wed, the sooner the storm would pass.

Not all of the interest in the coming nuptials was unkind. Friends of the baronet's family, and there were many, flooded the Anslowe townhouse, their delight in her having made such a grand match sincere—if astonished. At the townhouse of the Earl of Wyndham, grand and titled friends of the earl also came to call and they, too, seemed pleased that Julian had finally chosen a bride. And if they were mystified about his choice, who could blame them? Wyndham could have looked as high as he pleased for a bride, and after years of being the despair of every matchmaking mama in England, without warning he had offered his hand to the daughter of a mere baronet, albeit a wealthy, respected one.

There were, Nell supposed, some compensations for being handed over in marriage to the earl. Her father never stopped smiling and even her brothers seem to think that she had accomplished some impressive task for having snared Wyndham. Nell did not know whether to laugh or scream. She had never suspected that her father—or her brothers, for that matter—had lusted after a higher position amongst the ton, but to see them basking in the earl's aura of power and influence revised her opinion. I seem to be the only one, she thought sourly, not ready to fall down and worship at his boots. Which wasn't to say, she admitted, that she did not find him attractive . . . too attractive for her own liking. She was determined not to fall under his charm and she was having a hard time of it—especially when he smiled at her in that certain way . . . Damning herself for a fool she looked forward to her approaching wedding day with all the enthusiasm of sleeping naked in a nettle patch.

Julian viewed his coming wedding with an anticipation and impatience that surprised him. He told himself that it was only because he wanted the hubble-bubble surrounding his marriage behind him, but he knew that he was deluding himself. Every time he saw Nell, as he thought of her these days, or touched her hand, every time their glances caught and held, he'd swear that the air smelled of orange blossoms and that he'd developed an unsettling tendency to float across the room. It didn't matter that they'd never shared another private moment or that their meetings were always public. He had only to see her across the length of a room for his heart to leap and his step to lighten. He was not pleased with his reaction to her, particularly since he had set himself out to be at his most winning and the lady continued to treat him with cool resignation. But he was willing to bide his time—after all, they were going to be married for a very long time. The earl was a confident man, not a vain one, but occasionally he did wonder if he was being vain in assuming that he could win the heart of his lady. She certainly, he admitted wryly, seemed impervious to the lures he threw her way. He grinned. And her very imperviousness only whetted his appetite.

Not everyone was thrilled with the announcement of the earl's engagement to Miss Anslowe. Lady Wyndham tottered to her bed with her vinaigrette, convinced that Miss Anslowe was an ogre, and determined to wrest Julian's affections from her and her daughter. The coming wedding filled her with dread and when she could be pried from her bed and vinaigrette, she went about with such a lachrymose expression that most people assumed that the earl had indeed kept his interest in Miss Anslowe quiet because of his father's widow.

Elizabeth, of a far less dramatic mind than her mother, wasn't exactly *dis*pleased with the coming addition to the family, but she was aware that the life she and her mother had shared with Julian was changing forever and she suffered the occasional worry about the future.

Talcott, too, had reservations about the impending marriage, but on the whole, having met Miss Anslowe at a private dinner at the earl's residence on Thursday evening, found himself unexpectedly charmed by her. He was inclined to think that if his friend *had* to be married, the Anslowe baggage might do him very well. Considering her firm little chin and the intelligence gleaming in her fine eyes, she would certainly, he conceded with a smile, lead Julian a merry dance.

It took awhile, but even a few of the earl's friends and relatives who had already left London for their country estates or snug hunting boxes returned to town to see for themselves the little minx who had finally brought Julian to his knees. A week after the announcement had appeared in the newspaper, Marcus Sherbrook was shown into the library. Finding Julian alone, sprawled in a chair near the fire apparently lost in a brown study, he murmured, "Regretting it already, Cousin? And the wedding not two days away!"

A glad smile broke across Julian's dark features and he started to his feet. "Marcus! I had not thought to see you in town again so soon."

"What? And miss what bodes to be the most talked-about event of the year? Good God, do you take me for a flat?"

They met in the middle of the room, two tall, dark-haired men, their liking for each other obvious. Grinning at Marcus as he shook his hand, Julian said, "I'll wager you never thought this day would come."

Amusement gleaming in his cool gray eyes, Marcus admitted, "I'm afraid you have me there. I own that I can hardly wait to meet this paragon who has captured the one man I thought for sure would never stick his head in the parson's mousetrap again."

Showing him to a seat near the fire, Julian shrugged. "There are moments that I have trouble believing it myself, but when you meet her . . ." A wry smile crossed his mouth. "When you meet her you will either think me mad or curse me for finding her first."

Settling himself with careless elegance across from Julian, Marcus studied him, seeking for any hidden meaning in his words. He knew Julian well and what he saw must have satisfied him for he relaxed into the comfort of the overstuffed chair and stretched his long legs before him.

Only two years separated their ages, with Julian being the eldest. Marcus was the son of the eldest sister of the previous earl and it could be said that the cousins had known each other almost since the hour of their birth. Lady Barbara Weston had married Mr. Sherbrook, a very wealthy country gentleman of impeccable lineage whose estates lay not thirty miles from Wyndham Manor, and Marcus and Julian had grown up together. They'd shared the terrors of Eaton together, the joys of Oxford and holidays in the country, both equally comfortable in each other's homes. Beyond their dark hair and tall, athletic physiques, they shared few features in common, although there was a faint family resemblance about the eyes and nose.

Julian rang for his butler and conversation was desultory until after Dibble had brought in a decanter of brandy and two snifters and departed. Pouring his cousin a drink, Julian said, "I assume you read the notice in the newspaper."

Swirling the brandy around and letting the delicate fumes rise in the air, Marcus said, "Actually, no. The news came from one of our esteemed cousins." He made a face. "Charles appeared on my doorstep a few days ago—*he* had read the announcement in the newspaper."

"Hopefully Charles will use a little of the sense I know he possesses and not assume that I am marrying to spite him," Julian muttered. He shook his head, his expression rueful. "If only my uncle had not got a maggot in his head that my father had somehow cheated him out of the title and poisoned Charles's mind there would not be this bitterness between us."

"To put paid to any of Charles's lingering delusions, let us hope that your bride proves to be most fertile and that this time next year we are toasting the birth of your son," Marcus said. Raising his snifter, he smiled and added, "The first of many, I trust."

Julian raised his own glass. "As you said—we can hope."

The toast drunk, Marcus said, "So, tell me of this young woman—and your rapid courtship. I've racked my brains trying to recall if I have ever met her and, do you know, I cannot place her."

Julian laid out the same story that he had trotted out for Talcott and only by a sardonically lifted brow did Marcus betray that he thought it all hum. "What a rapper!" Marcus said when Julian had finished. "And too smoky by half, Cousin. Now tell me the truth and not this Canterbury tale."

Julian laughed. "I fear my lips are sealed, but know that I am not *un*happy with the turn of events and that I think you will like Miss Anslowe—and her family. Sir Edward is an affable gentleman, and her three brothers the same. Their breeding and fortune are above reproach and they don't appear to have any loose-fish lurking in the background." His mouth twisted. "Unlike our side of the family. One thing I can be sure of, knowing their worth, I'll not have them hanging on my purse strings. The Anslowes appear to be a nice, respectable family—far more respectable than certain members of ours."

"Ah, so the lady comes from a long line of paragons of virtue?"

Julian grinned. "Of course. Would the Earl of Wyndham expect any less?"

Marcus returned the grin. "And the lovely widgeon, your dear stepmama? How does she take this turn of events?"

"Oh, gad! I have been subjected to tears and spasms such as you never imagined. Diana is positive that Miss Anslowe intends to cast her and Lizzie onto the street with barely the clothes on their backs."

"Does she?" Marcus asked, with a cocked brow.

"I seriously doubt it. Miss Anslowe doesn't strike me as stupid or cruel." Julian made a face. "I'm sure that there will be a few, uh, changes that she will institute, but I see no major upsets."

"And here I thought that you were a downy one!" Marcus exclaimed, laughter gleaming in his eyes. "Might as well throw the cat amongst the pigeons. I don't envy you the domestic wars you're about to face."

Julian shrugged. "You may be right, but since Diana and Elizabeth have elected to remain here in town indefinitely, when they do return to Wyndham Manor, Nell should be well established as mistress of the house."

"And in the meantime? I assume that you will bring your bride here at least for a day or two before leaving for Wyndham Manor. Won't that be a trifle tricky considering Lady Diana's attitude?"

"That's already been taken care of—immediately following the wedding breakfast at her father's townhouse, my bride and I will be leaving for a week in the country," Julian said. "Talcott very kindly offered me, us, that little place of his in Surrey. If I'm lucky, Diana and my wife won't have a chance to come to fisticuffs for several weeks—if not months."

"Never tell me that Lady Diana is not attending your wedding!"

"Oh, no, she and Elizabeth will be there—never fear." His expression hard, Julian added, "After the most moving and tearful session that you can ever imagine, I told Diana that if she intended to have a friendly relationship with both my wife and myself, that it would be in her best interest to make an appearance at the wedding." He smiled grimly. "She saw my point . . . and I held out the added lure that since I am sending Dibble and several of the senior staff to Wyndham Manor for the winter, she has carte blanche to hire her own servants. I'm hoping by next spring she can be convinced that she'd like an establishment in town of her own—one I'll joyfully provide— and Nell and I will have this place to ourselves."

There was much left unsaid and Marcus did not envy Julian the coming months. The conversation went on to other topics, but eventually wandered back to the coming nuptials. "Have you heard from Stacey? I can't imagine him missing your wedding."

Thinking of the Honorable Stacey Bannister, the son of Julian's father's youngest and best-beloved sister, Julian smiled. "Stacey? No, I have not heard from or seen him, but I expect him to arrive on my doorstep any moment, just as you did."

"And Charles and his brother and dear Aunt Sofia? Will they arrive on your doorstep, too?"

Julian's lips thinned. "Aside from our other differences, Charles is aware that I hold him partially responsible for Daniel's death. I know that he loved the boy and I'm certain that in his mind he saw nothing wrong in introducing Daniel to Tynedale and that wild crowd of his—probably thought he was doing him a favor, but that favor led to Daniel's suicide. I doubt that Charles or any of his family will attend."

His gaze on the amber liquor in his snifter, Julian's thoughts were far away, dwelling on the tragedy of Daniel's death and the estrangement between himself and Charles—once considered one of his favorite cousins.

After a moment he shook away the darkness and asked abruptly, "Where are you staying? Surely you did not reopen your townhouse for this short stay?"

Marcus shook his head. "No, I've taken a suite of rooms at Stephens's and will return to my hunting box on Thursday."

The two men rose and, walking Marcus to the door, Julian asked, "Will you be my groomsman?"

"Indeed. I would be insulted if you had not asked."

The day of the wedding dawned wet and dreary and, staring at the unappealing weather, Nell rather thought that it fit her mood exactly. The past precious few days had vanished in a rush of preparation, but now all was in readiness. The Special License had been obtained, the church selected, and her father had ordered Chatham to see that all was in readiness for the wedding breakfast to be held at the house immediately following the wedding. The kitchen staff, prodded and berated by Cook had been working at a full gallop in the short time allotted them to prepare food and drink that would not shame a pasha.

The wedding was scheduled for eleven thirty that morning and, beyond the occasional flash of panic, Nell felt detached from the proceedings. She had taken little part, letting her father and the earl make plans as they wished. If she was going to be handed off like a piece of booty from one pirate to another, what difference did her opinion matter?

Entering the carriage for the short ride to the cathedral, she listened with only half an ear to her father's muttered complaints about the steady rain. In the cold, damp church, she removed her cloak, shook out her pale lilac gown, adjusted the small flowered headdress of yellow rosebuds and, with her father at her side walked down the aisle to meet the man who would be her husband.

The wedding party was small: only Nell, Julian, Sir Edward, Nell's brothers, Marcus Sherbrook, who acted as Julian's groomsman, Elizabeth and Lady Diana, who sobbed daintily into her lace handkerchief. Several of the pews were filled, though, with members of the ton who attended, Nell suspected, as much from curiosity as a desire to share in the celebration. The service was mercifully brief and passed in a haze for Nell. All she was aware of was the wide gold band that lay heavily on her finger and that the tall, broad-shouldered stranger at her side was now her husband. Not even her father's beaming face nor the proud expressions on her brothers' faces, nor even the kind smile bent upon her by Julian's groomsman, broke through the gloom that surrounded her.

For her family's sake, despite her detached air, Nell tried to partake in the festivities. At the wedding breakfast, she ate, chatted and graciously accepted the congratulations given to her by the various guests, all the while wondering if this was another nightmare, different, but no less terrifying.

The time finally came to leave, and amid laughter and good wishes, her sable-lined cloak billowing in the wind from the storm, she was handed into Wyndham's coach for the drive to Talcott's mansion some miles outside of London. She and Julian would remain there a week—long enough for her husband's formidable butler, Dibble, and others of the earl's servants to return to Wyndham Hall, her new home in the country, and for them to make everything ready for the arrival of the new lady of the house.

In the meantime, there was the present to be gotten through. Suddenly thinking of the night to come she swallowed and risked a glance at the tall, dark-haired gentleman sitting across from her. Good God! He, this stranger, this man she barely knew, was going to share her bed tonight and, if he so chose, all the nights for the remainder of her life.

In the murky, uncertain light inside the coach, she stared

across at him, feeling like a mare confronted by an unknown stallion. And I am not even in season, she thought almost hysterically.

Catching her eye, Julian smiled. "Everything must seem a little strange to you."

"A little," she admitted, dropping her gaze to her gloved hands.

"I am sorry for it—the haste of our marriage."

"Only the haste?" she asked dryly.

He shrugged. "Ours is not your usual match, but it is also not the first time that strangers have found themselves wed to each other." When she remained silent, he bent forward and she scooted back slightly, keeping a good distance between them. Julian noted it and his lips tightened. A skittish bride did not bode well for their future together. Quietly he said, "As I told you once, we can make of this what we want. I cannot force you into complaisance, nor can I make you, if not happy in our marriage, at least content. Only you can do that."

Her jaw clenched. "How very easy for you to say—your life is not the one torn asunder," she snapped. "It is in *your* home that I will be living, *your* servants that inhabit it. They are all strangers to me, used to your stepmother's ways, and now, suddenly, I am to supplant your stepmother in a place she has called home for years! I lief as face a pack of wild boars! Beyond my own maid, Becky, and my clothing, there will not be one thing that is familiar to me—and I am to be happy with that? Content?" Her eyes flashed. "I have left behind everything that I have ever known—my father, my home—for what? Life with a man I did not want to marry and do not know."

"I concede all of those things," he admitted ruefully, "but in time I trust that you will no longer think of them as mine, but as ours."

Irritated by his calm, sensible manner, she demanded, "Are you always so reasonable?"

He laughed. "No, not always—I have been known to lose my temper, though not often, I hope, and I'm not above sulking about when things don't go as I planned." Reaching across the distance that separated them, he took one of her hands in his. "I know that this not easy for you"—and when she would have spoken, he added hastily—"and that it is far easier for me than you." His eyes met hers. "But we are married, and while all is strange and unfamiliar now, we have our whole lives to learn of each other."

"Aren't you the least angry at having an unknown female foisted off on you as your bride?" she asked curiously.

"Not when she is a charming and agreeable as you, my dear," he replied, a twinkle in his eyes.

Despite herself, Nell giggled. "What a whisker! I have not been the least charming and I certainly would not call my conduct agreeable."

"Now how am I to reply to that? I am far too polite to call my wife, a liar—" the twinkle became more pronounced— "nor would I dare say, not if I value my life, that you are *dis*agreeable."

"A quandary, most certainly, my lord, but one from which a gentleman of your address should speedily extricate himself," she said, an impish smile crossing her face.

He laughed and her mood inexplicably lightened and she was able to enjoy the journey. The earl had set himself to entertaining his reluctant bride and when the coach swung to a stop in front of a charming mansion sometime later, Nell descended the coach, if not happy with the situation, at least no longer so glum.

The earl knew the servants, having stayed at Talcott's place many times before, and after Talcott's butler had shown them to an elegant salon, he asked, "Tell me, Hurst, has my valet and milady's maid arrived?"

Hurst bowed and said, "Yes, my lord, a few hours ago."

Julian turned back to Nell and said, "Perhaps you would

like to see your room and change and refresh yourself before dinner?"

Nell gratefully fell in with his suggestion. She was shown upstairs to her bedchamber, where she found Becky waiting for her. Becky, born and bred in the country, was still stunned by the sudden marriage. Her eyes big, she said, "Oh, miss . . ." She blushed and corrected, "Your ladyship, I am so glad to see you! I feared that I might well be waiting for you in the earl's bedroom and I was ready sink if his lordship should have come in!"

Relaxing for the first time since she'd woken this morning, Nell laughed. Glancing around the elegant rooms, she asked, "Is everything all right?"

"Oh, yes, miss—your ladyship! Everyone has been so kind."

With her open, freckled face and springy red hair, Becky Farnsworth was as far removed from the idea of a proper lady's maid as possible—and that suited Nell just fine. At Meadowlea Nell usually dispensed with a personal maid but for this trip to London, at her father's insistence, she had pressed Becky, normally an upper housemaid, into service. Becky, having never been more than five miles from Meadowlea in her life, had been elated, and with her sunny manner and lively willingness to throw herself into completing any chore, she had proven to be just the sort of lady's maid that Nell wanted.

"I wasn't certain how soon to order a bath brought or," Becky began, as she followed Nell into the actual bedroom, "how much to unpack, miss . . . er, your ladyship, but I did lay out your night things and had your bronze-green gown pressed for this evening."

"Thank you," Nell said as she wandered restlessly around the room. She felt helpless and, despite Wyndham's actions and conversation during their long ride here, just a little frightened. She dreaded the night to come. She was not a child and raised in the country—she'd been overseeing the breeding of her own horses since she was sixteen—she knew what was expected of her. The earl—and she would concede it—was a handsome man. She was relieved that she did not find him repulsive or disgusting, but she still wasn't looking forward to his lovemaking. He wasn't *un*appealing, reminding herself of those moments in the toll keeper's cottage just before her father and brother had interrupted them, and then there was that kiss . . . Perhaps if he was patient with her she could rouse some enthusiasm for the deed?

As Julian prepared to meet Nell in the dining room, her words in the coach came back to him and he tried to imagine how he would feel if everything familiar was swept away from him. Even this house and its servants, while not his, were well known to him; but for Nell, except for that maid of hers, everything was unfamiliar.

Attracted to his bride in a way he had not considered possible, Julian was eager for his wedding night, but it occurred to him that Nell might not share his eagerness. He had enough confidence in his lovemaking skills to know that he could make tonight, if not totally pleasurable, at least less of an ordeal, but uncertainty beset him at the idea of making love to an *unwilling* bride. His bride, he had realized during the coach ride to the house, was still not ecstatic with the marriage and was decidedly wary of him and her future. He smiled ruefully. So much for his vaunted position in the world, and he was pleased that Nell was not impressed by his title and wealth . . . but for tonight it might have made things easier if she had been. Yet when he thought of a fawning bride enamored of his position and money, allowing him her bed *because* of who he was, he found the idea distasteful. Recalling the stubborn tilt to her chin, he had no fears that Nell would ever fawn over him and he suspected that gaining her bed tonight with her delighted participation was not likely to happen. So how, he wondered wryly, did he get what he wanted and yet not make her more wary and aloof than she already was?

*   *   *

It was Nell herself who solved his dilemma. Both had partaken sparingly of the sumptuous feast spread out for them in the dining room. It was not a comfortable meal and the conversation between Julian and Nell was stilted, and when the meal was over, it was with relief that they both rose from the table.

Declining to linger alone over his wine, Julian followed Nell into a small sitting room. Once Hurst had shut the double doors after them, Julian wandered over to a gleaming table that held an array of crystal decanters and various glasses. Looking back at Nell as she sat stiffly on a small blue satin sofa, he asked, "Would you care for a small glass of hock?"

She nodded, deciding that holding a glass would give her something to do with her hands. After handing her the glass, Julian took his own glass and seated himself across from her in a chair that matched the sofa. An awkward silence fell.

Nell took a deep breath, a gulp of her wine and rushed into speech. "My lord, I must talk to you about tonight."

"Yes? What about tonight?" he asked, taking a sip of his wine.

Her cheeks blooming pink, Nell blurted out, "I do not want you in my bed."

Hiding his dismay, Julian replied, "Ah, unless memory fails me, we *are* man and wife and I believe that the joys of the marriage bed are much touted." He smiled charmingly at her. "I was rather looking forward to finding out for myself if it is true."

She gritted her teeth. "Well, would you mind not looking forward to it *tonight?*"

He studied her, noting the stiffness of her body, the glitter of half-fright, half defiance in the sea green eyes. He had feared an unwilling bride; he just hadn't realized how *very* unwilling she was. With a vision of his previous, unpleasant marriage in mind, he asked quietly, "Are you suggesting that the marriage never be consummated?"

Nell shook her head. "Not that," she said firmly. "I just beg your indulgence and that you allow us time to learn more about each other before . . ." She swallowed. "Before we consummate our marriage."

"Ah, and how much time do you think that would take? A week? A month? Six months?"

"I don't know but I don't believe we can set a time limit on it." She sent him an uncertain smile. "Surely, you yourself are not eager to take to bed a woman you barely know?"

Thinking of his anticipation for tonight, Julian would have disabused her of that notion and told her precisely just how very eager he was to take her to bed, if he had not thought that it would send her fleeing from the room. He was more used to women falling enthusiastically into bed with him than not and could hardly remember a time that he'd had to exert himself to accomplish that goal. On unfamiliar ground, he picked his way with care. Nell's request made sense—even if he didn't want it to. They would be married a long time. What was a week, a month or even two months of anticipation on his part when set against a lifetime together?

He glanced at her through lowered lids. She had no idea just how appealing she looked as she sat on the sofa, the candle-light gilding her hair, caressing the bare shoulders and casting a golden flicker across the entrancing bosom revealed by the gown. She would be soft and warm in his embrace, her mouth yielding, and his body tightened with expectation of the carnal pleasures that would be his. Every primal instinct urged him to close the small space between them and to show her just how very expert he was in the art of lovemaking, but caution, and the fear of destroying something he could barely guess at, held him back.

When he made no reply, Nell's chin lifted and she cleared her throat. "Well, my lord?"

Rising to his feet, he crossed the room to stand in front of her. Taking one of her hands in his, he pressed a warm kiss onto the back of it. "Perhaps your way will be best . . ." He smiled wryly at her expression—one would have thought she had escaped a fate worse than death.

"Oh, my lord! Thank you!" Nell exclaimed, snatching her hand back with a promptness that might have offended a lesser man. Standing up, she scooted away from him and said brightly, "Well, I am happy that we have that settled between us and since it has been a long day, I think I shall leave you now. Good night, my lord."

She fairly flew across the floor toward the double doors. Her retreat, however, was halted when Julian said, "There is one thing, my dear."

She froze and swung around, startled to find him right behind her. Eyes big and wary, she looked up at his dark, unreadable face. "Yes?"

He smiled and ran a caressing finger down her cheek. "I promise you I shall not force myself into your bed . . . but in return, you must allow me to court you."

"Court me?" she muttered. "What does that mean?"

"Why, only that I may touch you upon occasion"—and his hands slid around her waist as he pulled to her him—"and that I may now and then steal a kiss . . ."

His lips caught hers and his arms tightened around her. He kissed her long and deep, struggling to keep his passion in check, fighting back the desire to take more from the drugging sweetness of her mouth.

When he finally forced himself to lift his mouth from hers, she was pliant in his arms, her gaze unfocussed and her breath ragged. Pleased with himself, he turned her around and giving her a little pat on the rear, murmured, "Good night, my dear. Sleep well."

Chapter 7

As if chased by demons, Nell fled up the stairs to her rooms. And fled, she admitted, as she hurled herself through the door of her suite and shut the door behind her, was the only word for it. Heart banging painfully in her breast she stared at the door, searching frantically for a key, a lock. There was none. But even, she thought wildly, if she could have physically kept him away from her, nothing on this Earth was going to keep him from her mind—the memory of that long, sweetly seductive kiss seared like a brand into her brain.

Hardly aware of Becky bustling around in the background Nell prepared for bed and, despite her heightened senses, kept her thoughts away from what would *not* happen tonight. She felt a sham as she slipped on the fine lace and silk gown and with Becky's warm wishes ringing in her ears climbed into the big bed.

Alone in the dark room she lay there remembering that kiss. She was not, she reminded herself, a complete innocent. She was nine and twenty and she had been engaged once upon a time. She and Aubrey had been engaged only for a few months before her accident, but there had been the occasional stolen embrace and kiss in the garden or secluded nook, so it wasn't as if she'd never been kissed by a man not related to her. Remembering those few fumbling embraces with Aubrey, she snorted. Good heavens, Aubrey's kisses compared to Julian's were akin to comparing water to champagne. There *was* no comparison! Worse, she'd have sworn at the time that she was madly in love with Aubrey. So why, she wondered un-easily, did the kiss of a man she did not know, had not wanted to marry, was not even certain she liked, make her entire body feel as if she had been brushed by fire? Nell found no answers before she fell into a restless sleep.

In the morning, dreading the next sure-to-be-awkward meeting with her husband, she joined him in the breakfast room. To her relief he was the perfect gentleman, neither by word nor deed revealing that anything was amiss in the new marriage.

Not that anything *was* amiss, Nell reminded herself stoutly. To her relief, Julian made no further attempts to deepen their intimacy. As he was an entertaining companion, ever ready with a droll story or unobtrusively seeing to her comfort, she relaxed in his presence, finding that time spent with him passed most agreeably. So agreeably in fact that she looked forward to being with him and was, perhaps, not at all averse to another kiss . . .

By unspoken agreement, she and Julian met each morning for breakfast and together decided upon the plans for the day. They spent most days riding and enjoying the beautiful countryside of Surrey. It delighted Nell to discover that her new husband shared a love of horses and on those long, leisurely rides they whiled away hours at a time discussing horses, and their breeding and care. Some afternoons were passed strolling through the extensive gardens that sprawled out in all directions from the mansion, the roses still bloom-ing despite the increasing chill of autumn. They even shared a picnic on an especially fine day near the lake that had been built on the grounds of the mansion. Evenings were quiet and ended early as each sought out their own rooms and amusements, but as the days sped by, Nell lingered later and later in the dining room, laughing and chatting with Julian.

Julian chafed at the constraints put upon him by Nell, and acting the role of an avuncular companion, when every instinct he possessed sent a decidedly different message, was no easy task. Yet keeping his baser demands tightly leashed had its reward—at week's end as they prepared to leave for Wyndham Manor Nell treated him in a relaxed, confiding manner that had him torn between laughter and despair. There'd been no time prior to the wedding for even simple conversation. This week though, they had learned much about each other, and it had been good for both of them, the early awkwardness having mostly dissipated. Except for being denied her bed, Julian was, if not satisfied, at least, for the time being, resigned to the situation.

Nell was not sorry to leave Talcott's mansion. She had too much time on her hands, too much time to think about her husband and, to her astonishment, she found that she was looking forward to finally seeing her new home and taking up the reins as mistress.

The pleasant weather held: no storms bedeviled them or slowed them down and the journey to Wyndham Manor, not far from Dawlish and the Devonshire coast, was accomplished without incident. Nell fidgeted that last hour on the road, eager to escape the confines of the coach, eager to reach their destination, but as the coach finally swung down the long driveway lined with oaks, she experienced an unexpected attack of nervousness.

In a matter of days she had gone from being plain Miss Anslowe to being the Countess of Wyndham, and the enormity of her changed position suddenly assailed her. She glanced across at Julian, just able to discern his handsome features in the deepening twilight, and as their eyes met, her heart gave a small, uneven jump at the half-glimpsed expression in his. The situation, she realized, had changed between them. They were no longer on neutral ground, but on *his*, and would that, she wondered, change his treatment of her? Would he prove to be a tyrant in his own home? She had no reason to think that overnight he would become a different man than the one she had known these past several days, but doubts lingered and uneasiness stirred. What did she really know of him? A week, even a week as private as the one they had just spent, was not so very long. Perhaps he was a great actor? Hiding his true nature behind a polite smile, a courteous manner? She knew she was being silly but she could not entirely still the anxiety that churned in her breast.

Yet once the coach pulled to a stop and Julian helped her down from the coach in front of an ivy-covered, Elizabethan-style house her hand clung tightly to his. He had been her one constant in a changing world and whatever the future might hold, at this moment she was grateful for his presence as she faced her new world.

The house was huge and ablaze with light. In the gathering darkness of the autumn night, the yellow rays shone out from behind the many mullioned windows welcoming her, beckoning her closer. Nell's feet had barely touched the ground before the tall front doors were swung wide and more warm light spilled out, drawing her inside the house.

To Nell's discomfort, it seemed that all of the servants, from the punctilious butler, Dibble, down to the lowliest, simpering scullery maid, stood in the lofty, gray- and white-marble foyer waiting to greet her. Stiffening her spine and smiling warmly she greeted each of them, wondering if she'd ever remember half their names and positions, but as the moments passed and she moved on down the line of bobbing servants, she relaxed. To be sure, she was stared at with curiosity by some, studied covertly by others, but on the whole she felt welcomed and more at ease than she had expected.

*   *   *

After whisking away her cloak and gloves, Dibble showed them to a small saloon where a light repast awaited them; a fire danced on the marble hearth. Nell enjoyed her meal, thinking that she would have to ask Cook how she managed to make such a light and flavorful hot chicken mousse. The informal meal ended with, among other offerings, a pistachio cream, that fairly melted in her mouth.

Pushing aside her empty dish, she glanced around the charming room of green and cream silk. "You have a lovely home, my lord."

Julian smiled. "It is also your home now. Would you like to see more of it?"

When she hesitated, he added with a twinkle in his eyes, "Dibble, I'm sure, is most anxious to show it off for you."

Nell shot him a saucy look. "Well, never let it be said that I disappointed your butler. Ring for him, if you please."

Crossing to a velvet rope pull, Julian said, "He is also your butler, my dear."

Nell made a face. "I keep forgetting."

Well, that, Julian thought, as he rang for Dibble, certainly puts me in my place.

Dibble appeared instantly and when Julian explained the situation, the butler bowed low and said that it would be his pleasure to show her ladyship around the mansion. Amusement lurking in his eyes, Julian followed and watched Nell's expressive face as she was led from one stately parlor to the next. Seeing her eyes glaze over as Dibble proudly led her into yet another grand suite of rooms, Julian took pity on her and decided to bring a halt to the procession.

Taking Nell's hand in one of his, he smiled down at her and said, "It is a trifle overwhelming, is it not?" Glancing at Dibble he added, "I don't think that her ladyship needs to see any more this evening. This is her home now and she will have a lifetime to become familiar with it. It has been a long journey and I'm sure she would like nothing more than to re-tire to her rooms." To Nell he murmured, "Becky will no doubt be waiting for you." Dropping a kiss on the top of her hands, he said, "If you will excuse me, there are things I must see to—I shall see you in the morning."

Nell flashed Julian a grateful smile and followed Dibble up the wide marble staircase. Throwing wide the doors to her apartments with a flourish, Dibble murmured, "Your rooms, my ladyship. If you require anything, please ring and I shall see that it is taken care of for you."

Thanking him, Nell stepped inside the suite of rooms and shut the door behind her. Glancing around the large, ornately decorated sitting room done in shades of pink and gold, she leaned limply back against the door.

Well, here she was. Home. It felt strange to think of this huge, rambling place as home, but she might as well get used to it, she reminded herself, because that's what it was: her home from now on. Pushing away from the door and walk-ing toward a set of double doors that led, she supposed, to the bedchamber, she wondered how long it would take for this place to really feel like home and not just someone else's house that she was visiting.

Becky was busy unpacking when Nell walked into the bed-chamber. Seeing her mistress, a wide smile crossed her face. "Oh, your ladyship, did you ever see such a place?"

Nell laughed. "Yes, but I never expected to live in one." Catching sight of the huge pink silk-hung bed on the dais on the far side of the room, she blinked. Good heavens! It looked like an explosion of strawberry blancmange! Res-olutely ignoring the bed, Nell wandered around her suite, peeking inside the dressing room, which was was almost as large as her dearly familiar sitting room back at Meadowlea. Opening another set of doors, she found herself staring into her husband's room. Feeling like a snoop, she quickly shut the doors.

Turning to Becky, she asked, "Have you had a chance to get settled? Are the other servants treating you well?"

"Oh, yes, miss—your ladyship! Everyone has been so kind." Her expression awed, she added, "Only think—they have four scullery maids. Can you imagine?"

Nell smiled and made some light comment. Life at Wyndham Hall was going to be different than at Meadowlea, but Nell didn't see that it would be that much different. Running a household, even one the size of the earl's, gave her few qualms . . . being a wife did. She eyed the bed. Her husband had been more than considerate and she knew that most . . . many men confronted by a recalcitrant bride would not have hesitated in exerting their conjugal rights. But now that they were here in his home, amongst his people, would he continue to be so forbearing? She frowned. And would she mind if he was not? A little shiver of anticipation slid down her spine at the idea of Julian in her bed, kissing her as he had that first night, touching her, her touching him . . .

Cheeks flushed, her body tingling in a way foreign to her, she jerked her thoughts away from that path.

A sudden commotion from the direction of the dressing room caught Becky's attention and she said, "That will be your bath, your ladyship. I ordered it before I came upstairs."

Sometime later, after a warm, luxurious bath and tired from the journey, Nell approached the bed. Brushing aside the bed curtains, she gingerly climbed up onto the mattress, discovering that while the bed might look like an explosion of strawberries, it was most comfortable.

She'd thought that she might have trouble sleeping in the huge, unfamiliar room, but no sooner did her head hit the pillow than she fell asleep. She slept deeply for several hours, but insidiously, like a viper uncoiling from beneath a rock, the nightmare crept into her slumber.

The horror of the nightmare unfolded slowly in stark detail. The same smoke-stained gray dungeon again, the same shadowy figure of the man who practiced such terrible, savage cruelty on the weeping, pleading woman. A different woman tonight, Nell noted with one part of her brain. This one older, her hair dark, not blonde, but like the others her body was slim and smooth until that first flash of the blade . . . Nell thrashed amongst the sheets, moaning piteously, her head flinging from side to side as visions of brutality and ugliness swept across her brain. And the blood . . . Dear God, the blood . . . Fear, tasting bitter and foul, filled her mouth, and when the glittering blade slashed down for that final time, she jerked upright. Eyes wide and blind she screamed and screamed again, unable to stop.

At the sound of that first scream, Julian shot out of bed, prepared for battle yet confused and startled. A second scream sent a cascade of ice crashing through his body and immediately identifying the location of the terrified shriek, heedless of his nakedness, he paused only long enough to grab the knife that was never far from him and rushed through the door that divided their quarters.

Inky blackness met him but guided by the memory of the bed's location and the fearful sounds coming from Nell, he raced to the dais. Flinging back the bed curtains, he made out the white-clad form of his wife as she screamed once more and then began to cry in soft, low gulps.

"Oh, please," she begged in broken tones. "Please no more. No more. *Please*."

Realizing that she was in the grip of a nightmare, Julian pushed his knife under the pillow and climbed into the bed beside her. "Shush, Nell. You're safe. It is a nightmare, darling. No one can hurt you—I won't let them."

He reached out, intending to draw her into his arms, but at that first touch of his hand on her shoulder, she shrieked and fought him. Her fingernails bit into his cheek and she writhed like a wild thing, clawing at him, fighting frantically to escape.

Aware that she was still in the grip of the nightmare, he removed his hands from her, saying loudly, sharply, "Nell, wake up! It is a nightmare. Wake up."

His voice penetrated through the fog of terror that surrounded her and she froze. She blinked, shuddered and awoke. "J-J-Julian? Is that y-y-you?"

Moving from the bed, he lit a candle. Coming back to the side of her bed, he sat down. "Are you all right?" he asked quietly, his eyes moving over her, noting the streaks of tears, the pale features and the shudders that still racked her body.

More and more awake with every passing second, Nell nodded and scrubbed her cheeks. Forcing a smile, she glanced at him. "Yes. I am now." Conscious of the gloriously masculine body sitting only inches away from her, her gaze flitted away. "I woke you," she mumbled. "I'm sorry."

Julian shrugged. "That was quite a nightmare you had—indeed, I thought you were being murdered at the very least."

"Someone was," she said thickly. "Someone always is."

"What do you mean?" he asked, frowning. "Always? You have nightmares frequently?"

She nodded, then shook her head, adding, "Not exactly. More frequently of late, but for a long time . . ." She stared off into space.

"But for a long time . . ." he prodded gently.

She glanced back at him, her breath catching in her throat at his sheer physical beauty. His thick black hair was tousled and tumbled across his forehead as the candlelight flickered over him, highlighting and yet shadowing parts of the patrician face, the scrape on his cheek where her fingers had marked him, the broad shoulders and the long, elegantly muscular legs. Unbearably aware of him, aware of the slightest breath he took she tore her gaze away from him again. But the image of his body, his *naked* body would not leave her mind. She risked a glance at his cheek and mumbled, "I'm sorry I scratched you. I didn't mean to—I thought . . ." She swallowed. "I thought you were *him*."

"You didn't hurt me—I've suffered far worse in a fall from

my horse." She nodded, but he sensed that her thoughts were far away. He touched her lightly on the shoulder and she jumped, looking at him. He smiled but there was concern in his green eyes. "The man? In your nightmare? Do you want to tell me about it?"

She bit her lip and looked down at her tightly clasped fingers. "I didn't used to have them," she began. "But after I fell over the cliff, w-w-when I was crippled, ever since then, they come." She took a deep, shuddery breath. "Sometimes, not for months and then . . . T-T-They're always the same . . ." She frowned. "Well, in the first one a man was murdered . . . and not in the dungeon, but after that one, it is always women and always in the same place."

"The dungeon?" Julian asked, leaning forward, his eyes fixed intently on her.

She nodded. "I don't recognize it as anyplace I've ever been, but I recognize it from the nightmares. The size, the color of the stones, the chains on the walls, the bloodstains . . ." She swallowed. "The man, the creature hurting those poor women, is always in the shadows. It is the same man, but I never see his face, but I *know* he's the same one—there could not be two such depraved monsters in the world." Tears slid down her cheeks and she choked back a sob. "It's inhuman what he does to them in that awful place. And no matter how they plead, cry and beg, he never stops." Her voice shook. "He *enjoys* hurting them. Revels in it, the power he has over them."

She sobbed softly and with no more thought than to comfort her, Julian pulled her into his arms. Leaning back against the pillows of her bed, he cuddled her next to him, his lips brushing her hair. "Shhh," he murmured. "You're safe now. He can't hurt you."

Her cheek lying against his warm chest, she said, "But he hurts *them* and I cannot stop him. I can only watch and despair."

"It's not real, Nell," Julian said gently. "It's a nightmare."

She angled her head until her eyes met his. "I think it is real," she confessed. "It seems real to me and once I thought I knew one of his victims."

He shook his head, and said, "It may seem real, my dear, but it cannot be." He smiled at her. "Unless I married a witch and you can see things beyond the ken of normal man."

"Maybe I do see things, real things," Nell said, her expression troubled. "How else would I think I knew one of the women? Why would I feel that the woman was a real person and not the figment of a dream?"

"It is possible that you had seen her days or weeks before and for some reason, your memory put her in your nightmare," Julian replied reasonably.

"Do you think so?" she asked in a small voice, not convinced but wanting to be.

"I'm sure," he said, one hand absently rubbing her back as he would a frightened child.

They lay there together for several seconds bathed in the flickering light from the lone candle, Nell taking comfort from him, Julian quietly murmuring to her, his presence and manner helping to dispel any lingering effects from the nightmare. Precisely when the mood changed, precisely when Julian felt his body stir with something more than the need to comfort, or when Nell became aware of an insistent heat blooming low in her belly and a rampant curiosity about the long masculine body pressed against hers, neither one of them knew.

Whether Julian sensed the change in her or Nell sensed it in him, when she raised her head and their eyes met, the very air sizzled, an electrical sensation, as if lightning had struck nearby, crackled between them. And whether Julian kissed her or she kissed him, neither knew but the next second their mouths were melded together and they kissed as if life itself depended upon it.

Passion rode Julian hard and while one part of him counseled restraint, another part, a hungry, primitive part, would not listen. He kissed her deeply, his tongue conquering and making her mouth his own. That she returned the kiss with equal fervor destroyed the last of his thinly held restraint and his hand slid to her breast, her thigh . . .

Nell's fingers clenched against his chest when he lifted her nightgown, but she did not protest or stop him, not then nor when he whipped the offending garment over her head and in an instant had her naked next to him. The brush of her nipples against the coarse hair on his chest, the feel of his legs against hers sent a dizzying shaft of longing through her and she pressed closer, awash with sensations as old as time and as new as tomorrow.

His mouth worked magic on hers, his fingers plucking at her nipples, his hand cupping her breasts. Her response was everything he could have wished for and she moaned beneath his mouth and arched her back, pushing the soft flesh of her breast deeper into his greedy hand. He took it and all that she had to offer, his hand skimming over her slender body, exploring, touching, lingering, and then moving on to the next enticing curve, the next silky slope . . .

Need such as she had never experienced coiled and twisted low in Nell's body, Julian's kisses and his knowing hands stoking that unfamiliar feeling until it became an urgent, physical thing, clawing at her, demanding more of her, of him. And Julian gave her more, his fingers petting and stroking the thatch of curly hair between her thighs, sending tremors of delight streaking through her.

Uncertain, but unable to help herself, she caressed him, her hands discovering the contours of that sleek back, the muscular arms and chest. Driven as much by curiosity as by need, she reached for the rigid length of flesh that lay between them, a thrill shooting through her when he groaned pleasurably at her unsure touch. His hand covered hers and he taught the motions, the movements that pleased him best. She was an apt pupil and soon he was writhing beneath her hands.

Against her mouth he murmured, "One day, my sweet, you will teach me what gratifies you most—for now we shall just hope that I give you pleasure."

His finger delved inside of her and she arched up, gasping, "Oh! You do, my lord, you *do!*"

He gave something between a groan and a laugh. Laying her onto her back, he slid between her thighs, his fingers caressing and arousing her, making certain that she was ready for him. When she pushed up against his invading touch, he kissed her urgently and positioned himself. Lodged at the opening of her body, he rocked forward in gentle thrusts, driving himself half-mad at the slowness of his penetration. Inch by inch he sank into her soft, hot sheath, each thrust taking him deeper, giving him such pleasure that he thought he would gladly die of it.

Reaching the thin barrier of flesh that prevented further passage, he hesitated. Against her mouth, he muttered, "I may hurt you . . . but I promise you, never again."

Her eyes huge and luminous on his, she said, "I know." Her fingers clenched his shoulder and she wiggled against him, adding, "Please. Do it. *Now.*"

Her movement nearly destroyed what control he had and at her words he made a half-strangled sound and his mouth came down hard on hers. Thrusting deep he burst past the impediment and sank fully within her. Wrapped within her silken heat, her slender arms holding him tight, a growl of pleasure tore from his throat.

In a welter of pain and delight, Nell clung to him, the pain diminishing as the delight grew. Each time he thrust within her, a tremor of pleasure coursed through her and she twisted wildly beneath him. She was lost to the world and there was only Julian and what they were doing to each other, Julian's body driving into hers, her own answering the demand of his. As they moved together, something, something she could not name, curled and flexed in her loins. The incredible feeling increased and a sweet agony of sensation rippled through her. She gasped, stiffening as an explosion of pleasure burst through her.

Buried deep within her, Julian felt her release and with a shudder loosed whatever control he had maintained over himself. With one last thrust, he joined her in ecstasy.

Satiated as he had never been in his life, Julian dragged himself from between Nell's thighs, his breathing ragged and his heart pounding like a war drum. Eyes closed, he pulled her next to him, enjoying the supple warmth of her body as she curled confidingly against him.

Nell lay there listening to the beat of his heart, pleased to learn that hers was not the only one that raced. Deep within her little quakes of delight still rippled and she marveled at how such a simple, basic act could give such pleasure. She wrinkled her nose. And to think that she could have known this delicious part of marriage days ago!

Above her head, Julian asked, "What are you thinking?"

She grinned up at him. "That I was a ninny to hold you at bay."

He choked and half-smiled. "I assume that means that I pleased you."

"Oh, yes, indeed you did, my lord." A gleam in her eyes she murmured, "Will we do this often?"

Laughing, Julian brought his mouth next to hers. "As often as you like, my pet. I am always at your, uh, service." He kissed her and added, "But I trust you will give me a moment to recover before demanding that I exert my husbandly rights again."

Nell giggled and stretched. Perhaps, she decided, being married to Julian was not a fate worse than death. She glanced at his dark handsome face and her heart gave an odd little leap. She wasn't in love with him . . . at least she didn't think she was, but at the moment, she couldn't think of another man who held, or who had ever held, such an allure for her.

There could be no doubt that he held a potent allure for

her—how else to explain that she was lying naked in bed with him, her body still throbbing from his lovemaking? Their marriage had not been to her liking, she couldn't deny it, but now, would she escape if she could? She made a face. Probably. One delightful tumble did not a marriage make. And she had an inherent dislike of being *forced* to do anything.

From beneath her lashes, she studied his face. He seemed resigned to their marriage and she supposed that she should be grateful for that. She could have faced a man full of resentment, intent upon punishing her for their fate, but she had not—he had always been more reasonable about their marriage than she had. In fact he had never shown any sort of reluctance. She frowned. So why hadn't he objected? She had been a complete stranger to him and, even given the circumstances surrounding their marriage, shouldn't he have been a little bitter about it? Perhaps, it hadn't mattered very much to him who he married? That was a lowering thought. But it made her wonder about his motives for going along so tamely with their marriage. God knew, she hadn't and she still wasn't *exactly* resigned to it, but he seemed perfectly complacent with it. Oh, to be sure, being found in such a compromising situation had not left him much choice, even she was willing, albeit reluctantly, to admit that. But still . . . Was his easy acceptance of their forced marriage because he had been married before? Had he been so much in love with his first wife that no woman would ever hold his heart again? There hadn't been any children from that union, either; he had no direct heir. Had he begun to think that it was time he needed an heir?

At her movement, Julian glanced at her. Something in her expression sent his lazy satisfaction spinning away. "What?" he asked. "What are you thinking?"

"Did you love your first wife very much?" Nell blurted.

Julian stiffened and his expression grim, he said, "I'd rather not talk about her—she's in the past and has no place in our marriage—certainly not our bed."

"Oh, that means I can ask you about her tomorrow at breakfast?" Nell asked brightly, hiding the unease his response created.

Julian sat up and slid from the bed. His mouth tight, he muttered, "No. It means that I don't want to talk about Catherine, now or ever." Good God! How could he talk about the unhappiest time in his life, the despair at having made a terrible match, the anguish of losing an unborn child? Especially to this beguiling little minx who, somehow, miraculously made him believe that he might find happiness, great joy in this marriage? Nell deserved a better answer, he knew, but he could not bring himself to speak of those miserable days. At least not yet. Perhaps in time when they were both more confident in their marriage, but not *now!*

"Why not?" Nell persisted, knowing it was unwise, but unable to help herself. Unless Catherine mattered a great deal to him, he should be able to talk about her, and the fact that he wouldn't sent her heart sinking to her toes.

"Because," he said fiercely, reaching under the pillow to grab his knife, "she has nothing to do with our marriage. And I won't have her specter presiding over our marriage bed and at our table." He looked away, but not before Nell had glimpsed the pain in his face. "Catherine belongs to another time and part of my life. I do not want to share those memories with anyone."

He'd grabbed the knife, intending to leave before he said something he might regret, completely having forgotten Nell's nightmare and the fact that she had not seen him with it when he'd entered her room earlier.

At the sight of that naked blade in his hand, her breath sucked in. Eyes huge and wary, she scrambled off the far side of the bed. Poised for flight she stared across at him and questions, doubts flickered across her face.

Cursing himself and realizing what he had done, Julian quickly shielded the knife below the mattress. Softly he said, "I'm sorry. I didn't mean to frighten you. I brought the knife in with me when I heard you scream. I thought you were being attacked and I came to protect you, not harm you. And as for my refusal to disinter my first marriage—forgive me, but I do not wish to lay bare my soul—it is too painful."

The knife forgotten, her heart cold in her breast, Nell stared at him. Were his memories of his first wife so precious he could not even bear to speak of them? And again she wondered at the ease with which he had accepted their marriage. Could it be that after all these years only an heir mattered and as long as he married . . . and fathered a child . . . Thinking of the lovemaking they'd just shared, a chill went through her.

Julian knew that he had blundered, he just didn't know how badly. The passionate little creature who'd been in his arms only moments ago was gone and replaced by a woman who looked at him as if he had betrayed her in some manner.

"I think," she said in a voice that chilled him, "that you'd best seek your own bed, my lord. You accomplished what you came for."

Chapter 8

Conversation was strained the next morning when they met in the morning room for breakfast. In fact, the entire week that followed was uncomfortable for the pair of them as they attempted to settle into marriage.

Julian knew that he needed to repair the damage he'd done, all in innocence, he reminded himself bitterly, but the opportunity did not present itself. Certainly the reserved manner in which his bride treated him did not make it easy for him to broach the subject. That she also avoided him, throwing herself under Dibble's gratified tutelage in the customs and practices of Wyndham Manor didn't help and then there were the very real demands on his own time, which didn't help, either. He'd been away from the estate for months and there was much that needed his attention.

When he did have the spare moment to spend with his bride, except for the few meals they shared together, Nell always seemed in hurry to be somewhere else—wherever, he thought wryly, he wasn't. He'd considered bearding her in her bedroom, but that notion didn't find favor with him. He didn't feel that appearing at his wife's bedside as a supplicant was necessarily going to do him any good. In fact, he found the whole idea repugnant, reminding him as it did of those last months of his first marriage, when he had done everything within his power to make Catherine more resigned to her pregnancy. He didn't believe that Nell was cut from the same cloth, but having only his first marriage to go by, he was wary.

It didn't make him feel any better to know that he could have handled the entire incident better. Could have and should have. He shook his head. He was noted for thinking on his feet, for a quick response in the most complicated of situations, yet he'd reacted to Nell's question like the greenest paperskull.

His prior marriage, and he would be the first to admit it, was a deeply personal and painful subject for him. Nell's question, coming as it did immediately after the most glorious lovemaking he'd ever experienced, had caught him utterly off guard. He could have handled it more adroitly, but he hadn't. And the knife . . . Well, that had been an accident, one that if he hadn't already been rattled by Nell's questions about Catherine, he'd have been able to avoid.

I should never, he told himself for the hundredth time, have left her rooms with things unresolved between us. And the longer the estrangement continued, he realized gloomily, the more insurmountable it would become, the greater the barrier that existed between them would be. It was, he thought, a silly, impossible predicament.

Julian wasn't the only one who knew that mistakes had been made. Nell missed the easy companionship that had existed between them prior to that night and it did not set well with her that their current situation was as much of her own making as his. Not, she reminded herself, that Julian had set himself out to be particularly conciliatory. *He* didn't seem to care in the least that they both went their separate ways. Was this the way he wanted it?

Only half-listening to Dibble as he explained the history of the particularly fine Flemish tapestry that hung in one of the older parts of the house, Nell wondered how the breech between herself and Julian could be healed. It was unhappily clear that the subject of his first wife was painful for him and that he wasn't going to talk about Catherine anytime soon, which left her with the knife to consider . . . She shivered as the memory surfaced of Julian standing before her with a knife in his hand. She didn't know him very well but she didn't think it normal for a gentleman to have such easy access to a knife at that time of night—or to handle it with such a practiced ability. When she considered that he had come into her rooms prepared to defend her, she felt warm and protected, but she couldn't quite put aside her uneasiness at having him brandishing a knife in front of her eyes. She rather thought he'd told the truth, and while she was able to push it aside, every now and then the memory of that gleaming blade held so expertly in her husband's hand would resurface and she would wonder . . .

The knife was a problem, although, she sensed, a small one. But his first marriage to Lady Catherine Bellamy . . . He certainly hadn't been very forthcoming about that! And that, she decided, could become a very big problem. He'd refused bluntly to discuss his first marriage—which, she conceded ruefully, only made her more curious about it . . . particularly his feelings for his first wife.

She frowned as she followed Dibble down the long hallway. She supposed that was the crux of the matter. Their union had not begun in the best fashion and any chance they had of finding happiness together would not be helped by lingering shadows of his previous marriage. If he still loved his first wife, it would explain much, she admitted dejectedly. Such as his willingness to marry her—if his heart had been buried with a dead woman, it didn't matter who he married.

Marriage to a man whom she might come to love and who might come to love her was one thing; marriage to man in love with a ghost was another thing entirely. How can I compete with a dead woman? she wondered. More importantly, do I want to compete with a dead woman? Yes, she rather thought she did. While disliking the circumstances of their marriage, she intended to be happy and although affection could not be forced, she wanted to fall in love with her husband. With a start, she realized that not only did she want to fall in love with Julian, but that she wanted Julian to love her—not some woman moldering in a grave.

Thanking Dibble for his time, Nell wandered outside to stroll along one of the many paths that angled here and there through the extensive gardens. For nearly November the weather was exceptionally pleasant. Oblivious to the late-blooming roses and petunias, she walked without purpose, lost in her own thoughts.

Finding a charming stone bench that overlooked one of several lake-size bodies of water scattered throughout the enormous gardens, she sat down and considered the situation. The solution to one of the problems that lay between them was simple: ask him about the knife. Have him tell her how it had been so handy and how it was that he handled it with such ease. A pistol or a sword she could understand, but a knife . . . a knife wasn't the usual or normal weapon for a gentleman. In her opinion, knives were for the use of villains who skulked in dark, noxious alleys or monsters that inhabited nightmares. She shook off the disturbing thoughts.

Asking about Catherine was not so straightforward, she thought darkly. She'd already tried that and gotten her nose snapped off. No, she wouldn't be asking about Catherine anytime soon. But what was she going to do about the coolness that currently existed between them? Most of it, she reminded herself, of your own making, although the fact that Julian had not been falling over himself to mend matters between them had not escaped her attention. Perhaps, this was the way their life would be henceforth? Did Julian intend that they share the same house, occasionally the same bed, but that their paths would seldom cross, for the most part each one living a separate life? Depressed and feeling a little lost, she stared blankly out at the stretch of water.

The sound of footsteps broke into her thoughts and she glanced over to see Julian walking toward her. Ignoring the way her heart romped in her chest at the sight of his tall form clad in breeches and boots, she smiled and said, "Hello, my lord. Did you finish your business?"

Julian smiled at her and nodded. "Yes, I told Farley that it was too fine an afternoon to spend inside going over dusty estate books." Seating himself beside her, he took her hand and said, "Much too fine when I could be doing something much more to my liking . . . such as sitting beside my bride and enjoying the lovely view."

His gaze was on her face, those jade green eyes skimming over her in a way that made her cheeks bloom with roses. "You're not looking at the view," she said.

"Ah, but I am—and it is most delightful indeed."

Nell giggled. "Are you flirting with me, my lord?"

"With my wife? Why, yes, I do believe that I am. Do you mind?"

Her eyes met his. "No, not at all," she replied. Her fingers tightened on his and she added impulsively, "I've missed you, my lord. You have been very busy of late."

Hiding the pleasure her words gave him, he murmured, "And you also."

Looking at the placid extent of water before them, Nell said, "Perhaps, we won't be so busy anymore?"

Lifting her hand, Julian kissed it. "No, we won't be so busy anymore."

A silence fell between them, both of them uncertain what to say next. But unwilling to allow the moment to pass without making a push to right things between them, Julian said, "I'd like to explain about the other night."

"About the knife?"

Relieved that she did not mention Catherine, and knowing that he was a coward for being so, Julian seized the subject. "Yes. It must have frightened you, coming so soon after your nightmare. I'm sorry for it."

Her eyes fixed on his, she asked, "Do you always have a knife so handy?"

He made a face and releasing her hand, reached down and pulled forth a blade hidden in his boot. "Yes, I'm afraid that I do."

She recoiled a little at the sight of the knife. "Um, is there any particular reason for this? I don't think that most gentlemen go about armed thus. I know that my father and brothers do not—and two of them are in the military."

Replacing the knife, he said, "No, I'm sure that most gentlemen do not hide knives in their boots. But you have nothing to fear—it is simply a habit . . . an old one."

"And carrying a concealed knife in your boot became a habit because . . . ?"

"Because of a wretched, meddling old man by the name of Roxbury who thinks that it is very clever of him to send young, adventurous noblemen, in the guise of spies, to the continent to ferret out information for him," Julian admitted bluntly. "And the devil of it is—he's right. I know that I've brought him back a tidbit or two that have helped thwart Napoleon's efforts to swallow up the known world."

"You're a spy?" Nell asked, astonished.

"Not exactly and not anymore. But there was a time and not too long ago, that I did slip across the channel to discover what I could of Napoleon's plans."

Nell clapped her hands together. "Oh! How exciting!"

Julian made a face. "Believe me it was mostly dull work. Sometimes I did nothing more than carry messages to our allies in France, other times I merely sniffed around discovering what I could. But there was always the possibility of danger—part of the appeal of doing Roxbury's work, I might add—and because of that, a weapon, one easily hidden, but quickly reached, became a necessity." He flashed a twisted smile. "It is as simple as that—because of what I did for Roxbury, I grew used to having a knife always convenient and though I doubt I would ever have use of it now, it is, uh, comforting to know it is nearby." He looked at her. "And that, my lady, is the only reason that I came into your room armed with a knife—besides wanting to protect you." Taking her hand in his and kissing it once more he asked, "Am I forgiven for frightening you?"

"If you will forgive me for being a silly ninnyhammer and reacting badly," Nell said.

Pulling her into his arms, his mouth hovering inches above hers, he muttered, "Oh, I think that can be arranged with absolutely no difficulty at all."

Nell met his descending mouth and returned his kiss with equal fervor, her arms winding around his neck, her breasts pushing against his chest. Desire flooded Julian . . . Nell's generous response, the memory of that last night together, making him wild with need. Hungrily his hand closed over one breast and her soft gasp of pleasure incited an urgent passion. With her so willing and receptive in his embrace, it took all the willpower he possessed not to push up her gown and tumble her right there in the garden. Only the thought that a servant might come upon them stopped him.

His eyes glittering with desire, he set her from him. "It is," he said huskily, "a very good thing that we are married—otherwise, I am afraid that I would dishonor both of us."

"Is it a good thing, my lord? Our marriage?" she asked quietly.

He smiled. Running a caressing finger over her damp mouth, he murmured, "Ask me in twenty years."

It wasn't a very satisfactory answer, but Nell was happy enough to accept it for the present. The breech between them seemed to be mended and if questions about his first wife lingered like a small canker in the heart of a rose, she reminded herself that they had been married only for a few weeks. She had a lifetime to find out about Catherine . . . and her husband's feelings for a dead woman. I am the one who is married to him now, she told herself grimly, not Catherine.

And when Julian came to her that night, she welcomed him

into her bed and her body, determined to drive the specter of the other woman from his mind. She did better than she knew because the *last* thing on Julian's mind when Nell was in his arms was the memory of the woman who had caused him such pain and anguish.

Delighted with her husband's lovemaking and the reestablishment of friendly relations between them, Nell decided that marriage, especially to such a handsome and exciting man as her husband, wasn't a terrible thing. His nightly visits to her room became a ritual that she looked forward to with far more anticipation than even she thought seemly. I am, she admitted dreamily one night after a particularly satisfying bout of lovemaking, becoming quite, *quite* partial to this side of marriage.

Though she was still learning about the manor and adjusting to marriage, by the time November gave way to December and winter made itself felt with icy rain and blustery winds, she'd begun to think of the manor as her home. Recently, she'd met several of the notables from the neighborhood, and Marcus, accompanied by his mother, had called several times. She liked both and soon felt comfortable with them, treating Marcus like one of her brothers and Mrs. Barbara Sherbrook like a favorite aunt—if she'd ever had an aunt. She was learning her way around the district, but in many respects, Nell was aware that she was still a stranger. When she considered the events surrounding her marriage, she was surprised at how smoothly she had stepped into her new role as Countess Wyndham. She had a husband whose very smile made her spirits lift and whose touch she had grown to crave. Only to herself would she admit, and then only reluctantly, that she was halfway in love with him. His deepest feelings remained a mystery to her, but she knew he enjoyed her company and his many trips to her bed made it clear he did not find making love to her a chore. And if the shadow of Julian's first wife sometimes cast a gloom over her growing happiness, she fiercely pushed it aside. She was alive. Lady Catherine was not.

For all that, Nell was a little homesick. She missed her family, but every week the arrival of a missive from either her father or one of her brothers made them seem not so far away. Drew and Henry had remained in London and their letters were full of war news and their fervent hopes of getting in a few licks at Boney. Her father and Robert had left London shortly after the wedding and were back at Meadowlea, Robert taking over more and more of the running of the estate, leaving Sir Edward time to putter around in the small conservatory that had been built a few years ago. He was, Sir Edward informed her in one letter, developing quite the green thumb.

This particular cool, gray morning in early December, both Nell and Julian had received letters. Recognizing her father's scrawl on the envelope Nell had opened it and was soon happily lost in the mundane affairs at Meadowlea. Julian had also recognized the writing on his letter, but the sight of that dainty script had filled him with foreboding. Reading the contents, he knew his foreboding was justified.

His stifled curse caught Nell's attention and from the other end of the table, she glanced up. "Did you receive bad news, my lord?"

"That depends," he said carefully, "on how well you will like having your stepmother-in-law and her daughter taking up residence with us within weeks and remaining here until the Dower House can be refurbished to Diana's liking—an undertaking which is likely to last for months."

"I thought that Lady Diana was remaining in London for the winter," Nell said, her pleasure in the morning dimming. That Lady Diana did not like her had not escaped Nell's notice. The dowager countess had not said or done anything di-

rectly, but there had been a decidedly chilly note and a reserved manner about her whenever she'd been in Nell's company that had made it clear that Lady Diana was *not*
overjoyed with the match. Nell didn't think she'd have any
trouble with Elizabeth—Elizabeth had seemed a lively, good-
natured young woman—and Nell was confident that without
interference from Lady Diana, she and Elizabeth would be on
good terms in no time at all. Lady Diana was the rub.

"That was my understanding also. But it seems she's changed
her mind and is eager to return to Wyndham Manor."

Nell forced a smile. "Well, it *is* her home, my lord."

He cast her a brooding look down the length of the table,
Marcus's words about domestic wars coming back to haunt
him. Nell had settled into the routine of Wyndham Manor
without difficulty. She had a firm but kindly hand with the
servants and while no one would have dared to express
themselves one way or another to him, it was obvious that
the staff was very happy with their new mistress. But there
was no use pretending that the advent of his stepmother's unexpected arrival wasn't going to cause some disruptions. Not
only could Diana's fits and starts be a problem but he also
feared the feminine squabbles that might break out. If Diana
began to lord it over Nell . . . The hideous image of himself
torn asunder between two raging women rose in his mind.

"Isn't it, my lord?" Nell persisted when he remained silent.
"Her home?"

Julian shrugged. "Not exactly," he answered. "It *was* her
home and I would never want her to feel unwelcome. But it is
our home now—you are mistress of Wyndham Manor, not
my stepmother. She and Elizabeth will be our guests."

Several hours later Julian was still dwelling on Lady Diana's
unexpected desire to return to the country, when Dibble announced Marcus. Always glad to see his cousin, but especially
when Marcus's presence took his mind off of his problems,
Julian smiled as Marcus was shown into his study.

Julian's study was a large, masculine room, filled with books and mostly leather furniture. A Turkish rug in jewel tones of blue, gold and burgundy lay upon the gleaming wooden floor and midnight blue velvet drapes hung at the tall windows. The day had turned wet, drizzle had been falling since noon, and a welcome fire danced on the hearth, the faint scent of apple wood perfuming the air.

Greetings were exchanged and the two men chose a pair of large, overstuffed chairs covered in black leather near the fire in which to settle. Dibble served them tankards of hot whiskey punch and left the silver bowl full of the steaming potent drink behind when he departed.

Sprawled in the big chair, his booted feet resting near the fire, Julian said, "A nasty day for you to be out and about, isn't it?"

Marcus took a sip of the punch, the smell of lemons, cinnamon and cloves mingling with the whiskey rising to his nostrils. "Yes, it is, but this punch of Dibble's is almost reward enough for venturing out." Frowning, Marcus said, "I thought about waiting, and it probably isn't important . . . But I didn't want you to be blindsided as I was." He made a face. "Raoul, sly jackanapes that he is, would probably think it a great jest if you were, and Charles can be so . . . Well, Charles might just invite himself and the bounder to dinner here—if he was feeling particularly bold . . . and stupid."

"The, er, bounder? Obviously someone I'd not want to see."

"Obviously," Marcus replied with deep feeling. "I was in Dawlish yesterday afternoon," he said, "and who should walk up to me bold as brass on the street, but Charles and Raoul . . . accompanied by Lord Tynedale." Marcus's upper lip curled. "I'll give Charles his due, he didn't seem overjoyed to be in Tynedale's company, but that blackguard Tynedale fairly gushed how enjoyable he found Stonegate and how *very* much he was looking forward to an extended stay with his friends. Raoul was his usual foppish self—going on and on about how he intended to learn Tynedale's way with his cravat—as if Tynedale actually *knew* how to tie a cravat. It was nauseating. I tell you, Julian, I didn't know whether to cast up my accounts right in their faces or mill the three of them down." He looked thoughtful. "Should have milled them down."

Since Julian had first laid eyes on Nell, Tynedale had been the last thing on his mind. Guilt knifed through him as the realization hit him that, lost in the delight of his marriage, he had pushed Daniel's suicide and Tynedale's part in his young relative's ruin and needless death to the back of his mind. He hadn't forgotten that he had the power to ruin Tynedale, and thinking of all those vowels he held, some of his guilt faded. Daniel would be avenged—that was a certainty—it was only a question of *when*. Yet Nell's abduction by Tynedale complicated the situation. He didn't believe that Tynedale would be so foolish as to hold himself up for public condemnation in order to besmirch the reputation of the newest Countess of Wyndham. Yet Tynedale was in desperate straits and there was no guessing what he might do. Julian, knowing the man as he did, wouldn't put it past Tynedale to bring about his own ruination if in the process it harmed Nell, and through Nell, himself. Julian had no doubt that Tynedale was base enough to contemplate such an act.

And then there was Charles . . . Julian sighed. Charles may have introduced his nephew to Tynedale, but whatever other faults Charles had, and Lord knew he had plenty, Julian never doubted that his cousin had loved the boy and had never meant him any harm. His cousin was a rake, with all of a rake's bad habits, but Julian would acquit him of wishing Daniel evil. Julian sighed again. Charles was a problem, if only because one never knew which way Charles would jump. If Charles knew the truth of the marriage, he might be fiercely protective of the family name or he might wring whatever mischief he could from the circumstances of the unexpected marriage. With Charles one never knew.

Julian swore under his breath.

"My sentiments precisely," Marcus said. "Short of murder, I don't see how Tynedale can be removed from the castle. Of course, if you like, I'd be happy to run him through—I owe him for Daniel as much as you do."

Julian scowled as another problem presented itself. Marcus didn't know of Tynedale's involvement in his marriage to Nell. How the hell was he going to keep that a secret? Not that he feared Marcus would babble the specifics, but the more people who knew the circumstances, the more likely it was that someone would slip and say something. There'd already been enough talk about the suddenness of it—all he needed for a full-blown scandal to erupt was for Tynedale's part in the affaire to become public fodder.

"So what are you going to do?" Marcus asked. "You're the head of the family, but I hardly think that Charles would pay you any heed if you ordered him to send Tynedale about his business."

"It certainly is complicated—more than you know," Julian admitted. He studied Marcus as his cousin lounged near the fire. He would trust him with his life, so why not trust him with the full story surrounding his marriage to Nell? Because, he conceded wryly, it wasn't just his secret, it was Nell's, too.

Acting on impulse he stood up and rang for Dibble. When Dibble walked into the room, Julian asked him, "Is her ladyship about?"

"Why, yes, your lordship. She is upstairs in her sitting room, answering letters, I believe." Julian glanced back at Marcus, who was watching him with a small frown. "Indulge me, please," he said. "I won't be gone long."

Leaving behind a mystified Marcus, Julian took the stairs two at a time. Reaching his wife's apartments, he entered her sitting room. Nell was seated at a kneehole desk before a bank of windows, writing. Hearing the door open behind her, she turned and smiled when she saw that it was her husband who had disturbed her.

"Why, hello, my lord. Have you finished your business?"

"Not exactly," Julian said. Walking across the room, he pulled up a chair beside hers. Taking her hand in his, he said bluntly, "I have just learned that Tynedale is in the area, staying at my cousin's house."

Nell's face paled and she stiffened. "But how does this come about? I cannot imagine Marcus associating with such a vile creature."

Julian made a face. "You have not yet met the whole family—I have many cousins, but what concerns us now is the set of cousins I have who live not ten miles away, Charles and Raoul Weston. Their father was my father's twin and next in line for the title behind mine." Julian sighed. "For various reasons, not the least of it that I hold the title, there is little love lost between us—although it was not always so—but at present one or both of them might like it if the scandal caused me harm."

"I see," she replied, her expression troubled. The full import of what he was saying suddenly hit her and her eyes widened. "Do you think Tynedale would dare tell them that he abducted me that night?" Something else occurred to her. "Oh, goodness, surely we wouldn't have to meet him socially."

"That's what I don't know. He might tell Charles and Raoul. As for meeting him socially you have little to fear." He gave a hard laugh. "Charles is not a fool, he would know better than to allow Tynedale to attend any function where I would be. My main worry is that Tynedale might try to play a game of cat and mouse with us." Quietly, Julian added, "I have the means to destroy him—for motives of my own, I have managed to obtain enough of his vowels to ruin him financially. I'm sure he has learned of it and he might think that he could blackmail me into giving them up for his silence—he goes away and keeps his mouth shut if I give him the vowels."

Nell's hand tightened on his and she leaned forward, saying passionately, "My lord, you must not! He is a devil and cannot be trusted to keep his word. You would waste those vowels."

"I agree. I learned of his presence at Stonegate, Charles's home, only moments ago and have not yet decided on a way to handle the situation. But he is a danger to us and short of outright murder I want him gone—and his mouth shut. And if he tells Charles or Raoul of the abduction, I do not know what the consequences might be."

"Do your cousins hold their own name in such little esteem, that they would take part in any scheme to bring dishonor upon it? Wouldn't they dislike having *their* name besmirched?"

Julian smiled bitterly. "I sometimes believe from Charles's reckless escapades that except to inherit my title and fortune, he has no regard at all for the name of Weston, and I have no way of knowing if he will take our side or drag our name through the devil's cesspit."

"I've brought you nothing but trouble and you have been so very kind to me," Nell said mournfully. "And now through me, you stand to have your name and family held up to public disdain and contempt." She dragged her hand from his and rose to her feet. "Oh, if only I had not taken refuge in that toll keeper's cottage, then none of this would have happened."

"I have not been 'kind' to you," Julian said with an edge to his voice, also rising to his feet. "I have pleased myself."

She gave a little nod of her head that plainly indicated that she didn't believe him. Suppressing an urge to shake her, Julian said coolly, "Whatever the reasons, we are married, and Tynedale is on our doorstep. We are going to have to keep our heads about us, and gather our forces to us if we hope to get through this with our reputations intact."

"You make it sound like a battle."

"In many ways it is a battle, one I intend to win. But I need your help to do it."

She crossed to stand in front of him. Her voice passionate,

she declared, "You have it! Whatever you want, I will give it to you. We will beat Tynedale at his own game."

He smiled at her fierceness. "For now all I ask is permission to explain to Marcus Tynedale's part in our marriage."

Ready to take up the sword and confront Tynedale, she was startled by his request. Nell blinked, thought about it a moment, then flashed him a lovely smile. "If it will help us defeat Tynedale, then by all means tell your cousin."

That smile made his heart leap and pulling her into his arms, he kissed her. Putting her from him a long moment later, he said roughly, "And I am not *kind* to you."

Chapter 9

Leaving Nell to stare mystified after him, Julian departed her rooms and returned to the study. After shutting the door behind him, he walked to his chair near the fire and seated himself across from Marcus.

Marcus lifted one beautifully sculpted brow. "A task of some urgency?"

Julian grinned at him. "Not exactly, but the tale I have to tell you does not just involve myself and I needed my wife's permission before I told it to you."

"By all that I hold holy," Marcus marveled, his eyes dancing with glee, "can it be? Do my senses deceive me? Is the fellow standing before me not the much-sought-after Julian Weston, breaker of hearts from one end of England to the other? And is he not living tamely under the cat's paw? That I should live to see the day that he is brought to his knees by a mere female—shameful!"

"Enjoy yourself, but not too much. Someday our positions may be reversed—*you* may be the newly married man."

Marcus shuddered. "Please, no, I beg you! Never even mention my name in connection with the word 'matrimony.' I like my life just as it is and, unlike you, I have no title to worry about passing onto the fruit of my loins."

"There is that," Julian said, "but you do have a fortune and lands, and someday *someone* must inherit them."

"My eventual demise and the dispersal of my estate was not the subject of this conversation—your, er, consultation with your wife was."

Julian's humorous manner evaporated and leaning forward, he told Marcus of the events that had led to his marriage to Nell. When he finished speaking, he leaned back and waited for Marcus's reaction.

Marcus took a sip of his whiskey punch. "Do you know, I have always enjoyed being somewhat perspicacious, but this is one time I would have preferred being a corked-brained dunderhead. I knew that you were spinning me a Banbury story when you first told me about your coming marriage, but I never suspected something like this." He frowned. "Will Tynedale keep his mouth shut? Or do you think his whole purpose in coming here and staying with Charles is to make mischief?"

Julian shrugged. "It could be chance, but I doubt it."

"I wonder," Marcus speculated aloud, "if Tynedale realizes that Charles, if the mood took him, might be a powerful ally in the ruination of your lady's reputation." He shot Julian a keen look. "You do realize that she is the one most likely to suffer from this? You are, after all, the Earl of Wyndham, while she, until her marriage to you, was a little country nobody—albeit a lovely and rich nobody. She will be the most vulnerable to gossip and innuendo. People may pity you for falling into her clutches and some may think you a cuckold for marrying Tynedale's castoff, but your wife is the one who will be smeared the most."

A deadly note in his voice, Julian said, "I would be careful what I said, my friend. It is my wife you are talking about—and I do not appreciate you referring to her as 'Tynedale's castoff.' She was an innocent pawn caught up in his schemes and I'll not have you or anyone else refer to her in less than respectful terms. I'd run another man through for saying what you just did."

"Oh, don't fly up in the boughs with me! *I* ain't the enemy!

I hold Lady Wyndham in the highest esteem and will stand shoulder to shoulder with you on this—I'm merely telling you how others may view the situation." He grinned at his cousin. "Personally, I think your wife will be the making of you and if it didn't go against the grain, I'd shake Tynedale's hand for bringing about your marriage to her."

Julian flashed a twisted smile. "We are more alike than we know—that same thought, or something similar, has crossed my mind more than once."

"So what are we to do? I dislike standing about waiting to be attacked. I would far rather take the fight to the enemy."

"I agree, but I cannot, at the moment, short of murder, see a way out of this quagmire. If I confront Tynedale, it may make him believe that he holds a stronger hand than he does. Certainly I cannot tell him not to tell my cousins—he'd run to them with the tale the very next second. The vowels are, at present, useless to me. If I offer them to him for his silence, as Nell observed, once they are in his hands, there is nothing then to stop him from spreading the story of the abduction."

He scowled. "It occurs to me that he holds the best cards." At Marcus's skeptical look, he added, "By altering the story only slightly, he can make himself look to be the injured party. He could avow that because of her father's objections, he and Nell were making a runaway match of it—that there was no abduction, she was a willing participant and they were separated in the storm. My arrival on the scene ruined their plans and I am the villain of the piece. I compromised Nell and wrested her away from the arms of her true love." His scowl deepened. "That may even be what he plans to do—that way he blackens me, creates a scandal around Nell and emerges from the fray a figure of sympathy."

Marcus straightened. "Good God! You are right." Staring down at his boots, he muttered, "Well, then there is nothing for it. I shall just have to kill Tynedale." Glumly he added, "Probably Charles, too, but I tell you, Julian, it goes against the grain killing a relative."

Julian burst out laughing. "And I know you would, too, but I will not have you fighting my battles for me. I don't know yet how to resolve this, but we will manage, somehow."

The weather worsened, the drizzle turning into full-fledged rain and Marcus, at Julian's urging, remained for dinner. Nell had eyed Marcus uneasily when she joined the gentlemen in the dining room, but Marcus soon put her at her ease and her fears that Julian's cousin would think less of her once he knew the facts surrounding her marriage were soon banished. By the time the meal ended, Nell knew that Marcus was a dear and loyal friend, not only to Julian but to herself as well.

On the point of leaving the two men to their liquor, listening to the howling wind and driving rain, Nell suggested that Marcus remain for the night. He accepted her invitation gladly.

Nell retreated to the green saloon at the rear of the house. Unlike many of the rooms of the house, the green saloon was not large and it had a cozy informality that appealed to her. Not long after her arrival at Wyndham Manor, it had become her favorite room in which to spend the long winter evenings. When Dibble arrived with the tea tray, Nell informed him of their overnight guest. Dibble left, saying that he would immediately have rooms prepared for Mr. Sherbrook and would press one of the male servants into service to wait upon him.

When the gentlemen joined her in the green saloon, she mentioned to Marcus the arrangements for his comfort.

"I hope you will not mind having a footman acting as your valet?"

"My dear lady, I am grateful for your hospitality and since I am at your mercy for my wants, I appreciate your efforts."

"And I suppose," said Julian with a smile, "that I will have to give up some of my clean linen for you to wear home tomorrow."

"Well, I certainly wouldn't want to wear your dirty linen!"

The evening passed enjoyably and a few hours later, leaving the gentlemen as they started a game of piquet, Nell sought out her rooms.

Dismissing Becky after she'd changed into her nightclothes, Nell climbed into bed feeling more tired than usual. She always enjoyed Marcus's company, but until she'd seen him this evening and his manner had banished her fears of appearing less worthy in his eyes, she'd spent some anxious hours alone and they had taken their toll.

Yet, once abed, she lay sleepless, tossing and turning for hours. The faint feeling of nausea that she'd tried to ignore since dinner became more insistent and she sat up, thinking to ring for some hot milk. The upright motion was a mistake, the room swam and she bolted from the bed, barely reaching the chamber pot in time. Heaving and gagging she lost her dinner.

The door to Julian's chamber's opened and he stepped into the room. It was a woebegone face that turned in his direction. "Nell!" he cried and hurried to her side. "What is wrong, sweetheart?"

Mortified at being found heaving over the chamber pot, Nell motioned him to wait and tottered into her dressing room. From the rose and cream china pitcher that sat on the washstand, she threw water on her face and swilled some around in her mouth. Pushing back a strand of lank hair, she stared at herself in the mirror that hung above the marble washstand and made a face. She looked terrible, her eyes too big for her face and her skin pale and lifeless. Exactly what an amorous husband of only a few months wished to see, she thought wretchedly.

Walking back into her bedroom she sent Julian a wry smile. "I should have remembered that buttered lobster never agrees with me."

"Shall I have some hot tea or milk brought up for you?"

he asked, concerned, as his eyes roamed over her pale features.

Nell nodded. "Milk, please."

After helping her into bed, he rang for a servant. Shortly, a tray with a steaming glass of hot milk and some dry toast was placed on a table near the bed. Her stomach still rolling, Nell cautiously sipped the milk. Julian sat on the side of the bed only a few inches away, watching her. She still felt queasy and she prayed that the milk would stay down and that she wouldn't further humiliate herself by vomiting all over him.

It was a near thing, the milk hardly reaching her stomach before it was on a return journey. Nell scrambled frantically from the bed and Julian, having a good idea where this was going, leaped away and grabbed the chamber pot, presenting it to her in the nick of time.

If she'd been embarrassed previously that was nothing compared to her feelings now as Julian held her head and she gave up the milk into the chamber pot, her body racked by powerful spasms. When the ordeal was over, he took the chamber pot from her trembling hands, and setting it aside, disappeared into her dressing room, returning with a soft, damp cloth that he used to wipe her face and mouth. Her humiliation was complete. She'd never be able to look him in the eye again.

"I'm sorry," she said, her cheeks on fire.

"Don't be. Anyone can be ill. Are you feeling better now?"

She nodded, not looking at him, wishing him gone, so she could die in peace.

He smoothed back her hair and punched up her pillows. "Lie back and get some sleep. I shall see that the physician is here first thing in the morning."

"Oh, that's not necessary. I will be fine by then," she protested. "It was only the buttered lobster."

He smiled at her. "I'm sure it was, but I still think it will be a good idea if you see Dr. Coleman, our local physician. He is very good, you will like him."

Nell argued with him, but Julian only smiled. Pressing a kiss on her forehead, he said, "Go to sleep. If you need anything, call out. I will leave my door ajar and will hear you."

Nell eventually fell asleep.

She woke the next morning to a weak winter sun, but yesterday's storm was gone and with it, she thought happily, her upset stomach.

Bounding from bed, she luxuriated in a long warm bath. Sometime later, smelling deliciously of pink carnations, her tawny locks caught up in a green silk bow at the back of her head and wearing a charming gown of light green muslin, she hurried into the breakfast room. Marcus and Julian were there before her and both men rose when she entered the room. Waving them aside, she walked to the long sideboard and filled her plate full of several rashers of bacon, a slice of ham, scrambled eggs, some kippers and two pieces of buttered toast.

Seeing Marcus's expression at the amount of food on her plate, she grinned at him. "It is alarming, isn't it? But I've always had a good appetite and my father always insisted that the first meal of the day be a large one."

"I see that you have suffered no lasting ill effects from your, uh, disagreement last night with the buttered lobster," Julian commented after a thorough appraisal of her face.

"Indeed not. I told you that I did not need to see a physician."

"So you did," he agreed, "but I'm afraid that you shall still see him. I've already sent a servant requesting him to call upon us this morning."

Nell wrinkled her nose at him. "Has anyone ever told you that you can be very overbearing and dictatorial at times?"

"How very perspicacious of you, my lady!" Marcus said, leaning intimately in her direction. "I have told him that very thing time and time again." He sighed. "Alas, fair lady, he is the great Earl of Wyndham and cannot conceive of what we lesser beings speak."

"Tell me again," Julian said to Marcus, "why you are one of my favorite cousins?"

It was a merry meal and when it ended, Nell was sorry to see Marcus prepare to ride away. She and Julian waved him off from the broad steps of the house and as they walked back inside, she said, "I like him."

"I'm glad. Marcus is more like a brother to me than a mere cousin. I am very fond of him."

"But not Charles and Raoul?"

Showing her into his study, Julian remarked, "It is difficult to explain to someone who doesn't understand the family background my relationship with Charles. There was a time that we were very close but . . ."

"But . . . ?"

Inviting her to sit by the fire, he took the chair opposite her and said, "It is complicated and requires a bit of family genealogy to make it understandable." He made a face. "It is a long tale."

Leaning back into the supple leather of the chair, Nell said, "I'm not going anywhere."

He shot her a look. "You are a persistent little thing, aren't you?"

She grinned. "And you are dictatorial and overbearing."

Julian laughed. "Oh, very well, if you must know . . ." He hesitated, his light mood fading. Just when she thought he wouldn't continue, he said, "Like your brothers, my father was also a twin."

Nell looked surprised. "Identical like Drew and Henry?"

He nodded. "Yes, my father, Fane, and his brother, Harlan, were born only minutes apart and were alike as two peas in a pod—at least in looks. In personality . . ." He stared off. "In personality they were very different." He flashed her a wry grin. "My grandfather, the Old Earl, as we all called him, was a rake's rake, his reputation for seduction, inebriation and gambling was legendary, and I'm afraid that Harlan took after him, while my father was more like my mother's family."

"So except for your father arriving a few moments before him, Harlan would have been the heir?"

"Yes, and believe me, in his later years, Harlan dwelled far too long and often on that point. I remember one time, when he was in his cups shortly before he died, that he even dared to suggest that *he* was really the firstborn and heir, but for reasons that only made sense to a drunkard, he and my father were switched at birth."

"Not very logical."

"No, but then Uncle Harlan wasn't very logical at times. Other times he could be the best uncle in the world, but . . ."

"Not always," Nell said gently.

He cast her a grateful look. "No, not always. When I was young, my father and Harlan were very close, as twins often are. Oh, they sparred and fought, but there was a bond between them that seemed unbreakable. When Harlan's first wife died, and John and Charles were hardly out of leading strings, it was my father who steadied him during that wretched time. And when my mother died a few years later, it was Harlan who helped him the most during that sad time. Until around the time of John's death our two families were almost inseparable."

Nell frowned. "You mentioned John and Charles . . . Where does Raoul fit into the family?"

"Raoul is Harlan's son by his second wife, Sofia, a Frenchwoman."

"Ah, that explains the name. I wondered about it."

He smiled. "Harlan's marriage to her caused some raised eyebrows—not what it would do now with the war with Napoleon going on, but at the time it certainly caused a stir."

"Is she still alive?"

"Oh, yes. Aunt Sofia resides at Stonegate and gives the

place some respectability. Lord knows that without her there Charles and Raoul could very well turn it into a brothel."

"They do not sound very nice."

Julian made a face. "They're pleasant enough and as with my uncle, there was a time that I considered them in the same light that I do Marcus. In my youth, I spent as much time at Stonegate with my cousins as they did here. Marcus was part of the group—we all grew up together." His voice thickened. "John was the eldest of us by five years, with me next in age. John and I were extremely close, and when his son, Daniel, was born, John asked me to be his guardian should something happen to him. It was an odd request and we were, I think, both drunk at the time, but I agreed, never thinking I would actually find myself in that position."

When he remained silent for several minutes, his expression bleak, Nell prodded, "Something happened to John?"

"When Daniel was twelve years old, John was murdered," he said baldly.

"Murdered!" she exclaimed. "How horrible!"

"It was the worst tragedy that had ever happened in our family, even worse than the loss of my aunt or my mother— we were all devastated. John was . . ." He stopped, steadied his voice and then went on. "I can't explain the anguish we felt at the time. I often think that it was the loss of his eldest son that sent Harlan down his own path to destruction. He drank even more heavily than usual—he'd always been a heavy drinker—and he gambled . . ." Julian sighed. "He'd played ducks and drakes with his money all the time, but in a matter of months he'd gambled away most of a tidy fortune. Already furious that John had named me guardian of his grandson and heir, once he found himself in dun territory he resented my father and myself all the more."

"But none of it was your fault," Nell said hotly. "You didn't murder John or appoint yourself guardian, and you certainly didn't gamble away his fortune."

Julian gave a twisted smile. "You're wrong. Harlan

blamed my father and me for all his ills—and his poison corrupted Charles and Raoul. They were very loyal to their father and if Harlan resented and blamed us, so did they. Their attitude was not logical or reasonable and perhaps, if Harlan had lived longer, the breech might have eventually been healed." Heavily, Julian added, "Uncle Harlan died hardly a year after John . . . broke his neck while drunk by falling down the stairs at Stonegate."

Sympathy in her gaze, Nell said, "A terrible, sad tragedy, but again, not your fault—or your father's. Surely, Charles and Raoul cannot blame you for what happened. It wasn't *your* fault."

"That may be, but they are convinced that if my father had not selfishly—Raoul's word—refused to pay off all of Harlan's debts, that he would not have been drinking so much and wouldn't have fallen down the stairs." Julian shrugged. "Charles particularly resented my guardianship of his nephew. He felt slighted, and I believe was deeply hurt, that John bypassed him and left Daniel in my hands." He smiled ruefully. "And no one can hold a grudge like Charles."

"Well! They are fools the pair of them, and your uncle, too," Nell said firmly. She frowned. "And Daniel, your ward? What of him?"

Julian took a deep breath and told her of Daniel's suicide and the events surrounding it.

"*Tynedale!*" she spat, sitting bolt upright in her chair. "I cannot believe the infamy of that man." Her hands clenched into fists in her lap. "We must do something about him. First your cousin Daniel, and then his abduction of me. Oh, but his heart is black. I'd like nothing better than to run him through."

"I tried, but all I managed was to mark his pretty face," Julian said dryly.

Nell looked at him admiringly. "That was you? You gave him that scar?" At Julian's nod, she added warmly, "Oh, but that was well done of you, my lord!" A thoughtful expression crossed her face. "It is too bad that you could not have killed him."

Julian laughed. "My sentiments exactly." His face grew grim. "Because I had failed to kill him in our duel, I had planned to ruin him financially—hence my, er, collecting of his vowels."

She tapped a finger against her lips. "It is a very complicated situation and I see why you cannot use those vowels against him." She looked searchingly at him. "Are you so positive that Charles and Raoul would really take his side against you? Might not their sense of family unite them behind you?"

Julian shrugged. "It is difficult to tell. The relationship between us has grown, uh, uncomfortable during these past several years. We are not openly at daggers drawing with each other; we can still be in the same room with one another without coming to blows, but their resentment is deep and bitter."

"And Charles is your heir?"

"Yes . . . until, and if, we have a son."

Nell stared fixedly at her lap, the idea of a child, hers and Julian's, had not previously occurred to her. Remembering their passionate nights together made her heart race. Why, she could be pregnant at this very moment!

Terrified and elated at the same time by the thought of carrying Julian's child, Nell could think of nothing to say. For probably one of the first times in her life she was speechless. A child! Hers and Julian's. A warm glow spread through her body. To hold their child in her arms . . . She could think of nothing more wonderful.

Julian watched her face, wondering what she was thinking. Catherine had been adamantly against children, but it was a topic he and Nell had never touched upon. Would she, like his first wife, hate being pregnant with his child? A slight chill entered his heart. Surely he would not be unlucky enough to have a second wife who detested the idea of carrying his child? He did not want to believe it of Nell but, he reminded himself, for all the present easy intimacy that existed between them, they didn't know each very well—and she had not wanted to marry him . . .

A tap on the door broke into his thoughts and, at his command, Dibble entered the room. "My lord, the physician is here."

"Ah, show him to her ladyship's rooms. She will join him there."

The door shut behind Dibble. Sending Julian a speaking look, Nell stood up. "I told you that I didn't need to see a physician."

"And I told you that I thought you should see him," Julian replied equably.

"And if I refuse?" she asked, a speculative glint in her eyes.

He stood up. "I shouldn't like to," Julian said softly, "but if you refuse, then I shall be forced to carry you up the stairs myself and deposit you in your rooms."

She eyed his tall form and a delicious little shudder went through her at the idea of him sweeping her up in his arms and carrying her upstairs against her will. She considered forcing the issue, but in the end, she decided that this wasn't the battle in which to exert her rights.

"Bully," she said.

"But only for your own good," he replied with a crooked smile. "Come now, I will escort you to your rooms and introduce you to Dr. Coleman."

They walked up the stairs together and entered her sitting room. A tall man, his back to them, was standing staring out the long windows. Hearing the door open, he turned and smiled.

Nell's heart nearly stood still as she stared at the handsome man before her. She might as well have been facing her husband! She glanced up at Julian, then back at the other man.

No, on second thought, they did not quite look exactly the same, but they shared enough features in common to make her wonder.

Julian made the introductions and then after a few moments of polite conversation, discreetly left the room.

"Shall we adjourn to your dressing room, my lady?" Dr. Coleman asked with a smile. "I promise you that the examination will not take long."

He really did remind her of Julian, and that smile . . . She smiled back at him. "This really isn't necessary," she said. "It was only an upset stomach, from buttered lobster. I am the perfect picture of health."

"Yes, I'm sure that's true, but to keep his lordship happy, I think we shall at least"—a twinkle leaped into his very green eyes—"make an effort for it to 'appear' that I have made a thorough examination."

A gurgle of laughter escaped her. She liked this man. At ease with him, she led him to her dressing room. "Do you live nearby?" she asked as they entered the room.

He nodded, setting down the small black leather bag he carried. "Yes, not more than a couple of miles down the road at Rose Cottage."

"Oh, I remember the place. It is charming with all those rose-covered arbors around it."

"Thank you. It is a very comfortable home and the scent of the roses in the summertime is most delightful."

She would have liked to question him more, but he motioned her to sit down and said, "Well now. I shall, I'm afraid, have to ask you some questions and take your pulse in order to be able to look his lordship in the eye. Do you mind?"

She didn't. Keeping up a gentle flow of chatter, he quickly completed his task. His manner was such that it wasn't until they were walking across her sitting room that she realized she'd had a very thorough examination and that he had asked several searching questions about her health.

At the door, she smiled at him and said, "You are a very clever man, Dr. Coleman—hoodwinking me into allowing you to do precisely as my husband asked."

Bag in hand, he smiled down at her. "You have found me out. But please do not think too harshly of me. Lord Wyndham is a good patron. I would not wish to offend him." That twinkle leaped into his eyes again. "And it was not such an ordeal, now, was it?"

Nell laughed. "No, indeed, it was not. If I really have need of a physician in the future, I will rest easy, knowing that I am in your good hands."

"You are in fine health, my lady. Excellent, in fact, and I doubt that you shall need my services anytime soon but I thank you for the kind words."

In the magnificent entry hall, Nell watched as Dibble escorted him to her husband's study. She considered joining them—after all, it was *her* health they would be discussing—but decided it wasn't that important. She already knew she was healthy—even Dr. Coleman had said so.

Curious about Dr. Coleman's striking resemblance to Julian, Nell wandered around the green saloon, waiting impatiently for the doctor to depart. She intended to ask Julian some pointed questions about the very handsome Dr. Coleman.

Several minutes later, she rang for Dibble and upon learning that the physician had left, made a beeline for Julian's study. She found him seated behind his desk, several account books and papers scattered before him.

"I suppose," he said smiling, "that you've come to gloat. Coleman said that you are in perfect health and that if all his patients were like you that he'd soon be a poor man."

"I told you so," Nell replied, taking a seat next to the desk. "Perhaps, next time, you'll listen to me."

His eyes warm, he asked, "Was it so very bad?"

"No, his manner is most disarming and with me hardly

being aware of it, he made a very thorough examination."
She eyed her husband. "I liked him."

"I thought that you would. He is very popular with all his
patients."

There was no easy way around it and so Nell blurted out,
"He looks very like you . . . You could almost be twins . . ."

"You haven't met Cousin Charles yet," Julian said dryly.
"There is a strong family resemblance between all the Westons, but Charles and I could very well be twins."

"That's interesting, but unless I've misunderstood something, Dr. Coleman *isn't* a member of the Weston family. Or
is he another cousin?" she asked sweetly.

Julian hesitated. There was no reason for her not to know,
and Lord knew she'd find out soon enough from someone
else. And she was now a member of the family. He sighed.
She might as well know some of the skeletons and he should
be the one to tell her. "More of an uncle," he admitted reluctantly, "on the wrong side of the blanket."

Nell's eyes widened. "He's illegitimate?" she asked in
shocked accents.

He nodded. "Remember, I did mention about the Old
Earl? I'm afraid that you're going to notice several inhabitants of the area who bear a striking resemblance to the family. Coleman is one of several, uh, illegitimate children, to be
laid at my grandfather's feet. Fortunately, he's one of the
more respectable ones."

"Isn't it rather awkward?"

Julian shrugged. "It's never been a secret in the family. I
grew up knowing that I had several, ah, aunts and uncles
roaming about the area. Grandfather acknowledged them
and settled money on their families." Julian grimaced. "And
considered his filial duties at an end."

She stared at him a long time and Julian wondered if she
thought less of him for his grandfather's debauchery. He supposed he could have tried to hide his grandfather's various
by-blows from her, but that would have been, he admitted

grimly, an exercise in futility—their parentage was stamped on their faces.

"Well," she finally said, "you have a *much* more interesting family than I do."

Julian laughed, giddiness erupting through him. Would there ever come a time that she didn't make him laugh? That she didn't surprise him? Lord, he hoped not.

The creak of wooden wheels and the jingle of a harness carried into the room and they exchanged looks. "Were you expecting company?" Nell asked, rising to her feet.

"None."

A great commotion could be heard coming from the entry hall and upon stepping from the study, they discovered the area full of trunks and baggage, and Dibble giving orders to the various footmen and maids, which added to the chaos.

A figure attired in a sable-trimmed pelisse and wearing a saucy scarlet hat festooned with ostrich feathers stood in the center of the madness. Spying Julian and Nell standing at the edge of the hall, the figure gave a squeak and threw herself into Julian's startled embrace. "Oh, Julian," she cried, "I know I said I would not be here for *weeks* yet, but I could *not* stay away a moment longer. I *had* to come home. London is just too, *too* dreadful without you."

It appeared that Lady Diana, the dowager countess, had arrived.

Chapter 10

Following on the heels of her mother, her pretty face framed by a chinchilla-lined hood, Elizabeth said, "We are very sorry to arrive like this without notice, but mother really was pining for the country." She smiled shyly at Nell. "I hope you do not mind? And that we have not caused you any great inconvenience?"

"Well, of course we haven't," Lady Diana said crossly. "I should think that we can return to our home anytime we want without it causing a problem." She raised melting eyes to Julian. "Isn't that right, Julian? You'd never deny your stepmama a roof over her head, would you?"

Looking like a man facing a charge of a pride of starving lions, Julian glanced wildly about for escape.

Torn between amusement and vexation at Diana's antics, Nell stepped in. "Of course he wouldn't! I'm sure that, the Dower House aside, with as many properties as my husband owns that he would always be able to find a suitable home for you." Walking over to Diana, she delicately wrested the other woman's arms from around Julian's neck. Putting her arm through Diana's, she smiled warmly at her and said, "In the meantime, we are more than delighted to have you and Elizabeth stay with us."

Lady Diana and Elizabeth's outer clothing were deposed of and a moment later, Nell was determinedly guiding a lagging Diana across the elegant entry hall. "It will be so pleasant to have company. And after that long journey, I'm sure that you are longing to rest and refresh yourself," Nell said brightly as she led, *dragged* her stepmama-in-law away. "We had already begun to prepare in anticipation of your arrival, so that I'm sure with very little effort the staff will have your rooms waiting for you in no time at all." She glanced over her shoulder at Dibble. "Isn't that right, Dibble?"

Admiring her command of the situation, Dibble bowed and murmured, "Absolutely, my lady."

"Excellent! But first will you have tea and some biscuits served in the green saloon?"

Dibble bowed again. "I shall see to it immediately."

Nell beamed at Diana. "You see? Everything is taken care of. Now, if you and Elizabeth will come with me, we shall retire to the green saloon where you can tell me all about your journey."

Left standing in the entry hall surrounded by a mountain of trunks and valises, Julian watched the trio walk away. A smile lurked at the corners of his mouth as his eyes rested on Nell's slender form. By Jupiter! That had been a near thing! If Nell hadn't come to his rescue, he'd probably still be standing here looking like a wide-eyed hare pursued by hounds.

Feeling almost sanguine about having his wife and his stepmother under the same roof, he set off for his study. In any battle of wills between the two women, he rather thought he'd put his money on Nell. Recalling the masterful way Nell had cut the ground from underneath his stepmother, he grinned. Poor Diana! She had been bowled over before she knew what hit her.

Lady Diana and Elizabeth integrated into the household at Wyndham Manor without major incident. It helped that Nell kept her head about her and that Lady Diana, while silly and at times vexing, had no malice in her. There were a few tussles, but in the main, the addition of Lady Diana and Elizabeth proved to be a pleasant occurrence.

As the days passed winter increased its grip on the country-side and though they did not suffer the severe ice and snow that racked other less salubrious parts of England, there were many days that the weather made it impossible as well as impractical to be abroad. With Nell happily enmeshed in Lady Diana's planned renovation of the Dower House Julian was able to lock himself away in his study with his man of business and farm manager and concentrate on estate matters, of which there were a multitude. Most were routine, easily delegated and planned for spring when the weather broke—the marling of some fields felt to be deficient in lime, discussion of rotation of crops for better yields and some overdue improvements to certain of his tenants' houses. But the meeting with his gamekeeper was troublesome.

"What do you mean 'unusual depredations'?" Julian demanded.

Appropriately named, John Hunter, the Wyndham game-keeper, bore the stamp of the Old Earl on his harsh features and Julian had often wondered how his father had felt about having a half brother in service to him. He knew he felt dashed odd ordering about a man who was technically his uncle . . . another on the wrong side of the blanket.

John Hunter was a massively built man with a mane of shaggy black hair and with the family's piercing green eyes set beneath heavy black brows. He usually carried a stout staff in one hand and had no compunction about thrashing anyone caught trespassing on the earl's lands. With his height and size and that punishing staff held ever ready, he was a formidable figure. Just the sight of him tramping through the woods was known to strike terror in the hearts of any poacher foolhardy enough to step one foot on the earl's lands. Older than Julian by twenty-five years, he'd been gamekeeper at Wyndham Manor for almost as long as Julian could remember and his reputation for dealing swiftly and mercilessly with poachers was legendary and widespread in the neighborhood.

At Julian's question, John drew himself up and said with doleful satisfaction, "It's as I've warned you time and again, my lord. Your hand has been too light and now you are paying the price—your lordship's game is being slaughtered at will."

"Oh, come now, it can't be that bad. And you know I don't begrudge the occasional deer or leveret taken by poachers."

"Indeed, I do," said John regretfully, his expression making it clear what he thought of that sort of folly. "But this is not that sort of thing. In the north woods recently I've been finding places of the most wanton butchery." He shook his head in disgust. "I tell you, my lord, this is not some hungry poacher seeking to feed his family, this is a devil! A monster! The animals look . . . as if they've been torn apart and then discarded and left to rot."

"The game's not been taken?" Julian asked, shocked.

John shook his head. "None that I can tell, and there's been no attempt to hide his deeds—it is as if he wants his foul handiwork found."

Julian stared hard at John's weather-ravaged face. Leaving the game behind was unheard of . . . No poacher would do so. And no poacher with any sense would brave running into John by returning time and again. Yet, someone, Julian admitted, was entering his land at will, and if John was to be believed, senselessly slaughtering his game.

Rising to his feet, Julian said, "Take me to the most recent site."

Julian had hoped that John had exaggerated the situation, but riding home after accompanying John to the latest kill, he knew that his gamekeeper had not exaggerated. The deer had been savaged as if by a wild beast. A wild beast armed with a knife . . . Julian felt the bile rise in his throat. Good God! What sort of monster could be responsible for the carnage? And how, he wondered, was he to find him and stop him?

* * *

Lady Diana might very well be a silly woman, but she was not a stupid one and it had only taken her a matter of days to realize that while Nell was everything that was kind, this was the younger woman's home now. Of a docile nature and never one to pout or repine long on events unchangeable, Lady Diana had instantly turned her attention into making the Dower House into an elegant home for herself and her daughter.

The Dower House, situated a scant mile from Wyndham Manor in the middle of its own pretty park, had sat empty for the past twenty years or so, ever since Julian's great-grandmother had died. The sprawling house, built on the site of a much older building, was two storied, with a steep tiled roof and tall, arched windows, and surrounded by several terraces adorned with shrubbery that was overgrown. The entire place had received only a minimum of upkeep over the years and the renovations, both inside and out, would be extensive. Nell, after walking through the shadowy, echoing house with Lady Diana and Elizabeth, and seeing the changes that needed to be wrought, resigned herself to having Lady Diana and Elizabeth living at the manor for the foreseeable future.

Julian had promptly hired local builders and craftsman for the project but the weather delayed many things. Though the physical renovations were progressing slowly, there was much the ladies could do to help things along and Nell threw herself into the agreeable task of helping select fabrics and furnishings.

Gratified by Nell's interest in the project and discovering that her new stepdaughter-in-law had a good eye for color and style, Lady Diana was delighted to include her, and along with Elizabeth, they were deep into the changes that she had planned. Swatches of fabric, catalogs of furniture styles and advertisements for carpets filled Lady Diana's sitting room and, as winter deepened and the rain beat itself against the windows, seated near the cozy fire, there were intense discussions about wall coverings and fabric and color schemes for the Dower House.

Remembering Lady Diana's coolness to her the few times they'd met prior to the wedding, Nell had not been certain how she and Lady Diana would coexist in the same household together. It took Nell less than twenty-four hours to discover that though Lady Diana could be annoying and bird-witted, there was not a mean bone in her body. And as for Elizabeth . . . Elizabeth was a poppet and made Nell think that if she'd ever had a younger sister, she'd have wanted her to be like Elizabeth.

At Julian's invitation, Marcus came to dine one evening not long after Lady Diana and Elizabeth had arrived. The meal completed amid much lively talk, the ladies departed, leaving the two gentlemen in the dining room to enjoy their port.

Having noted the ease among the women, Marcus raised his glass in a toast. "You always were a lucky devil and if I had not seen it with my own eyes, I would not believe how easily you drive a unicorn. Congratulations!" He grinned over his glass at Julian. "I was certain that you would have been torn to pieces by now and I came, in pity, to dine over your corpse."

"It is my wife you should congratulate," Julian admitted wryly. "When they first arrived all I could do was stand there wild-eyed and wind-broken like a bayed stag at a cliff's edge. It was Nell who saved the situation. She keeps a cool head about her."

"Delightful though the subject is," Marcus murmured, "I have the feeling that she is not the reason for my invitation to dine. Don't tell me that Tynedale is causing trouble?"

Julian shook his head. "No. In fact, the neighborhood has been very quiet. I have neither seen nor heard anything of Tynedale or my cousins' activities. I suppose I should be wor-

ried but there is nothing that I can do until they make a move
. . . if they make a move."

"Then if not Tynedale or Cousin Charles, what has you in
a fret?"

His expression becoming grim, Julian set down his glass
and leaning forward asked, "Have you ever had any troubles
with poachers?'

Marcus looked surprised. "None other than the usual in-
cursions one would expect. Nothing serious."

"Never any senseless slaughter? The game left behind?"

"Never," Marcus said, frowning. "And I can't imagine
with John Hunter prowling your grounds that there would
be a poacher so lost to saving his own neck that he'd risk
falling into John's hands."

"Well, you're wrong there," Julian muttered and proceeded to explain the situation.

"An ugly business," Marcus said when Julian had finished
speaking.

Julian nodded. "I've given John permission to hire some
extra men to help him patrol the grounds at night. He wants
to set traps, but I'll not have the maiming and possible killing
of any man on my conscience just because he poached some
of my game."

"Doesn't sound like he's poaching," objected Marcus.

"You're right there. And damme if I know what to do! My
hope is that John can catch the fellow and we can put it behind us." He stared at his glass. "I haven't told the ladies—
don't want to worry them and there's no reason they should
know. Not hunters."

Marcus grinned. "Now are you so sure? I wouldn't put it
past that wife of yours to turn out to be a great huntress."

"Very possibly," Julian admitted with a smile. "She has
surprised me more than once."

"But not unpleasantly?"

Julian shook his head. "No. You see before you a grateful
married man."

"And a happy one?"

Julian hesitated. "Yes. And a happy one."

Marcus accepted Julian's claim to happiness, but in truth Julian was vaguely troubled, not *exactly* happy and yet not unhappy in his marriage. The state of his marriage had occupied his mind of late and he could not figure out why there lingered within him a disquieting feeling of dissatisfaction. He had a lovely, responsive wife, one who ran his household with skill and aplomb and whose eager, yielding body filled him with delight and yet . . . Something was missing. When he entered Nell's bedchamber she greeted him as passionately as any man could wish, yet he sensed that there was a part of her that she held back, a part of her hidden from him. There was, he admitted uneasily to himself, a barrier between them. It was not an obvious one, but it was there. It was there in the way Nell sometimes studied him, as if she was looking for something, as if she found something lacking in him. It was there in the way, with a smile and light comment, she would slip away from him whenever he paid her compliments or attempted to flirt with her. He snorted. It was a sad day when a husband was reduced to flirting with his own wife and his wife would have none of it. She was . . . elusive . . . yes, that was it. Elusive, that was the word. He could not explain it, but he felt it, was aware of it and more aware of it with every growing day.

The fear that Julian still loved his first wife had taken a strong hold of Nell. He was everything one could wish for in a husband, but that mattered little if there was no chance for her to ever win his heart. Admittedly she was halfway in love with him, but Lady Catherine's unseen presence haunted her and helped her keep a firm rein on her emotions. She would *not* wear the willow for a man who could not love her, nor pine over a man whose heart had been buried in a grave. She would be his wife in all ways and take pleasure in his company, but she would not allow herself to love him. Nell saw no advantage in loving a man who loved another, especially a man who loved a dead woman.

Lady Diana and Elizabeth's company made it easier for her to show the world, her husband included, an untroubled face. It was only at night, after Julian had left her and she was alone in her magnificent bedroom that her heart ached and tears clogged her throat. Julian's lovemaking banished her misery for awhile and she could lose herself in his embrace, revel in the joy he brought her body, but when he was gone . . . When he was gone from her bed, she felt empty, used. What they did was no different from a stallion breeding a mare in heat, she told herself fiercely, scrubbing away the trace of tears. Lust brought him to her. A primitive instinct. The drive to procreate. That was all that existed between them.

It did no good to remind herself how fortunate she was. That disastrous night Tynedale had kidnapped her could have turned out very differently. Tynedale might have succeeded in his wicked plans. Another man, one far less desirable than Julian, might have happened across her. Instead of disgrace and misery, she had a wealthy, aristocratic husband. She was a countess. She had an elegant home. Her husband was handsome, attentive, kind. But it wasn't enough. No, not nearly enough.

Her emotions dragged her down; behind the façade she kept for the world, she felt tired and out of sorts and though she kept them hidden, tears were never far away.

With the holiday season fast approaching, despite the delicious scents of evergreens and spices in the air, Nell's spirits drooped even further. She tried to take pleasure in the holly and mistletoe scattered throughout the house, in the fresh garlands draped along the banisters and over the mantels, but it was no use. This would be her first Christmas without her family and she was horribly homesick.

One morning a few days before Christmas, sensing that Nell's mind was not on the builder's plans they'd been looking at, Lady Diana pushed the paper away and said, "Oh, fiddle! I am sick to death of worrying about the changes to my house. Let us do something different today."

Nell, looking charming in a gown of olive green cashmere, glanced out the window at the spattering of rain against the windows. "Well, a walk, ride or drive is out of the question. The weather is frightful."

Elizabeth lifted her head from the swatches of silk she'd been studying and said, "I certainly agree with Nell. What shall we do?"

Lady Diana pouted for a moment, then brightened. "We can go explore the conservatory. It will be almost as nice as walking outside on a summer day."

"We did that yesterday," Elizabeth pointed out. "Don't you remember?"

Lady Diana made a face. "So we did. Surely there is something we can do besides pour over these boring plans and books?"

"I haven't explored all of the house yet," Nell began uncertainly, "perhaps there's some feature that is unusual you'd like to show me?"

Lady Diana and Elizabeth exchanged impish glances. "Have you seen the dungeons?" Lady Diana asked.

"D-d-dungeons?" Nell repeated, a chill blowing through her body.

"You mean Julian hasn't told you about them yet?" exclaimed Lady Diana. "Oh, it is too bad of him."

Just as if he'd withheld some great treat from her, Nell thought hollowly.

Leaning forward, Elizabeth asked, "Didn't you know that the manor is built on the site of an ancient castle? And that there is a secret passage leading to some old dungeons beneath us?" She gave a delicious shudder. "It is the most wonderfully terrifying place. Cousin Charles gave us a tour once and told us gruesome tales. We enjoyed it immensely, although Mama had nightmares for a week, and Lord Wyndham, Julian's father, was cross with Cousin Charles for scaring us so." She looked regretful. "Lord Wyndham said that all that talk of torture and murder was nonsense and that Cousin Charles made it up."

Nell frowned. "I thought that there was an estrangement between, er, Cousin Charles and Lord Wyndham."

"Well, there is no denying that the rift has gotten wider, but this was just after the late earl and I had married," explained Lady Diana, "and things were not so bad at that time. Charles was here often, although not so much after that."

Tapping a finger to her lip, Elizabeth said, "You know, exploring the dungeons might not be such a good idea. It was summertime when Cousin Charles showed them to us and I vaguely remember him saying something about them being damp, parts of them sometimes flooding in winter."

"Oh, that's right," agreed Lady Diana. "Oh, pooh! We shall have to think of something else."

"What about the gallery?" suggested Elizabeth.

"I think Dibble has shown me that," Nell replied apologetically. "Although it was only a quick tour—I didn't really have a chance to look at all those family portraits—"

Elizabeth jumped up. "Then you shall. It will be great fun. Wait until you see the portrait of the first earl—he looks a villain of the first order."

The first earl did indeed look like a villain, but Nell could see where Julian had gotten his green eyes and black swooping eyebrows. They started in the oldest part of the gallery and spent an enjoyable time viewing the portraits and commenting and laughing over the style of clothing and hair. As they came into the section that held portraits of more recent members of the family, one of them caught Nell's attention and held her spellbound.

It held a place of honor in a small alcove and a bouquet of

fresh, sweet-scented lilies from the estate's greenhouses sat on a small shelf below the huge gilt-framed portrait.

Nell noted the flowers, but it was the figure in the portrait that caught her attention and held her frozen to the spot.

The subject was a young woman, wearing a gown of sapphire blue with hair of gold and sky blue eyes. She was the loveliest female Nell had ever seen in her life and she could not tear her gaze away from that heart-shaped face and dainty form that would not have shamed a fairy princess.

Elizabeth noticed her interest and coming to stand beside her, said softly, "Lady Catherine, Julian's first wife. Isn't she just a perfect pocket-sized Venus? She was so lovely. Her death was such a tragedy."

"Lovely, indeed," Nell said in an empty voice. It was one thing to have a faceless rival, another to know that the woman who had taken her husband's heart to the grave with her had been an incomparable beauty. Nell's looks were not to be lightly dismissed, but she believed herself to be no more than passably pretty. Not for her that glorious mane of brilliant golden hair, and she suddenly hated her tawny locks, neither gold nor brown, but something in between. And as for eyes . . . Who would ever care for sea green ones when they'd stared into big eyes the color of a summer sky? And that rosy Cupid's bow mouth . . . Torturing herself, she studied Lady Catherine's perfect form. Not for Lady Catherine a tall, slim, boyish figure, no, Lady Catherine was everything she was not—perfect!

Lady Diana joined them and, staring at the portrait, sighed. "Her death was so sad, so terrible—a carriage accident, I believe. She was so young and so very beautiful. My late lord said that something died within Julian when she did. He was so worried about him he said he feared that Julian would throw himself into the grave with her." Her fingers caressed one of the petals of the lilies. "I see that Julian still has fresh flowers set before her. I wonder if he will ever . . ."

A pinch from Elizabeth reminded Lady Diana who was standing beside her and, laughing nervously, Lady Diana put her arm through Nell's. Patting Nell on the hand, she said, "I never knew her. She was already dead when I married Julian's father and what I know about her I learned from him. I know that Julian was devastated by her death, but now he has you and I am sure will be happy again."

Nell doubted it.

And that night when Julian came to her, she repulsed his advances for the first time. Lady Catherine's beautiful face lodged in her brain, she turned away from him and said in a low voice, "I am sorry, my lord, but I am not feeling well tonight."

Sprawled beside her on the big bed, Julian had already noticed that she seemed unusually quiet this evening and studying her face, he noted the shadows in the lovely eyes and the paleness of her complexion. "A headache, perhaps?" he asked, taking her hand in his.

Nell looked away from his handsome face and gently disentangled her hand from his. "Only a little one."

He studied her profile, conscious of her withdrawal. And the uneasiness that something was very wrong between them grew. "Have I offended you in some manner?" he asked slowly, his green eyes intent.

Her gaze flew to his. "Oh, n-n-no!" she exclaimed. She forced a smile. "I am just a little tired and out of sorts lately."

Julian accepted her words and dropping a chaste kiss on her forehead walked back to his own bedchamber. The door barely shut behind him before Nell buried her nose into the pillow and burst into tears. She was the most miserable wretch alive and she wished she was dead.

Julian did not sleep well that night. Only a fool would not have realized that Nell was unhappy and he was not a fool. Lying sleepless in his bed, he scoured his mind trying to put his finger on the moment that she'd begun to change, when he'd experienced those first twinges that there was something wrong between them. Not exactly wrong, he decided, but different. He could not recall an incident, a word, or an action, no matter how small, that could have brought about the changes he sensed in her. Tonight had brought it home, though, that his instincts were not at fault. Without having ever won her, he had the terrifying feeling that he was losing her. He smiled bitterly. First Catherine and now Nell. Of course, he'd never *wanted* to win Catherine.

Both times he'd married under pressure from outside forces, neither time had it been because he'd wanted a wife. With Catherine, despite his misgivings, he'd married to please his father. And just look, he thought savagely, how that had turned out! They'd both been miserable, the death of his unborn child adding to his misery. Although he'd vowed never to wed again, Nell's catapulting into his life had turned his world upside down and once again he'd married for all the wrong reasons, if noble ones. But with Nell he'd been . . . He'd been, he admitted wryly, eager, hopeful . . . And now, for reasons he could not explain, Nell was drawing away from him, putting him at a distance. What the hell was he to do? He would *not* again endure the angry fits and starts, the tears, the recriminations, the screaming arguments that had characterized his first marriage.

Comparing Nell to Catherine was unfair, he admitted— the two women were as different as chalk and cheese. With Catherine he'd never, that he could recall, experienced the pleasure, the delight that Nell gave him. Never.

Annoyed with himself, feeling that he'd been lunging at shadows where there were none, he punched his pillow and tried to get comfortable. Tonight was unimportant, he told himself. Nell had a headache and there was nothing in that to fill him with such disquiet. There was nothing in her gentle rejection to make him think that the ground had shifted beneath his feet. But she was . . . pulling away from him. He could feel it and was powerless to stop it. At least, so far, he reminded himself darkly, she has not started bursting into tears at the sight of me and blaming me for every ill in her life.

The holidays came and went and although Nell missed her family fiercely, she accepted the fact that Julian and Lady Catherine and Elizabeth were now her new family and she could be happy or she could be sad. She chose to be happy.

January began gray and dreary. Nell was surprised by the lack of snow and the temperate climate, but she longed for spring. After several weeks of rain, as January drew to a close, she felt like a caged animal. Oh, how she wanted to escape the confines of the house. She was not alone in this feeling—even Lady Diana and Elizabeth were moping around. Then, to everyone's joy, the rain stopped and the sun began to shine. Three days later the roads had begun to dry and the sun was shining brightly in a clear blue sky. Eager to escape the house, in the afternoon, the ladies, accompanied by two grooms, set out on a gentle ride. Julian was away in Dawlish on business.

Nell was riding a restive black mare, the other two women each riding a gentle hack that suited their abilities. The grooms followed sedately behind them.

The day was fine, cool in the shade, but comfortable, almost warm in the sunlight. After weeks locked inside the house, it was wonderful, Nell thought, to be outside and on horseback again. Stifling the urge to let her mare out into a full gallop, she managed to enjoy the plodding pace that Diana chose.

The countryside was not at its best—many trees leafless and barren-looking, and there were muddy, boggy patches in the road that had to be avoided, but still, it was pleasant. Nell had not yet had much of chance to explore and she looked about herself with interest, liking the glimpses of rolling terrain she spied through the various wooded areas. Fields, orchards and pastures lay beyond the trees, deep thickets of forests surrounding them, and she vowed that in the spring she'd spend hours and hours in the saddle acquainting herself with the area.

When Diana declared that she'd ridden enough, Nell sighed. Though they'd ridden several miles, her mare was barely warmed up and, unable to control the impulse, she turned to look at Diana. "If you don't mind, before we head back, I'm going to let my horse stretch her legs."

Ignoring Diana's shriek of dismay, Nell gave the mare her head and with a snort and a half-rear, the mare raced away like the wind, leaving the others behind. Feeling the powerful body surging under her, her face slapped by the streaming mane, Nell let the moment engulf her. It seemed magical as they flew past trees, fences and pastures, the mare actually taking flight as she jumped over the muddy patches in the road. Nell loved every moment of it and she wished she could ride and keep on riding forever. For a little while her melancholy vanished and she forgot her cares. Forgot the portrait of a beautiful woman hanging above a bouquet of lilies and a husband whose heart would never be hers.

Exhilarated and flushed, eventually Nell slowed the mare. Snorting and prancing the horse let her know that another few miles wouldn't come amiss, but laughing and patting the sleek neck, Nell turned her around and began to ride back to rejoin the others.

The mare traveled at a good pace but they did not cover much ground before one of the grooms, Hodges, riding at a mad gallop, came into view. "Oh, my lady! What a fright you gave Lady Diana," he cried when they met and pulled their horses to a stop. "She is convinced that your horse ran away with you."

"I was eight the last time a horse ran away with me," Nell said lightly. Patting the sweaty neck, she added, "And this little mare is far too good-mannered to try such a thing."

Nell ran her gaze over the groom and his mount. She knew Hodges from the stables and knew his reputation for being a neck-or-nothing rider and the neat bay gelding he was astride looked like he'd give the mare a good run. "How far back are they?" she asked thoughtfully.

"A couple of miles."

A mischievous smile lit her face. "Then shall we see which of us has the better horse?"

A light touch of her heels and the mare shot away. With a gleeful shout, the young groom followed.

The mare had a small advantage, Hodges was heavier and Nell had caught him by surprise, but within moments, as they careened down the road, the bay's head was at the mare's flank. They swung around a curve, lined by the forest, the bay fighting to take the lead when three does, eyes bulging from their heads exploded out of the woods in front of them. Nell desperately yanked on the reins trying to avoid a collision. The mare stumbled and the last thing Nell remembered was flying over her head.

She woke lying on the ground, her head cradled against a very broad masculine chest. Nearby she could hear Diana weeping and the young groom trying to explain what had happened. Blearily Nell glanced around and sighed with relief when she spied the mare contentedly cropping grass not six feet away, the bay beside her.

Her head ached and she knew that she'd have some impressive bruises to show for her spill. She struggled to sit up.

"No, lie still," commanded a man's voice, "and let me see how badly hurt you are. And for God's sake, don't wiggle and make things worse—Julian would have my hide if I let anything happen to you."

She jerked her head up. A stranger held her, but she knew him. "Cousin Charles," she said faintly.

He smiled. "Yes, it is indeed wicked Cousin Charles at your service, your ladyship."

Chapter 11

It was as well, Nell thought, as she lay staring up at Charles Weston that Julian had warned her that he and his cousin could pass for twins. The man looking down at her reminded her forcibly of her husband, yet there were differences. Both were harsh-featured, but Julian was by far the handsomer of the two. They shared other similar features: their coloring, their eyes, the formidable chin and nose and the general shape of their faces. She suspected that someone who did not know either man very well could mistake them for each other, something she did not. There was an expression in Charles' eyes that troubled her . . . The *lack* of expression, she realized. Charles Weston's eyes were as cold and unforgiving as the North Sea in December with none of the warmth and humor that her husband's gaze possessed.

Weston smiled at her and she noted that the smile did not reach his eyes. She didn't think that she liked him and she certainly did not like the intimacy of their position. Struggling in his arms, Nell attempted to sit up, but he held her in an iron grip.

"Be still. That was a spectacular spill that you took. Give yourself a moment," he said.

Startled, she asked, "You saw me fall?"

"Indeed, I did. I drove up behind you a split second before you went flying over the mare's head. Now, let me take a look and see how much damage you've done." Despite Nell's protest, he removed her dashing emerald green hat with its saucy yellow feather and tossed it carelessly on the ground. With surprisingly gentle fingers he probed Nell's head, grunting when Nell winced and cried out as his fingers touched an area near her temple. Moving even more gently he examined the area. His examination finished, he flashed her a singularly attractive smile and said, "You'll live, my lady. You'll have some bruising, but the skin is not even broken. A day or two of rest and you'll be good as new."

"Thank you," Nell muttered, "but I could have told you that myself."

Hearing Nell's voice, Lady Diana rushed over. "Oh, Nell, tell me that you are not dead!" she begged, her pretty face full of anxiety. She dabbed a scrap of lace to the corners of her eyes. "Julian will *kill* me if something happened to you while you were in my care." A sob broke from her. "Why, oh, why did we decide on this wretched ride?"

"Mother, hush!" said Elizabeth, sending Nell an apologetic look. "It is no one's fault. It was an accident and as you can see Lady Wyndham is certainly not dead."

"Are you sure?" Lady Diana asked doubtfully, her big velvet-brown eyes fixed on Nell's wan face.

Nell smiled at her. "I am fine. I will, no doubt, be sore and bruised, but it is nothing to fret over." She glanced at Weston. "May I get up now?"

He studied her features a moment longer, then shrugged and rose to his feet. "Whatever my lady wishes." Reaching down he easily pulled Nell to her feet.

Her head ached and the world spun when Nell stood upright. She swayed and her bad leg crumpled beneath her; Lady Diana shrieked a warning and a pair of powerful arms swept Nell off her feet.

"I think," said Weston, holding Nell against his chest, "that you are not as fit as you think."

Her stomach roiling and her leg aching like fire, Nell's

head drooped on his broad shoulder. "Perhaps, you are right," she admitted.

"What is to be done?" Lady Diana cried, wringing her hands and looking around helplessly. "How will we get her home? She cannot ride and Wyndham Manor is *miles* from here."

"I think you forget, my lady," said Weston dryly, "that Stonegate is only a few miles away; I shall take Lady Wyndham there in my curricle."

Lady Diana grabbed frantically at his arm. Alarm in her voice, she wailed, "Charles, are you mad? Julian will not like it at all."

Weston laughed. Not a very nice laugh, Nell thought. "Since when have I cared a farthing for what my esteemed cousin likes or does not like?"

Lady Diana moaned and disappeared into her scrap of lace.

Agreeing that Julian would not want to find her a guest of his cousin Charles, and paying no mind to her whirling head, Nell muttered, "It won't be necessary, Mr. Weston, for you to go to all that trouble. If you will set me down, I am sure that in a few moments I will be fine."

Ignoring her, Weston turned on his heels and said over his shoulder to Elizabeth, "Miss Forest, I beg you do something with your mother before I ring her pretty neck." He looked down at Nell who was struggling to escape his firm grasp. "And, you, my lady, quit wiggling around or I'll dump you on the ground for being such an ungrateful baggage."

Nell looked into his cold green eyes and immediately ceased her struggles. He meant it. Docile as a lamb, she allowed him to place her on the seat of the curricle.

Climbing into the curricle, Weston picked up the reins. Looking at the two grooms, shifting from foot to foot, he commanded, "One of you return to Wyndham Manor and inform your master of the accident. Assure him that his lady has not suffered any lasting harm, but that I have taken her to Stonegate to be tended by my stepmother until he can arrive with a suitable carriage to bring her home." Turning his attention to Lady Diana and Elizabeth, he added, "You and your remaining servant shall accompany us to Stonegate to await my dear cousin." He flashed a wintry smile. "You shall be Lady Wyndham's protection from my nefarious attentions. After all, everyone knows that I dare not be alone with any respectable woman without making an attempt to ruin her."

Clinging to the seat of the curricle, as Weston set his horses at a spanking trot, Nell fought to keep from disgracing herself by retching over the side of the vehicle. The fall had shaken her more than she had realized, certainly it had played havoc with her bad leg, and she tried to be grateful for Weston's assitance. It was difficult—knowing the estrangement between the families, she would have preferred just about anyone other than Charles Weston to have happened upon the scene.

Followed by Lady Diana, Elizabeth and the remaining groom, they traveled only a couple of miles along the road before turning off at the impressive stone gate that Nell assumed gave the estate its name. Another half mile of winding, forest-edged road and the curricle swept into a wide circular driveway. Pulling the horse to a stop before an elegant, three-story stone house of indeterminate age, Weston jumped down from the curricle. Walking around to the other side of the vehicle, he plucked Nell from her seat and effortlessly carried her up the three broad steps and strode across the stone terrace toward a pair of massive dark wooden doors with huge black iron hinges.

Leaving their groom to handle the horses, Lady Diana and Elizabeth followed right behind Weston. Three feet before they reached the doors, one of the doors swung open and a tall, cadaverous gentleman garbed in splendid black livery stood to the side, holding the door wide for Weston's entrance.

Without breaking stride, Weston walked into the house, saying to the tall man as he passed him, "Find my stepmother and tell her to come to the east salon. Also order some tea and refreshments for the ladies."

As if it was perfectly normal for the master to return home carrying in his arms an unknown female, the butler's face remained impassive. "It shall be done, sir, just as soon as I have seen to the ladies." Smiling at Nell, he said, "May I have your gloves, my lady?" Nell stripped them off and handed them to him. Turning to the other two women, he asked, "Lady Wyndham? Miss Forest?"

"Oh, yes, thank you, Garthwaite," exclaimed Lady Diana, giving him her gloves and riding crop. Elizabeth did the same. Both ladies then scurried down the long hallway to catch up with Weston's broad-shouldered form.

Her head and stomach having decided to behave, Nell glanced around her. Knowing his situation, Nell had expected Weston's home to reflect his squandered fortune, but such was not the case. So far she had seen nothing that bespoke a man on the brink of financial ruin. The driveway had contained no holes, nor ruts or other signs of poor upkeep, the vast expanse of lawns and shrubs surrounding the house had been meticulously trimmed and the house façade had appeared to be in excellent condition. Before Weston had whisked her away down a long hallway, she'd noted that the butler's raiment had looked expensive and that the walls in the foyer were hung in green figured silk. The hallway was well lit, gleaming gilt and crystal fixtures held brightly burning beeswax candles and the jewel-toned hall carpet showed no sign of wear or fading. Everything she had observed so far bespoke the home of a wealthy gentleman. Even the clothes Weston wore were of the first stare of fashion, his immaculate cravat arranged by the hand of a master and his coat of bottle green superfine fit him to perfection.

Weston pushed into a large room decorated in shades of blue, gold and cream, and again Nell was struck by the richness of the furnishings, from the elegant woolen carpet in shades of cream and blue to the sofas covered in gold damask scattered about the room. A fire crackled on the marble hearth and satinwood chairs and tables were placed about the room.

Striding over to one of the sofas near the fire, Weston eased Nell out of his arms and gently laid her down. Once Weston stepped away, she struggled upright, her head spinning as she did so.

Lady Diana and Elizabeth fluttered over to her, and sat down one on each side of Nell. Lady Diana took one of her hands in hers, pressing it anxiously. "Oh, my dear, tell me! Are you in pain? Perhaps you'd like some hartshorn and water?"

Nell shuddered. "No, no, thank you. I'm sure I shall be in excellent spirits in no time. I just need a few moments."

"My observation precisely," remarked Weston. Walking over to a marble-topped table he poured a drink from one of several crystal decanters that sat there. Returning to Nell, he stopped in front of her. Thrusting a snifter of amber liquid at her, he commanded, "Drink this. It's brandy. It will clear that spinning head of yours."

Nell thought about refusing, but reading determination in those cool green eyes, she took the snifter from him. "I suppose," she said wryly, "that if I refused you'd pour it down my throat."

A smile flickered across his dark face. "I do so admire intelligent women. Now drink it up. You'll see that I am right."

Nell took a sip, made a face and then, gamely, in one big gulp, swallowed the contents of the glass. She almost gagged, the liquor burning the length of her throat before flowing warmly down to her stomach. To her astonishment, in moments, she did feel better.

The door to the salon opened and a woman in a gown of puce kerseymere with an edging of cream lace around the neck swept into the room. She was a small, buxom female with startling fair skin that contrasted sharply to the mass of ebony-colored hair half-hidden by the charming lace and muslin cap she wore on her head. Black eyes full of lively intelligence surveyed the room, something deep in their depths flickering briefly as they rested on Nell.

The Frenchwoman, Nell thought, Harlan's second wife, the mother of Raoul, Charles Weston's younger half brother. If the Frenchwoman was surprised to find the Countesses Wyndham in her house, she gave no sign. Drifting up to where Nell sat on the couch, she said, "So we meet at last. I am Mrs. Weston and you are Lord Wyndham's bride, *oui?*"

Nell nodded. "Yes, I am. We are sorry to intrude upon you this way, but I suffered a fall from my horse and your, ah, stepson, was most insistent that he bring me here. I trust that our unexpected arrival will cause you no trouble."

The Frenchwoman shrugged. "It is my stepson's house. He may do as he pleases—even if I think it foolish." She cast a glance at Weston. "What were you thinking, *mon fils?* You know that the earl will not be happy to find his bride here."

"And why is it that everyone thinks that the state of my cousin's emotions is of any interest to me?" asked Weston with a raised brow.

Mrs. Weston's lips thinned. "You are a fool," she stated coldly.

"Well, at least we are in agreement about something," murmured Weston. "Ah, here's Garthwaite, just in time to prevent us from brawling in front of our guests."

Garthwaite entered the room carrying an ornate silver tray, followed by a footman carrying another larger tray arrayed with several types of small sandwiches, biscuits and sweets.

Nell was never so glad of a cup of hot, strong tea as she was at that moment. Taking the cup from Mrs. Weston, her fingers wrapped around the china cup as if she would never let it go. Mrs. Weston was a polite hostess and chatted aimlessly about the countryside, the weather and the latest fashions, in general making Nell feel comfortable. Lady Diana joined in and if one did not know better would have assumed that the ladies met regularly and were good friends. Weston amused himself by flirting with Elizabeth, with whom he seemed on excellent terms.

Nell had just finished her second cup of tea and was feeling more the thing when the sound of male voices could be heard coming down the hallway. She stiffened. It was far too soon for Julian to have arrived, so that meant . . .

Two men entered the salon, both wearing breeches and boots, one as dark as the other was fair. The Weston features, though altered by the infusion of French blood, made it easy for Nell to identify Raoul, Weston's younger half brother. As for the other . . . It was a face she would never forget. One of her hands clenched into a fist and only by the greatest of willpower was she able to keep seated on the sofa, controlling the feral instinct to fly across the room and claw out Lord Tynedale's very blue eyes.

Both men stopped, startled to find, except for Weston, the salon full of women. Raoul recovered instantly and rushed to the sofa.

"Never tell me," he exclaimed, smiling warmly down at Nell, "that this is my cousin's new bride come to call upon us?"

Lady Diana made a hurried introduction and explained the situation.

"Whatever the reasons for you being here, Lady Wyndham, it is a pleasure to finally meet you," he said. "My cousin is to be congratulated for choosing such a lovely lady for his wife."

Nell muttered something polite, bracing herself for Tynedale's approach. And approach her he did. A sly smile on his handsome mouth, he bowed over her hand and murmured, "My dear, dear Countess Wyndham, allow me to congratulate you on your marriage. Why you could have knocked me over with a feather when I heard the news—I, for one, never thought I'd see this day." Malice in his blue eyes, he added, "Here we all thought that Lord Wyndham had buried his heart with the beautiful Lady Catherine and what does he do, but steal the march on all of us and snatch another lovely heiress right from beneath our noses. His quick thinking and swift action quite took my breath away. So perspicacious of him to, er, seize the moment, don't you agree?"

Loathing him, Nell jerked her fingers from his grasp. "Yes, Lord Wyndham's intellect is of the highest order," she said. "And I do so admire and respect a man with cognitive ability, as well as charm and address." She smiled sweetly. "Compared to my husband, I must admit that most men seem . . . well, rather, ah, coarse and addle-brained."

Tynedale gave a hard laugh. "Ah, well, my lady, that remains to be seen. Some of us may upon occasion appear foolish and make mistakes, but I assure you, we seldom make the same one twice."

"Now why," complained Weston, coming over to stand behind them at the rear of the sofa, "do I have the impression that I have walked into the second act of a three-act play?"

Nell flushed and looked down at her hands. She had not meant to cross swords with Tynedale so openly, but the provocation had been great. From beneath her lashes she studied him as he turned aside Weston's comment with a laugh. He was a blackguard, an evil man, and she hated him. If not for him she would still be plain Miss Eleanor Anslowe. For just a second her heart stuttered. Did she really wish that she had never met Julian and married him? Yes, she admitted fiercely, if his heart is in the grave with Lady Catherine.

The conversation became general and Nell relaxed and let the others do the talking while she listened. She hated having to endure Tynedale's barbed conversation and she was very conscious of Weston standing just behind her. Weston puzzled her. He was nothing like she had thought he would be and under different circumstances, meeting him for the first time, she thought she might have liked him. And then again . . .

As the minutes passed she became aware that she was uneasy. Julian was not going to be happy finding her here, but it wasn't the anticipation of her husband's displeasure that troubled her. There was something about this house, these people, that bothered her and made her long for Julian's arrival and their departure for Wyndham Manor. Their *immediate* departure, she thought wryly.

She detested being in the same room with Tynedale, detested even more having to smile and treat him politely, and she wondered how Julian was going to react to his presence. It was bad enough that she had to be here in the first place, without Tynedale lurking nearby.

Her gaze slid to Raoul and she studied him from beneath her lashes. He was a handsome man, his features, while bearing the Weston stamp, more regular than either Julian or Weston's, but those black eyes of his reminded her of his mother as did the shape of his mouth. Raoul was far more handsome and charming than his half brother but watching Raoul as he laughed and teased Lady Diana, Nell decided that she preferred Weston's abrupt manner. It was possible, she admitted, for a man to possess too much charm.

Lady Diana rose from the sofa to take a chair next to Mrs. Weston and they were soon deep into a conversation about the merits of Pear's Soap for the complexion; Raoul carried Elizabeth off to view the gardens from one of the huge windows. Lord Tynedale promptly took the seat that Lady Diana had vacated and Nell froze. She was trying very hard not to cause a scene, but Tynedale's proximity was making it difficult.

"You really must tell me, my dear," he drawled in a voice for her ears alone, "how it is that your marriage to the earl came about. How did you manage to trap him?"

Her expression glacial, Nell stared at him. "And why," she asked tightly, "would I discuss something of such a personal nature with you? I'd sooner tie my garter in public. You know very well what happened!"

Tynedale clasped his heart as if struck. "Oh, fair lady, you wound me. Never tell me, that having made the match of the decade, that you begrudge my little part in it? For shame!"

Weston leaned over the back of the sofa and murmured, "Do you know, Tynedale, I am quite sure, no, I am positive that my revered cousin would find your attentions to his wife objectionable." His eyes locked with Tynedale's, he added, "I know I would . . . And my cousin and I, for all our differences, are remarkably alike . . . in some things." When Tynedale shrugged, Weston sighed. "Have you forgotten," he asked, "that Lord Wyndham is noted for his excellent swordplay?" Tynedale jerked and touched the faint scar on his face. Weston nodded. "Precisely. I suggest that unless you wish to meet him again in the very near future that you hedge off and find some other lady upon which to ply your charms."

The men exchanged glances. Tynedale smiled stiffly. "I'm sure you have misunderstood. Lady Wyndham and I are merely, er, renewing our acquaintance."

"Do you really think that Wyndham will care one way or the other?" Weston inquired dryly.

Before Tynedale could reply, Garthwaite strode into the room and announced, "The Earl of Wyndham."

Julian strolled into the doorway. A few steps into the room, he stopped, his gaze taking in the occupants. If the sight of his wife hobnobbing with Tynedale and Weston disturbed him there was no sign of it on his handsome face. His eyes raked over Nell and seeing that she appeared unhurt, he turned his attention to his hostess.

Greetings were exchanged and Julian was offered refreshments. Smiling, he declined. "Thank you, that will not be necessary. If we are to reach home before dark, it is imperative that we leave before the light fails."

"Afraid we'll corrupt you?" drawled Weston, as he straightened from the sofa. An odd smile on his lips, he walked toward Julian. "Surely, a cup of tea or a snifter of brandy will not come amiss before you tear your bride away from us?"

"Oh, Julian!" cried Lady Diana, jumping up and rushing over to Julian. "Do not be angry. It was not my fault! I swear to you." She cast an anxious glance at Nell. "And it wasn't Nell's fault, either. It was an accident. The mare stumbled and Nell could not keep her seat. It was most providential that Cousin Charles came along when he did." The scrap of lace reappeared and dabbing her eyes, she said, "If Cousin Charles had not been so helpful we'd probably still be there at the side of the road."

"I'm sure everything you have said is true," replied Julian in a soothing tone. Over Diana's head, he looked at his cousin. "And sometime in the very near future, I would very much like to hear how Cousin Charles came to be so, ah, conveniently at hand."

"Oh, think nothing of it, dear boy," remarked Charles, an unholy gleam in his eyes. "Consider it simply my good fortune. Anything to be of service to the head of the family. You know how I so try to curry favor with you every chance I get."

Julian burst out laughing. "Gammon! I sometimes think that your only redeeming quality is your bloody impudence." Smiling he extended his hand. "Thank you, Cousin. I am grateful for your service to my wife and family."

"At least you will concede that I have a redeeming quality," Charles said, as he shook Julian's hand. "And you're welcome."

"By Jove!" said Raoul coming up beside the other two men. "Does this mean that we are once again back in your good graces?"

Julian gave a twisted smile. "Have done! Suffice to say I am grateful for your help and hospitality and let us leave it at that for the time being."

He glanced around the room again, his eyes lingering for a moment on Tynedale, who still sat next to Nell. His mouth tightened, but he said only, "I am indeed sorry not to partake some refreshments, but nightfall is fast approaching and I wish to return home in all haste and apprise myself of Lady Wyndham's health."

Striding to the sofa, he put out an imperious hand to Nell. "My dear? Are you ready to leave?"

Nell was more than ready to leave. After thanking Mrs. Weston for her hospitality, she allowed Julian to escort her from the room. Lady Diana and Elizabeth were still taking their leave from Mrs. Weston and it was only the two of them that traversed the long hallway.

Aware that she was favoring her left leg more than usual, Julian asked quietly, "Are you really unhurt?"

Nell flashed him a look and nodded. "I was dizzy . . . shaken a little, but your cousin Charles made me drink some brandy and that seemed to solve the problem. I am sure that I will be stiff and sore for a few days, though." She hesitated. "Are you very angry to find us here? There really was no choice."

Julian sighed. "As Diana said, it is not your fault." Thinking of the exchange with Charles, he added, "And perhaps some good will come of it."

"But what of Tynedale?"

His eyes scanned her face. "I was surprised to see him seated next to you."

There was a question implicit in his words and Nell stiffened. "Do you think," she asked in a low, angry voice, "that I encouraged him?"

"No. No." Julian replied hastily. "I was merely surprised that he dared to approach you."

"You will find," she muttered, "that Tynedale will dare whatever he pleases. *I* have no control over him and short of causing just the sort of scene we wish to avoid, there was nothing I could do when he sat down beside me. I was never more grateful that Cousin Charles joined us."

Julian frowned. "Do you think Tynedale has told either of my cousins his part in our marriage?"

She shrugged. "I do not know . . . although I had the impression that your cousin Charles may know more than it appears."

Julian gave a bitter laugh. "That, my dear, is Cousin Charles all over. He always plays it close to the vest."

The sound of the others approaching behind them ended their exchange and they continued on their way down the hallway. They reached the foyer to find Garthwaite waiting with Nell, Lady Diana and Elizabeth's things. Pulling on her gloves, Nell thanked the butler. Her hat, she thought wryly, was probably still lying on the ground where Weston had thrown it.

Lady Diana and Elizabeth were putting on their own gloves and chatting to Weston and Raoul, who had followed them to the foyer, and Nell took the moment to cast another glance around the elegant area. A pair of doors she had not noticed previously were thrown wide and, glancing inside she saw that this room, like the rest of the house, reflected not only impeccable taste but also a sizeable amount of money. A massive, gilt-edged portrait hanging above the fireplace on the far wall caught her eye. The portrait drew her and un-aware of anything else, she walked slowly across the room to stop and stare at it. The subjects were a gentleman and a young boy of perhaps ten. The gentleman wore silks and satins well over a decade out of fashion; a stunning sapphire ring adorned one hand. She recognized at once the Weston features, the same features replicated in miniature in the face of the small boy who leaned affectionately against the knee of the gentleman.

Mesmerized as she stared at the darkly handsome features, her heart began to beat in hard, painful strokes. She knew that face. She had seen that smiling gentleman before . . . Only he had not been smiling . . . not when she had seen him. The room tilted and a wave of nausea swept over her, her left leg trembling violently. The pounding of her heart became al-most unbearable as memory clawed its way free from the deepest recesses of her mind. Oh, God. She remembered. She gasped, swayed and the world went black.

She awoke to find herself cradled in Julian's arms. Strug-gling upright, she became aware of movement and the rattle and jingle of a harness and realized that she was in the Wynd-ham coach.

Julian pressed her back against the dark blue velvet squabs of the coach, saying, "Easy, easy—you fainted." In the dim light of the coach, he stared into her face, brushing back a lock of her hair that had come loose. "How are you feeling now?"

"Oh, Nell, you scared us to death!" cried Lady Diana. "It was awful. You were standing there one minute and the next you were lying motionless on the floor. I thought you had died! I was never so terrified in my life."

Nell looked across at Lady Diana and Elizabeth as they sat together on the opposite side of the coach. Both wore anxious expressions, their eyes wide and worried as they stared at her.

She supplied a wan smile. "I'm sorry for frightening you— twice." Her gaze shadowed, she stared at her gloved hands in her lap. "I do not know what came over me. The fall must have shaken me more than I realized."

The two women took her words at face value and during the remainder of the journey they chatted away about the events of the day. Julian said nothing, but a peek at his shuttered face told Nell that he did not believe that the fall from her horse had caused her to faint. It hadn't. A shudder rolled through her and wearily she shut her eyes. It seemed that nightmares didn't only happen when one slept.

Arriving at Wyndham Manor, Nell sought out her rooms and Becky's eager services. A hot bath was waiting for her and later, wearing a nightgown of softest lawn and a warm dressing robe of amber velvet, she nibbled at the tray of food put before her.

"Now you eat that up right now!" fussed Becky, her big brown eyes full of anxiety. "What will his lordship say when he discovers that you haven't hardly swallowed a morsel?"

Nell pushed away the half-eaten bowl of broth. "I only fell," she protested. "No bones are broken. I'm fine. I was just . . . badly shaken."

Becky sniffed. "If you say so, my lady. And since you aren't going to eat anything else, I'll just take these things back to Cook, who will probably go off in a decline when she sees how little you appreciate her hard work."

"Oh, Becky, please don't scold so," Nell begged, her head beginning to throb, terrible memories crawling into her thoughts.

Becky's face softened. "Very well, my lady. You go get in bed now."

Nell followed Becky's orders and had just settled into bed with a huge bank of pillows at her back when Julian walked into her bedroom. He came up to the edge of the bed and sat down.

Taking one of her hands in his, he asked, "Feeling better now?"

She forced a smile. "Yes. I'm sorry that I caused such a disruption. It was only a fall."

His gaze searched hers. "That may be, but I don't believe that it was your fall that caused you to faint in such a dramatic fashion at the Westons's."

"It wasn't," she admitted. Looking away from him, she bit her lip. "My lord, that, that portrait where I fainted, who is it?"

He looked surprised. "My cousin John and his son, Daniel. Don't you remember? I've spoken of both of them to you." Staring at her averted features, he leaned forward. Catching her chin with one finger, he pulled her face around to him. "What is it, Nell? Tell me!"

Nell swallowed. "Do you remember," she began, "when I told you about my nightmares?"

He nodded, frowning.

"Well, do you remember that in the first one, I said that I dreamed that a man was murdered?"

Their gazes locked. Her voice trembling, Nell said, "I recognized the man in my nightmare . . . The man I saw murdered was your cousin John."

Chapter 12

Julian leaped up from the bed and took an agitated step away, only to swing back and stare at Nell with disbelief. "Impossible!" he burst out. "It was a nightmare. How could you have seen John in your nightmare?"

Looking miserable, Nell shook her head. "I do not know. I only know that I have never forgotten that man's face—and it was your cousin John's." She leaned forward, saying urgently, "I tell you that I recognized him! Your cousin is the same man that is in my nightmare. Julian, you must believe me! I *saw* his murder."

"Don't talk such fustian!" Julian ordered. "How can it be? My cousin was murdered ten years or more ago. You never met any of us until you married me. How could you have seen his murder?"

Nell pushed back a lock of tumbled tawny hair. "I cannot tell you, I do not understand it myself. I only know that after I was brought back from the cliffs and I began to have the nightmares that the first one was of a man being murdered. I swear to you that man wore your cousin John's face!"

Julian did not want to believe her, every instinct cried out against it, but there was no mistaking that *she* believed what she was saying. Approaching the bed once more, he reseated himself and taking her hand again, he said, "Nell, you cannot have seen John's murder. By your own admission, until today, you didn't even know who he was. How can he have been the man in a nightmare you had ten years ago? How can you be so sure now that it was my cousin John and not just a man who looked like him?"

"I cannot explain it," she admitted, "but I know it to be true—the man was your cousin." She swallowed convulsively. "I was unconscious for several days, but I dreamed all during that time, a horrible dream of a man being murdered. The same dream over and over and over. It was very vivid . . . as if I had actually seen it happen."

"It's impossible! You cannot have seen John murdered," he protested, his troubled gaze on her face.

Her sea green eyes met his steadily. "Tell me, where was your cousin murdered?"

Julian made an impatient gesture. "I don't remember exactly. Near some damn little provincial town. Somewhere in Dorset, near the coast." He stiffened, staring at her. "Meadowlea is in Dorset . . . near the coast," he said in an odd tone. Collecting himself, he muttered, "But that must be a coincidence."

She didn't argue with him. "And when? What was the date of his murder?"

"The tenth of October 1794."

She gave a twisted smile. "My accident occurred on October tenth that same year and my nightmares began around then. Another coincidence?"

"Yes, of course. It has to be," he insisted. "To think otherwise is utter madness."

"Very well, believe that if you will, but let me tell you the details of my nightmare and see if you still believe it is merely coincidence." He nodded curtly and she began softly, "I was riding my little mare, Firefly, that day, but she'd thrown a shoe and gone lame. I was leading her home, not two miles further down the road. We came upon a small copse of wood and as we began to walk through it, I heard the loud voices of men arguing ahead of me. I did not understand what they were saying, only that they were very angry. I was frightened, uneasy perhaps, but as this was the only way home I had no choice but to press on. Besides, I told myself, it was probably only some locals having a disagreement and once they recognized me, they'd stop their fighting until I'd gone on by or perhaps even give me a ride home. At worst, I hoped that I might pass them without incident.

"When I came around a curve in the road, I passed a small closed carriage parked off to the side and just beyond that, I saw two men, strangers, fighting." She took a deep breath. "They did not see me. I stopped and stared, transfixed by the violence. I had never seen men strike each other so savagely, so furiously before. They were both tall, evenly matched I would say. The man I now know to be your cousin gained the upper hand. He knocked the other man down and was kneeling astride him when the other man dragged forth a dagger and drove it into his chest. The man on the ground struck your cousin once more in the chest, then once in the shoulder and once in the throat. The blood . . . The blood seemed everywhere." Her voice shook. "I cried out, I could not help myself, and it was then that I became aware that there had to have been someone else in the copse. There was a sound, a whisper of movement behind me, and as I turned in that direction, I was struck on the back of the head."

Sinking against the pillows, she said, "The rest you know—they found me over the cliff, lying on a small ledge . . . Firefly dead on the rocks below." Turning her head away from him she added, "Believe what you will, but I know that the man I saw murdered was your cousin."

Julian's cool logic rejected her story, denied that her nightmare could be so accurate in the details surrounding John's murder. But he could not dismiss the impact her words had upon him. Against his will, he asked, "In your nightmare, how were they dressed—especially John?"

"The one who stabbed your cousin wore a green jacket and . . ." She frowned, trying to remember the other man.

How peculiar . . . Julian's cousin she could recall right down to the way his black curly hair was arranged, but the murderer . . . It was as if he had been blocked from her mind. But as the minutes passed and she concentrated, memory trickled back. "And buff breeches and boots," she finally said. "Your cousin John was garbed in Nankeen breeches, a dark blue coat with large silver buttons, a white waistcoat with black spots and upon his finger the same ring that is in that portrait at Stonegate."

Julian's breath sucked in as if he'd suffered a blow to the gut. He stared at nothing for several moments, fighting to understand. He could not judge the details of the murderer's clothes, but his cousin's he could. Reluctantly, he admitted, "John was dressed as you describe when his body was found. He always wore the sapphire ring—it was a family heirloom . . . It always puzzled me: if it had been mere robbery, as the local constable proposed, then why had the ring been left on his finger?" He rubbed his forehead. "The wounds you describe . . . John's were the same."

"Do you believe me now . . . Or do you think it is all just coincidence?"

He got up from the bed and stalked around the room, dragging a hand through his dark, unruly hair. "I do not know what to believe! This is beyond comprehension! What you tell me is incredible and I want to dismiss it out of hand . . . And yet you know too many things for it to be just a mere coincidence." He took another turn around the room. "Tell me," he demanded, "how did you end up on the cliff?"

"I have no idea," she replied simply. "As I told you, I was unconscious for days afterward and I have no memory of my fall or of even being in the vicinity where I was found."

"And the nightmare, the one where John is murdered, you had it ten years ago?"

She heard the skepticism in his voice, but she didn't blame him. Ten years was a long time to remember a nightmare. To remember a face. Even to remember a murder, but she did . . . as clearly as if it had happened yesterday.

"Yes," she answered, "ten years ago, repeatedly for weeks."

His expression harried, he stared at her. "And the other nightmares? Tell me about them."

She did so, trying to convey the horror, the fear, the unspeakable brutality that occurred in that terrifying place . . . those dungeons.

He was quiet for several minutes when she finished speaking. "And you are positive that it is the same man in all the nightmares?" he finally asked. "That the same man you saw kill John is also the man who savages these women?"

She nodded. "As best as I can tell." When he continued to stare at her, his demeanor giving nothing away, she said passionately, "You must remember that I've never seen the man's face. It was gloomy in the copse, thickly wooded, and when I first came upon them fighting, the murderer had his back to me. When your cousin knocked him down, your cousin was facing me, his murderer lying on the ground looking up at him. I was still several feet away and I only saw the top, the back, of his head. And in the dungeon, it is a dark, shadowy place and his face is always averted."

"Then how do you know they are the same man?"

"I sense that they are . . . There is something in the build, in the way the man moves, the shape of the head . . . that convinces me that they are the same person. And I find it easier," she confessed, "to believe that it is the same man rather than to think that two such monsters are abroad."

Wearing an expression of frustration, horror and anger, Julian loomed up next to the bed. His voice grim, he demanded, "If I believe you . . . If I accept that your nightmare reflects an actual occurrence . . . Do you realize what it means?"

Nell nodded. Bleakly she said, "It means that he is a real man, a real person, and that he's still out there somewhere, killing the women that I see in my nightmares." She bit her lip. "And that those dungeons actually exist, that I have not imagined them." She hesitated and flashed him a look before saying, "And I think I know where to look for them."

He glanced at her. "What are you saying?"

"Lady Diana and Elizabeth told me about the dungeons beneath this house," she said.

"And you dare to think that it is in the dungeons beneath my home that he does his killing?" he asked incredulously, his eyes blazing. "Isn't it enough that you're asking me to believe that by some unexplained black magic, witchcraft, you saw my cousin killed, that you see other women murdered? Must I now search out my own home to find proof of these vile crimes?"

"I don't know," she cried. "I don't understand any of it, but I do know that my nightmares cannot be dismissed as the results of my fall over the cliff any longer. I *recognized* your cousin! I *saw* his murder. And if his murder was real, then the dungeons are real and what goes on there is real, too."

Julian threw himself across the bed and lying on his back stared up at the silken canopy overhead. He lay there a long time, fighting against accepting her words as true. Yet what other explanation was there? It would be so much simpler if he could discard Nell's nightmares out of hand, blame them on feminine hysteria. If only he could convince himself that it was his misfortune to have married a woman of a nervous disposition, an excitable creature given to spasms and fanciful ideas, but he could not. True, he had not known Nell long, but he had seen her in a dangerous, difficult situation and she had kept her head. A smile lurked at the corner of his mouth as he remembered that first meeting. If she had been the type of woman to go off into screaming convulsions it would have been then, but instead she'd proven herself pluck to the backbone. While he wished violently that it was otherwise, he could not pretend that her nightmares were just the wild imaginings of a hysterical woman. She *knew* things—things for which he had no rational explanation.

"I do not want to believe you, but I find that I must," he said finally. He turned to look at her. "There are forces at work here that I do not understand. How you could have dreamed John's murder . . . !" He swore under his breath and sat up. "Upon my soul! This is an impossible situation! I must believe that in your nightmare you saw my cousin's death and that somehow you have a connection to the villain who killed him. A vicious villain who is still killing innocent women—in dungeons." His voice full of disgust he added, "Dungeons that you think might be beneath my very home."

"I don't think that I dreamed your cousin's murder," Nell muttered. "I think I actually saw it."

He jerked upright, his expression full of speculation. "And the events come back to you in the form of a nightmare?" he asked, a spark of interest in his eyes.

She nodded. "Yes, that's it precisely." She frowned. "The other nightmares . . . They feel different, as if I am watching them through a veil, but with your cousin . . . The colors are bright, vivid, I can smell the air, the forest, feel the coolness of the day, Firefly's reins in my hands—but not in the others."

It was Julian's turn to frown. "If you actually saw the murder, how did you end up where you did?"

Her fingers plucked nervously at the counterpane on the bed. "I think that your cousin's murderer, and whoever else was there in the copse with him—that after I was knocked unconscious, that they carried me to the cliffs and threw me over and then drove poor Firefly over the same cliff. They left me for dead."

An icy dagger ripped at his heart at the thought that she might have died that day . . . that he might never have known her. Rage against those faceless, nameless bastards filled him, but he throttled it back and coolly considered her words.

"Wasn't that dangerous for them? After all, your family is prominent in the area. Surely they must have known that you'd be missed, that within hours someone would be looking for you?"

"I am positive that they were strangers to the area, that they did not know who I was." She made a face. "I did not have a groom with me that day and I was wearing my oldest habit. There was nothing about me, other than perhaps Firefly's quality, that would give them a clue that I was anything more than some local female who had stumbled across something she should not have." A shudder rippled through her. "I feel that they did not plan on anyone, except mayhap a worried parent or husband, to go looking for me. Certainly they never thought that nearly everyone for miles around would be in on the search, or that I would be found alive."

Julian rubbed his forehead again. His thoughts crashing against one another like waves on the rocks, flying in all directions, splintering into a million pieces, only to re-form and repeat the process. He could see no good in what he had learned tonight. His wife, like the witches of legend, appeared to have the "sight" or whatever name one wanted to call it, and that this *gift,* he thought sourly, manifested itself in her dreams. Graphic, violent nightmares that woke her screaming and trembling from their black, bottomless depths.

Something occurred to him. "Your nightmares . . . the ones after John's murder, they're *only* in these dungeons, the same dungeons, and only when he is killing?"

Nell nodded.

Julian's eyes narrowed. "If you only see him at those times, then it must be the violence that is your link to him," he said more to himself than to her. "John's murder forged a link, and God knows how, between the two of you . . . and your nightmares, your connection to him, is triggered whenever he kills."

"Until today I did not believe, not truly, that I was seeing, dreaming of real people. I knew that the nightmares had to be connected," Nell admitted, "but it was my fall over the cliffs that I blamed for them, not your cousin's murder."

Julian studied her features, noting the purple shadows under her eyes and the air of fragility that surrounded her, and his heart turned in his breast. She looked exhausted; she'd suffered a bad toss today and needed to be coddled and comforted, not badgered about the horrible events they were discussing. He wanted to press on, there were questions upon questions that he wanted to have answered, but he drew back, deciding reluctantly that tomorrow would be soon enough to consider tonight's revelations.

He stood up, preparing to leave the room. "You need to rest, and talking about this subject is not going to help you sleep." His gaze traveled on her pale features again. "I want Dr. Coleman to see you tomorrow morning," he said abruptly.

Nell wrinkled her nose at him. "Will it do me any good to argue with you about that?"

"No, none at all," he returned, a flicker of amusement crossing his face. He ran a caressing finger down her cheek. "I do not want anything happening to you. When Hodges returned and told me of your fall . . ." Remembered terror washed through him, but he forced a smile and said, "Let us just say that I do not want to experience that sensation again."

Precisely what he meant Nell could not tell from either his voice or his expression. Had he been annoyed? Worried? Irritated? He had not been happy to find her at Stonegate, that much she easily surmised. Probing just a little, she looked away and murmured, "It must have been a shock for you to find us at Stonegate this afternoon."

"I can't deny it," Julian replied, and some imp of the devil prompted him to add, "but that was nothing compared to the shock I felt when I saw you sitting so cozily next to Tynedale."

Her head swung in his direction and her chin held at a pugnacious angle, she said, "As I told you, I did not have a choice. He sat down beside me. I could not prevent him."

Julian wanted to believe her in this, too, but the sight of his bride sitting and chatting so calmly beside the man who had supposedly kidnapped her not three months before had given him a start and aroused a green-eyed demon within him. He had wanted to jerk that silly popinjay, Tynedale, off that sofa and shake him like a terrier with a rat. As for Nell, he had barely contained the powerful urge to sweep her into his arms and demand that she *never* frighten him in such a manner again.

That Nell had affection, or a fondness, for him he did not doubt, but he was also conscious that she withheld a part of herself from him. He tried not to dwell upon it or give it importance, but he'd noticed those subtle withdrawals—the gentle removal of her hand from his and the slight turning of her mouth, so that his kisses fell upon her cheek. The nagging sense that she was moving further away from him filled him with helpless terror. He wanted to grab her and shake her and demand that she love him . . . as he, he realized, loved her.

Stunned he stared at her. He loved her! He shook his head, hardly able to believe what had happened to him. He, the man who had never considered falling in love, had committed that folly of follies and had done just that—with his wife!

He stared at Nell, his expression shuttered as he grappled with what had so inexplicably happened to him. He loved this slip of a woman with the big, misty-green eyes and tangled tawny hair. Loved her as he had never imagined loving another human being. In some mysterious way she had become his world . . . And unless he'd mistaken the situation, she was drifting away from him.

Remembering her sitting beside Tynedale this afternoon, jealousy stirred like a wakened dragon in his breast and for the first time, he wondered if Tynedale's kidnapping had been as one-sided as Nell had claimed. He had believed her . . . then. But now he wondered. Had the withdrawal he sensed started with the news that Tynedale was in the area? Could the so-called kidnapping have actually been merely a run-away match? Had there been a lovers' quarrel that had sent Nell rushing off into the storm to seek shelter in the toll keeper's cottage? And perhaps, the next morning, when confronted by himself and her father, she could not bring herself to admit it? Had events simply spun out of her control so she had decided to make the best of it? He winced. Bad enough to be married for title and wealth, but to be married because it was simply a solution to one's problem did not bear thinking of . . . especially now, when he was in love with her.

"My lord," Nell said, breaking into his wanderings, "surely you do not believe that I encouraged Lord Tynedale?"

Reeling from the sudden knowledge that he was in love with her, buffeted by pangs of jealousy and uncertainty, Julian muttered, "I do not know what to believe anymore."

Nell gasped, outraged. He doubted her word. Her green eyes glittering, she snapped, "Then I suggest that until you *do* decide to believe me that you not inflict yourself upon me."

"Inflict?" he demanded, her words flicking him like a cat-o'-nine-tails. Pride and temper goading him, he said, "Very well, my lady, I bid you good night. Do not worry that I shall *inflict* myself on you any longer."

Nell watched him stalk from the room, her volatile emotions flying from angry indignation to anguished despair and back again. The words to call him back, to make peace, hovered on her lips . . . and then it was too late. He was gone; the door between their rooms slamming shut behind his tall form with a thunderous boom that echoed around the room. The sound ringing in her ears, she buried her head in her pillow. A fist in her mouth, she choked back tears. Damn him! To doubt her word! To think even for a moment that she liked being in Tynedale's company. Oh, she hated him. And at that exact second she wasn't certain who was the true recipient of that hatred, Tynedale or her wretched husband, who did not love her—who had given his love and his heart to a dead woman. Damn and blast him!

While Nell fought her own demons, Julian paced the confines of his rooms. He had tossed aside his coat and cravat and removed his boots. His valet had left a decanter of brandy and a snifter and during the course of the hours that followed he made steady inroads into the liquor.

His thoughts were spinning. The import of Nell's nightmares, his newly discovered love, his jealousy and suspicions all fighting against each other like scorpions in his brain. John's death was a long-festering wound; Daniel's suicide the previous year only adding poison to the canker that ate at him. That Nell might really have seen John's murder, that she might be able to identify his murderer filled him with a savage exultance. At last, after all this time, he might be able to get his hands on the person who had foully murdered as fine a man as he had ever loved or known. Bringing his cousin's murderer to justice would help ease some of the guilt he felt for failing John's son, Daniel.

It did no good for Marcus or anyone to tell him that Daniel's suicide had not been his fault, Julian admitted wearily, taking a long swallow of the brandy. Whatever anyone else might think, in his heart he felt that he had failed John, that he had not kept his promise made on that long-ago day to care for Daniel should something ever happen to John. He had failed and failure did not sit easy with him.

He'd avoided thinking about Nell, but her image, the sweetness of her smile, the giddy joy of her kiss crept into his mind, driving out the darker thoughts. He stopped his pacing and stared blindly into the fire that crackled on the black marble hearth.

He was in love. With his wife. It was incredible and terrifying; glorious and confounding. He knew an insane impulse to toss the snifter on the hearth and charge into Nell's room, and taking her into his arms kiss her senseless, pour out what was in his heart and demand that she love him. With an effort he fought against acting so rashly. A bitter smile curled his mouth as he remembered their parting. Most likely he'd have his ears soundly boxed and only add to the estrangement if he dared to do so. His wife, he admitted, did not hold him in high esteem at the moment.

And Nell was right about one thing: he had to make up his mind whether he believed her . . . or not. Jealousy churned in his chest. Was it possible that Nell was in love with Tynedale? Had she perhaps not known her own feelings until she'd seen that bastard again? He did not want to believe it. He'd never once doubted Nell's word. He had believed implicitly her tale of being kidnapped and forced to accompany Tynedale. He had good reason to; he held the power to destroy Tynedale financially and he knew that Tynedale had been frantic for a way to escape his fate. Marriage to an heiress would be a perfect solution. And if Tynedale had been reduced to kidnapping and forcing an unwilling woman into marriage, it wouldn't have deterred him.

Julian took a turn around the room, rubbing his forehead. God! If only he could resolve the conflict within himself. Nell's nightmares were enough to drive a man to drink, let alone finding out he was in love with her and suspicious that she might be in love with a man he considered his enemy.

He tossed off the last of the brandy, his face grim. So, did he believe her or not? He recalled the glitter in her fine eyes, the outrage on her face, and a wave of remorse and shame washed over him. How could he have doubted her? He was a fool! The moment Tynedale's name had been uttered, he'd reacted like a callow youth in love for the first time—allowing insecurity and jealousy to rule him. A wry smile crossed his face. Well, he *was* in love for the first time, surely that gave him some excuse. But there was no denying that he'd let a green-eyed monster and, he admitted, his own temper, drive a wedge between them that they did not need. He took a deep breath. Even if he was not in love with Nell, he would not allow their relationship to deteriorate. He had failed at one marriage, he would not another. And he would not lose Nell to Tynedale without a fight. She was *his* . . . and he loved her.

Her nightmares, her link to the murderer, troubled him deeply. If John's murderer was to learn of that link . . . If even a hint of Nell's connection to him was discovered . . . A chill, a bone-deep terror enveloped him. Until this monster, this vile beast of her nightmares was caught Nell was in desperate danger, her very life could be at stake. At the idea of Nell being harmed a rage such as he had never known exploded through him. His fingers tightened on the snifter and the fragile stem of the snifter snapped. It was the stinging of his palm that brought him back from the well of black fury that he had fallen into and, staring at the blood welling from the deep cuts on his fingers, he made a vow: he would find this monster and kill him. For Nell's sake, this creature must be found and killed.

Julian did not sleep that night; he had much to consider and spent the intervening hours studying the problems before him. He had no clear plans, but shortly after daylight he rang for his valet. An hour later, bathed and ready to face the new day, he descended the staircase and headed for the breakfast room. A word with Dibble ensured that a message to Dr. Coleman was sent on its way.

After enjoying a quick breakfast of rare sirloin and a tankard of ale, Julian removed to the library, where he continued to pace, his movements no less restless than the thoughts tumbling through his mind. Of greatest importance, he needed to right things with Nell, ease the strain between them. He'd never considered himself a coward, but in the matters of the heart, he discovered that he did not quite have the nerve to blurt out his deepest feelings—not when doubts of the lady's affection for him remained. But if he could not declare himself, he could at least see to it that they were not at daggers drawing with each other.

And then there was the matter of the dungeons . . . He

scowled. Nell was right about that, too. His dungeons must be examined to determine if they were indeed the same ones in her nightmares. If they proved to be so . . . a feral gleam that his friends and family would not have recognized leaped to his eyes. A trap would be set, he thought, yes, a trap that would leave no room for escape, and this monster would be dealt with once and for all—by him. Only one of them would leave that dungeon alive.

Dr. Coleman's arrival interrupted his thoughts, and slapping on a polite smile he greeted the other man. Explaining the situation, Nell's fall the previous day, he soon sent the doctor on his way to see Nell. He smiled wryly. Something else she would hold against him.

Upstairs in her suite of rooms, Nell was not happy to see Dr. Coleman. Like Julian she'd spent a less than restful night, but she had managed to sleep for a few hours. Exhausted and her leg aching like the very devil, she'd put up with Becky's ministrations and scolds as she'd bathed. Not feeling robust, thinking that she would spend the day in bed, she'd elected to wear a pale yellow nightgown of finest cambric, followed by a lavender dressing gown festooned with lace. After Becky had combed her hair and tied the heavy locks back with a silk ribbon, she'd even managed to swallow a bite or two from the laden tray that had, at Becky's insistence, been brought to her.

She had just poured herself a second cup of tea when Dr. Coleman was announced. Putting a good face on it, she answered his questions and endured his examination. Nell was very conscious that this tall, dark-haired man who asked such probing questions and knew such intimate details of her body was her husband's uncle in blood, if not name; his resemblance to Julian only added to the awkwardness she felt. She thought of kindly, old, white-haired Dr. Babbington at Meadowlea, and suddenly longed to see his familiar face. A wave of intense homesickness engulfed her. She wanted her father. Her brothers. Tears welled in her eyes. What she really wanted, she admitted, averting her face from Dr. Coleman's impassive stare, was for her husband to love her . . .

His embarrassing questions and examination finished, Dr. Coleman left the bedroom for her sitting room, allowing Nell privacy to arrange her clothing. After what he'd just done to her, Nell wondered with flaming cheeks, why he bothered.

Her dignity intact once more, she joined him in the sitting room.

Hands behind his back, he was staring out the window, but when she entered and took a seat in one of the chairs, he turned to look at her and said, "Well, my lady, you are, despite your accident yesterday, in excellent health. A few days of rest and you will feel your old self." He walked toward her and a smile crossed his face. Wagging a finger at her, he added, "But no more reckless riding for you for awhile—it is not only your health that you put at risk now."

Nell frowned. "What do mean?"

His smile widened. "If all proceeds well, and I see no reason why it would not, I should think that you will deliver your lord a fine, healthy child sometime in July, possibly very early August at the latest. Congratulations."

Chapter 13

Nell sat there stunned. Feeling as if she'd been poleaxed, she was barely aware of the doctor's departure. She was pregnant! With Julian's child!

In amazement she stared down at her flat stomach. How could she be pregnant? A flush stained her cheeks as she thought of the nights of wild lovemaking in her husband's arms. Well, she knew how it had happened; she just couldn't believe it. She didn't feel any different . . . Although admittedly she *had* been tired lately and inclined to tears and her stomach had shown a decided queasiness that didn't seem quite normal . . .

She jumped up from the chair and ran into her dressing room to preen before her tall cheval glass. Tossing aside her dressing gown, she pulled her nightgown tight against her abdomen. A wave of disappointment washed over her. Her stomach still looked flat to her. She turned this way and that, studying herself. With a sigh, she let loose of her nightgown. Dr. Coleman might have said that she was pregnant, but at this moment, she saw no outward sign that a child grew within her. Still . . . There were all those other signs, and it was true that the last time she'd been aware of her monthly flow had been before Julian had come to her bed. A glow suffused her face. It was true. It had to be. She was pregnant.

Becky tapped on the door and peeked around the doorjamb. "My lady? I saw the doctor had left. Do you need anything?"

"No. Yes. I don't know," Nell confessed, still staring awestruck at her suddenly mysterious body. She made an impatient gesture for Becky to join her. "Look at me," she demanded. "Do I look different to you?"

Puzzled, Becky shook her head. "No, your ladyship."

A joyous smile on her lips, she looked at her maid and exclaimed, "Oh, Becky, I have just been given the most extraordinary news! I am with child!"

Her eyes growing round, Becky gasped, "Miss! I mean, your ladyship! How wonderful! You must be thrilled."

"I am," Nell admitted, "I just can't quite take it in yet." A note of awe in her voice, she said, "I am to have a child. In July . . . or early August." She laughed, and grabbing Becky's hand began to dance wildly around the room. "Can you believe it?" she demanded, giggling. "A child! Me!"

"Is his lordship pleased?" Becky asked, when they both collapsed breathless on the bed.

Nell's bubble of joy burst. She was to have a child fathered by a man who did not love her, a man whose heart and love belonged to a dead woman, a man who doubted her word. A heaviness of spirit overtook her. Julian should be pleased by the news of her pregnancy, though—he needed an heir and at least, she thought wryly, that was one thing she could do that the sainted Catherine could not. "He doesn't know yet," she confessed. "I imagine that Dr. Coleman is telling him at this very moment."

Nell was correct. Rejoining Julian in the library, Dr. Coleman related the news that her ladyship should give birth to a child in midsummer. Since a child was the last thing on Julian's mind at the moment, he stared at the doctor for several seconds before the other man's words made sense. A child. His wife was pregnant. His Nell was to give him a child. He would be a father. This summer.

The anxieties of the long sleepless night vanished. Wonderment and joy flooded him and a huge, silly grin broke across his face. His wife was with child.

Dr. Coleman, watching his reaction with a kind eye, smiled and said, "I see that my news pleases you."

"*Pleases* me!" Julian declared in jubilant accents. "You can have no idea! By Jupiter, Coleman, it is the very best news you could have given me."

Coleman laughed. "It is my pleasure, my lord, to give you good news." He picked up his small black valise and said, "I shall be on my way and leave you and your ladyship to contemplate the change in your future. Again, congratulations. If you need me, send a servant at a moment's notice." At Julian's worried look, he shook his head and laughed again. "Do not worry, your wife is young and healthy and strong. I anticipate no problems at all."

His lean face transfigured by delight, Julian vigorously shook the doctor's hand. "Thank you for coming so quickly." A dazed looked entered his eyes. "I cannot believe it. A child."

Alone in his study, Julian laughed aloud, feeling drunk with joy. He was to be a father! By midsummer he would hold his and Nell's child in his arms. Filled with exhilaration, his feet hardly touched the ground as he walked over to stand before the fire.

Gazing into the leaping red and gold flames, a soft smile curved his hard mouth. A child! How he had once longed for this day and had never thought that he would ever hear those wonderful words again. A pang went through him, the memory of Catherine's reaction to the news that she was expecting a child dimming his joy, clouding this moment of jubilation.

He and Nell had parted badly the night before and he admitted that it was his own damn fault. Anxiety, jealousy, doubt, pride and a temper that he usually kept under tight control had made for an unstable mixture and, unfortunately, it had caused him to lash out at the one person who did not deserve it. Remembering the flash in her eyes, he grimaced. His wife also had a temper and pride to match his and he considered just how much she was going to make him grovel before she allowed him back in her good graces. He frowned. *If* she let him back in her good graces . . . The coming child complicated matters and uneasiness stirred. Would Nell react as Catherine had done and use the pregnancy as a weapon against him, or would she share his joy, his wonder?

But he could not dwell on unhappy thoughts too long, his pleasure too intense, and it pushed aside those painful memories. Just contemplating fatherhood brought that same silly grin to his face once more. Surely, Nell would be pleased.

A knock on the door broke his concentration. Dibble entered at his command and murmured, "My lord, your cousin Mr. Weston is here to see you."

Startled, Julian exclaimed, "*Charles* is here to see me?"

Striding into the room and expeditiously moving Dibble aside, Charles said, "Yes, I am, and why you insist upon having Dibble announce me as if I were a perfect stranger is just one sign of how arrogant you've become since you inherited the title. It is a good thing that I am around to knock holes in your conceited ways and save you from becoming too stuffy by half."

Julian choked back a laugh. Talk about arrogance! And audacious in the bargain—Charles outdid him in spades. Waving Dibble away, he said, "Leave us . . . and in the future, please treat this overbearing jackanapes as you would any other member of the family."

"Which I am," retorted Charles, grinning, as he walked over to join Julian near the fire, "even if you'd like to pretend otherwise."

"Shall I serve refreshments, my lord?" Dibble asked.

"Well, of course you should," declared Charles, warming his hands by the flames. "In case you haven't noticed, it's bloody cold out there and I didn't ride over here without expecting some of that wonderful punch that you make. Be a good fellow, Dibble, and see to it, won't you?"

Well used to Mr. Charles's manner, Dibble hid a smile and

departed. It was good to see the cousins together again. And as for that punch . . . a gratified expression on his face, he hurried to the kitchen.

Smiling at his cousin, Julian said, "You know, if we are going to talk about arrogance—"

"Oh, hang it all, Julian, you know how much I dislike formality. I used to run tame through this place, and to be treated like someone who's never stepped foot in the house . . ." He looked rueful. "Sorry if I offended your sensibilities."

"Good God! Can it be? Charles Weston apologizing?"

Charles shrugged. "I do sometimes, you know." He grinned at Julian. "Just not very often."

Thinking of Nell and their unborn child, Julian wished his cousin at Jericho. If Charles had come to extend a further olive branch, he could not have chosen a more inconvenient time. Impatient to see Nell, to hold his wife in his arms and share the joyous news, he bit back a groan. Dare he send Charles on his way and make plans to meet later? Charles, for all his careless ways, could be devilish high in the instep and reluctantly Julian put away the idea of fobbing off his cousin. One never knew with Charles. His cousin might take offense and the moment would be lost. He and Charles had been at loggerheads for too long and Julian was surprised to feel a deep desire to lessen the chasm between them. Resigning himself to having to wait to see Nell, he took a seat not far from the fire and asked, "So what brings you to my house? Striking while the iron is hot?"

Charles shot him a keen look. "You mean building on yesterday's accord?"

"If you like."

"How would you feel if I said that it was true? That I want the discord of the past put behind us?"

Julian studied him. In many respects of all his cousins, at one time, he'd been the closest to Charles. Like he and Marcus, he and Charles had grown up together—practically in each other's pocket due to the proximity of Stonegate to Wyndham Manor. There'd been some rocky moments, but there was a bond between them not shared by other members of the extended family. The estrangement between them had hit him hard and while he had great affection for Marcus and enjoyed his company immensely, he missed Charles's sheer audacity and neck-or-nothing attitude.

"There have been some hard words exchanged between us," Julian said slowly. "If I remember correctly, you accused me of usurping your right to the title."

Charles made an impatient gesture. "Said in the heat of anger." He stared at Julian. "You cannot have thought that I meant it!"

Julian flicked a brow upward, a quizzical expression on his face. "At the time, it certainly sounded like it."

An embarrassed laugh was dragged from Charles. "Damn you! I suppose I did mean it at the time. But I didn't believe it. Not really." He looked away. "Father and I were deeply hurt . . . and angry that John named you guardian of his son." His mouth tightened. "By rights either my father or myself should have been—" He stopped, reminded himself that he was here to make peace, and muttered, "We said things then that should never have been said. I reacted badly." He flashed a thin smile at Julian. "As you may recall, I usually do when things don't go my way."

"Yes, I remember that trait," Julian said. "And while I'm willing to give a certain allowance for pride and temper— something I've become rather familiar with myself of late—it doesn't explain away all the other things that have been said and done over the years."

"I don't blame you for feeling as you do but I can't change the past—I can't unsay what was said or undo some of the things I've done." A thoughtful expression on his face, Charles murmured, "When John was murdered Father went a little mad for a while—we all did and in our agony we struck out blindly, foolishly. And even though he made those ugly claims about babies switched at birth and that your father had snatched the title from him, he knew that it was arrant nonsense." He sighed. "He was my father, I had no choice but to stand by him. And perhaps sometimes, for awhile, because I wanted it to be true, I let myself be dazzled by the thought that mayhap he was right. That I should be sitting where you are. That I should be the heir to the earldom and all that the title entails."

"You feel differently now?"

Charles grinned. "Let's say if I could prove any of father's wild claims, I'd turf you out of the house and title in a blink of the eye, but since that isn't likely to happen, I'm resigned to being plain Mr. Weston."

Julian laughed. It always amazed him that Charles could say the most outrageous things and one ended up amused by words that uttered by anyone else would have brought swords swinging from scabbards.

"That's very handsome of you," Julian drawled, "but it doesn't quite undo all that lies between us."

"You're speaking of Daniel," Charles said, all signs of good humor gone from his face. At Julian's nod, he admitted, "I cannot pretend that I am not a bad example, the worst, for any young man to follow—and you were right, though I railed against you, to keep Daniel from me. I am all that you think me—wild, profligate, reckless to a fault, a rakehell without parallel and careless of what other people think. But hear me, Julian: I loved my brother and I loved his son. I would not have deliberately led Daniel into ruin and danger." With a twisted smile he added, "Upon my honor—such as it is."

"Yet you did."

A muscle bunched in Charles's cheek and his hands clenched into fists. He took a deep breath and, not meeting Julian's eyes he said harshly, "Guilty. And I cannot blame myself any more than you do for what happened. You were out of the country. I should have watched him more carefully . . . I just didn't think that—" His mouth thinned. "It is my fault and no one knows that better than I." He glanced back at Julian. "No one regrets it more than I."

Julian tended to believe him—to his knowledge, Charles had never lied when confronted with his own misdeeds. Yesterday and today had done much to start the healing process between them, but he knew that they had a long and treacherous road to travel before their relationship would be as it had been in their youth. And while he was willing to cautiously meet Charles's extended hand, to take him at his word, one thing bothered him.

"And yet," Julian said, "you allow the man who caused Daniel's death to roam tamely through your house." A bite in his voice, he snapped, "You call him *friend*."

A wry expression crossed Charles's face and he tugged on the lobe of one ear. "You have me there and I can't quite explain it myself."

"Try," Julian said dryly.

Dibble's knock on the door and entrance into the room with a tray of steaming rum punch prevented Charles from replying. Both men watched as Dibble deposited the heavy silver tray and served them. The scent of rum, lemon, cinnamon and cloves drifted deliciously in the air.

After taking a sip of the warm, fragrant punch from the tankard served to him, Charles remarked, "Dibble, dear fellow, if you ever wish to change positions, please seek me out immediately. For this punch alone you are worth, I am sure, far more than my cousin pays you."

Dibble said nothing, but there was a smile on his face when he bowed and departed.

"Stealing my servants?" Julian asked, a twinkle in his eyes.

"If I could get away with it."

Julian shook his head. "Is there nothing that you would not dare?"

Charles appeared to give the matter some thought. "Hmmm, at the moment, I cannot think of anything," he said with a grin.

Julian took another drink of the punch. Staring at the

amber liquid in his tankard he asked, "So tell me, why do you allow Tynedale to roam like a pet through your home? Knowing that he ruined Daniel and caused your nephew, a mere boy you claim to love, to kill himself? How can you bear to even look upon him?"

"Needs must when the Devil drives," Charles growled, his gaze on the fire.

Julian's brows snapped together. "How badly," he asked, "are you dipped?"

Charles threw him an impatient glance. "That horse won't run. My finances, despite rumors and gossip to the contrary, are in order and I do not look to you to drag me from the clutches of the bloodsuckers. Believe me, I do not tolerate Tynedale because he has his hooks into me. I wish it were that simple."

"Then why, for God's sake? I curse the very ground he walks upon and if my blade had not slipped and I could have run him through—" Julian took a deep breath, choking back his rage and frustration. "Why?"

Charles tossed off a swallow of the punch. "Because it suits me," he said in a voice that brooked further discussion. He looked at Julian, a grim expression on his face. "I realize that I am in no position to ask you anything, but is it true that you hold enough of Tynedale's vowels to ruin him?"

Julian stared at him, his eyes hard and suspicious. "Why should I answer your question when you would not answer mine?"

"Because my question is less complicated? One that can be answered with a simple yes or no."

"Why would you care if I did? What business is it of yours?"

Charles waved away the questions with a careless hand. "If gossip is correct, you now hold the means to ruin him, yet you do nothing. Why is that, Cousin?" he demanded. "What holds your hand?"

"Needs must when the Devil drives?" Julian taunted, getting up to poke at the fire.

Charles laughed, but there was no amusement in it. "So we are at a stalemate, are we not? You will not answer my questions and I will not answer yours. We are a sorry lot, Julian."

"Indeed we are," Julian agreed.

Charles rose to his feet. "I must be going." Extending his hand, he said, "I shall look forward to dining here with you and your lady in the near future." A grin flitted across his hard features. "To cement our renewed relationship."

"As I have said before, only your sheer audacity makes you bearable," Julian said as he shook Charles's hand. "I shall see what night will suit my lady." His expression unyielding, he added, "You do realize that the invitation will not include Tynedale? That under no circumstances will he step foot into my house?"

Charles nodded curtly. "You have nothing to fear on that head."

Escorting Charles from the room, Julian mulled over the situation. He and Charles were speaking to each other again and unless he missed his guess, Charles was *not* Tynedale's friend. A mystery there, he thought as he opened the door to the hallway, its floor an imposing gray and white marble.

Nell and Lady Diana were coming down the staircase at that very moment and at the sight of Julian and Charles walking out of Julian's study together, they both stopped and stared. The two women made a fetching picture as they stood on the stairs. Nell's tall stature and tawny hair complemented Lady Diana's dark hair and smaller, rounder form, and Nell's simple cornflower blue-striped frock contrasted nicely with the cream and rose confection that Lady Diana wore.

"Good heavens, is that you, Charles?" Lady Diana blurted, her brown eyes very big and amazed.

"Why, yes, I believe so," Charles replied, amused.

Lady Diana drifted the remainder of the way down the stairs. Crossing to the two men, she presented her hand to Charles. "I cannot quite believe my eyes. Never say that you and my stepson have resolved your differences!"

"Some of them," Charles said as he bowed over her hand and dropped a polite kiss on the back of it. Grinning, he added, "He has even offered to invite me to dine one evening soon." Performing the same office to Nell's hand when she reached him he added, "That is, if your ladyship does not object?"

"Why should she?" demanded Lady Diana. Clapping her hands together, she said, "Oh, it will be famous! Company! I swear it has been so boring. Do bring your mother. I so enjoyed visiting with her yesterday. Oh, and your brother. I shall have to think of a few more people to round out the numbers. Tomorrow night, perhaps?" Suddenly remembering that it was no longer her house to arrange as she willed, Lady Diana flushed and cast Nell a guilty glance. "That is, if Lady Wyndham does not mind," she added hastily.

Nell cast Lady Diana an amused glance and murmured, "It sounds an excellent idea to me, but perhaps not tomorrow night." She looked at Charles. "Shall we say, Thursday, next?" At his nod, she added, "I shall send a note over to your stepmother. We will look forward to having you as our guests."

Throwing Nell a grateful look, Lady Diana took her leave and disappeared down the hallway in the direction of the breakfast room.

Taking his curly-brimmed beaver hat from Dibble, Charles said to Nell with a grin, "I shall not let you cry off, you know—mind, I expect that invitation within the week."

"Are you always so brazen, Mr. Weston?" Nell asked with dancing eyes.

"Always," Julian remarked. Looking at Charles, he added, "Go away, Cousin, before I change my mind about that invitation to dine."

Charles laughed and turning on his heels, departed.

Left alone with her husband, Nell fidgeted, intensely curious about his reaction to the news of her pregnancy but feeling awkward and unsure after their parting last night. He had obviously not told his cousin of the impending event, but then she realized that other than Becky, she had not mentioned it, either. She'd had every opportunity to inform Lady Diana of her state but she had not. A soft smile curved her lips. Her emotions were tangled—she wanted to shout it aloud and yet at the same time, she wanted to hug the knowledge of the child growing inside of her close, to savor it before sharing it with the world.

Julian's touch on her hand broke into her thoughts. "A word with you?"

Her silly heart leaped beneath the fabric of her gown at the expression in his eyes. And there was a note in his voice . . . "O-o-of c-c-course," she stammered.

Julian grinned and pulling Nell after him, made for his study. Shutting the door behind them, he leaned back and dragged Nell up against him. "My sweet," he murmured as he rained soft, teasing kisses over her face, "Dr. Coleman has told me. Are you happy with the news?"

Nell met his ardent gaze shyly. "Yes. Very. Are you?"

He laughed and catching her up in his arms swung her around the room until she was dizzy. "Happy?" he questioned, when he finally stopped. "Happy seems a weak, pitiful word to describe what I feel at the moment. I am, I think, drunk with joy. Ecstatic. And that *you* are happy only adds to my delight."

With Nell still in his arms, he sank down into one of the big overstuffed leather chairs near the fire. Her head rested on his shoulder and he caressed the tawny ringlets that tickled his chin. "I cannot remember a more rapturous time in my life," he confessed. "You could have bowled me over with a feather this morning when Dr. Coleman told me that I was to become a father. It took me a moment to understand what he was telling me and then, when I realized what he was saying, I was ablaze with joy." He kissed the top of her head. "You have made me an extremely happy man, my dear, and I am grateful to you for it."

At least one of her fears had been put to rest: he was thrilled with the news of her pregnancy. But Nell didn't want his gratitude, she wanted his love, and a little of the glow that suffused her ebbed away. Though it was the last thing she wanted to do, she pushed away from him and stood up. Catherine's ghost hung over her like a blade, slicing at her joy, and Nell was determined not to wear her heart on her sleeve—especially for a man who loved another. "I am pleased," she said primly, "that the prospect of our child makes you so happy."

It wasn't quite the reaction he had hoped for, but remembering their parting last night, he stood up next to her and caressing her cheek with a finger, he asked, "Are you still angry with me for last night?"

She hunched a shoulder, turning away. "Not angry," she admitted, "disappointed, perhaps." Walking to the fire, she glanced back over her shoulder. "You doubted my word." A spark kindled in her fine eyes. "Julian you *cannot* believe that I encouraged Tynedale yesterday! I loathe him! I was only polite to him because I had no choice. Would you rather I'd caused a scene and ordered him from my sight?"

"You are right to be cross with me," he admitted handsomely, "and you did exactly as you should. It is I who was at fault. I acted like a dolt, a blockhead." Wryly, he added, "You must forgive me—I was jealous and let jealously blind me to the truth."

Nell's mouth fell open. "Jealous?" she squeaked, delight spearing through her. "How could you possibly be jealous of a pompous blackguard like Tynedale?" She hurried over to him and, grasping the lapels of his claret jacket, shook him. "You are a good, kind, generous, honorable man—he is everything that you are not. You have no cause to be jealous of the likes of Tynedale!"

He grasped her hand and pressing a kiss on her fingers, he said huskily, "I was a fool last night in more ways than one. Will you forgive me?"

Despite her best intentions to hold him at a distance, Nell's heart melted. Forgive him? How could she not? Gruffly, she said, "Only because you are the father of my child—and if you promise not to act like such a dunderhead again."

He gave a shout of laughter and pulled her into his arms, kissing her soundly. "I cannot swear that I shall not act the fool in the future, I am, after all, only a mere man, but I shall try, my darling, I shall try."

Playing with a gold button on his jacket, Nell asked, "And the other?"

Julian sighed. "Your nightmares? The dungeons?"

She nodded.

"I intend to explore them with Dibble and a few stout groomsmen this afternoon," he said heavily. "Once I have seen that there is no danger to you, I shall walk you through them." His face grim, he added, "And I hope to God that they bear no resemblance to those in your dreams!"

On that note they parted.

Leaving Julian's study behind her, Nell's steps were drawn to the gallery. Wandering along its length, watched by the portraits of Julian's long-dead ancestors, the closer she came to her destination, the slower her tread became. Stopping before the portrait of Lady Catherine, she stared at the lovely face for a long time. There was no denying that Julian's first wife had been beautiful, but Nell could see nothing in those perfect features, that perfect form, that could explain Catherine's iron grip on Julian's heart.

He's *my* husband, she thought furiously, not yours. You're dead. Let him go. The limpid blue eyes still met hers serenely, the rosebud lips still held their alluring smile, and Nell knew an urge to tear the portrait from the wall and trample it to pieces. Her fingers curved into claws and she actually took a step forward before she caught herself, but the sight of the handsome vase filled with long-stemmed yellow roses from Julian's greenhouse was her undoing. With something like a snarl, she grabbed the vase and smashed it to the floor, kicking at the roses, scattering them in all directions.

Staring at the broken porcelain and the ruined roses, Nell was appalled. Good God, what had come over her?

Ashamed of her outburst, yet strangely elated by it, she cast one more look at Catherine's portrait. *I carry his child and I am his wife. I am alive. You are dead, damn you! Let him go!*

Julian kept his promise and accompanied by the others, he made the trek to the lowest, oldest reaches of the house that very afternoon. They found nothing in the damp, gloomy area not expected and deciding that Nell would come to no harm, the following afternoon, he guided her down the two sets of stairs to the remains of the dungeons.

Clinging to her husband's arm, in the flickering light from the torch he held, Nell glanced around. The dungeons consisted of two small cells that opened onto a larger room that still showed signs of its former use; a pair of manacles with chains and some terrifying objects hung from hooks driven deep into the walls. There was a large fire pit, and noticing the rusted, corroded items lying on the edge of the blackened hole, she shrank closer to Julian's comforting bulk. Everywhere she looked she was met with the thick, rough-hewn stone walls, signs of their age obvious, as were the dampness and soot stains from old torches, old fires . . . Staring at that depressing space, she noted the green scum on the floor, undoubtedly due to the flooding from time to time. She shuddered, it was an awful place . . . But it was *not* the dungeon of her nightmares and she didn't know whether to be glad or sorry that *this* dungeon was not *her* dungeon. It was a relief to know that the dungeons of Wyndham Manor bore only a superficial resemblance to that horrible place that appeared in her dreams. But she was conscious of disappointment, too. If only she could find where the demon of her dreams did his terrible work, then he could be caught and no more women would die screaming and writhing beneath his hands.

She glanced at Julian's grim face and shook her head. Relief flashed in his eyes and without another word, he hustled her away from the place.

Upstairs in his study, Julian paced the floor as Nell sat by the fire and sipped a steaming cup of strong tea. Noting the paleness of her features, he demanded, "Are you certain that you are all right? I can have Dr. Coleman here in an instant. I never should have let you talk me into letting you tour those blasted dungeons. I must have been mad!"

She sent him a wan smile. "Do not fuss. I am not sick. I am pregnant and it is your child who causes my discomfort, not the trip through the dungeons." An impish twinkle in her eyes she added, "Besides, if you hadn't gone with me, I'd have gone by myself and think how you would feel about that."

He closed his eyes in despair. "Has anyone ever told you that you are decidedly stubborn and headstrong in the bargain?"

"Frequently," she admitted with a laugh. Putting down her cup, she said, "I know that you didn't want me down there, but aren't you the least pleased that your dungeons are not the ones in my nightmares?"

"Thank God for little favors," he said piously and made her laugh again.

Her moment of lightheartedness vanished. "But today's discovery doesn't change anything," she muttered. "Those dungeons are still out there, somewhere . . . And we must find them if he is to be stopped." She glanced away. "If my nightmares are to be stopped."

Julian crossed to her and knelt on one knee before her. Taking her cold hands in his, he swore fiercely, "We will find them. And him—I swear it to you."

How much happier his words would have made her, she thought wistfully, as she left the room, if instead of swearing to find a madman, he'd sworn to love her . . .

Chapter 14

News that the countess was expecting a child come summer spread rapidly through the neighborhood and beyond. Nell was both flattered and amused at the profuse congratulations that poured in on her and Julian. Everyone it seemed was delighted with her pregnancy, from the lowliest scullery maid to the highest members of the peerage in England. Even the Prince of Wales had sent along a very nice note expressing his congratulations on their impending parenthood and Nell couldn't help be flattered. But the note she treasured most was the one from her father. She'd known that Sir Edward would be delighted and his simple pride and pleasure at the news came through in every word he wrote to her. He mentioned planning a trip to visit with her in early spring and Nell's heart leapt at the idea of seeing her father again.

Lady Diana was delighted with the news. When Nell told her of the pregnancy, she exclaimed, "Oh, my dear! How happy I am for you, for you both." A shadow crossed her pretty face. "My late lord and I had so hoped that we would have a child of our own but fate did not smile upon us." She shook off the melancholy memory and, beaming at Nell, added, "I know that he'd be over the moon with joy at the news. Why I remember how often he talked of Catherine and the child she carried, how ecstatic he said he'd been when he'd learned of the pregnancy and when she died how he mourned for her and the unborn child." Realizing she'd let her tongue run away with her, she flushed. "Forgive me! I did not mean to bring up the past." Earnestly, she added, "He would have been just thrilled, thrilled I tell you, by your pregnancy."

Smoothing over her mother's prattle, Elizabeth gave Nell a warm hug. Her eyes shining, she said, "You are so good for my stepbrother, and now you are to have his child. It is so exciting. And to think that Mama and I shall be only as far away as the Dower House." She grinned. "I warn you: we shall spoil your child in the worst possible manner."

Charles's dinner party, as Nell thought of it, went off without a hitch. To round out the numbers, and because she enjoyed them, she added a member of the local gentry, Squire Chadbourne, his plump, jovial wife, Blanche, and his heir, Pierce, a tall, handsome man, some thirty years of age. It was a most pleasant evening and Nell and Julian were again showered with good wishes and several toasts were drunk to their health and to that of their unborn child.

By the time the meal ended and the ladies withdrew to the gold saloon, leaving the gentlemen to their port and wine, she was well satisfied with her first dinner party as the Countess of Wyndham. Everything had gone just as it ought and the food—from the Mushroom Fritters, Crimped Cod, Pullets with Chestnuts, Veal Galantine, and Roast Loin of Beef to the melt-in-your-mouth perfection of the Gooseberry Cream, a Florendine of Oranges and Apples and a Duke of Cumberland's Pudding—was superb.

While she could take no credit for it, the apparent healing of the breech between Julian and his cousins gratified Nell. No one watching the three men would ever guess that until just a short time ago, there had been a long-standing estrangement between them.

Naturally as the ladies enjoyed their tea and nibbled from

a tray of sweets that Dibble had served before leaving the room, the conversation centered on Nell's pregnancy.

"Oh, my, how well I remember my first," said Mrs. Chadbourne, her blue eyes warm and friendly as they rested on Nell. "It is such an exciting time. And a summer birth is the best. I know—my last was born in December and I swear she had nothing but the croup and colds and sniffles from the moment she was laid in my arms until the following June."

"*Ma foi!* I prefer a spring birth, like my Raoul," chimed in Mrs. Weston. "I felt so heavy and clumsy those last weeks." She gave a delicate shudder. "Carrying a child into summer will not be pleasant—I do not envy you, *ma belle*. Your back will ache and your feet will swell—if you can see them—and the July heat will make you miserable."

Lady Diana, sitting beside Nell on a gold brocade sofa, patted her on the arm and said, "Oh, pooh, don't pay any attention to her, none of it will matter when your child is laid in your arms." She smiled at Elizabeth sitting in a chair across from them. "I know the moment that my dear daughter was placed in my arms, I forgot everything that had gone before except the joy of actually holding her." She patted Nell's arm once more. "You'll see that I am right."

"Indeed she is," added Mrs. Chadbourne cheerfully. "There is nothing to compare to that first sight of your own child." She beamed at her. "It has been a long time since these halls have rung with the laughter of a child—I'm sure that his lordship is overjoyed by the news."

"Yes, he is," Nell agreed. Julian might not love her, but she couldn't deny that he was thrilled at the prospect of becoming a father. This past week or so his sheer exuberance and open pleasure had done much to soothe her heart. He might never love her, but he would adore their child and she could forgive him much because of that. A small, private smile curved her mouth. There was an added pleasure to her state: Julian's lovemaking had been so exquisitely tender these past days that her body quivered with delight just thinking of it.

Her black eyes fixed on Nell's face, Mrs. Weston murmured, "But one must remember, that this is not the first time his lordship has had his hopes buoyed by such news. *Enfin,* let us hope that he is not disappointed as he was the last time."

"What a ghastly thing to say!" Lady Diana burst out, looking at Mrs. Weston as if she'd turned into a viper.

"Now, now, I'm sure she didn't mean that like it sounded," said the squire's wife sharply, her amiable features marred by an expression of disapproval. She glared at Mrs. Weston. "I'm sure she has an explanation that will make it all clear."

"Then perhaps," Nell said quietly, her eyes steadily meeting the Frenchwoman's, "Mrs. Weston would like to explain what she did mean?"

"Why I meant nothing by it," protested Mrs. Weston. "But it is true, is it not, that this is not the first time that his lordship has been expecting a child? And that the child and, alas, his poor wife died? He cannot help but think of it."

"But that tragedy has nothing to do with my child, does it?" Nell replied. "I am sure that you did not mean to alarm me, but how else am I to interpret your comments?"

"*Je vous demande pardon!* You have misunderstood me," Mrs. Weston said stiffly. "I meant no harm—let us talk of other things."

Mrs. Chadbourne and Lady Diana were amenable to that suggestion and in a few minutes the conversation had veered to Lady Diana's plans for the renovation of the Dower House. Elizabeth, sitting quietly as befitted a proper young lady in the midst of matrons, smiled warmly at Nell and joined the discussion. Mrs. Weston was quick to follow their lead and in no time the ladies were deep into debating the use of various fabrics and the other changes Lady Diana planned for the house.

Nell listened with half an ear, her thoughts on Mrs. Weston. She was trying very hard to like Julian's relatives but there was something about this Frenchwoman that didn't sit well. Perhaps, she shouldn't have been so prickly about Mrs. Weston's comments? If Lady Diana had said such a thing, she would have lightly dismissed it as merely Lady Diana's artless chatter, but with Mrs. Weston, she could not. One thing Nell was certain of: Mrs. Weston's words had been deliberate—and there was nothing innocent about them.

When Lady Diana moved to a chair by Mrs. Weston to explain in greater detail some of the remodeling that was under way at the Dower House, Mrs. Chadbourne took the seat she had vacated.

"Don't pay Sofie any mind," Mrs. Chadbourne said in a low voice. "She can be a proud, disagreeable woman, but I don't believe she means any harm. She doesn't care a fig what people think and speaks without stopping to consider other people's feelings."

"Have you known her a long time?"

"Oh, Lord, yes! Ever since she married his lordship's uncle, thirty years or more ago." Mrs. Chadbourne sighed. "Not that there haven't been times I'd wished he'd married someone a trifle more comfortable, I can tell you that! But there was nothing for it: she had a fortune and Weston needed it." She looked thoughtful. "I think they had a good marriage, though. There was never any question about it being a love match. Harlan adored John and Charles's mother, Letty, and when she died . . ." A sad expression flitted across her face. "It was a bad time for all of us. We'd all grown up together and when Letty died . . . Well, when she died something died within Harlan."

She shook herself and continued briskly. "Sofie was what Stonegate needed and Weston knew it. He was, I think, content with the bargain he'd made." She smiled. "He was thrilled to be a father again and certainly happy to let her lavish her money on the place. Believe me, if it hadn't been for Sofie's fortune, he'd have been in desperate straits. She saved him from ruin and Stonegate, too. Her son is nicely fixed thanks to Sofie's fortune and I'll give Charles his due—he's never held it against his younger brother that he's the one who will inherit a handsome fortune someday and not Charles. Charles, for all his wild, arrogant ways, has always watched out for Raoul." She shook her head. "Lord, the scrapes he's pulled that boy out of. Sofie has spoiled Raoul almost beyond bearing. And the tales of his women—" She stopped and looked a little flustered. "Er, you do know about the Old Earl, don't you?" she asked.

When Nell nodded, she added, "Well, there's some who say that Raoul is the Old Earl all over again—and far less generous. The girls that young man has ruined." She looked across at Mrs. Weston. "I lay the blame squarely on her shoulders—she dotes on her son and will not hear a word against him—she simply adores the ground Raoul walks upon. But then I suppose it's only natural with Harlan marrying her for her fortune—who else could she love? But, as I said, Sofie and Harlan did well together—even if it wasn't a love match, they had respect and liking, even a fondness for each other."

"I see," Nell said slowly, identifying with Sofie. Her husband hadn't loved her, either . . . Mayhap there was a reason for her cold manner.

The gentlemen entered the room and the moment for further private conversation was lost. The remainder of the evening passed pleasantly and Nell was almost sorry when her guests departed. But it had been a long arduous day and after she and Julian had waved first the Chadbournes and then the Westons away, she was very glad to seek out her bedroom.

Mrs. Chadbourne's words gave her much to think about and after she crawled into bed and had blown out the candle, she considered them. While Julian had not married her for her fortune, it was true that, like Sofie and Harlan Weston, theirs was not a love match. She sighed. When she looked at Mrs. Weston was she seeing herself in thirty years' time?

Lud! She hoped not. She sighed again. The Weston men it seemed were only capable of loving once, that first love ruining them for all others. Harlan and his Letty and Julian and Catherine . . .

Julian's entrance into her rooms ended her unhappy thoughts. Tossing aside his black silk robe, he slid into bed beside her. Nell's pulse leaped as he drew her next to his warm, naked length.

Brushing back a few curls that tumbled over her cheek, he kissed her ear and asked, "Happy, Madame wife, with your first dinner party at Wyndham Manor?"

Trying to ignore the wayward response of her body, she snuggled nearer to him. He did not love her, she thought with an ache in her heart, but he *was* a good husband. Toying with the thick dark hairs that covered his chest, she said, "It went well, did it not?"

"Indeed, it did, especially when you consider the dicey proposition that it was—there was every chance that Charles and I would be at each other's throats—nagged on by Raoul and cheered by Aunt Sofie," he murmured, a smile in his voice.

"I like your cousin Charles," Nell confessed. "He is not as cold and uncaring as he pretends, is he?"

In the darkness Julian made a face. He'd much rather make love to his enticing wife, but it appeared that she wished to talk first. "That's Charles's problem," he admitted, "he cares too much, but he hides it behind that stone face of his."

"But why?"

"I think, perhaps, because . . . Aunt Sofie has not always been kind to her stepsons and when her own son arrived . . . She will do anything for Raoul, but John, Charles and later John's son, Daniel, could have been torn apart by lions right in front of her and she wouldn't even have noticed." He sighed. "It is very hard to like Aunt Sofie at times, but in the main, I'm grateful to her for saving Stonegate and for exerting a bit of stability in that branch of the Westons. I really don't know what would have happened with my Uncle Harlan if Sofie hadn't been there. And with Charles . . . There may be no love lost between them, but she has in the past exercised some control over his reckless ways—even if her methods were not the kindest."

"Her fortune?"

Julian gave a harsh laugh. "Oh, yes, she has beaten him over the head with it more than once. I sometimes wonder how Charles has kept from wringing her neck." He buried his nose in her hair. "But come, let us talk of other things besides my pack of disreputable relatives."

"Such as?" she asked lightly, aware of the growing bulge of his member at her hip.

"Such as how beautiful you looked tonight . . ." His hand roamed across her abdomen, "and how nicely my son is growing within you."

"Your son?" she hooted. "How do you know I am not carrying a girl?"

He nuzzled her ear. "Fine, let it be a girl. I have no objections to having a house full of charming Amazons. I shall look forward to it, but I trust that in time you will give me an heir." His mouth found hers and he kissed her deeply, passionately. His hands slid up and under her nightgown, cupping her breasts. "And it is not," he breathed against her soft mouth, "as if making a baby is such an arduous task." Lifting her gown off of her body and tossing it aside, he murmured, "In fact, I can think of nothing more pleasurable."

His head bent and he captured one tempting nipple between his teeth. "Hmmm, sweet," he muttered, curling his tongue around the swollen nub. "Sweeter than spring strawberries." He suckled, pulling hard, sending streaks of delight shooting through Nell's body.

In the summer, she thought dreamily, it would be their child who suckled so lustily and her breath caught as she imagined a tiny dark head buried against her breast. Then one of Julian's hands slid lower to the thatch of curls between her thighs and thoughts of summer and babies vanished like smoke in the wind and she gave herself up to the magic of making love with her husband.

Later, they lay together, replete and languorous, basking in the sweet aftermath of their mating. Nell's head rested on Julian's shoulder and she savored the moment. They were so right together in so many ways, she thought, and yet there was a chasm between them. A chasm that had a name: Catherine.

Nell's enjoyment in the moment disappeared, just the mere idea of Julian's first wife destroying her peace. Sofie Weston's words came back to bedevil her, to taunt her, adding to her unhappiness, and she moved restlessly at Julian's side.

"Be still," muttered Julian. "You are wiggling like an eel."

Nell concentrated on keeping her body motionless, but the harder she concentrated, the stronger the urge to wiggle grew. Finally she gave up and scooted away from him.

Julian raised up. "What is the matter?"

"Nothing," Nell answered quickly. "I just cannot be still. I have, I suppose, too many things on my mind." Like your first wife. Your Aunt Sofie's comments. And the knowledge that you will never love me—no matter how kind you are, how *fond* you may be of me. Nell wrinkled her nose. Odd how she'd never realized before what a milksop word 'fond' was. She suddenly hated it.

In the darkness Julian frowned, sensing that there was more behind her words. "Does something trouble you, Nell? The nightmares, perhaps?"

"No. Not the nightmares. I have not had one in weeks." She hesitated. "Which means, no doubt, that I will have one soon."

She hoped she'd distracted him, but he pulled her back against him and asked, "If not the nightmares, then what else is on your mind that will not allow you to lay peaceably by my side?"

Nell detested tattletales, but she couldn't help blurting out, "Your Aunt Sofie reminded me tonight that this was not the first time that you had looked forward to the birth of a child . . . and that those hopes ended in tragedy."

"That *woman!*" Julian growled, a note in his voice making Nell very glad that she was not Sofie Weston. "I may save Charles the trouble of wringing her neck." Nell believed him. He took a breath, saying in a calmer tone, "Rest assured that I shall have something to say to my dear Aunt Sofie when next I see her. In the meantime, put her nonsensical and, I might add, vicious comments from your mind. She has always been a troublemaker—pay her no heed. This is *our* child and what is between us has nothing to do with the past."

Nell wanted to believe him. Part of her did. Yet he was wrong. The past had *everything* to do with them and as long as Catherine's specter hovered between them . . .

Nell was not a coward, yet she was clutching her courage in both hands when she asked, "Did you love her so much?"

"Who?" Julian inquired, completely at sea.

Baldly she said, "Catherine."

Julian stiffened. Biting back a curse, he jerked upright and running an agitated hand through his hair, demanded, "What the hell does she have to do with us? She's dead, Nell. She's dead and buried. Forget her!"

"Can you?" she asked tightly.

Just the mention of Catherine's name filled him with rage and remorse. What he and Nell had together was precious and clean and honest. He wanted nothing to touch that, nothing to tarnish it. And bringing Catherine into their lives, their marriage, could certainly do that, he thought mirthlessly. Remembering the ugliness, the lies, the lovers she'd paraded before him, he wondered how he could ever explain to Nell everything that Catherine had been without sounding weak and pitiful—or like the cuckold he'd been? Nor could he bring himself to speak aloud his darkest fear: that the child Catherine carried and that he mourned to this day might not even have been his. How could he ever speak aloud of his loathing for a woman he had sworn to respect and protect all of his life and had failed . . . miserably, completely? If there was one thing he did *not* want to discuss with his second wife, it was his first wife. But Nell had asked a question and she deserved an answer. Could he ever forget Catherine? No, he thought wearily. She had sunk her claws into his very being and had stripped away his pride, his manliness, and very nearly destroyed him. No, he would never forget Catherine.

"No, I cannot forget her. I will remember until my dying day her and the child that she carried when she died, but she has nothing to do with us," he said heavily, standing up and pulling on his robe. "This is our marriage . . . and our child. I beg you, leave my past where it belongs. Understand me: accept as I have the fact that she is dead and buried and nothing will change that."

Well, there you have it, Nell thought bleakly. He's admitted it. He will never forget the heavenly Catherine. What hope is there for me? None. Defeat washed over her and Nell turned her head away. "Oh, I understand perfectly," she muttered, wishing him a thousand miles away. She made a great act of yawning. "Forgive me, my lord. I am very tired."

Julian hesitated, but the note of dismissal in her voice was not encouraging and he did not want to part from her this way. He didn't, he realized, want to part from her at all. What he wanted was something he'd never wanted from any other woman; he wanted to lie beside Nell the entire night, to feel her warmth against him, to listen to her soft breathing and to know that she was near his side all through the long, lonely, dark hours of the night.

Just the mere mention of Catherine's name, he thought savagely, had ruined any chance of Nell welcoming him back into her bed tonight. By heaven, but he wasn't going to let that witch reach out from the grave and destroy his only chance for happiness. Damn her black soul! Try your wiles, Catherine, but you will *not* win this battle, he vowed.

Surprising both of them, he tossed aside his robe and climbed back into bed beside Nell. Pulling her against him, they lay spoon fashion. Julian kissed the top of Nell's head. "I, too, am tired and can think of no more delightful place to sleep than at my wife's side."

Nell tried hard to cling to her hurt and anger, tried hard not to be pleased by his words, but it was impossible—she loved him. Her breath caught sharply as she realized that it was true: she did love him. Madly. Passionately. Completely. Awed she lay there reveling in his big, warm body pressed against hers. She loved this man. When it had happened she did not know. Perhaps from the moment she had first seen him looking like a desperate highwayman? Or had it been on their wedding night when he had kissed her so passionately? Made her so very aware of him as a man? Mayhap later still, when he had first made love to her? She didn't know when the fierce emotion that beat in her breast had begun, she only knew that she loved him with every fiber of her being.

Her jaw clenched. And he loved another. But it was with her that he lay—not a dead woman, and she took hope from that. She had months, years in which to make him love her . . . and Catherine had none. A little smile curved her mouth. And she carried his child. She fell asleep, a smile on her lips, her husband's arm wrapped around her, his hand lying protectively over her womb.

There was no warning. One second she was sleeping deeply, dreams of her child, dreams of the day when Julian would declare his love for her drifting rosily through her mind and the next . . She was there, watching in that smoke-stained dungeon, her ears assaulted by the woman's shrieks, her eyes fixed on the bloody rampage only a mind devoured by feral madness could inflict upon another human. Nell fought to escape the ripping talons of the nightmare, but they held her fast, forcing her to watch the horrible things done in that horrible place. She shuddered as the Shadow Man turned aside from his victim and reached for a different toy, a thin-bladed knife honed to razor sharpness . . .

As always he was in shadows, no way for her to identify him beyond his height and breadth of shoulder and yet when he had turned for that knife, something tugged at her brain and her breath caught. *She knew him.* She could not name him, but a bone-deep certainty flashed through her that she had met this man, had talked with him. Her Shadow Man was someone she knew.

In her sleep, Nell tossed wildly, panting softly. Julian awakened the second she had shuddered. Cursing under his breath, knowing it was the nightmare, he found a candle on the bed stand and quickly lit it. In the faint light, her face was contorted by fear and revulsion, and he reached out to touch her, to reassure her. But at his first gentle caress, she screamed and jerked upright, her eyes wide-open, but seeing nothing.

"Nell," he cried softly, "wake up. It is the nightmare. You are safe. Wake up, darling. Wake up."

But she could not, her gaze locked on a vision of unbelievable savagery. In all the nightmares, over all the years, she had never witnessed such ungovernable violence. Always before, no matter how vicious the act, there had been a pitiless curiosity emanating from him, as if he was intrigued by the reactions of the women to each new torture. But tonight there was no curiosity, there was nothing but a blind, mad urge to hurt, to rend and tear.

Kind words and gentle strokes were having no effect on Nell and in desperation, Julian slapped her across the cheek. She gasped, gagged and her gazed cleared. White-faced and shaking, she threw herself into Julian's arms. Sobbing against his shoulder, she muttered, "It was awful. Awful. I cannot bear this."

Julian held her, waiting for the worst of the storm to pass.

All he could do was give comfort and he did that by holding her close, murmuring to her and stroking the tousled tawny locks. "Hush, sweetheart. You are safe. I have you and I will not let anyone hurt you. Hush, now."

Eventually her sobs lessened, but her clutch on his arms did not. She raised her head and in the flickering golden light from the candle she whispered, "I know him, Julian."

His eyes locked with hers. "You saw his face tonight?" he asked sharply. "You know his name?"

Nell shook her head. "No. Not that, it is just that at one point I felt instinctively that I knew him. That I had met him, talked with him." A shudder rippled through her. "He is someone we may have talked with in our very home."

Julian frowned. "But if you didn't see his face, how do you know he is someone you've met?"

"I can't explain it," Nell admitted. "It's just something that I know to be true." Urgently, she added, "We *know* him. He is no stranger to us."

Julian studied her pale face, seeing the streaks from her tears, the remembered horror in her eyes. He had already accepted the fact that by means and methods that went beyond normal understanding his wife had an unexplainable connection to the man who had murdered his cousin and tried to kill her by throwing her over a cliff. Nell's nightmares revealed that the same man, a monstrous creature, had for years been murdering innocent women in some dark dungeon. Having accepted all of that, it was not so hard for Julian to believe in what Nell claimed: that the man they sought was someone they knew.

"Very well. He is someone we know." He sent Nell a grim look. "But that helps us little if you cannot identify him."

"I know," Nell said mournfully. "If only we could find the dungeons! If we knew where they were, whose they were, we would know the name of this monster."

"Has it occurred to you that we have no idea *where* these

dungeons might be?" Julian asked. "To be sure, we have explored the ones here at Wyndham Hall and excluded them, but good God! There are old, forgotten dungeons spread across the breadth and length of England! We could search out every dungeon in Devonshire and your madman could be in Cornwall for all we know."

Nell sat very still, her head cocked to one side as if she was listening to some faraway voice. Eventually she looked at him and shook her head. "No. I cannot identify him or them, but he is from this area and the dungeons are here, too."

Julian sighed. "And how do you know this?"

"I just know it!" she snapped. "I've told you—I can't explain it. Any of it. I only know what I feel, what my instincts tell me. And my instincts tell me that he and that hellish place are here in this area." She bit her lip. "The nightmares have always been terrible, but the ones I've had here . . . I cannot explain it, but they are more intense . . . as if I am nearer to the source and because of that the impressions, the *feel* of them is so much stronger, more powerful." Mournfully she added, "I don't know how to make you understand, but I am not imagining any of this. You do believe me, don't you?"

Wearily Julian nodded. "Yes, I believe you. I don't want to, I'll admit that much, and everything that you've related to me flies in the face of reason but what you've told me about John's murder convinces me that there is some link between you and his murderer. And if I believe that much, then it is not so difficult to believe all the rest, incredible though it may be." He covered her hand with his. "We are in this together, Nell, and together we will find this monster . . . and his cursed dungeons."

She leaned against him, needing his warmth, his strength. "You are very good to me," she said in a husky voice. "Few husbands would be so understanding."

Flushed with pleasure by her words, Julian kissed her forehead. "It is a good thing that I am such an exceptional husband, is it not?"

Despite the gravity of the moment, Nell smiled, "Are you fishing for compliments, my lord?"

He smiled. "No, but it is nice to have you speak well of me."

They sat together for several moments, enjoying the closeness that existed between them, but all too soon Julian's thoughts returned to the matter at hand and sighing he said, "I dislike asking you this, but is there anything else from tonight's nightmare that you remember that may help us?"

"Only that he was enraged. He was like a terrible savage, brimming, boiling with fury."

"I wonder," Julian mused, "what set him off."

"I cannot even hazard a guess." She shuddered and pressed closer to Julian. "That poor woman."

"It is clear that we have our work cut out for us." Julian shook his head. "I am not, I can assure you, looking forward to exploring every wretched, abandoned, damp, filthy dungeon in Devonshire. And the mendacious tales I shall have to concoct to convince my hapless friends, family and acquaintances to allow me to explore the lower reaches of their house doesn't bear thinking about."

She smiled wryly at him. "At least you can rest easy that your own dungeons are not suspect."

He nodded. "Yes, there is that to be thankful for." He glanced down at Nell, his features grave. "Are you positive that he is someone we know?"

Nell nodded. "There is no doubt in my mind."

"Well then, let us hope," he growled, "that our madman turns out to be that bastard Tynedale."

Nell shook her head. "It is not Tynedale. Tynedale is blond. The Shadow Man has black hair, much like your own . . ."

Chapter 15

Julian did not waste time. The next morning, seated in his library, he composed a list of the estates that he knew possessed dungeons. On that list he marked the properties owned by people that Nell had met. The fact that he knew them was of secondary importance, Nell was the key.

Having been born here he was familiar with the various properties. When his initial list was completed, he was surprised to discover that there were so many homes owned by friends and family that had been built on the sites of former Norman keeps or castles, with dungeons. Some of the owners, such as Squire Chadbourne, took great delight in the gloomy dungeon beneath his grand home and would without any excuse at all drag unsuspecting visitors down to view them. Others like himself forgot that they existed unless reminded of the fact. Viewing the ones at Chadbourne would not be a problem. As for the others . . . he sighed. Everyone was going to think he had gone mad unless he could fashion a plausible excuse for wishing to see their dungeons. He looked wry. He could picture the expression on Charles's face if he asked to stroll through the extensive dungeons he knew lay beneath Stonegate. Dr. Coleman wouldn't be best pleased either to be asked to throw wide the doors of Rose Cottage to let him poke around in the bowels of the place. Now Lord Beckworth, his neighbor to the north, was like Squire Chadbourne, rather proud of his family's dungeons, and could probably be induced to give him a tour without so much as raising an eyebrow.

And last on his list was John Hunter, his gamekeeper. Not that Hunter owned a grand estate, but his home and several acres surrounding it, bequeathed to him by the Old Earl, had once been a handsome hunting lodge and was said to be built on the site of an old Saxon castle replete with the requisite dungeons. Julian didn't know about the Saxon castle part, but he did know that the dungeons existed—as boys, he, John, Marcus and Charles, with a fearful Raoul in tow, had explored them. Julian smiled at the memory. Oh, they'd had a grand time roaming through that vast, ghostly place until John Hunter had discovered them and nearly scared them out of a decade's growth when his huge form, cudgel in hand, had risen up out of the shadows and he had chased them away.

He frowned. In addition to those already listed, he supposed he should add the remains of the old Norman keep near Dawlish and the crumbling remnants of a monastery deserted since the times of Henry VIII. Both sites, if he remembered correctly, were rumored to have dungeons beneath them. If there were other places nearby that had dungeons or dungeonlike areas beneath them, he could not think of any. Feeling that his list was as complete as he could make it, he put it aside and went in search of his wife.

He could not find her and an inquiry to Dibble informed him that all of the ladies were presently at the Dower House. "They wanted to see how the work was progressing," Dibble added, "and I believe that there is some disagreement about the color of silk to be hung in the main saloon."

Since the day was fine for the second week of February and the Dower House was less than a mile away, Julian decided to walk. He had paid little heed to the comings and goings surrounding the renovations and because the Dower House sat back nearly a quarter of mile from the main road leading to Wyndham Hall, and was well concealed by a mass of tangled forest, he had not noticed any changes. Strolling down the badly pitted road that led to the house, avoiding the largest of the potholes, he concluded that work had not yet begun on the outlying areas.

The wild woodland pressed close, in some cases actually encroaching onto the roadway, making for a narrow, gloomy walk, the branches of trees meeting overhead. When leafed out they would block out the sunlight. If I were of a nervous disposition, he told himself, I certainly wouldn't be taking a stroll along this road. As he reached the final turn of the ambling lane, the Dower House rose before him, the roadway circling around in front of a steep-roofed, half-timbered, three-story house with mullion windows.

He crossed the roadway and standing at the base of the bottom step, he stared around, amazed at the difference that the freshly trimmed shrubbery made in this area. No longer half-hidden beneath mounds of ivy and vines the beautiful lines of the house were apparent. The massive oak and lime trees that had brooded over the house had either been removed or trimmed back and after the suffocating murkiness of the roadway leading to the house, the openness was a most welcome change. Julian smiled. At least from the outside the place no longer looked like the abode of a warlock or an evil sorceress. A wide brick walkway, lined with expertly pruned roses and newly weeded perennial beds, dotted with the cheerful nodding heads of yellow daffodils, angled off to one side of the house. An offshoot of the main driveway disappeared in the opposite direction leading, Julian remembered, to the stables. No one had lived here since the days of his great-grandmother and all of his memories of the place had been of a deserted, overgrown, decaying place. Only the most basic upkeep had been done to the place in decades.

He was pleased to see the changes and a bit ashamed that he, along with his father and grandfather, had let the place almost fall into rack and ruin.

The sounds of pounding and hammering carried through the air and when his knock went unanswered, he tried the massive door and, finding it unlocked, let himself inside. In contrast to the outside, the interior of the house was chaos. Plaster, lumber, ladders, ghostly covered furniture loomed up here and there, and scrapes of wallpaper, buckets with mysterious substances in them and bolts of expensive material were everywhere.

But there were signs of progress: the large entry hall floor had been redone in a striking rose-shot marble; the walls were covered in a cream-colored satin embossed with pink rosebuds and all the moldings had been either retouched with gilt or repainted a gleaming white. The long curving staircase, which he vaguely recalled having sported several broken steps with a railing that trembled at the lightest touch, had been expertly repaired and repainted. The hammering came from the left side of the house and Julian followed the sound to its source, glancing into several rooms along the way. He smiled ruefully. His stepmother did indeed love pink.

In a handsomely appointed room near the rear of the house, he found his wife and the other two women arguing over the merits of a pink watered silk as opposed to a soft blue fabric enlivened with a faint gold stripe. He stopped in the doorway, a smile twitching at the corner of his lips. From their intent expressions, this was serious business.

"But Diana," exclaimed Nell, "you've already used pink in several rooms, in fact nearly every room in the house is pink, don't you think it would be better to use the blue here? Won't you get tired of pink?"

Lady Diana made a moue. "But I like pink. It is my favorite color. Besides, it is my house, why can't I do every room in pink if I want to?"

Nell and Elizabeth exchanged a look. "Of course, Mother, you can do exactly what you want," Elizabeth agreed. "But don't you think others, perhaps some friends and guests, who aren't as, uh, fond of pink as you are, might not find it a bit, er, overpowering?"

"Even perhaps boring and predictable," Nell added quickly. "You certainly wouldn't want that, now would you?"

Lady Diana looked torn. Naturally, she didn't want her family and friends to think her taste in furnishings was boring and predictable. Her gaze went from one fabric to the other.

"It would make a refreshing change," urged Nell. "A statement even."

"What sort of statement?" asked Lady Diana, intrigued.

Julian decided to enter the fray and, walking across the room toward the ladies, he said, "A clear statement that here lives a lady of refinement and elegance that possesses the most exquisite taste."

All three women turned at once, the warm smile Nell sent his way making Julian feel oddly breathless and light as a feather, as if he were floating. Certain that his feet were not touching the floor, he joined the ladies in front of the big window, still in need, he noticed, of a great deal of work, that overlooked the garden.

"Oh, do you really think so?" Lady Diana asked, her big brown eyes fixed on his face.

"Absolutely," Julian murmured, fingering the blue fabric. "Yes, the blue with the gold stripe is the way to go. I'm sure that friend of Prinny's, the one who is making such a name for himself amongst the ton, that Brummell fellow, would go into raptures over the blue." He looked thoughtful. "And no doubt despise the pink."

Lady Diana drew in a sharp breath. "That must not happen! Brummell can ruin a hostess by just a lift of his eyebrow." Turning back to Nell, she said, "It will be the blue, definitely the blue." A worried expression crossed her pretty face. "Mayhap I should redo all the rooms and remove any sign of pink?"

As one the other three said, "No!" There were still months of renovations in front of them and if Lady Diana began tearing out already completed areas, they'd be having this same conversation, or one appallingly similar, a year from now. There'd been a few accidents that had caused delays and several bolts of fabric for the drawing room had inexplicably gone missing, necessitating its reordering from London as well as a roll of lovely new carpet for the library, which had also disappeared.

"The other rooms are fine," Nell said glibly. "There is no need to tear everything down and start anew. You only need a touch of another color here and there to make all perfect."

Lady Diana nodded. "I believe that you are right, but I may change the walls in the dining room to that gold figured silk that I thought I didn't like. And the chairs—they could be recovered in that gorgeous green damask I bought and didn't know where to use. What do you think?"

She was looking to Julian for an answer and seeing his wife frantically nodding her head in the affirmative, he said, "An excellent idea! After all, one wouldn't want to be thought insipid and flat. Especially not by Brummell."

Not wishing to be embroiled in further decorating decisions Julian expertly cut Nell out from the others and whisked his wife away, leaving Lady Diana and Elizabeth to their own devices.

As they left the house behind them, Nell said, "I cannot tell you how grateful I am for your intervention. She has such good taste in so many things, but when it comes to the color pink . . ." She shook her head. "It has been all that Elizabeth and I can do to keep her from wrapping the house in the most vulgar and shocking shade of pink silk."

"Has it been a trial for you?" he asked, tucking her hand under his arm as they walked.

"Oh, no. I did not mean it that way." She glanced up at him. "I am very fond of your stepmother. I didn't think that I would be, but she is very sweet and biddable and has a kind heart."

Julian nodded. "And a brain filled with goose down."

Nell chuckled. "Well, perhaps her intellect is not the highest, but she sometimes surprises me with her observations. Just about the time that you think she is a perfect pea-goose, she will say something that makes you take a second look at her."

They walked away from the house, entering the section of road that had not yet been improved. Nell shivered a bit as the gloom closed around them. "I will be quite happy when work is begun on this road. It is so dark and depressing that one can almost imagine fierce beasts staring at one from the concealment of the forests."

Julian kissed her hand. "I shall order it cleared immediately. It will be one of my contributions to help speed along Diana's removal from our home."

Nell looked up at him. "Do you dislike having her living at Wyndham Manor?"

"No, not really. I am, like you, very fond of my stepmother, and especially so of Elizabeth, and will always keep a watchful eye on them. But I think for everyone's sake it is important that she have her own household." He smiled down at Nell. "I have new and delightful demands on my time and purse that take precedence over her and Elizabeth's claims."

"Very prettily said, my lord," Nell replied with an impish smile.

"I certainly thought so," he murmured, his eyes full of laughter.

Quite in harmony with each other they continued their walk. Julian told her of the list he had compiled and they discussed different methods by which Julian could gain access to the various dungeons. None of them sounded very good and they soon abandoned that topic and went on to a bone of contention between them.

"I still think you should take me with you," Nell argued. "I know exactly what to look for—you don't."

"It is going to be devilish tricky as it is for me to inveigle my way into these places without having you trailing at my heels." His jaw tightened. "Besides, I do not want your Shadow Man to have the slightest inkling that you may be involved."

"I will have to see the dungeon eventually, you know," Nell said stubbornly.

"Yes, after I have eliminated as many as I can, you shall certainly have to see the ones that have the characteristics of your nightmare. But until then, you will remain safely at Wyndham Manor and keep your delightful little nose out of trouble. I will not have you, or our child, endangered in any way."

Nell threw him a look. "I'm not made of crystal, you know."

He stopped and pulled her into his arms. Smiling down at her, an expression in his eyes that made her heart race, he murmured, "But you are pregnant with our child and I would have no harm come to you—ever."

Julian might have said more, but at that moment, John Hunter, riding a neat bay and accompanied by a pack of mastiffs and hounds, came around a curve in the road. To Julian's surprise, Marcus, astride a stunning black stallion, was with him.

Nell was not of a nervous disposition, but the sight of those two big, dark men, so similar in looks, riding toward her, coupled with the size and fierce look of the dogs that surrounded them, made her cling tightly to Julian's arm. She eyed the huge mastiff leading the pack and she suddenly wished she was riding her own horse . . . or had a pistol in her hand.

Spotting them, the dogs gave tongue and, as one, surged

forward. A sharp command from John Hunter stopped them in their tracks.

When they were within speaking distance, Julian exclaimed, "Marcus! What are you doing here? This is a most pleasant surprise—I had thought not to see you here again for months."

Marcus pulled his horse to a stop and dismounted. Bowing low over Nell's hand, he said, "Ah, but that was before the news that our family was expanding reached me. Congratulations, my lady. I hope that all is well with you and the heir?"

"Why is it," demanded Nell with a smile, "that everyone assumes that I am carrying a boy? You know it is possible that I shall present my lord with a girl."

"Possible," Marcus agreed, "but the Wyndhams seem to be singularly lucky in that their firstborns are almost universally male."

John Hunter, after a snarled command to his dogs that had them slinking to the ground on their bellies, dismounted also. He acknowledged Nell and Julian and then said, "I am sorry to interrupt you, my lord, but might I have word in private with you?"

Julian shot him a sharp glance. "Yes, of course. Allow me to escort my wife back to the house and get my cousin settled and we can meet in my office in thirty minutes."

Hunter appeared ready to protest, but his gaze fell upon Nell's face and he apparently changed his mind. Looking at Julian, he nodded curtly. "Thirty minutes, my lord, I will be there."

His reply sounding more like a threat than a confirmation, he remounted his horse and, his dogs obediently following behind him, disappeared down the road.

Watching him go, Marcus remarked, "He was preparing to go in search of you when I arrived. Seemed rather perturbed to find you gone from the house. He was, uh, most insistent that he find you right away." He looked at Julian. "My curiosity was aroused, but, alas, he revealed nothing to me."

Julian grinned. "I suppose you would like to be present at our meeting?"

Marcus flashed his charming smile. "I never thought you'd ask."

"What do you think he wants to see you about?" Nell asked.

Julian glanced down at her. "I have no idea. Something simple I am sure."

"Yes, I'm positive that your husband is correct," drawled Marcus, taking her other arm, his horse trailing behind them. "Dear Hunter does take his duties most seriously, always has, and I am sure that we shall discover that it is nothing more than some pilfering by the locals of leveret or partridge—a hanging offense in Hunter's mind."

But Hunter was oddly loathe to explain exactly what it was that he had to report when they met in the library, precisely twenty-nine minutes later. Marcus was lounging in the chair by the fire and Julian was seated behind his desk. Julian had asked Hunter to take the other chair, but the older man would have none of it.

Standing stiffly in front of Julian, his impatience barely concealed, Hunter growled, "Enough time has been wasted as it is, my lord. You must come with me immediately and see for yourself." He shot Marcus an unfriendly glance. "And that one, too."

"Is it another slaughter?" Julian asked, dread in his voice.

Hunter gave a harsh bark. "Worse, my lord."

He would say no more and irritated as much as curious and uneasy, Julian ordered his own horse, and a fresh one for his cousin, brought round to the front of the house.

*   *   *

Hunter set a swift pace, Julian and Marcus riding on his heels as his horse veered off the roadway and struck out into the wooded area. It was a wild ride as the horses jumped over streams and galloped through the forest. When Hunter finally pulled his horse to a snorting stop, they were in a section of the forest that Julian seldom visited.

As one the three men dismounted and tied their horses to a tree. With Julian and Marcus following, Hunter led them to the edge of a small clearing where he stopped. Stepping up to Hunter's side, Julian paled as his gaze fell on what lay in the center of that clearing.

"Dear God," he breathed. "What manner of beast did this?" But he knew. Even more appalling he knew with a deep conviction that he was staring at the remains of the woman Nell had seen killed in her nightmare last night. Bile rose in his throat. Merciful God, she'd had to watch *this* be done to another human being.

Marcus, his eyes frozen in horror on the woman's body, almost lost the excellent ham and ale he'd stopped to enjoy on the road only a few hours ago. Taking careful breaths, he said, "It would appear that our fellow has gone from venting his rage on your game to taking human prey."

"I warned you, my lord," said Hunter, gloomy satisfaction in his voice. "I warned you if you didn't take steps that something terrible would happen."

"I do not remember you telling me that I would find a poor woman slaughtered if I didn't allow you to set your man-traps and loose your dogs on trespassers," Julian replied sharply. "This is something that no one could have foreseen or prevented. This is the work of a madman."

Hunter nodded. "You are right, my lord, forgive me, I forgot myself."

Neither Julian nor Marcus was eager to approach the body, but eventually they did. The remains were so torn and mangled that it was difficult to tell much about them, other than that they were female and that she had suffered agonizingly before dying. Her killer had thrown her naked body like so much refuse on the forest floor. Beyond the pitiful body in the center of the clearing, there were no obvious signs as to how she'd gotten there. None of the three men could identify her.

Since Hunter was expert at reading the signs and tracks of the forest, Marcus and Julian followed him as he inspected the site. It seemed he searched for hours, in ever-widening circles, but he found little beyond a few broken and snapped branches, the thick debris of the forest floor in this area hiding any footprints—human or animal. But there was a trail of sorts and with Hunter leading the way, they followed it, finding the spot where a horse had been tied to stout tree, the hoofprints and a pile of dung revealing its presence. Julian surmised that the killer had left his horse and then carried the body to the clearing where he'd left it to be discovered.

Weary and discouraged, they made their way back to the body. The first wave of horror had passed and Julian stared down at the woman, his heart full of pity for what she had suffered. Rage at what had been done to her choked him and he turned away.

"Get the bailiff and the magistrate and your best hounds," he snapped to Hunter. "After that, alert the household to our delay. Tell them that we are hunting—hot on the heels of a handsome stag." He looked hard at Hunter. "Not one word of this to anyone. My cousin and I shall remain here until you return with the others." He glanced back at the body. "And bring something to wrap the poor thing in. She deserves that at least."

It was very late when Julian and Marcus finally returned to Wyndham Manor. The bailiff and magistrate had been badly shaken at being confronted by the body of the young woman done to death in such a vicious manner and on the Earl of

Wyndham's land. After swearing them to silence, Julian and the others left the bailiff to deal with the removal of the body. With the magistrate joining them, Julian, Marcus and Hunter gathered up their horses and rode to where the killer's mount had been tied. Hunter's hounds were loosed and the hunt for a killer began. They pushed on well after sunset despite the rising wind and the hint of rain in the air, but the night closed in on them. The weather worsened, rain falling steadily, the wind biting through their clothes, and when the scent had gone cold at the edge of the river that crisscrossed Julian's lands, the hunt was abandoned. Discouraged, they turned their horses toward home. It was agreed to keep the matter quiet—at least the manner of death. That a young woman had been murdered could not be kept secret, but no one else need know how she had died.

Leaving their horses at the stables, Julian and Marcus walked silently to the house. Entering, they were greeted by Dibble. "Her ladyship requested that I prepare a cold buffet for you. She said that you might be late. I have placed everything in your study. She said that you would no doubt prefer to eat there in private." Politely Dibble asked, "And did you kill your stag, my lord?"

"No. The animal managed to elude us." Dismissing the butler, Julian added, "Good night, Dibble, we will not need your services further."

In his study, both men tossed aside their muddied and soiled jackets, loosened their once-pristine cravats and removed their boots. Sitting before the fire, and looking at the condition of his formerly gleaming boots, Marcus remarked, "If my valet doesn't give notice when I hand him these, I am in for tears and recriminations the like of which you have never seen."

Pouring them both a snifter of brandy, Julian said over his shoulder, "Truesdale may despair of your lack of desire to join the ranks of the Fancy, but I know that nothing less than a charge of the Light Brigade would separate him from your side."

Tossing aside his boots, Marcus laid his head back against the chair and sighed. "This is a very bad business, Julian."

Handing Marcus a snifter of brandy and taking the other chair, Julian stretched his feet out toward the warmth of the crackling fire. "I agree and I don't know what the bloody hell I'm going to do about it."

Julian found himself once more in an invidious situation. Holding back vital information from Marcus was dangerous, but he could say nothing of Nell's nightmares or what they revealed. He trusted his cousin implicitly, but this, even more than the Tynedale kidnapping, was not his secret to tell. Nell had agreed for Marcus to know the truth surrounding their wedding, but he suspected that sharing her nightmares with a man who was almost a stranger, no matter how highly Julian thought of him, was not something that she would readily agree to. He could vouch for Marcus but while she appeared to like his cousin, she did not know him well. It had been hard enough for him, who loved her and knew her, to accept the truth of what she had told him. How much more difficult would it be for Marcus to believe that she actually saw grisly murders committed . . . including John's? He would not ask it of her.

The two men were exhausted after their hours in the saddle and for some time they sat and stared at the fire, sipping their brandies, each man busy with his own thoughts. Neither was hungry and they ignored the cold buffet, but from time to time Julian would rise and refill their snifters. By the time they'd finished off several snifters of brandy, some of the horror of the day had lessened.

Though he'd said nothing, Julian had been thinking very hard about Nell's nightmares and his inability to reveal all to Marcus. He took a sip of his brandy considering how best to handle the situation. He would, he realized, have to find a way to lead Marcus in the right direction without divulging Nell's part. He closed his eyes, weariness washing over him, his thoughts returning against his will to that ghastly sight in the forest. That poor woman! Little more than a child, really. And to have been so brutally and senselessly murdered. His fingers tightened on the snifter. He wanted this monster, wanted him dead with a violence he had not thought himself capable of.

"So what are we going to do?" Marcus asked, as he stared morosely down into his swirling amber liquor. "How do we find such a monster? Where do we start?" He took an ungentlemanly gulp of the very expensive French brandy. "You realize that if he has left off killing game and has begun killing humans that he may not be willing to go back to the mere slaughter of deer. They may no longer satisfy him."

Seizing on a way to give Marcus a glimmer of the truth, Julian said, "I don't believe that he has just *begun* killing humans—I think that he has been doing it all along and that poor unfortunate woman we saw today is only the first one we've found. The slaughtering of the game was merely a diversion for him. Perhaps, he went looking for a human victim and not finding one vented his fury on some four-legged victims."

"You may be right," Marcus said thoughtfully. "This is beyond my ken—I've never dealt with anything like this. Outright murder, I understand. Killing your man in a duel, I understand. Bloodshed I understand—the war with Napoleon is a good example—but what we saw today . . ." He sighed heavily. "It has to be the work of a madman."

"I agree. But finding and stopping him is our problem." Having finished his snifter of brandy, Julian rose up and poured them each another one. Sipping his brandy, he sat back down. He brooded over the situation for a few minutes before saying, "He has to have somewhere that he does his filthy handiwork. Someplace private where he can practice his vile arts. A location where no one will hear his victims' pleas and screams. A secret place that no one will stumble across."

Marcus considered Julian's words for several minutes, nodding his head thoughtfully. "Yes, I can see that," he admitted finally. Running a hand tiredly across his face, he added, "And that leads us to one conclusion: this is not the handiwork of a peasant living in a one-room hovel. He is either a man of property and owns the place where he kills or he has unfettered access to such a place and fears no interruptions. He also," Marcus said slowly, "must be free to come and go as he pleases with no one questioning his movements."

Their gazes met. "Which means," Julian said, "that he could very well be a gentleman. Someone with property and independent means, or employed in such a manner that he can move about freely with no one keeping account of his whereabouts."

"Oh, good God! Do you realize what we're saying?" Marcus demanded. "If we go by that, we could very well find out that Dr. Coleman, or even John Hunter is our madman. Or the vicar. Or even the squire."

"Yes, you're absolutely right. And isn't it interesting that all of them, except for perhaps the vicar, happen to have homes that have been built above or near long-forgotten dungeons. Except, of course, the squire—he delights in showing his off—but that doesn't mean that there are parts no one knows about, now does it?"

Marcus stared at Julian as if he'd gone mad. He took a deep, calming breath. There was silence in the room, except for the pop and crackle of the fire as Marcus stared at it for several minutes. He swallowed some more brandy and looked at Julian. "You've given this some thought," he finally said, "haven't you?"

Julian smiled sleepily. "Indeed, I've thought of little else for some time now." He tossed off the remainder of his brandy. "What do you say that tomorrow we start touring the area, looking at dungeons?"

Marcus threw him a disgusted look. "Now just suppose I agree with you—how are we to do that without giving away what we're up to?"

Julian thought for awhile. "Didn't there used to be a dungeon beneath Sherbrook Hall?"

"Which I had filled in years ago. Don't you dare, even for one minute, consider *me* a candidate for your madman," Marcus said grimly.

Julian waved a hand. "Wasn't. Was thinking that you might like to restore your dungeons. Need to gather information to do it right. You want to see what some of the ones in this area look like—see how they compare to yours."

Scowling Marcus stared at him. "You're drunk as a wheelbarrow."

Julian shook his head. "No—a bit bosky, perhaps, empty stomach, you know. But my idea might work."

"Drunk *and* mad," Marcus muttered.

"Hmmm, think you're right, but that doesn't mean my idea won't work," Julian agreed amiably. He stood up, swaying slightly. "Going to bed." He smiled seraphically at his cousin. "We have dungeons to explore tomorrow. Early."

Chapter 16

Nell pounced on Julian the moment he entered his bed-chamber. Despite their intimacy and the fact that they had been married nearly four months, this was the first time she'd ventured into his bedchamber. His rooms had not been denied her, but until now, there had never been a reason to enter them.

Under different circumstances she might have noticed that they were attractive. But tonight she had no eye for draperies of burgundy velvet and masculine furniture made of fine mahogany. She paced the floors heedless of the elegant rug in tones of burgundy, black and gold beneath her feet, her thoughts on Julian and John Hunter's odd manner. Occasionally she stopped to stick her hands out to the warmth of the fire, her gaze blind to the leaping orange and yellow flames.

Nell was convinced of one thing: Julian was hunting no stag. This unexpected hunting trip coming right on the heels of last night's nightmare made her suspect that his absence was somehow connected to the brutal death of the woman she'd seen in her nightmare.

She and Julian had much to learn of each other, but she knew him well enough by now to be positive that it was unlike him to suddenly take it into his head to disappear from home for hours on end without warning. The terse message delivered by John Hunter had roused all her suspicions. She had considered demanding more of Hunter before dismissing him, but she had not. She made a face. If she'd dared to question Hunter, he'd most likely have glared at her and ignored her.

Upon Lady Diana and Elizabeth's return from the Dower House, she'd informed them of Marcus's unexpected arrival and made light of the gentlemen's bloodthirsty desire to go haring off after a stag. The other two women were full of their ideas and plans for the continued renovations of the Dower House, and without question they accepted her excuse for Julian and Marcus's absence from the dining room.

Nell got through the evening, smiling and making appropriate comments, but with one ear cocked for the sound of her husband's arrival home. The evening dragged on, the hours on the clock passing with excruciating slowness.

Around eleven o'clock, Lady Diana politely stifled a yawn. Standing up and shaking out her gown, she said, "Oh, dear, I fear that my bed is calling for me. Who knew that decorating a house could be so fatiguing?"

Elizabeth stood up and also prepared to leave for her bedroom. Glancing at Nell, she asked, "Are you coming to bed, too?" Adding with a smile, "I would not wait up if I were you. From past experience, Mama and I know that when Lord Wyndham and Mr. Sherbrook are hunting they can lose all track of time."

"Oh, my, yes!" said Lady Diana. "Why I remember one time that they disappeared for three days chasing after a fox they'd jumped. Naturally the fox escaped and Julian's horse threw a shoe and they ended up stranded in some little country village until they could find a blacksmith. My husband thought it a huge joke, but I was most anxious. We had no idea where they were or when they would return." She patted Nell on the cheek. "But return they did, starving and dirty and none the worse for wear—all my fretting was for naught. Come along with us, dear, there is no need for you to wait up for them."

Nell allowed herself to be convinced and the three ladies retired to their bedchambers. After changing into her nightclothes, Nell dismissed Becky. She'd eyed the glass of warm milk that Becky had brought to help her sleep and wrinkled her nose. Warm milk would not help her tonight.

Determination in her step, she had crossed the room and entered her husband's domain. And there she'd remained, pacing and speculating as the hours ticked by.

Nell had not heard Julian and Marcus's return and when the door to his room swung open and he walked inside, she gasped as his tall, broad-shouldered form loomed up out of the shadows.

They stared at each other a second, both surprised to see the other, and then relief coursing through her she flew across the room and hurled herself into his arms. "Oh, thank God, you are home," she cried, clutching him as if she'd never let him go. Burying her nose at the throat of his opened shirt, she drank in the beloved scent. "I have been so worried," she said finally. "You have been gone for hours and hours."

She felt wonderful in his arms, her slender body soft and warm, driving out the ugliness of the day. How different, he thought, was Nell's sweet greeting from that of Catherine's. Even now he could still hear Catherine's bored tones and picture the indifferent expression on her face when he returned after being away, sometimes for a week or more. Catherine, he thought wryly, had certainly never worried about him. That Nell was anxious for him touched him deeply and he hugged her close, savoring the feel of her against him. Trying for a light note, he said, "Why should you have been? I sent word with John Hunter that Marcus and I would be delayed. Do not tell me that I have married a shrew who begrudges me a bit of hunting now and then?"

Nell took a long look at him, noting the scent of brandy in the air, the careful articulation and the suspiciously innocent expression on his face. Raised in a household of men, she was aware of the signs of a gentleman who had imbibed a trifle overgenerously. Exasperated, she said, "Not only gone hunting for hours, but bosky in the bargain." There was a twinkle in her eyes that told him that she was not truly angry.

He grinned, a slow, lazy grin that made her heart turn over in her breast. "Perhaps, a bit," he admitted. "We didn't intend for it to happen, but Marcus and I were, uh, very friendly with the decanter of brandy in my study." He kissed her nose. "I appreciate your anxiety, my dear, but you see before you your husband returned unharmed."

He looked weary and devilish attractive with his shirt half-undone and his black hair mussed and tangled. There was a shadow of a beard darkening his lean jaw and for a moment Nell was transported back to her first sight of him. He looked a brigand then, albeit a very appealing brigand, and he looked a brigand now—one she adored. Trailing a caressing finger along that jaw she asked, "Did you eat anything? I had Dibble prepare a cold buffet for you."

Guiding her to a chair by the fire, Julian sat down, pulling her into his lap as he did so. With Nell nestled near to him, her tawny curls brushing his chin, he said, "I thank you for your kindness, Madame wife, but we were not hungry. The brandy filled our needs."

Her eyes on the fire, basking in the comfort of his nearness, she asked, "Julian, what was the real reason that John Hunter came for you?" She looked up at him. "And please, do not lie to me."

Julian hesitated. He'd wanted to keep the horror of the day far away from his home, especially from her, but her words made it impossible. His voice bleak, he said, "Hunter found the body of the woman you saw murdered in your nightmare. She was spread out in a small clearing near the north end of my lands."

Nell bolted upright. "But it cannot be! He never leaves the body where it can be found. He always . . ." She stopped, frowning. "There is a sluice hole in the dungeon," she said after a moment, "and he always throws the bodies down it."

"Well, he didn't this one," Julian said. Wearily he added, "Unless there are two such monsters at work in the neighborhood and that I cannot believe." He stared into Nell's eyes.

"There is no mistaking his work—not from what you described to me last night. She was torn apart," he said, "and tossed on the ground like so much refuse. I cannot prove it, but I am convinced that she is the woman you saw murdered last night."

Nell's gaze fell and her fingers dug into the palms of her hands. "But he never . . ."

"I know that it is hard for you, but think back to last night," Julian said gently. "Did you actually see him put the body down the sluice hole?"

"The dreams always end the same way, with him putting the bodies down the sluice hole," she explained patiently. "And last night was no diff—" She paused, a puzzled expression on her face. "I did not see him do that last night," she admitted. Her eyes flew to Julian's. "What he did last night was so frightening that I woke before . . ." She shivered. "If the woman you found is indeed the woman in my nightmare, why did he change his custom? He has done his awful work for years in secrecy because the bodies are never found. Why did he leave this one out where it can be found?"

Julian's arms tightened around her and he pulled back next to him. His lips brushing her hair, he said, "Have no doubt, the body was indeed the victim of your recent nightmare. As for his reasoning . . . perhaps, something has changed and he wanted her to be found." He frowned. "It could be that he underestimated Hunter's knowledge of the land and he assumed the place he had chosen to dispose of her body would never be discovered—or least not for months. Or, worse, he did know of Hunter's devotion to the estate and for his own twisted needs he wanted everyone to be aware of his work. It could be that after years of doing his deeds in secrecy, he wanted someone to find her—wanted people to see what he did to her."

"I wonder why he left the body on your land," Nell mused. "How is it that John Hunter found her so quickly?"

Julian rested his head back against the top of the chair. "You have to understand Hunter. He breathes the land and he has been its lover, its caretaker for decades. He grew up here. He knows every inch, every hollow, every dell, every glen . . . He knows everything about the forest right down to the number of fox, stag and hares at any given time—and where they can be found. I exaggerate, but I swear that not a leaf can fall that he doesn't know about it." He ran a hand through his hair. "I did not ask him how he came to be in that area, but I'll wager that he'll have a good reason."

"So what happens now?"

"The magistrate and the bailiff have been notified and the body has been taken away. In fact the magistrate spent a fruitless afternoon and the better part of the evening with us trying to follow your Shadow Man's trail. We used Hunter's dogs, but the trail went cold at the river. By then we were soaked and chilled from the rain and wind and it was dark and late. Since there was very little moonlight, and we were all tired, wet and discouraged, we called the hunt off."

"What will happen to her body? Do you think that she is a local?"

"I have asked Dr. Coleman to examine her. Once she has been . . . cleaned, it is possible that Coleman will recognize her. He is the only physician for miles around and if she is a local woman, it is possible that he will know her. The magistrate as well as the bailiff will be making inquiries about any missing women." Julian hugged her against him. "God, Nell!" he said in shaken tones, "but this is a curst, ugly business. And terrifying that you are so closely linked with it."

"Harder for you than me," Nell said. "I have lived with the knowledge of this monster for a decade or more, but you . . . You have just learned of him."

"And wish to God that I had not!" His lips brushed her temple. "But most of all, I wish that you had never been subjected to the horror of his handiwork."

She smiled sadly. "I, too, wish the same, but perhaps, there is a reason behind my having the nightmares. Remember: from what we learn from them, we may find a way to stop him."

Julian stifled a yawn. "That is the only saving grace I can find in this whole ugly business."

Standing up, she reached for his hand. "Come to bed," she urged. "I can see that you are exhausted."

The firelight behind her silhouetted her form and a gleam entered his eyes. "Bed sounds a fine idea . . . especially with you in it and in my arms," he said huskily as he rose from his seat and pulled her into an embrace. He kissed her long, hard and deep. "Most especially," he breathed against her tingling lips, "with you in my arms."

He swept her up into the air and carried her to the huge, canopied bed. Lying her in the center, he smiled down at her. "I do not know how it comes about, but I have never made love to you in my bed. I shall have to rectify that omission."

And he did. Most enjoyably and quite, *quite* thoroughly.

Despite his intention for an early start the next morning, Julian's plans were foiled by the weather. The weather that had bedeviled them the previous night had become a howling storm and the notion of riding out in blowing rain and screaming wind was promptly put aside.

After a long, leisurely breakfast wherein Marcus paid all the women extravagant compliments and brought a blush more than once to Elizabeth's cheeks, the gentlemen closeted themselves for several hours in Julian's study. Nell sent them a dark look as they exited the morning room, knowing that she was being abandoned to feminine pastimes while they discussed more weighty matters.

The ladies spent the day going over more pattern books and craftsman catalogs in search of furnishings for the Dower House. Nell chafed at sitting on the sofa looking at swatch after swatch of fabric and page after page of furniture when she longed to join the gentlemen in the study. She knew that they would be discussing how best to proceed with finding out the identity of the slain woman and how to catch the killer. She scowled. She knew more about the Shadow Man than anyone did, but did they ask her opinion? She snorted. Of course not! She was only a mere woman to be petted and cosseted. Grudgingly she admitted that Julian was only trying to protect her, but it was ridiculous. She was already deep in the middle of it. She *should* be in that study with them instead of here listening to Lady Diana's joyous exclamations as yet another swatch of fabric or chair was found that pleased her eye.

Unable to stand it a moment longer, she leaped to her feet and after making an excuse to the other two women, with her spine ramrod straight, she went in search of her husband. She found Julian and Marcus still in the study, and from the grim expressions on their faces when she entered the room, she knew that they had been discussing the murdered woman.

Both men immediately rose when she entered, but she waved them back to their chairs and seated herself on a small, channel-backed sofa not far from the fire. Fixing both men with a determined stare, she said, "Forgive me for intruding, but it is ridiculous to pretend that I do not have something to offer concerning this matter." At the stubborn expression that appeared on Julian's face, she said quickly, "You know that I am right, my lord, and that I have a personal interest in finding out who murdered that poor young girl. A more personal interest than either one of you."

Marcus appeared stunned. He stared incredulously at Julian. "You *told* her?"

"Not exactly," Julian said grimly. He studied Nell's set face and sighed. He had married a strong woman and she was not going to let him wrap her in ermine and silk and keep her safely in the background. No, he thought with rueful admiration, his Nell was pluck to the backbone and, it appeared, resolute in throwing herself in the midst of deadly peril.

"Not exactly? What the hell does that mean?" demanded Marcus, his gaze moving from one taut face to the other. "What the devil is going on here?"

Julian sighed. "Do you want to tell him, or shall I?"

Nell had known when she walked into that room that she would have to share the secret of the nightmares with Marcus. She just hadn't realized how hard it would be to convince a stranger that she was not a candidate for Bedlam. It helped that Julian supported her. And that he believed her. She began her story . . .

It was Julian's belief in her that eventually convinced Marcus. Like Julian he had been skeptical and disbelieving in the beginning. From the looks he occasionally shot his cousin, it was clear that for awhile he thought that both of them were mad. But gradually, as she and Julian laid it all out for him, he became a believer.

"I cannot believe it! You saw John murdered?" Marcus asked several times. "You actually saw it? In your, er, nightmare?"

Patiently Nell assured him that this was so, and tried not to be annoyed when he would glance then at Julian for confirmation of what she said.

Once he was receptive to the idea that she had indeed seen the murder of John Weston a decade ago, it seemed easier for him to accept that she had dreamed the murder of several innocent women by the same man who had slain his oldest cousin. "And the place is always the same?" he demanded. "You are positive of that? There is no mistake?"

"Yes, it is always the same. And no, I am not mistaken," she answered sharply, "and I have never seen his face."

"You do realize, don't you, Lady Wyndham, that you are in grave danger?" Marcus asked slowly. "Should this monster learn that you watch him through your nightmares he would stop at nothing to silence you . . . You could end up in the ghastly dungeon of his."

"That will never happen," said Julian with quiet determination. "I will keep her safe." He stared at Marcus. "*We* will keep her safe."

Marcus nodded, and for once there was no sign of his usual ready smile. He took a deep breath. "And the best way to do that is find those bloody dungeons and the madman who inhabits them."

"I agree, but until this weather breaks we cannot go forward," Julian said.

A speculative expression in his gaze, Marcus looked at Nell. "These nightmares of yours: are you certain that you will recognize the place if we actually find it?"

It was obvious to both Nell and Julian that though he was trying gamely to believe in Nell's nightmares and what they revealed, Marcus was not totally convinced.

"She will recognize them," Julian said flatly.

Julian and Marcus were aimlessly playing a game of billiards several hours later when Dibble appeared with the news that Dr. Coleman had come to call. The two men exchanged glances and as one threw down their cues and left the room with swift strides. Julian called over his shoulder to Dibble as he walked away, "Some of your rum punch, Dibble. We will have need of it."

Dibble had shown Dr. Coleman into Julian's study and he had been standing and staring at the fire, but at the entrance of Julian and Marcus he turned and looked at them. Greetings were exchanged and Julian's offer of warm punch was gladly accepted. Polite conversation flowed as Dibble returned with the punch and served it.

After Dibble had departed, Julian said, "Tell us all that you have discovered."

"In all my years, I have never seen anything like it," Dr. Coleman said in shaken tones. "It is as if a beast ravaged her, tried to tear her apart."

"It was a beast," Julian said grimly. "A human beast with a heart of evil."

Dr. Coleman nodded. "Yes, I agree. But I was not certain as to the cause of death until I examined the body closely— then it became clear that her terrible wounds were made by the hand of a man and not an animal."

"A debatable point," murmured Marcus.

Dr. Coleman grimaced. "Yes, yes, indeed." He took another sip of the punch as if fortifying himself to go on. "Her features were unrecognizable to me at first," he continued, "but once I had washed away the blood and debris I realized that I knew her. Her name is, er, was, Ann Barnes and she works . . . worked at a small family inn not far from the coast, some ten miles north of here. I treated her last year for chicken pox when it swept through the county." He sighed. "Poor, poor child! She was only seventeen. Such a tragedy! A waste. All the more so since I discovered that she was pregnant." At Julian's sharp look, he added, "I found the remains of the fetus. From its development, I suspect that she could not have been more than four months pregnant."

It was agreed that Dr. Coleman would notify Ann Barnes's family of her death. There was some discussion about the burial, and not wishing for her family to look upon those mutilated remains, as much to spare them the awful sight as to disguise the murder, Julian requested that the doctor take care of all the arrangements.

"I do not want her parents to see what that monster did to her, nor cause panic in the area," Julian said. "So I think it would be best if her body was returned to them in a sealed coffin. Naturally I shall pay for it."

"I shall have to tell them something concerning her death," Dr. Coleman protested.

"Tell them that she fell from the cliffs," Marcus said, "and that his lordship wished to spare them the sight of damage done by the rocks and the sea."

Julian looked thoughtfully at Marcus, wondering if his cousin realized how closely that story tallied with Nell's brush with death a decade ago. It made him uncomfortable, the similarities, but he agreed that the tale would explain much. Aloud he said, "I shall write to the magistrate immediately and the bailiff to let them know what we propose. And hope to God they have not already spread the manner of her death."

Dr. Coleman bowed. "I spoke with both of them late last night and we agreed that the less said abroad, the better. They are discreet men, my lord. You have nothing to fear of them speaking of things they should not. No one wants the populace frightened and starting at shadows." He pulled out his pocket watch and glancing at it, said, "I have a meeting with both of them at my house in an hour. I shall be happy to relate to them what has been decided here."

Having delivered his report, and the meeting with the magistrate and bailiff looming, Dr. Coleman did not linger.

After he had left, Julian stood up and walked to the window that overlooked the driveway. The weather was still beastly and he did not envy Dr. Coleman the ride to his house.

It wasn't until late that night when they retired that Julian was able to relate to Nell all that had been revealed by the doctor's visit. Curled up by his side in bed, she listened as he told her what they now knew about the victim. When he spoke of the fetus, Nell's hands instinctively curved around her belly. She and the dead woman had not been very far apart in their pregnancies. It hurt to think of not only the wanton death of a young woman with everything to live for, but also the innocent creature that had grown in Ann Barnes's belly.

Julian's warm hand closed over hers. "I know," he said softly. "I thought the same thing. You and young Ann would have given birth within weeks of each other."

"We must stop this monster," Nell said fiercely. "He must not be allowed to continue to kill at will."

"Have no fear, we will find him and we *will* stop him, no matter where he runs or where he hides." There was silence for a moment as they both considered the formidable task before them. Then Julian said, "Marcus and I will poke about, and we may learn something that will put us on his track."

The inclement weather continued almost unabated for over two weeks and since there had been no urgent reason for him to return home, Marcus accepted Julian's invitation to stay at Wyndham Manor. By the time the series of storms had blown themselves out, everyone was heartily sick of rain and wind—and more wind and rain. There had not been a day that it had not rained, sometimes it had rained the entire day and night. But then the skies cleared and while every roof, fence, twig, branch and leaf dripped water, the sun had finally shone. The storms had lashed the neighborhood hard—all the area rivers and streams were swollen and roaring, some spilling their banks and flooding the adjacent lands; nearly every road, path and walkway was knee-deep in mud and littered with puddles. On that last Monday in February, the inhabitants of Wyndham Manor greeted the sight of the sun shining in the blue sky with grateful pleasure and delight. Meeting at the breakfast table that morning, everyone was full of plans and impatient to be gone and busy with their affairs.

While the storms had precluded any work being done on the exterior of the Dower House, the workmen had been scheduled to continue work on the interior and Lady Diana and Elizabeth were eager to see the progress.

"If there has been any progress," Lady Diana said gloomily. "The roads have been atrocious and the only time we were at the house since this awful weather started the foreman indicated that he might send everyone home until the weather cleared." She sighed. "He said that the paint and plaster was not drying and that the wall hangings were slipping because of the dampness in the air." She sighed again. "And that the chimneys were blowing smoke into some of the newly redone rooms—something that must be repaired when the weather breaks." She put down her cup of tea. "Sometimes I wonder if my house will ever be habitable. It seems that there has just been one delay after another."

Lady Diana's complaints were valid, Julian thought with a frown. Besides the weather, which no one had any control over, there had been several vexing delays. He had not paid a great deal of attention to Lady Diana's grievances and, as he remembered, they'd been little things. There'd been some missing fabric, he recalled, and a carpet? A word with the head carpenter would not come amiss, he decided as they rose from the table.

They all exited the room together and walked to the front of the house, where a small trap drawn by a stout pony was waiting for Lady Diana and Elizabeth, and soon the women were happily driving to the Dower House. Having declined Lady Diana's offer to join them, Nell waved them on their way.

No less eager than Lady Diana and Elizabeth were to escape the confines of the house, Julian and Marcus stood by Nell as their horses were led up from the stables. Their plans included a visit to Squire Chadbourne and the hope that the squire could be maneuvered into showing them the dungeons beneath Chadbourne House.

Turning to say good-bye to his wife, Julian frowned. "I do not like leaving you here alone."

"I will not be alone," Nell said. "How could I be with a house full of servants? Besides, you'd be horrified if I demanded to go with you."

The guilty expression that crossed his face made her smile, but it was the appalled look on Marcus's face that had her bursting into laughter. "Go away," she said to the pair of them. "Do not worry about me, I will find something to amuse myself. In fact, I am looking forward to a pleasant day alone."

Nell wasn't pretending. Despite the soggy ground she did want to walk around the gardens and perhaps down to the stables. After two weeks of being housebound, she was eager to stretch her legs and be out and about in the sunshine.

Left to her own devices, Nell did as she planned, wearing a fur-trimmed pelisse to keep out the cold and a charming bonnet on her head, she strolled about the gardens, avoiding those pathways that seemed too muddy. It was wonderful to be outside, she thought, as she lifted her face to the sun's rays and took a deep breath of the clean, country air. She patted her abdomen, pleased that there was an increasing bulge where her child grew. Except for the horrors associated with the Shadow Man and the specter of Julian's first wife, Nell was happy. She did miss her family, her father in particular, but Wyndham Manor and its ways and people were feeling more and more like home to her. She adored her husband; he was a good, generous man and just the mere sight of him made her blood race and her heart lift. And there was the birth of their child in the summer to anticipate.

She had, she realized, much to be grateful for. Picturing the expression on Lord Tynedale's face if she was to thank him for kidnapping her, she nearly laughed aloud. Without his interference, she thought, I'd never have known Julian, never married him and never fallen in love with him. But then she remembered Catherine and the fresh bouquet of roses or lilies carefully arranged every morning beneath the portrait in the gallery and her spirits plummeted.

You could stop torturing yourself by checking whether Julian was still ordering those those bloody flowers, you know, she told herself sternly. You do yourself no good and only hurt yourself every time you prowl the gallery and see the new bouquets.

She'd tried to break the habit of going to the gallery, but just as Julian seemed unable to break his tradition, so did she hers.

Miserably, she walked back to the house, her enjoyment in the day and gardens ruined. I should have gone to the Dower House with Lady Diana, she thought bitterly. Her eyes turned in that direction and her breath caught at the sight of a huge, billowing cloud of black smoke rising in the air above the trees.

It took a second for her to understand what she was seeing, but then she did, and a thrill of horror went through her. The Dower House was on fire.

Chapter 17

Picking up her skirts, Nell ran back to the manor, her heart slamming hard against her ribs. What had happened? She glanced again in the direction of the Dower House, hoping that her eyes had deceived her. They had not. If anything the cloud was blacker, larger, more terrifying.

As she neared the front door, she heard the babble of the servants, the sounds of people running and calling out and realized that they too had seen the ominous cloud of smoke rising in the air and were sounding the alarm. Already there was the clatter of vehicles and horses as every able man and woman sped away to fight the fire at the Dower House.

Nell joined in the rush, only to be brought up short by someone calling her name. "Your ladyship! Your ladyship! Wait—I have brought a horse for you."

She whirled around and there was Hodges astride a dancing chestnut and holding the reins to her favorite black mare. She flashed him a grateful smile and heedless of modesty or position, she easily vaulted into the saddle. Neck and neck, swerving to avoid those on foot and slower vehicles, she and Hodges careened down the road, mud flying from their horses' hooves.

Reaching the rear of the Dower House where the fire raged, Nell discovered a scene of ordered chaos. Horses and wagons and carts were parked willy-nilly along a line of trees at the side of the house. Lady Diana, her dark hair mussed and wild, a black smudge on one cheek and the hem of her gown stained and torn, was organizing the newest arrivals. Now and then Lady Diana risked a horrified glance at the leaping flames coming from the rear of the house before seeming to gather herself once more and attend to the matter at hand. Elizabeth, looking as if she'd fought with a flaming coal bucket and lost—if her sooty face and scorched gown were anything to go by—was beating the flames with a wet rug as she and several others tried to keep the fire from spreading. Buckets and pails soon appeared; a straggling line of volunteers was formed and using the well at the back of the house, pail after pail of water was thrown onto the raging fire.

Nell joined in the fray, taking her place in the middle of the water brigade, eagerly accepting the sloshing pail of water passed to her and turning to pass it on to the next person. They worked tirelessly, the only thing that mattered being that next bucket of water that was swiftly hoisted from the well and passed on to the next pair of willing hands.

The unrelenting rain of the last few weeks was a godsend. The roof, the walls, the ground itself and the exterior were still soaked and that slowed the fire's reach and gave them all hope that it could be stopped before engulfing the entire house.

A second line was formed as more volunteers arrived. The fight continued unrelentingly and Nell's shoulders and arms were screaming for relief as she reached for what seemed like the hundredth bucket, but before her fingers touched the handle, a pair of masculine hands closed around her waist and lifted her bodily from the line.

Astonished she stared up into Charles Weston's face. "Charles!" she exclaimed. "What are you doing here?"

He flashed a grim smile. "Saving my cousin's heir and taking your place in the line. Go join my stepmother and Lady Diana on the sidelines. Raoul and I shall add our bit to the fight."

Looking around, Nell noticed that Raoul, having apparently dispatched Elizabeth the same way Charles had her, had joined the other line of the water brigade. Mrs. Weston, garbed in a dark blue riding habit, was standing next to Lady Diana and Elizabeth was trudging over to where they stood staring at the fire.

Nell protested, but Charles gave her a warning look and said: "Now we can stand here arguing, an argument you shall lose, or you can let me go to work. Which shall it be, my lady?"

Nell knew when she was beaten—Charles was quite capable of picking her up and carrying her away from the line if need be. "Very well," she said. "I shall join Lady Diana and the others."

Reluctance in every step, Nell walked over to join the other ladies. Lady Diana embraced her. "Oh, Nell, it was so brave of you to help fight the fire." She turned a proud maternal smile on Elizabeth. "And you, Elizabeth, my darling, you were splendid."

Elizabeth smiled wanly. "I just hope that the house can be saved."

"With my son and stepson adding their might to fight the fire, you have nothing to fear now," said Sofia Weston with irritating assurance. "They will stop the fire."

None of the other three ladies made any reply, but Elizabeth and Nell exchanged glances. Under her breath Nell muttered, "And I suppose our efforts were meaningless."

Elizabeth choked back a laugh and looked away.

Sofia studied Nell for a moment, and Nell wondered if she had overheard her comment to Elizabeth.

"It is a good thing that my stepson and I decided to come to call this morning," Sofia said after an awkward moment.

"Yes, it was," Nell said meekly. "We are grateful for their help."

It was feared that the fire would spread internally and gut the house, but as the time passed, and more people arrived and a third and fourth line were formed, the battle to save the Dower House was won, bucket by bucket, pail by pail. Though there was still an appalling cloud of smoke billowing skyward, the yellow and red flames subsided.

Water continued to be thrown on the remains of the fire, but eventually there was no longer any obvious sign of flames. Smoke lingered heavily in the air and a hiss and a sizzling snap greeted each new bucket of water.

The small wing at the rear of the Dower House that had consisted of the kitchen, scullery, pantry, larder and coal yard was a total loss, but the main structure, connected to the kitchen by a covered walkway, had been spared. There was much comment on how lucky it had been that the coal yard had been almost empty at the time, else the fire in that area would have burned so hot that there would not have been any stopping it.

The fight won, amid much backslapping and self-congratulations, most of the servants gradually drifted away, back to their usual chores. While the Westons remained off to the side, Nell, Lady Diana and Elizabeth stood in a bedraggled reception line in front of the house thanking each person as they left the scene of the fire.

Having a private word with Dibble, Nell said, "Everyone was magnificent! Will you see to it that all are given an extra half day off within the week?"

Despite a streak of soot smearing his cheek and his usual immaculate livery stained and smelling of smoke, Dibble rose nobly to the occasion. Bowing regally, he said, "It shall be done, my lady."

When the last of the volunteers had departed, the three ladies walked to the back of the house to survey the damage. The Westons joined them. The foreman, the head carpenter and several of the men who had been working inside of the house when the fire started continued to monitor the smoky skeleton that had once been the kitchen area.

"How did it start?" Nell asked as she walked beside Lady Diana.

Her face wearing an expression of complete dejection, Lady Diana shrugged. "I don't really know. Elizabeth and I were going over some newly arrived samples of fabric from London when we smelled something burning. A few moments later we actually saw wisps of smoke curling around the edges of the doorway. We immediately fled out of the room where we met the foreman and some others running from the back of the house. They yelled at us to leave, that the house was on fire."

"Everything happened so fast," Elizabeth said, "that there was no time to ask any questions. We just ran. It wasn't until we got outside that we saw the flames and realized how dangerous the situation was." She shuddered. "Thank goodness we were able to stop it before the whole house was consumed."

A tear dripped down Lady Diana's cheek. "It is all ruined. Everything. All my beautiful rooms. I shall never be able to live here."

"Oh, now don't be hasty," Nell said, slipping an arm around Lady Diana's waist. "This is indeed a horrid setback, but just think—you will have a whole new kitchen wing."

Lady Diana looked at her. "I never go into the kitchen," she said in a small voice.

"Ah, but stop and think," Charles said as he walked up to join them, "with a new kitchen in which to work, your servants shall serve you meals whose praises will be sung by everyone fortunate enough to dine at your table."

When Charles's comment aroused nothing more than a heavy sigh in Lady Diana, Nell said bracingly, "I know it is a huge disappointment but you know there were some things that you'd had second thoughts about, now you will have a chance to do them over."

Lady Diana regarded her with big brown eyes swimming

in tears. "But the cost will be astronomical. And you know that we purchased the last bolt of cream silk with the pink rosebuds—it cannot be replaced." She choked back a sob. "Julian will be so angry. He is likely to banish Elizabeth and me from Wyndham Manor. Whatever shall we do? We will be homeless on the streets."

"Oh, good God!" Charles burst out. "Spare me these theatrics."

Nell sent him a speaking look and he shrugged. Followed by Raoul, he walked over to speak with the foreman. Turning to Lady Diana, Nell regarded her fondly. In the midst of the crisis, Lady Diana had been superb, organizing everyone with the skill of a great general planning a crucial battle, but now that the danger was past . . . Nell sighed. She supposed that her stepmama-in-law could not help being a pea-goose. She smiled. A very practical pea-goose, though.

Giving her a hug, Nell said, "You know very well that Julian will not toss you homeless onto the streets—besides, I would not let him if he were so shatterbrained to even consider such a thing. As for the cost—fiddle! I'm sure that he can stand the nonsense, and be happy to do so. His only concern will be that you and Elizabeth were unharmed." When Lady Diana still looked unconvinced, Nell added, "The fire was not of your making—it was an accident. Julian will not hold you accountable." Her jaw hardened and she glanced over to where Charles and Raoul were talking to the foreman. "He will be asking some hard questions of the workmen, though, of that you can be assured."

"Yes, of that I am sure," said Sofia Weston. "My nephew does not suffer fools gladly. I would not like to be in the shoes of those workmen."

Eventually, Nell, Lady Diana and Elizabeth, accompanied by the Westons, arrived back at Wyndham Manor. Excusing themselves to wash and change out of their sooty and stained gowns, the three ladies of the house disappeared up the stairs, leaving Dibble to serve refreshments to the Westons in the front drawing room.

Returning downstairs once more, Nell joined her guests. Lady Diana sent word that she was too fatigued to join the guests and begged their forgiveness. Elizabeth elected to stay with her mother. Everyone understood the situation.

Handing Nell a cup of tea, Charles said, "After this morning's event, you must be wishing us at Jericho."

She smiled at him. "No. No. I am just so grateful that you arrived when you did." An impish gleam leaped to her eye. "I *was* becoming tired."

He laughed. "And I'll wager that it cost you to admit that to me."

"But why should it?" demanded Sofia Weston. Her upper lip curled. "It must not have been pleasant working in the midst of one's servants."

With an effort Nell kept her smile in place. "It was most fortunate that you happened along," she said, taking a sip of her tea.

"Yes," replied Charles dryly. He glanced across at his brother. "And that Raoul decided to leave Lord Tynedale to his own devices and join us."

Raoul flushed. "He is our guest and our friend."

"But that doesn't mean that you have to dance attendance on him," Charles said.

Raoul looked as if he would have liked to continue the argument, but he said nothing. The look he shot his brother, however, was *not* fond.

"With the weather so fine, we had hoped to invite you to join us in a ride," Charles said. "Since that is out of the question, we shall be on our way." He glanced down at his own soot-stained clothing. "I, for one, am not fit to be seen in polite company."

Nell did not encourage them to stay but she did walk with them to the front of the house. Once Mrs. Weston had been settled on her horse, Charles and Raoul mounted their horses and the trio trotted away.

Arriving home late that afternoon from a fruitless quest, Julian was shocked at the news of the fire. His first concern was for his wife and it took all of Nell's persuasive powers to convince him that she and the baby were unharmed and that tearing the foreman from limb to limb would accomplish little. His main fears allayed, Julian didn't bat an eyelash at the information that Nell had promised Lady Diana a lavish budget to prepare the Dower House for her installation—including a new and enlarged kitchen wing. Having heard a concise report from Nell concerning the situation, he was quite able to endure Lady Diana's tears and to assure her that he had no intention of flinging her out of the house. Seeing that the ladies were unharmed, while there was still daylight, he and Marcus set out for the Dower House to examine the damage themselves . . . and, as Nell had suspected, to have a word with the workmen.

Work had already begun on clearing away the rubble that remained of the kitchen wing and Julian had no trouble finding the foreman. Leaving Marcus to poke around in the ruins, Julian took the foreman aside.

Standing several yards from the house, Julian asked, "Would you care to explain to me how this happened?"

The foreman, Jenkins, was a local man whose reputation for honest, hard work had convinced Julian to hire him instead of using someone from the estate. He was a sturdy fellow with a thatch of rusty-red hair just beginning to be threaded with gray and a workman's brawny arms and rough hands.

His weathered features grim, Jenkins rubbed his jaw. "Explanation's easy enough, my lord: someone left a burning candle in the kitchen near a pile of rags and some beeswax that had been used to polish the wainscoting we'd just installed the day before in the upper hallway."

"And how do you know that?

"Because when I smelled smoke I went in search of the source," Jenkins said. "When I entered the kitchen the fire was already burning steadily and the candle and rags were still in the middle of the room. I shouted for help and kicked the rags apart and began stamping on the fire. Two of my fellows heard my call and joined me, but it was no use. By then it was so smoky that we could hardly see and when the fire reached the north wall and began climbing, we knew that there was nothing we could do but see to it that everyone escaped safely."

"It would seem that you hire careless workmen," Julian said coolly, holding back the rage he felt that Lady Diana and Elizabeth had been put at risk and, more damning from his standpoint, that *Nell* had been placed in danger.

Jenkins's calm blue eyes met Julian's hard stare. "I do not," he said firmly, "hire careless workmen. These men have worked for me for years and there's not a fool or a careless man in the bunch. I've questioned them—in particular the man who left the rags and beeswax in the kitchen—and he swears that last night he threw the rags and such in the middle of the floor to be gathered up later today and taken outside. He swears that there was *no* candle in that room, or anywhere near that room."

"If it was not one of your men, then how do you think the candle ended up in the kitchen, conveniently near a pile of rags reeking of beeswax?" For a moment some of Julian's rage and fear leaked through. "Good God, man! The countess, endangering herself and the baby she carries, was here fighting to save the house!"

Jenkins dipped his head. "Indeed, my lord, and I am sorry for any danger your lady may have been in." Stubbornly, he added, "But the blame for the fire does not lie at my feet. It was no man of mine who left that candle burning in the kitchen."

"Then who?"

"I can't answer that, my lord." Jenkins hesitated, then cleared his throat. "There's been some gypsies in the area lately, they've been camping near Lord Beckworth's place, and you know how they are. A worst set of pilfering thieves I've never seen—nothing is safe with them around. It's possible that one of them set the fire to distract everyone so that the rest of them could steal things from anywhere they wanted while we were all busy fighting the fire."

Julian scowled. Gypsies would explain the missing items from the Dower House . . . but, the fire? It was possible. There seemed to be nothing more to be learned from Jenkins, so he dismissed him.

Looking for Marcus, he found him studying the remains of the kitchen wing. At Julian's approach he turned. "Did you discover anything of interest?" Marcus asked.

Julian related the news about the candle, the rags and the gypsies.

"Hmmm, it's possible," Marcus said, frowning. "Most are known to be light-fingered and crafty. The fire would have provided a great distraction and with everyone here, they could steal at will—the stables, the henhouse, the orangery and, if they dared, even the manor itself, all would have been worthy targets."

Julian's mouth grew grim. "You may be right. I'll talk to Farley and have him investigate."

Marcus glanced at the blackened ruins. "It's going to cost you a pretty sum to rebuild. Not to mention the work that must be redone because of the smoke damage."

"My wife has already informed me that she expects me to meekly meet any of Lady Diana's demands on my pocket-book and to not only gladly pay for all damages, but to have the kitchen wing enlarged and rebuilt with all speed." Julian grinned. "And it shall be worth every penny it will cost me if it keeps the females of my household happy."

"Aha! I told you that you would live under the cat's paw."

Julian laughed and motioned Marcus toward their horses. "Yes, it is true," he said, as they mounted, "but it is such a dainty paw, that I find I do not mind its weight at all."

Marcus sent him a narrow-eyed stare. "My God! Don't tell me you've gone and fallen in love with your own wife?"

Julian only smiled and would not be drawn. He spent the remainder of the day talking with his steward, his stable master and his butler. What he learned from them gave him little to smile about.

It was late when Julian went in search of his wife. Everyone had gone to bed and, wearing a heavy black silk robe, Julian entered Nell's rooms and found her halfway across the room, walking in his direction.

"Were you coming to call, my lady?" he asked, a warm light leaping to his eyes at the sight of her with her hair tumbling around her shoulders and only a diaphanous negligee of some misty-green color cloaking her body from his gaze.

"I was," Nell admitted with a laugh. "Did you think that you would escape telling me what you discovered today?"

"That thought never crossed my mind." Reaching out a hand, he added, "Come. We shall sit by the fire in my room."

Julian seated Nell near the cheery fire that burned on the grate in his rooms and handed her a small glass of ratafia. After serving himself a snifter of brandy, he sprawled comfortably in the chair next to hers, his long legs stretched toward the leaping flames.

"What a bloody wasted day," he said after taking a sip of his brandy. "When I think of the fire and what could have happened . . ."

"I was terrified when I saw all that black smoke and realized that it came from the Dower House," Nell admitted. "But once I was actually there and saw that Lady Diana and

Elizabeth were unharmed . . ." A faint smile crossed her face. "After that I was too busy to be frightened."

He reached out and took her hand. Kissing the back of it, he said huskily, "Dear God, Nell, when I think of you fighting that fire . . . If anything had happened to you and the babe, I do not think I could bear it."

Nell's heart swelled with delight. Catherine's reach from the grave *must* be fading. Why else would there be that note in his voice, that look in his eyes? More hopeful than she had been for a long time, she said cheerfully, "Do not worry about me. Remember, I survived a fall over a cliff. I am sure that throwing some buckets of water on a fire will not harm me, or our babe." When Julian remained silent, his gaze fixed moodily on the fire, she asked, "And your day? Were you able to see the dungeons at Squire Chadbourne's home?"

Julian's head dropped back against the chair and a smile curled his lips. "Oh, Lord, yes. Chadbourne fairly leaped at the idea of showing us around his prize. But Pierce looked at us as if we were candidates for Bedlam, I can tell you that."

"Was it . . . Did it resemble the place in my nightmare?"

Julian shook his head. "No. It was as clean and neat as our front drawing room. It had no sluice hole as in your nightmare, but there's a cistern down there that was used to store water in case of siege." He glanced at her. "Nell, the place was pristine—no smoke-stained walls, no stone . . . altar, for lack of a better word." He grinned at her. "He *did* have an iron maiden that sent him off into raptures when he showed it to us. I'm sure that he'll be happy to show it to you. Perhaps even let you fit inside it."

Nell shuddered at the thought of even viewing one of those iron-spiked monstrosities, much less trying it on for a fit. "No, thank you." She grimaced. "So your day was not very productive, either."

"I wouldn't say that. Squire was so delighted with Marcus's interest that he suggested that we see the dungeon at

Lord Beckworth's. Even offered to talk to Beckworth about it himself."

"Excellent! How wonderful for us that Squire will be the one to approach him."

"Yes, I suppose so," Julian said slowly. "I know Beckworth, but not well. He is closer to the squire's age than my own and I had been racking my brain for an excuse to pay him a visit." He took a sip of his brandy. "The squire's invitation seemed fortuitous, but Jenkins's mention of gypsies camping on Beckworth's land has also given me an excuse to call—and a more timely one."

Nell looked at him, her expression troubled. "Do you think that it was the gypsies that started the fire?"

"They're the most likely culprits. Unless you believe in ghosts." He took another sip of brandy. "I talked to Dibble and Farley and I found it most enlightening—there has been some minor pilfering over the past few weeks. And Hunter admits to having run several of them off my land, more than once. So, yes, I do think that the fire was caused by the gypsies. And I intend to call upon Lord Beckworth tomorrow to discuss the matter with him."

"Will you try to view his dungeons then?"

Julian shook his head. "No, I'll let Squire arrange that." When Nell looked disappointed he added, "I'll get to Beckworth's dungeons soon enough. In the meantime, Marcus and I can eliminate the ones that are rumored to be beneath the old Norman keep and the remains of the monastery." He frowned. "And those beneath Hunter's place." He looked across at her and smiled crookedly. "Believe me, I shall have plenty of dungeons to examine." He stood up and pulling her out of the chair, he kissed her neck. "But right now, there is this enticing bundle in my arms that requires my fullest examination."

Pressed next to him Nell could feel his bulging member. Heat swarmed through her lower body and when Julian's hand swept down over her hips and cupped her buttocks and pulled her even closer to him, her breath quickened and desire rose within her. Just the touch of his hands and she burned with hunger, her breasts swelling and excitement churning low in her belly.

Julian's lips brushed her ear. "I assume that you have no objections, my lady?" His teeth closed lightly on her lobe and Nell shivered, imagining them on her nipples.

Her arms went around his neck, her head fell back and with eyes already glazed with passion, she murmured, "I cannot think of even one, my lord."

His teeth a white flash in his dark face, Julian laughed and swung her up into his arms. He carried her to his bed and dropping her down on the soft, feather-filled mattress, he joined her. Plucking at the sash of her negligee, he said, "Now, where was I? . . . Ah, yes, I remember, I was *examining* you."

And examine her, he did. Twice. Very, very thoroughly.

The next morning the other ladies were not inclined to rise early, but Nell rose at her usual time. While Becky laid out her clothing for the day, Nell, wearing only a chemise, preened in front of the cheval glass, noting with pride that her once-flat abdomen now had a nice, noticeable bulge. A smile curved her mouth and she patted the little bulge.

Wearing an apricot gown of fine woolen material, her hair caught up in an olive green ribbon, she hurried down the stairs. Entering the morning room, she discovered that the two gentlemen were just finishing their breakfasts. She joined them and they remained, keeping her company while she sipped her tea and ate her usual hearty meal. The conversation was about the fire and Julian's plan to call on Lord Beckworth and talk to him about the gypsies. Marcus declined to accompany him, both men having privately agreed that it might be wise for one of them to remain at the house for the time being.

Nell knew very well what they were about and with a

sparkle in her sea green eyes, she asked, "Do you really think that the gypsies are going to launch a raid on the manor? Or that the moment your back is turned the Shadow Man is going to materialize and whisk me away to his dungeon?"

"No," Julian replied grimly. "But why take chances?"

Nell had no argument against that and shortly Julian departed to call upon Lord Beckworth. Since the weather held and the day was agreeable she and Marcus spent a pleasant morning touring the gardens. Nell suspected that he was bored but his innate politeness kept any sign of it from appearing in his manner. She took pity on him and excused herself, telling him that she wished to rest.

Upstairs in her rooms she wandered around restlessly. There were a thousand little tasks that she should be doing or overseeing, but none of them appealed. Absently patting the place where her child grew, she stood staring out the windows, thinking of Julian and their relationship. A faint blush pinked her cheeks when she thought of the way he had made love to her last night.

He must care for me, she thought for the thousandth time, and it *must* be more than respect and fondness that he holds for me. It cannot be mere kindness, or *just* lust that brings him to me. She turned last night over in her mind, considering his anxious features and his gratifying words: *"If anything happened to you and the babe, I do not think I could bear it."* Surely that denoted a deep feeling? Dare she hope that Catherine's hold on him had weakened? Or was it just the coming baby that aroused such strong emotions within him? Did he value her only as the vessel that carried his child? Her heart shrank a little in her breast. She'd rather die than be held in esteem for her abilities as a brood mare. And liking, respect, fondness and kindness were not enough. She wanted him to love her.

She sighed. Heaven knew she'd brought up Catherine's name often enough and had been firmly repulsed for it, too, she thought grimly. What was it that Catherine possessed that she didn't?

Her jaw set, she crossed the room and stepped out into the hall and surreptitiously headed for the gallery. It would have mortified her if anyone noticed that she spent an inordinate amount of time staring at the portrait of Julian's first wife.

But someone did notice the furtive air about her as she hurried to the gallery. Puzzled, Marcus discreetly followed her.

Reaching her destination, Nell stood in front of Catherine's portrait. Nothing had changed since the last time she'd been there—Catherine was still as petite, still as blonde, still as ethereally lovely as she had always been. For a second Nell's gaze rested on the fresh, lush bouquet of huge red roses beneath the portrait. She kept hoping that one day she would come here and there would be no roses—at least that would be a positive sign. But, no, she thought viciously, the bloody roses are here again.

She glared at the portrait. Catherine had been beautiful, of that there was no doubt, but so beautiful that her allure extended from the grave? How could she fight a dead woman? Nell wondered with despairing anger. Why couldn't Julian love *her*? At least she was *alive*. Rage shook Nell and forgetting not to let her angry despair get the upper hand, she once again snatched up the crystal vase of roses and smashed it on the floor. Shattered glass, water and roses flew everywhere. Heedless of the destruction she'd wrought, she stormed from the gallery. And this time she wasn't even ashamed of her actions.

Hidden in the shadows, Marcus watched the entire scene. Once Nell fled, he left his place of concealment and walked over to stand in front of Catherine's portrait. He looked at the portrait for several minutes, then at the ruined flowers. His gaze came back to Catherine's portrait. He stared a long time at that lovely face. And what, my pretty bitch, he wondered, are you up to now?

Chapter 18

By the time Julian had reached the driveway that led to Beckworth's home, he'd not yet decided precisely how he would present the situation to Lord Beckworth. He wished that he knew the man better. The only memory he had of him was of a dark, taciturn gentleman near his father's age, and some of those old gentlemen could be as stiff-rumped as they come and take offense at anyone daring to complain about decisions they made. His lips tightened. Like allowing gypsies to camp on their land.

As he was shown into a handsome library by Beckworth's butler, he decided that the easiest ways were usually the simplest and once the social niceties were dispensed with he plunged into his reason for calling. Bluntly he said, "Yesterday there was fire at the Dower House . . . and the suspicion was raised that it might have been started by some gypsies that are in the neighborhood."

Lord Beckworth grunted and shot him a look from under his brows. "The gypsies camping on my land?" he asked.

"Unless you know of any others in the area?"

Beckworth ran a hand over his face. "No, I'm afraid that I don't. Damme! I suspected there'd be trouble one of these days if I let those fellows camp in the south meadow." He shook his head. "When the poor buggers first showed up they seemed desperate and a decent lot, for gypsies, and I decided to take a chance on them. During the spring and summer I've let them camp there for the past couple of years now, but I should have known that sooner or later . . ." He grimaced. "Must be getting totty-headed in my old age." He took a long swallow of the ale that had been served. Slapping down the tankard hard on his desk, he said, "I'll have them run off before nightfall."

Julian hesitated. The reputation of gypsies for thievery of all sorts, be it livestock, jewelry or food, even small children, was legendary and their arrival in a new neighborhood, usually having been driven out by their previous unwilling hosts, was never greeted with joy by the local populace. Julian's sympathies lay with his tenants, but he realized that in bringing about the eviction of the gypsies, he was putting women and children on the road—and there was not yet any solid proof that they had started the fire, or stolen one item.

"Milord," he said, after a moment's reflection, "we do not know positively that it was the gypsies that started the fire or that they are responsible for the petty thievery that has been going on. Perhaps I could ride out and interview them first? I do not want to cause them any trouble if it can be avoided."

Beckworth nodded. "I appreciate that, my lord. I don't hold with liars and thieves, but I can't blame the wretched devils for trying to feed their families. As I said earlier, this particular tribe has camped here for a couple years now and except for some minor pilfering, have been a good lot." He cleared his throat. "I've grown to like the leader, Cesar, and occasionally I've hired him and some of his fellows to do some work for me. They've always done a good job for me, and I've yet to find anyone that has as good a hand with horses as Cesar."

Julian was surprised. Most landlords, at the first sight of the gaily colored gypsy wagons, didn't hesitate to run them off. That Beckworth had allowed them not once but several times to camp on his lands, and had a good word to say about them, made him an unusual man.

When Beckworth offered to show him where the gypsies were camped, Julian gladly accepted.

It was a lovely spot where the gypsies made their summer home: a big, grassy meadow ringed by the remnants of an old orchard with a burbling stream running along the edge of it. There were a half dozen or so brightly painted—green and yellow, scarlet and gold—gypsy wagons parked in an irregular circle near one side of the meadow; several stout, flashy piebald horses were staked out here and there with a couple of scrawny milk cows and some goats mingled amongst them. A dozen chickens and a pair of geese scratched for food around the wagons; six or seven men, some with scarlet and blue handkerchiefs wrapped around their heads and gold earrings dangling from their ears, lounged near an open fire that burned in the middle of the camp. Three women were busy washing clothes in the creek and several children ran yelling and laughing throughout the camp followed by a pack of skinny mongrels.

The dogs got wind of the newcomers and gave tongue. Instantly, the women stopped their tasks and grabbed the nearest child and hurried to the wagons. The men leaped to their feet and watched with wary, suspicious eyes as Julian and Beckworth rode toward them.

They were, Julian thought, a defiant, ragged little group, and pity stirred in his breast. Their lot was not a happy one, and while they brought most of their misery on themselves, he wondered what it would be like to be shunned and viewed with contempt and mistrust everywhere one went. Most of his concern was for the children, though, the expression in their big dark eyes making him uncomfortable.

The leader, a tall, strikingly handsome man, with wings of silver at his temples and hoops of gold at his ears, stepped forward. "Milords. How may I serve you?"

Julian studied the green-eyed, swarthy-faced man standing before him and recognizing those familiar features, his heart sank. Damn his grandfather! When the offspring of his grandfather's dalliances were of honest folk, it was difficult enough to know how to deal with them, but now it appeared that the Old Earl had at some point, lusted after a gypsy maiden. How, he wondered, was he going to break the news to Charles and Marcus that they now had a gypsy uncle?

Staring at the other man, he sighed. Oh, bloody hell. What did he do now? It went against the grain to turf out a relative—even one on the wrong side of the blanket. Particularly, he thought wearily, one on the wrong side of the blanket.

It was apparent from the narrowing of the other man's green eyes that he, too, saw the similarity in their features and recognized their significance. A wry smile tugged at the corner of his shapely mouth. "I am called Cesar and you can be none other than the Earl of Wyndham, yes?" His tongue in cheek, he added, "I believe that my mother was perhaps acquainted with your father?"

"Grandfather," Julian said in clipped tones, then cursed himself for even acknowledging the other man's impertinence. What the devil did he say now? Pleased to meet you . . . Uncle?

Beckworth, noticing for the first the time the undeniable resemblance between the two men, was nonplused. Deciding hastily that only a fool would step into *that* situation, he harrumphed loudly and cleared his throat. "Yesterday some property of the earl's caught fire," he said. "Do you know anything about it?"

Cesar appeared genuinely taken aback. "No, milord. We were at a peddlers' fair near the village of Lympstone. We were gone all day—left before first light and returned at dark." He smiled again and waved toward the men near the fire. "Hence you find us resting and taking our leisure."

Gypsies were known to learn to lie at their mother's breast, but something in the way Cesar's eyes met his made Julian think that he was telling the truth. "It's been discovered that several items are missing from my estate," Julian said carefully, "including some bolts of expensive material . . . Would you or your fellows know anything about that?"

Something flickered in Cesar's eyes, but then he shrugged. "How could we, milord?" he asked, his face the picture of innocence. "We are but poor gypsies. We know nothing of a grand lord's estate—you may search our wretched belongings if you wish." Amusement glittered in the depths of those green eyes. "I can assure you that you will find nothing of yours amongst them."

Looking down into that guileless face, Julian fought back a laugh. Whatever they might have stolen from him, they had, no doubt, sold at the peddlers' fair yesterday. Cesar was an impudent cur and brazen in the bargain but much against his will, he could not help liking him.

"Then I won't waste my time," Julian said. "I came to Lord Beckworth's with the intention of having you driven from his lands . . ." Julian paused, and his gaze hard and direct, locked with Cesar's. "However, if I can be assured that there will be no more, er, missing items from my estate, I will intercede for you."

Cesar studied Julian for a long minute, then nodded. "You have nothing to fear from my tribe—this I promise you."

They regarded each other for another moment, each man taking the other's measure before Julian turned his horse away. To Beckworth, he said, "Shall we leave, my lord? I believe the matter is settled—unless you disagree."

"No, no, fine with me." Beckworth bent a stern eye on Cesar. "I trust there'll be no more complaints from any of my neighbors."

A shameless smile curved Cesar's mouth. "I assure you, my lord, that no one of great esteem will come calling with complaints."

Beckworth gave a bark of laugher. "Watch your step, you brazen dog—I may have to throw you off my lands yet."

Cesar bowed. "I shall do my best to see that does not happen, my lord."

Leaving the gypsies behind, Julian and Beckworth rode toward Beckworth's home. They rode in silence for a moment, then Beckworth said, "Don't mean to intrude, my lord, but did you, uh, know about Cesar?"

Julian sighed. There was no use pretending that he didn't know what Beckworth was referring to—nor in being offended by it—the Old Earl's proclivities were well known. "No. I'm afraid that my grandfather did not leave a list of all the ladies who caught his, er, attention."

"Devilish situation," Beckworth said with sympathy.

"You don't know the half of it, my lord," Julian muttered.

Returning home that afternoon and finding that Lady Diana and Elizabeth were still in their rooms, he quickly arranged a meeting with Marcus and Nell. Briefly he related what he had learned, including the fact that he and Marcus had a new relative.

"A damn gypsy!" Marcus exclaimed. "My God, was there nothing in skirts that our grandfather ignored?"

"I do not believe . . . as yet," Julian said mildly, "that we have discovered an aunt or uncle birthed by a nun."

"Well, thank the good Lord for that!"

Nell looked at Marcus curiously. "Does it bother you to have a gypsy uncle? I would find it exciting. They are the most romantic of creatures."

"Romantic! You wouldn't think so if it were your relative." Looking austere and shaking a finger at her, he said, "Just you wait until Julian has to intercede to keep this curst new uncle of ours from swinging on the gallows—then we'll see how exciting you find it." His expression changed in a twinkling and grinning, he admitted, "Devilish situation, can't deny it. But it's not the gypsy blood that I object to so much as I fear the day that Julian finds them camped on his front steps and he's saddled with the care and feeding of the whole lot of them."

"You don't think that they shall search you out and batten

down on you?" Julian asked, a glimmer of amusement in his eyes.

Marcus looked innocent. "Me? Oh, no, they won't bother me—you're the one with the title and the soft-hearted one in the family." He grinned. "And the richest."

"Perhaps all that is true, but I believe I have Cesar's measure and I doubt that he will come to call with his hand out." Julian smiled and added, "Now, pilfering a chicken or two and snagging some eggs, *that* I am more than certain he would do—with impunity."

The weather turned ugly again the next day and February faded into March with little change in the gray, wet skies. Work continued on the Dower House, but nothing could be done about rebuilding the ruined kitchen wing until the weather broke. The weather also kept Julian and Marcus from continuing their search for the dungeon site of Nell's nightmares, although they had, taking advantage of one clear day, eliminated the ancient Norman keep as a possibility. If there had been a dungeon on the site, the stone walls of the keep had fallen in on themselves and obliterated any signs of it.

Staring out the window at the drizzling rain one morning near the middle of March, Nell sighed. The rain had not been the steady onslaught that it had been in February, but there was never more than a day of dry weather—and very little sun—before rain returned. It wasn't even, she thought wryly, as if it was actually storming all the time, although there'd been a few of them, but if they weren't in the midst of a storm, they were treated, as they were today, to persistent drizzle that made outside activities unappealing and unpleasant.

Turning away from the window, she considered the plans for the day. Lady Diana and Elizabeth would be full of chatter about the Dower House; Julian and Marcus would, no doubt, since hunting or any outside activity was precluded, lock themselves away in the library or the billiard room, and that left her as odd man out. She glanced down at her nicely swelling abdomen and smiled. She might have time on her hands right now, but once the baby arrived, there'd be few free moments—she could hardly wait. Caressing the little lump, she murmured, "So what shall we do today? Join the other ladies? Inventory the linen closets? Mend? Count the silver with Dibble? Read? Harass the servants?"

Not receiving an answer she glanced outside again. Oh, but how she would love to go riding or for a long walk. Yes, even on a day like today. She was so tired of winter.

But if she was bored and tired of being locked inside, she took comfort from the fact that there had been no new nightmares. Ann Barnes had been buried and her family left to grieve. The locals had accepted the story of a fall from the cliffs and beyond bemoaning such a sad and needless fate there was no further talk.

The arrival of the mail that afternoon further damped her spirits. Her father wrote that his visit to her would be delayed—he'd fallen from a horse and, dashed if he hadn't broken his leg. It would be summer before he could come to Wyndham Manor. Nell tried not to be disappointed, but she was. Terribly.

She missed her family. She was very fond of Lady Diana and Elizabeth and Marcus . . . She smiled. Marcus was a great friend and a good companion. As for Julian—her pulse leaped—she loved him more than life itself, and if it was not for Catherine's presence in his heart, she'd be almost content. Her lips drooped. What a hen-hearted creature she was! Rebuffed every time she dared to mention Catherine's name to him, she'd given up trying to get Julian to talk about his dead wife and beaten a craven retreat. She had, she admitted dully, even reached the point where it didn't matter, at least not too much, that Julian did not love her, she just wanted him to stop loving Catherine!

As often whenever her thoughts turned to Catherine, she walked out of her rooms and made her way to the gallery. She stared glumly at the latest bouquet of fragrant scarlet rosebuds, unable even to rouse the rage that had shaken her a few weeks ago. She glanced again at the lovely face in the portrait and then, sighing, drifted away.

Since the day of the shattered vase, Marcus had made it a point to determine if Nell's visit to Catherine's portrait had been an aberration or something she did frequently. Spying discreetly on Nell, he discovered that it was indeed a habit, one he thought was decidedly unhealthy. His first instinct was to tell Julian of his wife's odd obsession with Catherine's portrait, but he hesitated to run to Julian bearing tales. Tattling or interfering between a man and his wife was not something any man with any sense considered with pleasure, and at a loss to understand Nell's fascination with Julian's first wife, Marcus watched and waited, hoping inspiration would strike. It did not.

Yet watching Nell's slender figure disappear into the gray gloom of the hallway, he decided grimly that he could wait no longer. Something must be done. There was an unwholesome air about this entire situation and he wondered that Julian had not put a stop to it. He started as it occurred to him that Julian might not even know of Nell's fascination with his first wife. His gaze fell upon the fresh arrangement of rosebuds and another thought struck him: what the devil did Julian mean by sending flowers to a woman dead and buried? Particularly, a woman who had made his life a living hell?

That night after the ladies had retired from the dining room, leaving Julian and Marcus to their port, Marcus could keep a still tongue no longer. He and Julian were lounging near the table, glasses of port at their elbows, when he took the plunge.

Having decided that there was no easy way about this,

Marcus asked bluntly, "I do not mean to pry, but will you tell me why you have a monstrous bouquet of newly plucked flowers placed before Catherine's portrait every day?"

Julian jerked as if he had been stabbed. "What the bloody hell are you talking about?"

Marcus cocked a brow. "You didn't order the flowers?"

"This is the first I've heard of them," Julian snapped, scowling. "Good God! She's been dead for years—why would I still be doing such a damn silly thing?"

"Guilt, perhaps? Or because you still care about her? Honoring her memory?"

Marcus had never feared Julian before, but he found himself actually bracing himself in his chair at the expression on his cousin's face as Julian leaped to his feet and loomed in front of him.

Through clenched teeth, Julian said, "By the time she died, as you damn well know, there was nothing between Catherine and me *to* honor."

Leaving Marcus to stare after him, Julian stormed out of the room. Marcus followed on his heels as Julian took the stairs two at time, heading for the gallery.

The gallery was in darkness, but Julian lit a candelabrum and strode over to where Catherine's portrait hung. In disbelief he stared at the roses, the buds just opening and perfuming the air.

Biting back a curse, Julian found the black bell rope and yanked so hard that Marcus feared he would tear it from the wall. Throwing Marcus a violent look, Julian said, "I never ordered these curst flowers, but I certainly intend to find out who did!"

Dibble appeared a few minutes later, an expression of concern on his face. The clatter of the bell summoning him had been quite dramatic. "Milord, is something amiss?"

Julian pointed to the bouquet. "Would you please explain those?"

Dibble looked at the bouquet, then back at Julian's taut

features. "Uh, it's a bouquet of roses beneath Lady Catherine's portrait."

"I see that," Julian snapped, "but upon whose orders are they placed here?"

"Why yours, my lord," Dibble answered, looking mystified. "I assure you that I have always had a new bouquet sent up from the greenhouse every day."

"Odd, but I do not remember *ever* asking for flowers to be placed here."

Dibble looked even more mystified, then his brow cleared. "I beg pardon, my lord, it was your father who originally asked for the bouquets." He smiled fondly. "He came to me the day after Lady Catherine was buried and said that you would like it if she had fresh flowers every day." When Julian just stared at him, his smile faded. "Have I done wrong, my lord? Perhaps after your father died I should have consulted with you, but I assumed . . ." He cleared his throat, clearly distressed. "I just assumed that if you had wanted me to stop preparing a fresh arrangement every day, you would have said so. Have I erred in some way?"

Aware that it was not his butler's fault, Julian's fury ebbed. "No, you have not—the mistake was mine," Julian said with an effort. "I should have cancelled those orders long ago—it never occurred to me that you were still carrying them out."

"You wish me to stop bringing the flowers, my lord?"

Julian nodded. "Yes. No more flowers for Lady Catherine. Take that bouquet with you now and dispose of it."

Dibble lifted the huge bouquet and quietly departed, leaving the two men alone.

"Did you know that your father had made the request for the flowers?" Marcus asked.

"What do you think?" Julian demanded. "Of course, I didn't—if I had I would have countermanded the order immediately." Julian shook his head. "My father never saw any of her faults and he turned a blind eye to the problems in the marriage. He wanted me to be happy and simply ignored anything that ran contrary to that belief." He made a face. "I certainly never disillusioned him—I let him think that I adored her and that she adored me. I'm sure he went to the grave believing that a part of me died with Catherine."

Marcus stared at him, comprehension dawning. "Er, you don't think that he might have said something to that effect to Lady Diana, do you?"

"Probably," Julian replied carelessly. "I'm sure he spun her a tale of my undying love for Catherine. Why?"

"Because I believe your lady thinks just that," Marcus said slowly.

Julian's brows snapped together. "Don't talk fustian! I doubt that beyond a brief tour that my wife has been to the gallery or even knows where Catherine's portrait hangs. And as for the other—don't be ridiculous!"

"Oh, you're wrong there," Marcus said. "Your wife knows exactly where this portrait hangs. I've seen her studying it, more than once."

"Why the devil would she do that?"

"Oh, I could imagine that Lady Diana and Elizabeth probably showed her the gallery one day . . . and that they stopped to admire the portrait and lamented Lady Catherine's tragic death . . ."

Julian paled. In hollow accents, he said slowly, "And Lady Diana, no doubt, repeated the fairy tale that my father had told her . . ." He swallowed convulsively and his fist clenched. "The flowers, the bloody flowers would give the story credence."

"Come along," Marcus ordered gently. "Let us return to the library and I shall tell you what I have observed. You may make of it what you will."

Nell was lying in bed looking at some new fashion plates that had arrived from her modiste in London when the door to her room was flung open so violently that it banged like a thunderclap against the wall. She sat upright as Julian, pale and shaken, charged into the room. Striding across the room, he grabbed both her arms and jerked her against him.

"You silly little fool," he muttered, "you cannot believe that I am still in love with Catherine—not when just the sound of your voice leaves me breathless with delight!" He shook her. "Don't you understand? Until you came into my world, I thought that my life was complete, that I was content, but oh, God, I was wrong, so very wrong." His lips brushed her brow. "Nell, darling, I love you. You are *everything* to me!"

Nell stared stunned up into his dark, beloved face. "You don't love Catherine?" she asked urgently, her fingers tightening on the lapels of his mulberry jacket. "Everyone says so."

He smiled tenderly at her. "I don't know who everyone is, but believe me, my darling, everyone is wrong. I do not love Catherine. I never loved Catherine."

"But the flowers—a fresh, beautiful bouquet every day!"

"A miscommunication. There will never be another vase of flowers delivered to the gallery again."

Nell couldn't quite take it all in, but stars began to peep into her lovely eyes. "You love me?"

"I adore you! I do not remember the exact moment I fell in love with you, but you have been in my heart almost from the moment I laid eyes on you." He shook her again, not gently. "How could you possibly think that I still loved Catherine? Didn't my lovemaking, my pleasure in your company tell you anything?"

She rested her forehead against his chest. "I thought that you were merely making the best of our marriage and that you were only being kind . . ."

Sinking down onto the bed beside her, Julian pulled her close. "Making the best of—! What a little goose you have been! You are the best thing, the most wonderful thing that has ever happened to me and when I am with you *kindness* is the last thought on my mind."

"But that could just be lust," she argued, a little smile curving her mouth, dizzy joy spiraling through her as belief in his words took root. *He loved her!* And *not,* she thought happily, Catherine!

"I do have lust aplenty for you, Madame wife, oh, but Nell, I do adore you!" He pulled her to his chest and cupping the back of her head, brought their mouths together. He kissed her, holding nothing back, hiding nothing, letting his kiss reveal the depth of his emotions.

When he released her, Nell was thoroughly dazzled. His gaze traveled over her features and a teasing gleam entered his eyes. "And have you nothing to say to me? I have just lain my heart at your feet—I hope you do not intend to trample it."

Nell gave an enchanting gurgle of laughter and, raining soft kisses over his face, she said, "I love you! I love you! I love you! I have been sick with love for you for months."

What could he do after that but kiss her again?

For a long time they lay together cocooned from the world, speaking of those things that only lovers know. It was magical, in between sweet kisses, all the anxieties, the doubts, the fears and the uncertainties that had plagued them explained and swept aside.

What seemed like hours later, Julian said, "I still find it astonishing that you believed that I was still in love with Catherine."

"What else could I think?" Nell argued. "Every time I mentioned her name, you became cold and refused to talk about her. And Lady Diana told me how much you loved her and how your heart was buried in Catherine's grave."

Julian snorted, making it clear what he thought of Lady Diana's opinion. Nell pinched him. "And what about the flowers? Seeing that new bouquet every day—anyone would have thought so!"

He turned his head and smiled lazily at her. "Only a little

goose like you—anyone with any sense would have known that I was mad about you."

Nell's breath caught in her throat. "Are you really?" she asked shyly.

"Completely besotted," he murmured against her mouth. "Utterly and completely captivated by you." He kissed her. "I will be in love with you until the day I die—and beyond." He kissed her again. "Never doubt it, Nell, never."

That something momentous had happened overnight was obvious to the entire household. While there was no overt change between Nell and Julian, there was a difference, something in the air around them, a lightness of spirit, a quiet joy that accompanied them and filled the house like the perfume of lilacs on a spring day.

Marcus commented on it that evening. The ladies were in the drawing room and he and Julian were once again enjoying a glass of port before joining them.

Grinning across at his cousin, he said, "The smell of April and May has been overpowering today. I take it that all is well with you and your lady?"

Julian smiled at him, a soft inward smile that Marcus had never seen before. "You could say that." He glanced at Marcus. "She loves me," he said simply. "As I love her."

"And that, my friend, definitely calls for a toast." Raising his glass, Marcus said, "To your happiness."

The gray, rainy weather continued nearly unabated for the entire month of March. There were never more than two days in a row that it did not rain. The sun did manage to show its great golden face a few days but they were few and far between.

Locked inside as they were and unable to do much but speculate about the Shadow Man and watch the rain, Marcus seriously considered returning to his own home. "I might as well," he said to Julian one night. "I can do nothing here."

"You would leave me to the mercies of a household of women?" Julian demanded.

"Who adore you and have given you the mistaken impression that the world revolves around you!"

"Precisely why you should stay—think how insufferable I shall become without you to remind me that I am only a mere human."

Marcus had laughed and there was no more talk of his leaving.

As April, with her promise of spring, rolled around everyone became hopeful that winter was over. Eventually the skies did clear and with exception of the occasional small shower, the days that followed were filled with bright sunshine. At the end of the second week of April, when it did indeed seem that winter had departed for good, like birds released from gilded cages, the inhabitants scattered in all directions. Lady Diana and Elizabeth immediately set out for the Dower House and Julian and Marcus decided that they would eliminate the old monastery from their list of prospects. Feeling there was no harm in it, Julian invited Nell to accompany them. An invitation she promptly accepted, giving him no time to have second thoughts. The day was fine, and though an exploration of the remains of the monastery revealed no dungeons, it proved enjoyable.

Returning to the house, Nell discovered that Mrs. Weston had sent over an invitation to dine at Stonegate the following week. While things were better between Julian and the Westons, Tynedale's continued presence as their guest created problems.

Going in search of Julian, she found him in his library reading a note, the contents of which had brought a frown to his face. Seeing Nell, his expression instantly cleared, a warm light leaping to his eyes.

Waving the invitation at him, she said, "Mrs. Weston is having a party and she has invited us. The whole neighborhood is invited it seems and I hate to decline, but if Tynedale is there . . ."

"And he is," Julian replied, pointing to his own note. "Charles wrote me, warning me of that fact."

"Now why would he do that? Do you think that Charles knows what part Tynedale played in our marriage?"

"No, it is because of Tynedale's part in Daniel's death that he warns me—he knows how I feel about him."

"Doesn't he hold him in abhorrence also?" Nell asked, curiosity in her face. "Wasn't he fond of Daniel?"

"I have no doubt about Charles's feeling for Daniel. He told me himself that he loved Daniel, and that he also blames himself for what happened," Julian said. "And I asked Charles to explain why he tolerates Tynedale but he wouldn't say." He frowned. "One thing I do know: Charles has his own reasons for befriending Tynedale, but what they are, I cannot even guess."

Nell made a face. "So what shall I do about the invitation?"

Julian came from around his desk and pulled her into his arms. Dropping soft kisses over her face, he murmured, "Do not fret over it. There will be other parties, ones without Tynedale to mar our enjoyment."

Nell leaned her head against his shoulder. "What would you say if I accepted the invitation?"

Surprised, he looked down into her face. "Why?"

She wrinkled her nose at him. "To show Tynedale that he has no power over us." She kissed his chin. "In fact we owe the wretched man a debt of gratitude—without his wicked actions, we might never have met, or married . . . or fallen in love."

"Or fallen in love," Julian repeated huskily, his gaze warm on her face. "Do you know, I think we shall attend that party." He kissed her. "And Tynedale be damned!"

Chapter 19

The weather continued mild and sunny and the night of Mrs. Weston's party was a delightful spring evening. With great anticipation the ladies of Wyndham Manor had looked forward to the night and especially to mingling with friends and acquaintances. New gowns had been procured from a pair of local seamstresses in Exmouth and as the carriage pulled away from the manor, each lady knew that she looked her best.

Nell, wearing a confection of periwinkle and lace, had never appeared lovelier. Her sea green eyes sparkled and she fairly glowed, the soft color of the gown intensifying the natural beauty of her skin. A white silk cape cloaked her shoulders, white gloves were on her hands, and with her tawny hair piled high on her head and wearing a necklace of pearls and diamonds that matched the gleaming jewels at her ears, she looked every inch a countess. The rounded curve of her belly was not so pronounced as to detract from the elegant picture she made. In fact, Julian thought the signs of her advancing pregnancy only added to her beauty—but then, he admitted wryly, he was somewhat prejudiced when it came to his wife.

Mrs. Weston had invited nearly the entire neighborhood. Squire, his wife and eldest son, Lord Beckworth and Dr. Coleman were in attendance as were several other notables in the area including the magistrate and his wife, and one of the largest landowners in the area, Mr. Blakesley, along with his wife, his eldest son and only daughter. Mrs. Chadbourne had a niece visiting who was around Elizabeth's age and, coupled with the vicar's wife, his widowed youngest sister and his two eldest daughters, the numbers rounded out nicely.

Stonegate was aglow, every sconce, candelabrum and chandelier glittering brightly from the dancing flames of hundreds of candles. The party had turned into a small ball; there was music from hired musicians and dancing in the ballroom at the side of the house. Crystal punch bowls and trays laden with dainty finger food rested on long tables adorned with white linen and orchids and lilies grown in the estate's greenhouses; servants in crisp livery moved silently and swiftly through the guests, offering even more variety of food and drink.

When it became too warm in the ballroom, French doors thrown wide beckoned the guests to wander outside; the garden paths were strewn with gaily colored paper lanterns that cast a soft glow over the area. After several dances, Julian escorted Nell for a brief walk through the gardens.

"Tynedale," Julian said as soon as they were out of earshot of anyone else, "seems to be on his best behavior—or at least he's keeping his distance from us. Perhaps we will get through this night without scandal . . . or bloodshed."

Nell shot him an anxious glance. "You don't think that he would be foolish enough to—"

Julian shrugged. "So far he seems to be behaving just as he ought. He has kept discreetly in the background and has made no move to interject himself into any group of which I am a part." He looked down at her. "More importantly, he has not been foolish enough or brazen enough to solicit your hand for a dance."

"Indeed not!" Nell exclaimed. "Once he came toward me and I thought he might dare, but then he seemed to think better of it and asked the vicar's sister to dance instead."

He ran a caressing finger down the side of her cheek. "A good thing, too—I would hate to call him out." He stole a brief kiss. "Tynedale aside," he said, "are you enjoying yourself?"

She smiled at him. "Most assuredly. Charles is a wonderful dancer and full of the most amazing tales. Did you really put a dead fish on the collection plate when you were nine?"

Julian laughed. "Guilty. Lord, I'd forgotten about that. Leave it to Charles to bring it up."

"It is a good thing that the troubles between you have been resolved, is it not?"

Julian rubbed his chin. "I don't know that they've been resolved, but we are certainly on a better footing than we have been in years—and that, my sweet, is indeed a good thing."

Eventually the guests were escorted into the dining room and a lavish meal was served. Everyone was in high spirits and laughter filled the room. At the end of the meal, Mrs. Weston arose from the table and regally led the ladies into the front salon, leaving the gentlemen to enjoy their liquor.

Nell was tired. Despite her enjoyment, the party was not without anxiety. Avoiding Tynedale without appearing to and keeping an eye out that he never edged too close to where Julian stood took their toll. She had no doubt that she could depress his pretensions should he dare to approach her, but Julian's reaction to his close proximity worried her. She was enjoying the party, but not as she would have if Tynedale had not been present. Secure at last in Julian's love she no longer worried about the possible scandal that Tynedale could cause by alluding to the real circumstances surrounding their marriage, but he was still a snake, albeit one with most of his poison spent. As she and Julian had discussed, without exposing himself as a bounder beyond the pale, Tynedale could not say much, although if he pretended that the kidnapping was really an elopement, it might prove awkward.

She smiled. She didn't even worry about that anymore—

together she and Julian could face down any gossip that could arise. Yet Tynedale still represented a possible threat to her future happiness and as the ladies left the dining room, she was apprehensive that he might goad Julian into unwise action. Knowing that Tynedale and Julian were in the dining room together, even amongst several other level-headed gentlemen, made her uneasy. That drink would be flowing freely added to her unease—gentlemen in their cups were known to act foolishly . . .

Nell had reason to be uneasy. Tynedale had covered his true emotions all evening, hiding the resentment, hatred and jealousy that raged in his breast behind exquisite manners and a polite smile. Surreptitiously, he'd noted the interplay between Julian and Nell, the tender expression in Julian's eyes when they rested on his wife's lovely features, the glow on Nell's face when Julian led her out to dance and the air of sweet intimacy that existed between them. Only a fool wouldn't have recognized the fact that they were deeply in love. And Tynedale was no fool.

The sight of Nell's expanding pregnancy added to his fury, knowing that except for a trick of fate, it could be his child growing there, *his* heir, not Wyndham's. From under lowered lids, he'd glared at Wyndham, cursing him for not only being wealthy beyond compare, but for stealing the heiress that he'd chosen for himself. Nell's fortune and child should have been *his!* Wyndham had stolen it all from him. Cheated him. Brought him to the brink of ruin—his estates were so encumbered that he doubted he'd ever tow them from the River Tick—and just as devastating: Wyndham could demand payment of all those vowels whenever the whim suited him.

Bitterly Tynedale admitted that if he'd not forced an invitation from Raoul to visit, he'd have been at a standstill. The situation was so bad, he dared not even show his face at his own estate—the bloodsuckers were probably even now clamoring at the gates, dunning him to the very steps of his ancestral abode. Marriage to Nell would have changed all that and when he considered the difference that marriage would have made, his malice and hatred of Wyndham grew. Damn Wyndham. Damn him!

After the ladies left the dining room, Tynedale continued to brood. His predicament was all Wyndham's fault and he dwelt again on Wyndham's crimes against him: Wyndham had stolen a fortune from him. Wyndham had married the woman who should have been his bride. And it was Wyndham who had scarred him for life. Unconsciously he fingered that puckered red mark.

Julian saw Tynedale touch the scar and a cool smile lifted the corners of his mouth. At least I did that much for Daniel, he thought as he sipped his port, regretting that he could not have done more. In different circumstances he might have been willing to let bygones be bygones. Tynedale had brought Nell into his life and, despite the circumstances of it, for that Julian could have forgiven him much, but not for the ruination and death of an innocent youth. Julian's jaw clenched.

"Let it be," Marcus said quietly, interrupting and guessing his thoughts. "Tynedale's fate shall be none of your making now."

"Though it galls me to admit it, you are probably right," Julian said. He glanced again at the scar. "At least his face is not so pretty anymore."

"Yes, I agree," drawled Charles from behind Julian, "but it is a pity you didn't finish the job. He wants killing."

Charles had been roaming around the room, being the perfect host as he stopped to chat with first this gentleman and then that. His circuit had eventually brought him to the area where Julian and Marcus were sitting with their chairs pushed away from the table.

"Now why do you feel that way?" Julian asked with a raised brow, as Charles came to stand beside him.

His eyes on Tynedale, Charles took a sip of the brandy he was drinking. "Daniel is not the only young fool to come under Tynedale's spell."

Julian's breath caught and he looked down the long table where Raoul sat in the group around Tynedale. "Are you saying that *Raoul* has fallen into his clutches?"

Charles shrugged. "There has to be some explanation for his sudden fondness for the man. Raoul is not the gambler that I am, and I know that his mother has warned him that she will not tolerate massive losses at the gaming table." He smiled thinly. "If I had to guess the reason for my brother's present predilection for him, I'd say it's because he owes Tynedale money." Charles looked across the room where Raoul was laughing at something that Chadbourne had said. "I suspect that Raoul is postponing the evil moment that he has to go to my dear stepmother for the money to cover this latest batch of gaming debts. In the meantime, he allows Tynedale to batten down on him."

"Is that why you wanted the vowels? To bargain with him?"

"It had crossed my mind."

"Well, why the devil didn't you say so?" Julian demanded. "You know that under those circumstances I would have gladly given them to you."

Charles looked at him, an odd smile curving his hard mouth. "Perhaps, I just wanted you to trust me to do the right thing."

"Oh, good gad!" burst out Marcus. "Of all the maudlin . . ." He glared at Charles. "You always were too arrogant and puffed up with yourself for comfort."

"And you were always too bloody smug of your own worth," Charles said, smiling sweetly at Marcus.

Julian sighed. How often as children had they scrabbled thus? "Gentlemen," he said softly, "could we please leave these infantile insults behind us?"

Marcus and Charles stared at each other, neither giving an inch until Marcus made a face and laughed. "I will . . . if he will."

Charles grinned and bowed. "You have my word."

"So what," Julian asked, "are we going to do about Tynedale?"

His eyes once again on Tynedale, Charles said, "Kill him."

"I'd be happy to," Julian murmured, his gaze also on Tynedale, "but short of murder, I see no way of that happening."

"I suppose I could challenge him to a duel," Marcus offered, looking in Tynedale's direction.

Tynedale must have felt their collective gazes, because he glanced in their direction, his practiced smile freezing when he realized that all three men were staring at him. He recovered himself almost immediately and turned away, laughing apparently at some quip offered by Pierce Chadbourne. Made uneasy by the knowledge that the other three men were watching him, he managed to move his chair so that he was obscured from their view by a hideous sterling silver epergne that Mrs. Weston insisted gave the table elegance.

Why were they staring at him? he wondered. That they held no fondness for him, he didn't doubt. That they would shed no tears if misfortune was to befall him, he also knew. So what were they thinking? Were they planning some attack against him? He gulped down a glass of wine, stoking his courage, considering the possibilities. He had no argument with Sherbrook or Weston, either one, but by God! He would welcome the chance to meet Wyndham again . . . and kill him.

The possibilities blinded him. If Wyndham was to die . . . And Nell was to miscarry or the child was to be born dead, which would be easy enough to arrange . . . Weston would step into his cousin's boots. Raoul would then be only one person away from inheriting the title and the enormous fortune that went with it. Tynedale smiled. He would be very happy to help Raoul waste it away. Best of all, Nell would be a widow, with a fortune of her own. His first attempt to coerce her into marriage had failed, but he was wiser now and he'd plan better. A crafty gleam entered his eyes. Why not?

Why the bloody hell not? Time was against him; the sooner Wyndham joined the ranks of the dead, the sooner the grieving Countess Wyndham could be rid of the brat she carried and become Lady Tynedale—and gossip be damned!

Tynedale stood up. Everything was falling into place. He even had his dueling pistols with him . . . He smiled again. They were very special, those pistols—one pulled ever so slightly to the right, the other to the left, but only he knew which one did what and could compensate for it, while poor Wyndham . . . He almost laughed aloud, picturing the expression on Wyndham's face when *his* bullet found its mark and Wyndham's did not. A febrile glitter in his blue eyes, he strolled over to where Julian, Marcus and Charles were still gathered.

Approaching them, he bowed. "A most enjoyable event. Your mother is to be congratulated on her abilities as hostess," he said to Charles, coming to stand beside him. Smiling at Julian, he said, "I do not believe that I have ever congratulated you on your recent marriage. What is it . . . six months now? Oh, and an heir on the way, too—congratulations." He sipped his wine, his eyes never leaving Julian's rigid features. "She is a lovely little thing—you are a lucky man," he added genially. "Very lucky, indeed . . . So easily could she have slipped from your fingers and, alas, become the bride of another man."

Julian's nostrils flared and Marcus grabbed his arm. Staring at Tynedale, despising him, Julian said flatly, "If you value your life, I would suggest that you take your loathsome self far away from me."

Tynedale's eyes widened girlishly. "Oh, my, are you insulting me?" It was not his plan to be the challenger. He needed to be the one challenged—then the choice of weapons would be his.

"Can you be insulted?" mocked Julian.

They were not speaking in low tones and several gentlemen alert to brewing trouble turned to stare at them.

"Oh, yes, I'm quite certain of it . . . if I allow myself to be," Tynedale said, taking another sip of his wine. "But, you see, I have great command of my temper and do not allow myself to be goaded by the trite comments uttered by commoners."

Charles's face turned to marble and Marcus started to his feet, only to be halted by Julian's apparently careless but bone-crushing hold of his arm.

"You are to be commended," Julian drawled, his long body deceptively relaxed. "I, too, am somewhat impervious to insults, especially when they are uttered by offal like yourself."

Everyone was watching and listening to them by now and there was a collective gasp at Julian's words.

The squire rushed forward, followed closely on his heels by the vicar and Lord Beckworth. "Oh, I say now," said the squire uneasily. "None of that, this has gone on too long."

Tynedale tittered but his eyes burned with hatred. "Dear me. Are you trying to force a duel upon me?" He glanced around the room. "I am afraid that poor Wyndham isn't content with having already shed my blood. It would appear that he is lusting for more."

"You are wrong," Julian murmured, "I do not want your blood, you licentious knave, I want you dead so that you can no longer swindle and cheat green boys out of their fortunes."

Tynedale went white with fury, but he held on to his temper. "Goodness! I had so hoped that you had gotten over your displeasure with your ward's foolish acts, but it appears that I am wrong. You hold a grudge, my lord—how unsporting of you."

With a flick of his wrist Julian tossed the contents of his glass into Tynedale's face. "And you, my Lord Blackguard," he said quietly, "are a cur and a coward, nothing short of vermin that should be stamped out."

Enraged, Tynedale lost sight of his goal. "You smug bastard," he snarled, "name your seconds!"

"Gladly," Julian said. His eyes never leaving Tynedale's livid features, he said, "Marcus? Charles?"

Not waiting for their assent, Julian drawled, "I believe that weapons are my choice—swords . . . and the time and place, here and now."

"Oh, no, no, we can't have that!" exclaimed the squire, appalled at this turn of events. "Tynedale has not even named his seconds, " he added desperately.

"Mr. Raoul Weston and Mr. Pierce Chadbourne will act for me," Tynedale snapped. Both Raoul and Pierce looked dismayed, but they could hardly refuse, and both nodded and came to stand beside their man. "And I am ready," Tynedale said, "whenever Lord Wyndham is ready."

"Upon my soul! This is highly irregular," protested Lord Beckworth. "You must allow your seconds to attempt a peaceable outcome."

Julian had not moved from his relaxed position by the table, but like a tiger with his prey in his sights, his eyes had never left Tynedale's face. "Irregular it may be," he said, "but protocol has been met; by good luck, we have a physician in attendance and certainly we have enough respectable witnesses, in addition to our seconds. There is nothing to prevent the duel from taking place—here and now."

Tynedale gave a curt nod. "I concur. There is nothing for our seconds to discuss."

To Charles, Julian said, "I believe that you have an exceptional pair of swords—we shall use those." His lip curled in contempt. "Unless, of course, Tynedale or his seconds have some objections."

"None," said Tynedale, cursing inwardly that he had lost the advantage.

"Then while Charles goes in search of the weapons, let us prepare," Julian said.

It was clear that there was nothing more to be done; the duel would be fought. Here. Now.

While Charles disappeared in search of the swords, the other gentlemen, some muttering their displeasure, others voicing anxiety and still others with growing excitement, a few even placing wagers on the outcome, swiftly prepared the room. Candelabrums were placed out of danger; the table was moved to the far end; and chairs were shoved out of the way until there was a sizable space cleared in the middle of the large room, revealing in full glory the colors and design of a costly Turkish rug. When Charles returned with the swords, they were examined by the seconds and deemed acceptable. The principles and their seconds retreated to opposite ends of the room, the witnesses lining themselves up along the walls.

"Are you mad?" Marcus hissed the moment he, Charles and Julian were alone.

Shrugging out of his jacket, Julian murmured, "We are agreed, are we not, that he wants killing?"

"Yes, but who decided that it would be you? Charles or I could do it just as easily. You have responsibilities . . . Or have your forgotten your wife? What about the babe your wife carries?"

Taking the sword Charles handed him, Julian said, "I have not forgotten them and I trust that if the worst happens that you and Charles will look out for them." He hesitated, an anguished expression crossing his face. Thinking of Nell and her grief should he die would do him no good. Nor was this the time to consider the wisdom his actions. He needed a clear head, but he could not leave Nell without a final word. He took a deep breath. "If I should die, tell my wife that I love her, that she brought me immeasurable joy and that my last thought was of her and our child."

"Oh, bloody hell!" Marcus burst out. He glanced at Charles in exasperation. "For God's sake, do something."

"Me? Why should I?" Charles asked. "If my esteemed

cousin were unlucky enough to die tonight, I inherit." He flashed Julian a lopsided grin. "Rest assured, my lord, that I shall grieve deeply and I swear to you that I will see that your lady is protected and that no harm comes to her."

Julian sent him a look. "Do you know, I never realized before," he marveled, "that you have, at the most inopportune times, a decidedly flippant attitude."

"Better that than wringing my hands like that old maid, Marcus."

Marcus surged forward, violence in his eyes, but with a swift movement Julian prevented him from reaching his target. "I believe that I am the one fighting a duel," he said quietly. "You two may cut each other to ribbons afterward if you wish, but for now, remember that you are my seconds."

Julian started to turn away, but Charles caught his arm. His expression grim, Charles said thickly, "You do know, my lord, don't you, that if you fall, Tynedale will not outlive you by many moments."

Julian smiled faintly and nodded his dark head. "I never doubted it for a moment—despite your infernal impudence."

Turning away, Julian took off his embroidered waistcoat and laid it on top of his jacket. After rolling up the sleeves of his fine linen shirt, he picked up the sword and tested its balance, finding that memory had not played him false. It was an exquisite weapon. Too exquisite, he thought viciously, to use on Tynedale.

While Julian had been preparing himself, Tynedale had been doing the same and a moment later the two men faced each other. They met in the center of the cleared space, their swords kissing as a prelude to the duel.

In spite of several gentlemen being in the room, the air was hushed as the swords sang against each other for the first time. No one doubted that the duel would go beyond the drawing of first blood; many believed that they would see a man die.

As Julian and Tynedale stalked each other, there was no

stylish maneuvering, no intricate footwork meant to draw the admiration and respect of the spectators—this was a duel in which each of the opponents' only thought was to kill the other. It began slowly enough; they had met before and had the measure of the other, and in an elegant dance of death, they tested each other's strengths, looking for an opening, a weakness.

Beyond the muffled sound of the booted feet of the swordsmen on the Turkish rug and the occasional scrape of blade upon blade, there was silence. Julian easily parried Tynedale's feints as they fought, their blades flashing silver in the candlelight. For endless minutes the duel continued: feint, parry, thrust, disengage—only to begin again with neither man finding a clear opening for attack. Then, suddenly, Tynedale's blade slipped under Julian's guard and a long crimson slash appeared on Julian's upper arm.

"Enough!" cried the squire, his features anxious. "You have bloodied your man."

"But I do not claim satisfaction," snarled Tynedale, and lunged at Julian.

Julian danced away from Tynedale's onslaught, only to come back at him, their blades shrieking as steel clashed against steel. His face dark and grim, Julian kept up the attack, relentlessly driving Tynedale backward, his blade striking like lightning, leaving Tynedale's shirt torn and bloody from a dozen small nicks. Tynedale's shirt hung in ribbons on him and he was gasping for breath, but Tynedale was an excellent swordsman and though Julian had been able to inflict insulting damage, he had not been able to find a chink in Tynedale's defense that would allow him the killing thrust.

Perspiration rolled down Tynedale's face as once again his blade met Julian's attack. His wounds stung and bled. His arm ached and his breathing was ragged. He had held Julian off so far, but he knew that he could not do so indefinitely. Fear uncurled like a snake in his belly and any thought of killing his opponent vanished—Tynedale was fighting for his life.

Fear and rage clouding Tynedale's mind, his defenses wavered and in that moment, Julian broke through, his blade whistling across Tynedale's as Julian went for the heart. At the last second, Tynedale moved slightly and instead of finding its mark, Julian's blade sank deeply into Tynedale's shoulder.

Tynedale shrieked and fell to the floor as Julian pulled his blade free. Disgusted Julian stood over his fallen opponent as Tynedale writhed on the floor. Of all the damn things! Julian thought as he stared down at Tynedale. He had failed again. Tynedale would live. To continue the duel would be to commit cold-blooded murder and Julian's honor balked at that— no matter how badly he wished Tynedale dead. Damn and blast!

"Once again you seem to have the Devil's own luck, my lord," Julian said grimly.

Pierce and Raoul ran to their man and helped Tynedale to his feet. Sagging between them, his sword held limply by one side, Tynedale retorted, "Luck had nothing to do with it, my lord. Skill is the thing."

"Indeed. Believe that if you will." Julian glanced around the room. "Tynedale cannot go on. The duel is ended." Turning his back on Tynedale, he began to walk to the other end of the room.

Seeing his enemy walking away from him, realizing that all his schemes and dreams would not come to fruition unless Wyndham died, Tynedale went mad. "No!" he screamed. "It does not end thus!"

Astonishing everyone, Tynedale threw off the hands of his seconds and stood swaying in the middle of the room.

Julian turned back to Tynedale. His cold gaze swept up and down Tynedale. "Even the desire to eradicate vermin such as you will not compel me to commit murder." Contempt in every movement, Julian spun on his heels and walked away.

Tynedale gave a strangled cry and charged after Julian. It was clear that in his maddened state Tynedale intended to drive his blade into Julian's unprotected back.

There was a horrified gasp from the gentlemen watching and Charles and Marcus lunged forward simultaneously, Charles shouting, "Julian, your back!"

Julian whirled around and dropping to one knee, countered Tynedale's attack, his blade thrusting clean and true straight to Tynedale's heart. With Julian's sword sunk deep into his heart Tynedale staggered backward, his eyes full of disbelief. His sword dropped; he tried to speak and fell to the floor, dead.

Standing over Tynedale's body Julian stared dully at him, wondering that he felt nothing. He had thought with Tynedale's death that the despair and guilt over Daniel's death would lift, but it did not. Even the knowledge that Tynedale had paid dearly for the upheaval he had wrought in Nell's life did not bring him gratification. There was no exultation of having beaten his enemy, not even a feeling of satisfaction or one of relief that he had finally kept his vow and avenged Daniel. He was aware only of a great weariness and of a powerful need to see Nell, to hold her in his arms and feel her soft body next his.

A babble arose in the dining room, some gentlemen rushing forward to congratulate Julian; others shaking their heads and muttering direful prophesies and deploring the lack of decorum and manners in the younger generation . . . and it was several moments before order was restored. Silence reigned when Tynedale's body was carried from the room. There was no question that the death was justified and Julian need not fear that there would be any repercussions from this night's work. Too many gentlemen had seen the duel itself to keep it a secret and Julian never entertained any idea of being able to muzzle those in attendance. As for gossip, and there would be an abundance . . . Well, that couldn't be helped. He would, he decided wearily, just have to deal with it.

It was some time before the room was set to rights, but eventually all signs that a deadly duel had been fought on the very floor beneath Mrs. Weston's long mahogany table were erased. Julian's wound, amidst much low-voiced scolding by Dr. Coleman, was cleaned and dressed; Marcus helped him into his waistcoat and jacket. Charles expertly twitched his cravat back into some semblance of its former elegant arrangement.

"A bad business," Squire Chadbourne said to him shortly as several gentlemen gathered around him. "A very bad business."

Julian nodded. "I cannot deny it and I take no pride in my part in it."

Lord Beckworth snorted. "But you meant to kill him, didn't you?"

"If fate was kind," Julian murmured.

"Well, you are very lucky to have escaped with nothing more than a scratch," remarked Coleman sternly. "I hope that you will take my advice and rest that arm for a few days." A faint gleam of amusement leaped into his eyes. "And avoid fighting another duel anytime soon."

"I don't think you have anything to fear," Julian said dryly. "Dueling is not my forte and if . . ." He looked away, thinking of young Daniel and Nell. "There were reasons," he finally offered, taking a sip of his brandy.

"There always are," Beckworth commented. "Let us hope that whatever your reasons were that they were worth a man's life."

Standing beside Julian, Charles said, "Oh, they were worth it."

"Without a doubt," added Marcus, lounging nearby.

Beckworth stared at the three cousins. "Like that, was it?"

"Like that," Julian said.

When the others wandered off and Julian, Marcus and Charles were left standing alone, Charles asked, "That went rather well, don't you think?"

Marcus made a face. "I'd have liked it better if Julian had not been wounded."

Several of the gentlemen were preparing to leave the dining room and Julian was not looking forward to the next half hour. In theory, gentlemen did not discuss duels with the fairer sex, but Julian didn't doubt that once the gentlemen joined the ladies that the cat would be out of the bag—and amongst the pigeons. He groaned. What had he been thinking of? A duel fought in his aunt's dining room! Good God, he was not some hotheaded youth ripe for excitement and danger! He was a soberly married man, with a child on the way. It didn't matter that Tynedale needed killing—surely he could have thought of another way?

He caught Charles looking at him, a smile on his lips. "What?" Julian demanded.

Shaking his head, Charles said, "For once you acted without thinking of the consequences and you're already regretting it."

Marcus glanced at Julian. "Are you?"

Julian made a face. "Not Tynedale's death, but I could have chosen a more, ah, respectable venue."

"My stepmother's dining room isn't respectable enough for you?"

"You know very well what I mean," Julian replied irritably. "You're the rascal in the family, I don't do this sort of thing—you do!"

"Hmmm, yes, I do," agreed Charles looking over the rim of his snifter at Julian, his eyes bright and amused. He grinned at Julian. "And I must say, dear fellow, I couldn't have done it better!"

Chapter 20

Julian's fear that news of the duel would fly like wildfire around Mrs. Weston's saloon was unfounded. Apparently none of the gentlemen felt compelled to whisper a word of the stunning occurrence in the dining room into the receptive ears of their female companions when he and the others rejoined the ladies. But the party, to Mrs. Weston's mystification, did seem to end rather abruptly. Julian was glad that it would be left to Charles to break the news of the duel to her—if Raoul didn't beat him to it.

His shoulder ached but Julian was able to act normally until he and Nell had bid the others good night and driven home. After that there was no hiding from her what had happened, unless he intended to avoid any intimacy with her until he was fully healed. A slow smiled crossed his mouth as he gingerly slipped into a heavy silk robe. It would take a great deal more than a wounded arm to keep him from Nell's bed.

Nell was horrified when he confessed the evening's events. When he showed her where Tynedale's blade had cut him, she stared for a long time at the white bandages that covered the wound, her hands clutched to her heart.

"You might have died!" she finally managed. "You could have been killed while I sat drinking tea in the saloon." Rage shook her and she pounded his chest with her fists. "How dare you risk your life that way! How dare you!"

"But, sweetheart, aren't you happy that Tynedale is dead?" asked Julian nonplused. "He is no longer any sort of a threat to us. Doesn't that make you happy?"

"Happy?" she shouted. "Happy that you nearly got killed? Are you mad?" Her rage faded as quickly as it had arisen. "Oh, Julian," she cried, throwing herself into his arms with such force that he winced. "I love you! My life would have ended if he had killed you." Her head against his chest, she gulped back a sob and held him tighter. "Promise me you'll never do something so foolish again. Promise me! I could not bear it if something happened to you."

Julian smiled and pressed a kiss on the top of her head. "Nothing is going to happen to me—I swear it."

With one hand she caressed the site of the wound. "Does it hurt terribly?"

He started to deny it but then a crafty thought entered his head. "Perhaps a little . . . If I could just lie here on the bed beside you for a trifle longer?"

Her face full of tender solicitation, Nell helped him shed his robe and slide into her bed. Mindful of his wound, she snuggled next to his naked body, careful not to cause him any pain by her movements on the bed. "Is this better?" she asked.

His fingers plucked at the hem of her gown. "Perhaps if you would just . . . ah, much better," he murmured, urging her gown upward, his hands skimming over her body before lingering at the juncture of her thighs, clearly revealing his intentions. With delight his fingers discovered the sweet, hot moisture between her legs.

"What of your wound?" Nell got out, her eyes blurred with desire.

He smiled lazily at her in the glow of the candle near the bed. "If you will help me I promise that we shall do just fine."

Bending his head, he caught her lower lip and bit gently just as his fingers stretched her and pushed into her. Nell arched up against his hand, pleasure flooding her. She reached for him, almost purring when her fingers closed around the hard length of him.

Already wild for her, he shifted and with his good arm, pulled and urged her astride him. It took only a moment to sheathe his swollen length within her and after that, as he had promised, they did just fine.

The news of the extraordinary duel and Tynedale's death caused a stir—not only in the district but also throughout England. The death of a peer in a duel was not unheard of, but the circumstances and the history between Tynedale and Julian made it a topic of great speculation and interest. It helped that the Season had just begun and that many members of society were still away at their country estates, most busy closing down their great houses and packing up their families for the trek to London. Because a large portion of the ton was scattered throughout England, the news did not reach everyone at once but traveled erratically through the countryside.

If the residents of Wyndham Manor had not already decided not to make an appearance in London this particular Season, the duel and its attendant scandal would have certainly made them do so. The advisability of changing plans and going to London to let the Polite World know that there was no reason for Julian, or any of his family, to hide away in the country, was discussed by the family. Nell had never liked the Season and since her advancing pregnancy gave her an excellent excuse to remain at Wyndham Manor, she was adamant: the others could go if they wished, but she was staying home.

Ordinarily, Lady Diana and Elizabeth would have been all agog to return to London, but both of them were excited about the renovations to the Dower House and neither particularly wanted to run the gamut of gossip their appearance in town would cause.

As Lady Diana had said, "It is one thing to be invited to all the most exclusive balls and soirees because of one's rank and position and another to be invited because everyone wants to know every unsavory detail of a disgusting duel."

That Lady Diana might have another reason for remaining in the country only dawned on Julian three weeks later when he realized that Lord Beckworth was a frequent visitor these days to Wyndham Manor—and to the Dower House. Discovering his lordship wandering around the grounds of the Dower House with Lady Diana hanging on his arm as Beckworth patiently explained the various stages of construction of her new kitchen, Julian didn't think much of it. But then finding Beckworth at his dinner table for the third evening out of five, even Julian became aware that something was going on right in front of him.

Walking through the gardens late one morning with Nell, Julian remarked, "Is it my imagination or is Beckworth practically living in my stepmother's pocket?"

Nell giggled. "No, it is not your imagination. Isn't it wonderful? I wonder if he will make her an offer? Elizabeth and I are most hopeful that there will be a wedding this fall."

Julian looked aghast. "Diana marry that old man?"

"He's younger than your father and she married him, didn't she?" Nell responded tartly.

"Well, yes, but that was . . ." He stopped, at a loss.

"Different?" Nell supplied and when he nodded, she asked, "How so?"

Julian shrugged. "I can't explain it." He shook his head. "I guess whenever I even considered the possibility of her remarrying I assumed that it would be to someone nearer her own age."

Nell glanced at him curiously. "Would you dislike it if she were to marry Lord Beckworth?"

"No, I suppose not—if that is what she wants."

Nell smiled. "I think it is exactly what she wants, although she is being very coy with Elizabeth and me whenever we tax her about her new swain. She denies that there is anything between them, but there is a look in her eyes . . ." She sighed, a dreamy expression crossing her face. "I'm sure that when they marry he will make her very happy."

When Julian continued to look skeptical, she said, "If you stop and think about it, it makes perfect sense."

"How did you come to that conclusion?" he asked with a lifted brow.

"Her first marriage to a man her own age was . . . Well, I gather from things Elizabeth let slip that her parents married very young and were not happy together. It's obvious that Lady Diana adored your father and that *their* marriage was a happy one. So when another older, respectable gentleman expresses an interest in her it is only logical that she would be receptive." Nell looked thoughtful. "In fact I would hazard a guess that she would repulse the advances of a younger man—equating him with her first husband."

Julian digested this theory and concluded that Nell probably had the correct reading of the situation.

Something occurred to him. "Does this mean that I can expect a formal visiting from Beckworth one of these days?"

Nell chuckled. "Most likely."

His eyes opened to the romance blooming under his nose made Julian more aware of the comings and goings of others and it dawned on him that there was a steady stream of gentlemen in and out of his house these days. It seemed that Charles was continually underfoot, while Raoul and Pierce appeared to have taken a liking to the hospitality of Wyndham Manor. It didn't take him long to realize that the allure wasn't his home but rather his entrancing young stepsister, Elizabeth. It shouldn't have surprised him, but it did and he wasn't quite certain how he felt about the situation. He goggled at the notion of *Charles* marrying at all, let alone a chit just out of the schoolroom! As for Raoul . . . His younger cousin's reputation with women and his gambling habits left him with some misgivings. Squire Chadbourne's heir, Pierce, would be a nice catch, but on the whole he thought that all three men were a little old for his young stepsister.

An opportunity to approach Charles on the subject occurred during the last week of April. An early-morning ride had been arranged among the cousins, but both Marcus and Raoul had begged off, leaving Julian and Charles the only riders. The morning was lovely, the sun warm and comfortable, the trees were full of bright green leaves, wildflowers carpeted the meadows in every hue imaginable and birdsong filled the air. Julian enjoyed it but he was distracted as he considered how to broach the subject of Charles's apparent romantic interest in Elizabeth. It wasn't until they were riding back to the house that Julian brought himself to the sticking point.

Out of the blue, he just asked, "Are you dangling after my stepsister?"

Charles stopped his horse. He simply looked at Julian.

Julian flushed. "Well, what else am I to think? This time of year you would normally be back in your old haunts in London, but here you are still in the country and, unless I am much mistaken, part of the court flitting around my stepsister. I know that there are several other local young cubs calling on her, but you, Raoul and Chadbourne seemed to be the main contenders for her attention."

"Hmmm, yes, I've noticed that too," Charles said, urging his horse forward again. "I think Raoul and Pierce are too old for her, don't you? She's, what, seventeen?" He slanted a sly glance at Julian. "Unless you think she's following in her mother's footsteps and prefers older men? Which reminds me, do you think Lady Diana is going to become Lady Beckworth this year?"

If that wasn't just like Charles, Julian thought half-annoyed,

half-amused, to ignore his question and then change the subject. "According to my wife," Julian admitted, knowing it was
useless to expect more out of his cousin, "in all likelihood we
shall be hosting a wedding this fall."

"Ah, yes, I rather thought so—his pursuit has been somewhat obvious and she has shown no signs of repulsing him.
Are you pleased?"

Julian nodded. Having accepted the idea of his stepmother's
eventual marriage to Lord Beckworth, he discovered that he
was more than pleased—he was elated. Beckworth was a good
man. Steady. Reliable. Clearly smitten with Lady Diana. And
the lady herself seemed to have a glow about her these days
that he hadn't seen in a long time . . . not since his father had
died. Yes, Julian was pleased. There wasn't much that didn't
please him these days, as a matter of fact. He was married to
a woman who loved him and he adored; he would become a
father in a matter of months and the care and responsibility
of his stepmother and stepsister seemed about to be lifted
from his shoulders. A smile curved his mouth. Leaving me,
he thought happily, able to concentrate exclusively on my
wife and our child.

There was just one black spot on Julian's horizon: the
Shadow Man. During the time since Tynedale's death he and
Marcus had dutifully managed to search out every possible
site for a dungeon, causing the pair of them to be recipients
of some raised eyebrows and probing looks. Getting a look
at the dungeons beneath Stonegate had been the most difficult and Julian knew that Charles hadn't bought Marcus's
story for a moment. The afternoon of the tour, Charles had
been a perfect host and while Mrs. Weston had accompanied
them to the lowest reaches of the house, her manner had
been stiff and unbending and it was obvious that she was still
greatly annoyed about the duel during her dinner party.
Raoul, plainly thinking them mad had hastily absented himself. Of course the Stonegate dungeons bore no resemblance
to those in Nell's nightmare and as far as the Shadow Man

was concerned the only good thing that Julian could say was that Nell had had no more nightmares—nor had John Hunter approached him with news of another grisly find.

"What are you going to do about the Dower House if Lady Diana does marry Beckworth?" Charles asked, breaking into Julian's thoughts. "It seems a pity to let it return to rack and ruin again."

"That won't happen," Julian said. "I should have been a better landowner and never allowed it to deteriorate. Now that it will be in prime shape, I shall see that it stays so."

"And the new kitchen? It is progressing nicely? No more, er, setbacks? No vandals or unexplained thefts? No mysterious visitors in the night?"

Julian looked at him. "Why do you ask?"

Charles grimaced. "The other night coming home from your place, I noticed a horse tied to tree near the Dower House. I investigated, but couldn't find a soul. Made me wonder."

"There have been no problems since the fire," Julian said thoughtfully, "I talked to the gypsies and that seemed to be the end of it."

"Those fellows camping at Beckworth's?"

Julian nodded. "Their leader is named Cesar and while I realize that the word of a gypsy is suspect, he swore that I would have no trouble with them—and I believed him."

Charles grinned. "Are you talking about the latest of our uncles to surface?"

"How did—! Oh, Marcus, of course," Julian murmured. "I wondered if he would keep it to himself."

"He felt I should know in case Cesar tried to batten down on you and he wasn't around to slap his nimble fingers away from your pocket."

Julian smiled. "I think Marcus worries too much about nonsensical things."

"Oh, undoubtedly. Always did." They rode in silence a moment. Then Charles asked, "Does he intend to remain with you much longer? I would have thought that the demands of his own estate or the delights of London would have lured him away by now."

"He has a competent steward to take care of things at Sherbrook. As for London . . . Its siren call was always more powerful for you than Marcus. He likes the country."

"I don't dislike the country," Charles snapped, scowling. "I think you forget that my stepmother makes it plain that she doesn't want me underfoot. She endures me for the winter, but come spring . . . Turfed out of my own home, what the bloody hell am I to do but take myself off to London and lose myself amidst the hells and fleshpots?"

Startled not only by the admission, but the pain and frustration in his cousin's voice, Julian halted his horse. He stared at Charles's averted features, so many things that had puzzled him about Charles's actions becoming clear. Mrs. Weston, Julian thought grimly, has much to answer for. Aloud he said merely, "It *is* your home."

Charles gave a bitter laugh. "You might try telling her that!" He shook his head. "No, it is far better for me to be in London and away from her—it keeps me from wringing her neck and throwing her body in the river."

Returning to the house, Charles's question about the duration of Marcus's stay was answered by Marcus himself. Having bid Charles adieu, Julian had closeted himself in his study to go over the estate books that Farley had left on his desk. It was a boring, mundane task but a necessary one and from a young age Julian had taken his duties as the owner of a grand estate seriously. But when Marcus knocked on the door and walked into the room, Julian welcomed the interruption.

He set aside the books filled with Farley's cramped writing and, smiling at Marcus, invited him to take the overstuffed leather chair near the corner of his desk.

They exchanged pleasantries for a few minutes before Marcus said, "I am reluctant to leave you without a satisfactory conclusion to the, er, Shadow Man, but I fear that I must leave for a few weeks."

"Trouble?"

Marcus smiled wryly. "No. My mother. She demands my escort to London."

"Ah, I understand." It was well known in the family that Marcus's mother, Barbara, a charming, complaisant woman, made few claims on her son's time, but the one thing she did insist upon was his company whenever she traveled any distance from Sherbrook Hall. A trip to London was a great undertaking for her and since the death of Marcus's father several years ago Marcus had good-naturedly escorted his mother on her annual trek to and from the city. No amount of persuasion by Marcus could convince her that the roads were not littered with highwaymen bent upon attacking her coach and her and ripping her jewels right off her fingers.

"I should not be gone longer than I can help," Marcus said, his expression troubled. "There has been no sign of your wife's madman since we found that poor butchered girl. Perhaps he has moved on."

Julian grimaced. "Believe me, I would like to think so, but I doubt it. Unfortunately, we have no way of knowing when or where he will strike or even *if*—although my wife is convinced that it could be any day. She says that the times between his murderous rages are shortening. It has been nearly three months since the death of Ann Barnes and she fears another nightmare any day." Julian sighed. "The problem is that you could remain chained here at Wyndham indefinitely waiting for something to happen. There is no predicting his actions." He smiled faintly at Marcus. "I have been most grateful for your support, but you have other demands on your time—go escort your mother to London."

Marcus hesitated, his expression unhappy. It was clear that he was torn. "I suppose," he said slowly, "I could write Mother that I have broken my leg and would be of no use to her . . .

Julian grinned. "And that would bring her posthaste to our doorstep to ascertain for herself the extent of your injuries." When Marcus smiled ruefully, Julian added, "Until and *if* he strikes again there is nothing you can do. Go. And return with all speed."

Marcus rose to his feet. "I shall do that, especially the speed part." He looked worried. "Let us hope that he remains quiet while I am away."

Julian nodded. "Yes, let us hope."

Marcus departed that afternoon and Nell was surprised at how empty the house felt without his presence. She said as much to Julian as they took an early evening stroll around the gardens.

"He would be flattered that you say so," Julian replied.

"He is very different than Charles, isn't he?" she asked.

Julian laughed. "Indeed! Marcus is staid and steady and Charles is a profligate gambler and impudent in the bargain." He shook his head. "While Marcus lives a calm, ordered life, Charles lurches from one near disaster to the next and thinks it a great game. He has the Devil's own luck, too. How he escaped drowning last year when his yacht sank, won on the turn of a card, I might add, is beyond me. Marcus was appalled by the incident and Charles thought it an amusing jest. I can think of no two men less alike than Marcus and Charles, but I also could not name two other men that I would like at my side when facing adversity." He paused and a smile curved his mouth. "Except, perhaps, my cousin Stacey. Do you remember meeting him at our wedding?"

"Vaguely," Nell admitted. She wrinkled her nose. "It seems a long time ago, doesn't it?"

He smiled down at her. "Yes, and yet, it seems just yesterday. Any regrets?"

She shook her head and leaned her cheek against the sleeve of his coat. "Not one . . . now that I know that you love me."

He took her into his arms. "And I do. With all my heart. With every breath of my body."

Starry-eyed she melted into his embrace.

Charles's mention of finding a horse tied near the Dower House aroused Julian's curiosity. For several nights afterward, long after Nell had fallen asleep, he would slide noiselessly to his feet, hastily dress and, although feeling ridiculous, he would creep out and make his way to Diana's future home to watch it for any signs of activity. Deciding that he was on a fool's errand as he made his way from the manor this particular night, he swore to himself that tonight would be the last he spent lurking like a thief in the shrubbery that surrounded the Dower House.

The moon was waxing full and there was plenty of light for Julian to see as he slowly walked. Before the rooftop came into sight, he slowed his pace and kept his ears open. Stopping in the shadows of a large lilac bush a short distance from the rear of the house, he surveyed the scene but saw nothing to arouse his curiosity. He hadn't expected to see anyone, but he remained concealed in his spot for over two hours before deciding that he was indeed on a fool's errand. He was about to leave and seek out his bed when just the slightest flicker of movement near the back entrance caught his eye.

He stiffened, his gaze locked on the spot, but as the minutes passed and he saw nothing out of the ordinary, he relaxed again. Imagination? His eyes playing tricks on him? He smiled. Or perhaps he just wanted to see something? A moment later, he jerked upright, his smile gone, certain this time that he saw something moving in the shadows near the house. Yes, there at the corner, where the construction of the new kitchen was well under way, he could make out the form of a man. From his post near the lilac tree, Julian watched as the man slid from the shadows and stepped into the moonlight for a second before disappearing into the house. There was something familiar about that tall form, but the glint of moonlight on the golden earring in the man's ear told Julian exactly who he was watching: *Cesar!*

Expression grim, Julian worked his way through the shrubbery until he was only a few feet away from where Cesar had disappeared inside. He hesitated, not relishing charging into the unknown. The interior would be black as Hades and he had no way of knowing if Cesar was alone or if he was meeting someone. He could wait for Cesar to return and confront him, but then he wouldn't know what the gypsy was doing, and there was no guarantee that Cesar would leave the same way he had entered.

Undecided, Julian waited in the shadows, wishing he was armed with something more than the knife hidden in his boot. The minutes passed and he was just about to creep nearer the house when a whisper of sound warned him that he was not alone. He moved, but he was too late and an arm closed around his neck, choking him.

Throwing his head back with great force, Julian heard with satisfaction the grunt of pain that came from his attacker, but the chokehold around his neck loosened only fractionally. Julian swiftly bent forward almost double and his assailant went flying over his head, landing hard on the ground. Julian was on him in a flash, the knife from his boot already in his hand.

His blade was at his attacker's throat when the moonlight fell full on the man's face. With a curse Julian removed the knife and rolled over to lie beside the other man on the ground.

"Do you know," Charles said conversationally, "that I'd heard rumors that you were a dangerous man, but until tonight I never knew how dangerous."

"I could have killed you, you fool!"

"Yes, but you didn't and that's all that concerns me at the moment," Charles said as he bounded to his feet.

Julian followed his lead and almost as one the two men moved quickly back into the shadows.

"Did you see him?" Charles whispered.

"Yes. Recognized him, too—Cesar, the gypsy chief from Beckworth's."

"How disappointing. Here I thought I would uncover some notable crime and it is merely a pilfering gypsy."

"How did you know that Cesar would be here tonight?" Julian asked sharply.

"I didn't. I've been watching the house for the past week from that blasted hawthorn hedge and tonight is the first time I've seen anything."

Julian grimaced. "It would appear that neither one of us is very adept at this—I have been watching from the lilacs for almost the same amount of time."

"Oh, I wouldn't say that—we were adept enough not to alert each other."

"Until tonight . . . What gave me away?"

Charles pulled on his ear. "Nothing gave you away. I decided to try a different vantage point and discovered you, quite by chance. Gave me a start I can tell you."

Julian felt marginally better. At least his old skills had not failed him completely.

"So? What do we do now?"

"Split up," Julian replied. "One of us watches the front, the other the back." His voice grew grim. "And we capture anyone coming out of the house."

Before they could put that plan into action, the sight of Cesar slipping from the house galvanized both men and like a pair of hunting leopards, they slunk through the tangled shrubbery until they were in position to strike. Both leaped at the same time and their prey went to the ground with a groan and a thud.

Having used the kerchief from around Cesar's neck to gag him and Charles's cravat to bind his hands, they dragged him to where Charles's horse was tied. Throwing Cesar like a sack of potatoes onto the horse they led the horse to Julian's stables. As Julian said to Charles, "We need somewhere private to talk and I don't relish having this fellow in my library. Uncle or not!"

The stables reached they hustled a struggling Cesar inside the stable office. Julian quickly lit a candle and Cesar got his first look at his attackers.

Ripping off the gag, Julian said, "I think you have some explaining to do—you swore that I had nothing to fear from you."

"And you do not—if you will notice I had nothing of yours when I came from the house."

"And what were you doing there?" Charles asked mildly. "Taking a midnight stroll, hmmm? Or checking to see what else you could steal from my cousin?"

"If you will untie me," Cesar said, "perhaps we can discuss this like rational men."

Charles snorted. "Next I suppose you will suggest that we share a glass of wine."

"Yes, that would be an excellent idea." Cesar's gaze slid toward the massive oak desk that dominated the office. "I believe that there is a most exceptional decanter of brandy in the lower right-hand corner of the desk and several rather nice crystal snifters."

Unable to help himself, Julian laughed. There was something about Cesar that reminded him remarkably of Charles. Their impudence? Undoubtedly! Aloud, he merely said, "Know about those, do you? I wonder what else you know."

Cesar grinned at him, his white teeth flashing in his gypsy dark face. "If you will untie me and pour me a snifter of brandy, I shall be happy to tell you."

Julian glanced at Charles, amusement in his gaze. "Now, who, I wonder," he asked of no one in particular, "does this fellow remind me of?" Not waiting for an answer, Julian walked over and untied Cesar.

Then, opening the drawer of the desk Julian brought out

the decanter of brandy and three elegant snifters. Often, after a long day in the saddle, he and friends would linger here in the office, sipping brandy, discussing the hunt.

After pouring the snifters and handing them out, Julian sat on a corner of the desk and asked, "When did you search the stables?"

Cesar sighed. "Prior to our meeting in Beckworth's meadow." His dark gaze met Julian's. "I spoke the truth when I said that you had nothing to fear from my tribe."

"Then explain to me how it is that I find you creeping around my property in the dead of night."

"I will not deny that some of the more, er, exuberant members of my tribe did, before you paid us a visit, uh, help themselves to some things that were lying around—in particular, some rolls of fabric from the house that I was in tonight. I will admit to those thefts." His eyes locked on Julian's, he said, "But I swear to you, on the blood that we share, that it was no gypsy who started the fire."

"That's all very interesting," remarked Charles, "but it still doesn't explain what you were doing there tonight, now does it?"

Cesar looked surprised. "I thought it was obvious—I was following the man in the black cloak. Didn't you see him?"

Chapter 21

Julian nearly called him a liar, but then he remembered those few seconds before he'd spotted Cesar when he'd thought he'd seen something near the back entrance. He played the scene back in his mind, trying to recall exactly what he'd seen—or thought he'd seen. Could it have been the flicker of a cloak as someone disappeared into the house?

"He's lying," Charles snapped, breaking into Julian's thoughts.

"No, I don't believe that he is," Julian said slowly, his gaze on Cesar's face. "A few minutes before I spotted Cesar, I thought that I saw something by the back entrance."

Charles's brows rose. "You saw something?"

"I *thought* I saw something—and the more I think on it, it could have been the edge of a cloak as someone entered the house."

Julian sent Cesar a hard look. "Assuming you are telling the truth, would you recognize the man you saw enter the house?"

Cesar shook his head. "No, the lower half of his face was covered by a dark scarf and he was wearing a black . . . a dark hat that obscured most of his other features."

"Even if you saw this fellow, that still doesn't explain what you were doing on the Dower House grounds in the first place," muttered Charles.

Cesar stared down into the amber liquid in his snifter. "Gypsies make their living by telling half truths, sometimes outright lies," he said simply. "Our reputation for being light-fingered thieves is not undeserved, but"—he lifted his head and looked at Julian—"we do have our own honor, and lying to a blood relative is not an inconsequential act. When I told you that you had nothing to fear from us, I meant it." He grimaced. "We are thieves, rascals if you like, but we do not set fires endangering lives. I knew that the damage done to your fine house was not the work of the gypsies and I was curious as to the identity of the real culprit." He shrugged. "So I watched—and *that* is why you discovered me at that house tonight."

"Too smoky by half," growled Charles. "And something else: for a damn rascally gypsy you have an excellent command of the King's English."

Cesar smiled thinly. "My . . . father saw to it that my mother was given an adequate sum of money—some of which, at his insistence, was to be used to educate me. I may not have attended one of your prestigious schools, but I am not unlearned."

Charles looked uncomfortable. "I apologize," he said. "My remark was rude." He grinned. "Especially to a, er, relative of sorts."

"Is tonight the first time that you've seen this fellow?" Julian asked abruptly.

Cesar nodded. "Yes. Once I had spotted him, I did not intend to let him out of my sight. When he entered the house I followed him to try to see where he went or what he did." The muscles in Cesar's jaw clenched. "But I failed. Except where the moonlight came in through the windows, the interior of the house was too dark to see anything. I lost him the moment he stepped inside. I stopped and listened, hoping to hear his movements, but I heard nothing. I could do nothing but retreat, fearful that if I continued I would blunder into him or alert him to my presence. I came out of the house, intending to wait for his return." He flashed Julian a wry glance. "But you put a stop to that."

"Do you mean to tell me that while we're here wasting time with you the fellow's escaping?" demanded Charles, incensed.

Cesar shrugged. "It is possible. I do know that once inside the house he seemed to vanish." He smiled crookedly. "As if by magic."

Julian looked thoughtful. "There's no point in returning to the house tonight—he probably heard our capture of you and ran away. He could be anywhere by now." He made a face. "But at least we know that someone *is* using the Dower House for his own purposes. It occurs to me that the fire may have been done to stop or slow work on the house, perhaps to drive my stepmother away. For the time being, we shall have to assume that the man tonight is the same one who started the fire since it is unlikely that it was caused by yet another party."

Julian took an impatient turn around the small office, thinking hard. Guilt ate at him for not sharing with the others information that he knew would shed light on tonight's events. There was no doubt in his mind that he'd nearly come face-to-face with the Shadow Man tonight.

Leaving that problem aside, he wasn't certain what to do about Cesar. His first instinct was to thank him for his efforts and send him on his way, but he realized that in his own way, Cesar had an interest in the comings and goings of the cloaked stranger. Because of the man in the cloak, Cesar and his people had come under suspicion and Julian didn't hold it against the man that he wanted to know who and why.

After much discussion among the three men, it was decided that Charles and Cesar would return to the Dower House and retrieve Cesar's horse that was hidden in the woods nearby. It was agreed that the three of them would work in unison instead of independently of each other. Julian felt he owed them both that much and with Marcus gone, he was going to need their help. Which didn't solve his dilemma: How could he send them up against a monster like the Shadow Man without letting them know what they were facing? And did he trust them both enough to tell them Nell's secret?

His thoughts heavy, Julian slowly walked back to the main house. He tried to view tonight in a positive manner. Until tonight they'd been grappling with shadows, and half-formed suspicions, but now they knew that someone was indeed afoot in the hours of darkness. In his mind, that person could be no one but the Shadow Man, and a chill trickled down his spine as he considered those implications.

Nell's Shadow Man was too bloody close for comfort, he decided as he mounted the steps to the house and entered. And thinking of the many times that Nell, Lady Diana and Elizabeth blithely wandered through the Dower House he cursed under his breath. A monster had entered it tonight. How many other times had he been there? How many times had Nell or one of the others come within inches of him?

But for what purpose, he wondered, was the Shadow Man creeping about the Dower House? Enlightenment struck him like a blow as he opened door to his room. Dungeons! Could it be? He and Marcus had eliminated all the sites known to have dungeons . . . but what if . . . ?

Stripping off his clothes, he made his way to Nell's room. Tomorrow, he swore grimly, he would examine the Dower House and its history very, *very* closely. The idea that the dungeons of Nell's nightmares could be beneath the Dower House was terrifying. The knowledge that while he and Nell slept less than a mile away unspeakable things were being done to innocent victims horrified him.

Slipping into bed beside Nell a few moments later, Julian pulled her close to him, needing the warmth of her soft body to drive out the chill. She slept deeply, not even stirring when he pressed a kiss to her temple. His hand caressed the growing mound that concealed their child and with her and their child safe in his arms for a little while, the evil went away and he fell asleep.

Cradled against her husband's big body Nell moaned and fought against the insidious power of the nightmare that seemed to have had her trapped in its talons for hours. In the nightmare, different from any other she'd ever experienced, she was confronted by inky blackness, unable to see or even guess where she was. Walls closed in on her and she had the sensation that she was in a narrow passage of some sort. With a spurt of fright, she sensed that the Shadow Man lurked nearby, concealed in that veil of darkness. She could not see him, but she could *feel* him, could hear him breathing as if he was standing next to her. She knew that the Shadow Man was *there* in the darkness. And he was waiting . . . for her? She shuddered, a scream rising in her throat at the mere idea that somehow she had become his next target, but the nightmare held her too tightly in its grip and the scream died stillborn.

The total darkness terrified her, that and the certain knowledge that the Shadow Man was standing there listening, calculating his next move. He stood for what felt like hours but finally he moved—Nell could hear the rustle of his garments—and a second later pale light flickered from the small torch he'd lit. In the faint light Nell could see now that he was standing in a narrow hall with stone steps that led downward. The walls were the familiar smoke-stained stones of other nightmares and she realized that they were in the passageway leading to the dungeon.

With sure steps the Shadow Man rushed down the stairs, the passageway ending at a gated entrance. He pushed open the iron gate and stepped inside the dungeon. Nell braced herself for the sight of another victim, but to her relief, except for the Shadow Man, the dungeon was empty. His black cloak swirled around his tall, broad-shouldered form as he lit another, larger torch that hung on the wall. For a split second she had a glimpse of his profile, but a scarlet scarf obscured the lower half of his face and with his wide-brimmed black hat pulled low on his forehead, he could have been any one of a dozen men.

Suppressed violence emanated from him as he prowled the confines of the dungeon before stopping beside the slab that dominated the area. His back was to her and she watched, mesmerized by revulsion and terror, as time and again he caressed the blood-stained slab where so many of his victims had screamed away their lives, his hand moving over the stone like a lover's.

For once not distracted by the plight of a victim, Nell studied the Shadow Man intently, trying to imprint in her mind anything that would help her identify him when she was awake. What was there about him that made him unique? she wondered. What would make him identifiable?

As if sensing her concentration, he froze. Slowly he turned his head and looked over his shoulder directly into her eyes. The scarf and hat almost totally hid his features, leaving uncovered only a narrow band above and below his eyes, but those eyes, those mad, malevolent eyes met and held hers. Stark terror filled her as their gazes locked and a terrible knowledge shook her. *He could see her!* She watched the dawning awareness strike him, saw the widening of his eyes, the realization flooding through him. Then, as if a candle was blown out, the image vanished and she hurtled free of the nightmare.

The horror of what had just happened was too powerful for her to escape; she could feel his hand upon her, hear his voice in her ear, and she bolted upright, screaming in mindless terror.

Attune to her in ways Julian had never thought possible, at the first movement of her body, he instantly awakened. It was only seconds, but even before she jerked upright and screamed he had known that she was in the grip of another of those dreadful nightmares. His hand had been on her shoulder and he had been speaking quietly to her when that first scream was ripped from her throat.

Only gradually did Nell realize that the hand on her was Julian's and that it was his voice that she heard and not that of the Shadow Man.

"Nell, sweetheart, wake up," he said softly, his hand caressing her arm and shoulder. "You're safe. You're at home with me. I am by your side. Wake up."

She gulped back a sob and her body shaking, she flung herself into his warm embrace. She tried to speak, but could not—fright made her mute. Under Julian's gentle guidance she fought to compose herself.

"Was it very bad?" he asked, anxiety in his voice.

"A light. Please, a light," she managed. "I cannot bear the darkness."

He left her long enough to light a candle kept near the bed; returning to the bed, he wrapped his arms around her and murmured, "You are safe, darling. I will not let him hurt you."

Against his big body, she shuddered. "You cannot stop him," she said mournfully. She lifted her head and stared at him with horror-clouded eyes. "Julian, he saw me. He knows who I am."

Julian frowned. "What do you mean?"

Terror rushed over her as she relived those awful moments when her gaze had met that of the Shadow Man. Almost gibbering in fright, she shook Julian, crying out, "Don't you understand? *He saw me!* He looked right at me." A sob rose in her throat. "He recognized me. I know he did." She glanced wildly around the room at the shadows dancing ominously in the faint light from the candle, terrified that the monster of her nightmares would step out of the darkness. "He'll come after me. He has to—he knows that I know what he does. He cannot let me live."

"Nell, hush, darling. You're talking nonsense," Julian said

gently, trying to understand and make sense of her words. "How could he see you?"

"I don't know," she answered in a small voice. "But I know that he did. We looked right at each other and I could see in his eyes . . . an awareness . . ."

Excitement in his voice, he said, "But if he looked at you, you must have seen his face, too. Did you recognize him?"

She shook her head. "No. He wore a scarf over the lower half of his face and a hat pulled low across his forehead." A shudder racked her. "I only saw his eyes . . . his horrible, horrible eyes." Her gaze searched his. "You must believe me!"

Julian nodded, thinking of Cesar's description of the man he had followed into the Dower House tonight. Incredible as it seemed, Nell, in her nightmare, had been there with the Shadow Man.

Easing her back from him, Julian said, "Let me get you some brandy and settle you by the fire in my room. We will talk then." He smiled crookedly at her. "You were not the only one to have a sighting of the Shadow Man tonight."

When he would have slid out of the bed, she clutched his arm. "No. Don't leave me—even for a moment."

Picking up the candle, he held out a hand and said, "Then come with me."

In his room he stirred up the fire, adding wood from the neat stack held ready. He lit several more candles and after grabbing a blanket from the bed and wrapping Nell in it, he nestled her in a chair near the now cheerfully burning fire. He shrugged into a robe and poured them both generous snifters of brandy. Taking the chair next to hers, he asked, "Which of us shall go first?"

"You," Nell said quickly, wishing to put off the moment of reliving her nightmare.

Julian nodded and related all that had happened that evening.

When he had finished speaking, she exclaimed, "Oh, to think that you were that close to catching him!"

"Believe me," Julian said, "I've wished a thousand times that we had known what Cesar was about earlier. If we'd all been working together . . ." He shook his head. "It is unfortunate, but we have learned something from tonight: the Dower House holds significance for him."

"You think that the dungeons of my nightmare are in the Dower House?"

"Yes, I do. It is the only thing that makes sense. And tomorrow I intend to start looking for them."

"There must be a passage from inside the house," Nell said slowly. "When the nightmare began, he was in what seemed like a tunnel, a very narrow passageway. I know now from what you have told me that he was hiding there and listening for Cesar. He waited there a long time, I assume, wanting to make certain that it was safe before he continued on into the dungeon."

His gaze on her face, Julian asked quietly, "Can you talk about it now?"

Nell took a big gulp of her brandy. "Yes. Yes, I can. I must." And so she told him all that had occurred in her nightmare, her voice breaking only a little when she described the moment when she had looked into the eyes of a madman.

When she finished speaking, Julian asked, "I do not doubt you, sweetheart, do not think it, but are you certain that he actually *saw* you?"

Nell nodded. "Oh, yes. He saw me. I cannot describe it to you, but I *know* that he saw me, that he knew me."

Frowning, Julian stared into his half-empty snifter. "I do not understand the half of it, but it would seem that the link between you is no longer one way." He glanced at her, cursing under his breath when he saw the terror in her face. Setting down his snifter, he rose from his chair and in one easy movement scooped her up. Resettling himself in the chair by the fire, with her in his lap, his strong arms holding her securely, he said fiercely, "Nell, I will not let him hurt you! I swear it."

She buried her head into his shoulder, her hair tickling his chin. "Without locking me up or putting me under guard I do not see how you can protect me."

"Don't be ridiculous!" he snapped, fear sharpening his tone. "He is not going to snatch you out of your very home. You are safe here."

She smiled sadly. "Perhaps. Do not forget: I did not recognize him. Even though I stared into his face tonight I could see nothing beyond those eyes of his. We know little beyond the fact that he is a tall man, a well-built man, in the prime of life—that description could fit hundreds of men."

Julian could not argue with her and for the first time he was frightened. Terrified that this nameless monster would tear her from his arms, and instinctively they tightened around her. No, he vowed, the Shadow Man shall not have her.

The next week that followed was tense and frustrating. Julian was up at first light pouring over all the old construction plans that had been stored in his library. He'd never paid them any heed but he'd been excited to discover that his great-grandfather had been a meticulous preserver of the past. And when his hand had closed around a fragile roll marked "Dower House" he was certain that the mysterious location of the dungeon would soon be revealed. It was not. The plans he scanned dealt with the building of the covered walkway that connected the kitchen to the main house. He found nothing that gave him a clue as to the location of the dungeons or any sign that there had ever been dungeons at the Dower House.

Disappointed but not discouraged, Julian set out for the Dower House, determined to find the entrance to the dungeons that he knew must exist. Finding the workmen busy with the renovations, he dismissed them with little explanation, telling them that work was suspended indefinitely. Grimly, he probed and poked and prodded every wall, every nook and cranny that might have concealed a secret entrance. Aided by the knowledge gleaned from Nell's night-mare, he was convinced that the entrance to the dungeon had to be somewhere within the Dower House. Day after day he searched the interior of the Dower House but to his increasing frustration and anxiety he found nothing.

Those days were no less anxious and frustrating for Nell. Not one given to hysterics, Nell found herself starting at the slightest sound or movement, and unless Julian was at her side she rarely strayed beyond the main rooms of the house. Fear was her companion and it shadowed her every step. There was never a moment that she was not aware of danger, not aware that the Shadow Man was there, perhaps watching her, planning his next move . . .

Despite her fear, she tried to prevail upon Julian to let her accompany him to the Dower House to search for the entrance, but he was adamantly against it. Glaring at her, he growled, "Under no circumstances do I want you setting foot in the blasted house! The entrance to the dungeons is somewhere within and wherever it is, it is well hidden. I'm not having him spirit you away when my back is turned."

She made a face and only her growing child kept her from arguing with him. She had not only herself to protect but a child as well, and aware that her pregnancy made her dangerously vulnerable she did not protest further.

Lady Diana had been puzzled by Julian's dismissal of the workmen, but she had merely looked shy and murmured, "Since it appears that I may not live there after all, perhaps it is for the best."

Julian grinned at her and lightly pinched her cheek. "Be happy, little puss—Father would have wanted you to be."

"Of course," she said quickly, a faint blush staining her cheeks, "nothing is settled. Do not think that it is."

"Of course not," Julian replied gravely, a twinkle in his eyes, and her blush deepened before she hurried away.

*   *   *

Elizabeth was a different matter and one morning not long after that, Julian was surprised by a visit from her. It was awkward, as his stepsister found him down on his knees in the library of the Dower House poking around in the back of a bookcase.

Amazement on her face, she asked, "What on earth! What are you doing?"

Rising to his feet with what dignity he could muster, Julian dusted the knees of his breeches and turning to look at her, he mumbled, "I, er, was, ah, checking for signs of, um, termites."

Elizabeth looked unconvinced. "You don't think that the workmen would have discovered some sign by now?"

Julian shrugged. "It never hurts to make certain of some things," he said.

Hands on her hips she studied him. "You have been acting most strange lately. Nell can hardly take a step that she is not shadowed by you, and when Mother and I want to take a perfectly safe walk through the lower gardens, you insist that one of the footmen accompany us. You hover over us as if you expect a monster to leap out and attack us. What is going on?"

"Nothing!" He forced a smile, for once wishing that Elizabeth was not quite so intelligent. "I did not realize that I was 'hovering' over you. Put it down to expectant-father nerves."

She hooted. "You?"

He nodded shamefaced. "I find that the thought of impending fatherhood has made me most protective."

"As if you were not before." When he offered nothing more, she stood on her tiptoes and pressed a kiss on his cheek. "Very well, I will not tease you further, but do please try to curb your, er, protectiveness."

Elizabeth probably suspected that there was more to it than that, but she appeared to accept his explanation and Julian was relieved. Keeping Nell out of danger was hair-raising enough, but if he was faced with two determined damsels . . .

Smiling at Elizabeth, he said, "Will you call it 'protective-ness' if I escort you back to the house?"

She wrinkled her nose at him, but allowed him to walk her back to the house.

Though Julian, Charles and Cesar took turns watching the Dower House, there was no further sign of the man in the cloak, and as the days passed, Charles grew disgruntled.

Accompanying his stepmother and brother one day when they came to call on the ladies of Wyndham Manor, Charles paid his respects and then inquired after Julian. Informed that Julian was at the Dower House, Charles decided that listening to his stepmother prattle on about Raoul as an infant, and watching Raoul flirt with Elizabeth was not to his liking, so he excused himself and set off to find Julian.

He found him outside wandering around the back of the house, specifically poking around the parts of the old foundation that had been incorporated into the new kitchen wing.

"What are you doing?" Charles asked as he walked up.

Julian started. "Must you creep up on a fellow so?" he demanded testily.

Charles's eyebrow rose. "I didn't realize that I was 'creep-ing' up on you."

"You weren't," Julian admitted. "I think it is the thought of our cloaked stranger creeping about that prompted my comment. I apologize."

"None needed." Charles nodded to the foundation that had appeared to hold Julian's attention. "What are you look-ing for?"

Julian hesitated. Keeping Nell's secret was playing havoc with his instincts to let Charles and Cesar know what they were up against and he struggled with a way to give them a hint without revealing all. An idea occurred to him and he said, "I've been thinking about the way that Cesar said that our man disappeared—as if by magic—that night. Granted the house was in darkness, but what if there was a secret stairway or a secret compartment?"

"Have you been reading one of those gothicky novels from the Minerva Press?" Charles asked suspiciously.

Julian grimaced. "No. But think about it. If there was a secret passage, it would explain how he just seemed to disappear."

Charles did not appear convinced, but he shrugged and said, "Very well. Where have you looked so far?"

"Everywhere," Julian replied disgustedly. "I've spent the past week sticking my nose into every crevice and cranny I can find. You see me reduced to kicking at the foundation."

"Then you've overlooked it," Charles said, adding dryly, "if it exists."

"It does," Julian said grimly. "It has to—it is the only explanation."

Watching Raoul pay court to Elizabeth was not one of Nell's favorite pastimes, either, and this afternoon was no different. He'd been at the house nearly every day this week and his courtship of Elizabeth was becoming quite marked. Whether it was because Nell would pity any young woman saddled with Mrs. Weston for a mother-in-law or simply because she wished to see Elizabeth established with gentleman with more to offer than Raoul Weston, she could not say. Raoul was handsome and personable, but he was not a landed gentleman, and while he had a generous allowance from his mother and would one day inherit a large fortune from her, Nell would have preferred a gentlemen who already had his own estate, and perhaps . . . a title? She smiled to herself, understanding for the first time her father's desire to see her settled with a man of means and position.

Nell was not sorry to see the Westons leave and with her first really genuine smile of the afternoon, she bid them goodbye as they drove away at a smart pace in a small closed carriage. Shortly afterward, Lady Diana and Elizabeth left on a visit to the squire's wife.

After waving Lady Diana and Elizabeth away, Nell realized that except for the servants, she was alone in the house. Some of her terror following the latest nightmare had faded but she remained uneasy. Today was no different and she suddenly wished that Julian had returned or that she'd gone with Lady Diana and Elizabeth. Which is ridiculous, she decided firmly, her spine stiffening. She was perfectly safe. And she had no intention of doing anything foolish. Chiding herself for being silly, she turned toward the gardens, reminding herself that there were a dozen servants within the sound of her voice.

It was a lovely day for a stroll in the gardens and walking down the steps Nell entered by a path at the right side of the house. After several minutes of wandering through the neatly maintained grounds, she found a stone bench near a small pool shaded by some willows and sat down, enjoying the sound of the bees and the scent of lilacs and roses that perfumed the air. The gentle murmur of the insects and the warmth of the day had a drugging effect and before she knew it, Nell's head drooped and she dozed off.

She woke with a start and nearly jumped out of her skin when she discovered Mrs. Weston sitting beside her on the bench.

Patting her hand, Mrs. Weston said, "Ah, I did not mean to startle you, *petite.*"

Fighting off the remaining vestiges of sleep, Nell sat up straighter and murmured, "I must have nodded off for a moment." She frowned. "Did you forget something?"

Mrs. Weston smiled and said, "*Mais oui!* It is so fortunate that I spied you sleeping here in the garden and did not have to have your so-proper Dibble announce me." The smile faded and with those shiny black cobra eyes fixed on Nell's face, Mrs. Weston said, "And now, *ma amie*, before anyone discovers that I have returned, I think it is time that we were

going, don't you? This has been postponed long enough."
Her voice hardened. "Ten years too long."

Horror washed over Nell as comprehension struck. Her
voice hushed, she said, "It was *you* that day! You were the
one who hit me in the back of the head." Her eyes widened.
"And that means ..." She swallowed, unable to say the
words aloud.

Mrs. Weston stood up. "We shall have time to talk later,
but for now, you shall come with me quietly or I shall shoot
you."

Nell rose slowly to her feet, her eyes on the small pistol
held in Mrs. Weston's hand. Only one thing was clear to
Nell: She was *not* going anywhere with Mrs. Weston. Not,
she thought sickly, as long as she was alive. And if she could
keep Mrs. Weston talking ...

"Why?" she asked. "Why did he kill John?"

Mrs. Weston looked impatient. "Because my eldest stepson was a fool and determined that my son marry some un-
washed farmer's daughter. The little slut had been stupid
enough to get with child and thought to entrap my Raoul."
Her face darkened. "My Raoul. My son! Married to a common farmer's daughter."

"And he killed his brother for *that?*" Nell demanded incredulously.

"It doesn't matter," snapped Mrs. Weston. "Enough! Start
walking toward the back of the garden. He is waiting there
for us with the coach."

Her feet rooted to the spot, as much from fear as from
sheer determination, Nell said, "No. Not until you answer
some questions."

Mrs. Weston's fingers tightened on the pistol and Nell feared
she'd be shot where she stood. Better that, she thought wildly,
than to be torn apart by Raoul Weston ... the Shadow Man.

Confronted by Nell's obstinate stance, Mrs. Weston found
her attitude unexpected and she appeared uncertain as to her
next move. Glaring at Nell, she said, "Raoul didn't mean to

kill John. Raoul was only going to talk to him, to make him see that he was carrying honor to a ridiculous degree. But John would not have it. He spouted some nonsense about not having another such as the Old Earl in the family. He swore that Raoul was going to do the honorable thing and marry her—or he'd tell their father. They came to blows and John . . . died."

"And me? You tried to kill me—and nearly succeeded."

"What else could we do? You had stumbled into something that was none of your business. We could not leave you alive to tell everyone what you had seen." An expression of hatred crossed Mrs. Weston's face. "That you lived is a miracle. That you reappeared in our lives, married to my nephew was beyond bad luck. The agonies Raoul and I have suffered, fearing that you would remember something and recognize him. You should be dead and done with and this time we shall not fail." She took a step forward, motioning with the pistol. "You either walk to the back of the garden or I'll shoot you where you stand."

Growing up in a household of males had some advantages, Nell thought savagely as her fist came up and she socked Mrs. Weston with as pretty a right hook as there ever was.

Mrs. Weston rocked back on her heels and went down like a sack of cabbages.

Despite the clumsiness of her pregnancy, Nell was on her like a tigress on an ox and she tore the pistol from Mrs. Weston's grip. The pistol held firmly in her own hand, she struggled to her feet.

Breathing heavily, she stood over Mrs. Weston's prone form long enough to see that the woman was out cold. Nell was turning to run to the house when the world exploded in her head. As everything went dark, she thought, Raoul, I forgot about Raoul . . .

Chapter 22

Nell woke with a blinding headache in pitch-darkness. Dizzy and disoriented, she groped to make sense of her situation. She was lying down and as she struggled into an upright position she puzzled over the fact that her hands were tied and that she was lying on the floor . . . on a stone floor . . . and then she knew. She *knew*.

Fear clawed up her throat and with a low whimper she fought it back. She was in the dungeon. The Shadow Man's domain.

Fright blasted any lingering dizziness from her brain and sitting on the floor she awkwardly scooted as far back as she could. Only when her back touched a wall did she stop.

For a moment, she wondered why she'd not been gagged . . . But then she realized—because it doesn't matter. Because, like those other poor women, I could scream until kingdom come and it wouldn't make a parcel of difference. No one can hear me.

Terror churned in her breast, but she vowed not to let it overcome her. Concentrate. Concentrate on getting free. At least then you'll stand a chance. Against two? A shudder went through her. In her nightmares it had been only the Shadow Man . . . Raoul. Pray God that his wretched mother doesn't come with him.

Working at the ropes that held her hands together in front

of her, she listened intently for any sound. Think, she told herself. Think. Raoul hit you. He and his mother have brought you to the dungeon. But how long ago was that? What time is it now? How long have you been here? And where exactly in the dungeon are you?

She gnawed at the ropes to no avail. The knots were tight and after several fruitless moments she gave up. Head back against the wall she stared into utter blackness.

You're in the dungeon. But where? Struggling to her feet, keeping her back to the wall, she traversed her prison, gasping in surprise when she reached the iron bars. From her nightmares, she vaguely remembered that there were two small cells that faced the main area. She was in one of them.

Further, cautious exploration gave her the dimensions of her cell. She calculated that it was less than eight feet square with three stone walls and the bars across the front. It was also empty—there was nothing in it that she could use for a weapon.

Defeated for the moment, she slumped against the wall near the bars and began to gnaw again at the knots that kept her hands tied. Freeing her hands wouldn't help her situation, but it would certainly make her feel better and at least she would not be completely helpless. With renewed vigor her teeth bit into the coarse rope.

While her teeth were busy with the knots, she considered a timeline. It had been late afternoon when she had been taken. The greatest danger to the Westons had been getting her from the garden into the coach, but once that was done they were safe.

She frowned. Julian had been at the Dower House so she doubted that they'd headed immediately for it. No. They'd wait until he had left. It was unlikely that they'd risk moving her from the coach to the house until it was dark, so several hours had to have passed.

By now the alarm would have been raised, and a trickle of warmth ebbed through her. At this very moment Julian was looking for her and he would move Heaven and Earth to find her. That thought comforted her and energized her efforts to free herself.

A thrill passed through her when she felt one of the knots loosen just the faintest bit. Feverishly she worked at the knot and a moment later it came undone. It took her several more minutes, but eventually, she managed to free her hands.

Feeling more confident, she stood up again, one hand touching her belly where her baby grew. More than her own life was at stake, she reminded herself. Julian would come for her. She knew this. All she had to do was keep herself and their baby alive. Julian would raise the alarm and people would be looking for her.

Nell was not wrong. Coming home from the Dower House, Julian had been greeted by Lady Diana and Elizabeth who'd returned only moments before from their visit to Squire Chadbourne's. Leaving them in the front parlor, he'd gone in search of his wife, thinking she was napping in her bedroom. Not finding her, with increasing anxiety, he'd raced through the house looking for her, eventually enlisting the entire household in the search. When a search of the house, the grounds, the gardens, even the stables produced no sign of Nell, Julian had been like a man possessed. Fighting back his own fear, the nausea that roiled in his gut, he'd ordered nearly every man, woman and child on the estate to start looking for Nell, keeping only Lady Diana, Elizabeth, Dibble and a skeleton staff at the house.

Lady Diana was quick to organize a chart to keep track of all the search parties and their locations. To Julian she said, "All information must come here. We need to know what is going on everywhere so that we can get word of changes to the others as soon as possible." She smiled gently at Julian. "Never fear. We shall find her. I am sure that she has just wandered off farther than she meant to and will, no doubt, when we find her be much embarrassed to have caused such a fuss. Do not worry, my lord."

That part of the operation under way, Julian had sent word to Charles, the squire and Lord Beckworth that Nell was missing and that he desperately needed their help in finding her. In a matter of a few hours an army of volunteers from the outlying areas had been gathered and had joined the search. Unwilling to trust anyone for fear he could be talking to the Shadow Man himself, he kept his terror tightly leashed. No one seeing his grim face, however, had any doubts that there was something very serious afoot.

Charles and Raoul answered the call immediately and were among the first of the neighbors to arrive. After Charles told Raoul to join the group of people just leaving to search the north woods, and that he would catch up with him as soon as he'd seen Julian, he bounded up the steps and into the manor. Inside he nearly collided with Julian in the entry hall. Having done what he could at the house, Julian was preparing to leave to begin his own search. Charles took one look at Julian's face and grasping his arm, said calmly, "Do not fear. We shall find her. She has probably simply gotten lost in the woods."

His voice full of suppressed fear and rage, Julian said, "Yes, we shall . . . and if anything has happened to her . . ." He took a deep breath. "This is connected to the man in the cloak," he said flatly. "I am on my way to the Dower House. We must find how he disappeared so easily even if I have to take that damn house apart brick by brick."

Charles frowned. "You think that he has abducted her?"

"Yes. Believe me when I say that Nell would not have wandered off—not willingly." Julian ran a hand through his disordered hair. "I cannot explain everything to you right now, but there are reasons, good reasons why I believe that this is true." He closed his eyes. "Charles, if you love me, do not ask questions, only know that my wife is in danger of losing her life and that the only way to find her is to find the trail of the man in the cloak."

Charles nodded curtly. "Very well. Let us be off."

Turning to an anxious Dibble who had just entered the hall, Julian said, "Should word come—*any* word—we shall be at the Dower House."

Dibble nodded.

As they exited the house, Julian asked, "Are you armed?"

"Always," Charles said.

Once at the Dower House, they concentrated their efforts in the area near the kitchen, the place where Cesar had lost the man in the cloak. His features taut, Julian tackled the wall in front of him, prepared if necessary to tear the house apart, stone by stone, board by board . . .

Nell glimpsed the faint flicker of light in the blackness and swallowed back a gasp. The Shadow Man was coming! She could hear footsteps approaching and like a dove mesmerized by a viper, she watched as the yellow glow increased and came closer. Shrinking back against the stone walls, she tried to melt into them and disappear.

The footsteps stopped in front of the cell and light flooded her prison. Nell blinked, blinded by the sudden light. After a second she could make out the form of the man standing behind the lantern and her heart raced.

"Well, well, well, what have we here?" Raoul drawled from behind the lantern. "Why, can it be? Her ladyship?" He laughed. "You'll be happy to know that your husband is tearing up Heaven and Earth trying to find you." He laughed again. "But he won't . . . at least not in time."

Nell slowly stood up. Throttling back her fear, she said coolly, "I would not be so certain. He knows about this place . . . and what you do. He *will* find it—and you."

"And if he does," said Mrs. Weston, stepping beside her

son, "then he shall die—which will be just as well. My son will make an exceptional Earl of Wyndham."

"Aren't you forgetting Charles?" Nell asked, not even surprised by their mad plan. "Even if you kill me, my husband and my child, Charles will still be in your way."

Raoul laughed. "Believe me, I have not forgotten Charles." He appeared to think about it. "Charles, I fear, will have a tragic accident. A fatal one this time."

Something niggled at the back of Nell's brain. Something about Charles having the Devil's own luck . . . She gasped. "The yacht. *You* did that!"

Turning away, Raoul hung the lantern from a peg on the wall. "Oh, yes. That was indeed my work. He's proven to be a tricky bastard to kill, but I'll get that chore done soon enough." He paused. "Not too soon, though—we don't want to arouse any suspicions."

"He's your brother! How can you?"

"Half brother," snapped Mrs. Weston. "And I would worry about your own fate if I were you and not waste any time over the demise of my stepson."

Nell glanced at her and couldn't help being pleased to see that Mrs. Weston sported a beautiful purple and black bruise on one side of her face.

Mrs. Weston caught her expression and her lips thinned. "You think you are so clever catching me by surprise like that, but you were not clever enough to escape from my son, were you?"

Nell shrugged. "At least I didn't act like a coward and sneak around and hit you from behind."

"My son is no coward!" spat Mrs. Weston, her face darkening with fury.

Wondering if she could use Mrs. Weston's blind devotion to her son in some way, Nell pushed harder. "I beg to differ with you. Anyone who attacks those weaker than himself can be nothing but a coward." Her gaze slid to Raoul. "A skulking, repulsive coward who hides in the dark and is only brave when his victim is helpless and held powerless."

For a moment, Nell thought she'd gone too far. Mrs. Weston was gripping the bars of the cell as if she'd tear them apart with her bare hands. Panting with rage, Mrs. Weston said, "Brave words. Wait until he has you under the knife, then you won't have such a saucy mouth on you."

Quelling the spurt of fear that went through her, Nell asked carelessly, "Would you like to place a wager on that? Or aren't you going to stay for the finale? Too messy for you?"

Raoul walked up to the bars. "Yes, I'm afraid that's the case," he said easily. He looked fondly at Mrs. Weston. "Poor mother—she has a queasy stomach."

"You've known all along what he does here?" Nell asked, horrified.

Mrs. Weston shrugged. "Of course. I do not approve of his, ah, amusements, but it gives him pleasure. Those women were nothing, only stupid creatures of the *canaille*. Piffle. They are better off dead." She stared at Nell. "As you will be very soon."

"But she has to answer a question for me first," Raoul said. His expression puzzled, he asked, "What happened between us the other night? You saw me and I saw you. How is that possible? I could feel someone watching me and when I looked around, I saw your face. Is it some sort of magic? Witchcraft?"

Nell considered not telling him, but in the end she said simply, "I don't know—I only know that since that day you threw me over the cliffs that I have had some sort of . . . link with you . . . with the violence you do here."

He looked uneasy and angry at the same time. "Whatever it is," he said, "it ends tonight."

Inserting the key into the lock on the cell, Raoul unlocked the door and pushed it open. So frightened she could hardly breathe, Nell backed away from him as he stepped inside.

Don't make it easy for him, she told herself. Don't let him walk away unscathed. Kick him! Bite him! Scratch him! Mark him! Fight for your life!

As the moments passed and he and Charles discovered nothing to help them, Julian's rage and fear and frustration built until he thought he would explode with it all. Sledgehammer in hand, he struck again and again at the seemingly solid wall before him, fighting to hold his emotions in check. He was working in a promising spot at the back of the old kitchen pantry, something about the way the wall was constructed having aroused his attention. Besides, he thought viciously, attacking mortar and brick is the only thing keeping me sane. Nell was in there somewhere. Held captive, perhaps even being tortured by the Shadow Man at this very moment. Only rigid control kept him from howling aloud in fear and misery. I have to find her! I promised her. I swore I would keep her safe!

He and Charles had given up on probing carefully for a secret entrance and had opted for brute-force demolition. He'd already wasted days looking for the bloody catch, latch, whatever it might be that revealed the entrance he knew existed and hadn't found anything and now they'd run out of time. Utter destruction was the only way.

And yet no one was more astonished than he was when his heavy sledgehammer suddenly smashed though the wall and instead of finding himself in another room or staring outside, he was looking into yawning blackness. His heart nearly leaped out of his chest, and throwing aside the hammer he yelled for Charles.

Charles, busy elsewhere in the kitchen, ran to his side. Together the two men stared at the opening.

"Well, I'll be damned," said Charles. "There really is a secret entrance."

"You didn't believe it?" Julian asked as he began to tear bricks out of the way to widen the hold.

"Not really," Charles admitted. "But you seemed so convinced and Cesar's story made sense so I believed in the *possibility* of it."

"Well, help me clear this *possibility* so we may go down it."

With the entrance breached, it took them only a moment to find the mechanism that worked the door. The damaged door swung slowly open revealing the narrow stairs that Nell had seen in her nightmare.

When Charles would have taken a candle, Julian shook his head. "No. He must have no warning that we are coming."

Charles stared at him. "You are certain that he's down there."

"Yes. And that he means to murder to my wife." Foot on the first step he pulled free his pistol from his clothes and looking back at Charles said, "Have your weapon ready—we are going after a monster. This man is a killer, a vicious murderer. Do not hesitate when dealing with him because he will kill us if he can."

Charles studied him a moment. "There is more to this than you have told me."

"Yes. And I apologize—it is not my tale to tell—just believe me when I tell you that this man murdered your brother and countless innocent women. He is a monster."

Charles's eyes turned icy. "You know that he killed John?"

When Julian nodded, Charles's hand tightened on his pistol. "Then lead on—I've waited a long time to meet this bastard."

Nell fought valiantly but she was no match for Raoul and Mrs. Weston. She was determined not to make it easy it for them, and her teeth, fingernails and feet had left both Westons bloodied by the time Raoul managed to wrestle her from the cell and throw her across the room into the main part of the dungeon. She landed heavily on the floor, groaning in pain as her body met the unyielding stone, but she could take satisfaction from the damage she'd inflicted. Among other sundry wounds, Raoul's handsome face was now marred by a long, bloody gash where she'd clawed his cheek; his right ear bled freely courtesy of her teeth and his lower lip was split where she'd butted him with her head. Mrs. Weston had added a cut eyebrow and a blackening eye to the ever-widening bruise on her jaw. They will have trouble explaining those marks away, Nell thought grimly, attempting to get to her feet.

"Infernal bitch!" Raoul shouted, his fingers feeling along the gash. "You'll pay for that, and pay dearly before I am through with you."

He glanced at his mother. "Mother. Are you hurt?"

Mrs. Weston staggered out of the cell, gasping for breath. "She kicked me. Knocked the air out of me."

Having struggled upright, Nell kept a wary eye on the pair of them. She had not escaped unscathed; her wrists were bloody and bruised from the ropes, her ribs hurt, her gown was ripped from one shoulder and her damn bad leg was aching. A scrape across her chin stung and she knew that eventually her right eye would be as black as Mrs. Weston's—if I live that long, she thought.

Her back against the stone wall she faced the pair of them, considering her next move. Her gaze fell to the floor, resting for a second on the sluice hole off to one side, that same sluice hole where she'd seen Raoul toss so many bodies. From there her eyes traveled to the bloodstained stone slab in the middle of the room and she swallowed painfully. Her nightmares had been accurate, too accurate, she admitted almost hysterically. Images of other women flashed through her mind and she swore that she'd die before she'd allow Raoul to fasten her down on that slab as he had all the others.

Frantically she looked around for a weapon, for anything that could be used as a weapon, but there was nothing. Except . . . Her gaze stopped at the lantern hanging on the wall only a few feet from her hand and at the old debris and rushes upon the floor. Her eyes flickered across the room to the doorway that she knew must lead up the stairs to freedom. *If I could* . . .

Raoul noticed the direction of her gaze and laughed. "You'll never make it." An ugly smile crossed his face. "But go ahead—the chase will add a certain piquancy to the outcome."

"Just kill her and be done with it," said Mrs. Weston. "You cannot be gone long or you will be missed and your absence commented on."

Raoul touched his face. "This will have to be explained. I cannot return looking like this."

"This is all your fault," Mrs. Weston hissed, glaring at Nell. "If you'd never married my nephew none of this would have happened. You've nearly ruined everything. Everything."

Nell stared. This was *her* fault?

"I fail to see how this can be my fault—after all, you brought me here," she pointed out.

"You're in our way," Mrs. Weston said flatly. "It was going to be so simple before you appeared. I had always hoped that fate would allow Raoul to obtain Wyndham's title one day, but in the beginning there were too many people ahead of him for it to become reality. But Julian's wife died leaving him no heir, then John . . . and my husband and Julian's father died. Daniel's death was providential, a stroke of luck, and made us realize that the dream was within our grasp—with Daniel dead, and Julian without an heir, only Charles was between Raoul and the title."

"And no one," added Raoul, "would have been surprised if Charles had died when his yacht sank or if he'd broken his neck in a hunting accident—or even if a jealous husband had killed him. We'd planned for Julian to die a year or two later—when we felt it was safe to kill him without arousing suspicion."

"An accident, of course, and then my son would have been the earl," said Mrs. Weston, the complacent note in her voice making Nell wish she could get her hands around the other woman's neck. "Wyndham would have been his." She shot Nell a vicious look. "But then you came along. You and that brat you carry, and nearly ruined everything."

"I'm surprised," Nell muttered, "that you didn't kill me before this."

"Well, I would have," admitted Raoul carelessly, "but it had to look like an accident and you were never alone. You were always safely within Wyndham Manor or with one of my cousins or Lady Diana and Miss Forest. There was never a good opportunity to arrange things to my satisfaction." He shrugged and added, "If it weren't for that . . . that thing that happened the other night—your ability to watch me—if not for that I would have waited for a better time, but my hand has been forced." A dreamy expression entered his eyes. "But it makes little difference—I did not intend for you to live to give birth, so your time was already short."

It appeared that conversation was at an end and warily Nell tracked Raoul's movements and that of his mother. They were splitting up, coming at her from two different directions. She risked a glance at the lantern hanging so tantalizingly near. Time had run out and Nell knew that if they got their hands on her again, then it was over—she'd die.

Her pregnancy and her bad leg made her clumsy, but with surprising speed and agility she lunged for the lantern, the opposite direction they thought she'd take. Her move caught them off guard and they froze for a split second but it was all the time that Nell needed.

Wrenching the lantern from the wall, Nell pitched it with all the strength she possessed at Mrs. Weston, who was closest to her. It hit Raoul's mother full in the chest, knocking her backward. Fire erupted across the front of Mrs. Weston's dress and shrieking and beating wildly at the flames she tripped and fell to the floor.

Nell forgotten, Raoul cried out and rushed to his mother's side as she rolled on the floor, spreading the fire along the dry rushes and debris. Smoke drifted upward from a dozen smoldering pieces of debris, and taking advantage of the distraction Nell flung herself forward, stumbling and running toward the unprotected doorway.

Seeing what she was about, Raoul leaped for her, catching her hair in one hand. "No!" he screamed. "You'll not escape."

Nell twisted and fought his grasp, heedless of the pain. "Let me go! Let me go!" she shouted, aiming a solid kick at his leg.

Coming down the stairs, Julian heard Nell's voice and with a roar, Charles at his heels, he plunged down the few remaining steps and charged into the room.

Pistols ready, Julian and Charles stopped just inside the dungeon, staring stunned at Raoul holding Nell prisoner by her hair.

Pushing aside his shock and horror at the identity of the Shadow Man, Julian focussed on the only thing that mattered: Nell. "Let her go," he said in a deadly voice. "Let her go now."

His face white, a muscle clenched in his jaw, Charles exclaimed in horror and disbelief, "Raoul? *You* killed John?"

"I had to," said Raoul. "He was going to force me to marry some bloody farmer's daughter and would not listen to reason. He left me no choice."

"Let her go," Julian repeated, his gaze fixed on Raoul.

Raoul smiled and dragged Nell's head back. "Or what? You'll shoot me? I don't think you dare—what if your bullet misses? Are you willing to risk her life?"

Nell winced as he pulled her hair tighter. As long as Raoul had her, they were at a stalemate. Julian or Charles could not risk a shot. She had to do something to tip the balance. Locking her hands together Nell drove her elbow as hard as possible into Raoul's abdomen. The move caught him off guard and he gasped as the breath left his body. His hold on her hair slackened ever so slightly, but it was enough, Nell shot free, running to her husband.

Julian's pistol never wavered as he clamped Nell to his side with his other arm. A dangerous smile on his face, Julian drawled, "I think the situation has changed, don't you?"

"You won't shoot me," Raoul said with a sneer, his hand edging inside his jacket. "I'm your cousin. The great Earl of Wyndham wouldn't want a scandal, now would he?"

Near the stone slab, Mrs. Weston staggered to her feet. She had beaten out the flames and though she had some painful burns, they were not severe—her clothing had protected her from the worst. At her feet a few of the rushes still smoldered, sending wisps of smoke into the air.

"He's right," Mrs. Weston gasped. "How will you explain shooting him? Will you want everyone to know what he does here?"

"And what," asked Charles in a quiet tone, "does my brother do here?"

"Ask her," retorted Raoul, pointing at Nell. "She seems to know everything."

"I have nightmares," said Nell, "and in them I have seen Raoul, although I did not know it was him, murder your brother John near my home and later, kill and torture young women here . . . on that slab."

"Prove it!" taunted Raoul. "I am sure that the earl will enjoy having it known that his wife has dreams, visions like some witch of old. Won't that be wonderful fodder for all your fine friends."

A muscle twitched in Julian's cheek. "You think that I will allow you to escape to protect my name and reputation?" he asked, his pistol never wavering from its target.

"Not your name—but to protect her you would."

He has me there, Julian conceded bitterly. Without revealing Nell's nightmares, there is no proof of what he does—and I cannot shoot the bastard down in cold blood. To protect

Nell, I would do anything, even let a vile creature like Raoul live. But not free, he thought, not free to kill at will. Never that. The solution escaped him at the moment and unbearably aware of Nell's trembling body next to his, all he wanted was to get her from this foul place and away from Raoul's poisonous presence . . . and that of his dear Aunt Sofia. What part she played had yet to be revealed, but it was clear that she was as guilty as her son—at least as far as the abduction of Nell was concerned. As for the other . . . Bile rose in his throat at the knowledge that Mrs. Weston had known and condoned Raoul's actions.

"So what is it to be?" demanded Raoul. "Either kill me or let me go."

"Let us go," urged Mrs. Weston. "We will go away—far away. You will never hear from us again."

The hand Raoul had slipped inside his jacket suddenly came free. Julian glimpsed the pistol in his hand and pushed Nell behind him and fired. The sounds of three shots rang out in the small room, Julian and Charles firing simultaneously.

Raoul's shot went wild, smashing into the wall behind Julian's head, but both Julian and Charles's found their mark. Shot twice in the upper body, Raoul flew backward, falling to the floor near the sluice hole. His expression incredulous he looked at the blood flooding across his waistcoat and then at Charles.

Staring at Charles he muttered, "You've killed me! Me! Your own brother."

His face grim, Charles said levelly, "Yes . . . as you killed our brother."

With a feral shriek Mrs. Weston launched herself at Charles. "My son! My son! You've hurt him! I will kill you!"

Her hands closed around Charles's double-barreled pistol and she sought to turn it against him. She was a strong woman and fury gave her enormous strength as they fought for control of the weapon. Locked in mortal battle they swayed together, their bodies as close as lovers embracing.

Julian shoved Nell aside and leaped to join the fray, but it was over in a second. Between the intertwined bodies of Charles and Mrs. Weston, the pistol exploded. For an agonizing moment they clung together and then, her skirts billowing out around her Mrs. Weston sank to the floor. Her eyelids fluttered once and a moment later she was dead.

Transfixed by horror Charles stared down at the body of his stepmother. "I didn't . . ." he began, took a breath and tried again, "I didn't mean . . . It was an accident."

"No one will think anything different," Julian said, looking down at Mrs. Weston's still form. "Nell and I will testify to what happened." He clasped Charles's shoulder. "I am sorry this had to happen. All of it."

"Julian!" Nell cried. "Look! He's gone."

Julian spun around and looked to where Nell pointed. Taking advantage of their distraction by his mother's attack on Charles, Raoul had disappeared.

Julian cursed and ran to the spot where Raoul had fallen. Shot twice, badly wounded, if not fatally, Julian had thought him disabled, but Raoul had proved him wrong. He followed the widening trail of blood to the sluice hole. The rim was stained with fresh blood, telling its own tale. Rather than face justice, Raoul had thrown himself down the sluice hole . . . the same hole that he had so carelessly thrown the bodies of so many young women. They'd find his body down there, he knew, lying amongst the scattered remains of his victims. It was, Julian thought bleakly, a fitting end to a monster. He glanced back to where Mrs. Weston's body lay. Two monsters, he decided.

Walking back to Nell, he embraced her and then, his wife beside him and followed by Charles, they left the blood and death behind them and climbed up the stairs.

Standing outside the Dower House and staring up at the

glittering stars in the sky, Nell took a deep breath of fresh night air. She ached in every bone in her body, but she was safe. Her hand went to her belly. Feeling a strong kick, she smiled. Dr. Coleman would only confirm what she knew to be true, that her baby was safe. Resting her head against Julian's shoulder, feeling his arm tighten around her, she sighed with contentment. They had won. The monsters had been beaten. Never again would she have to endure another of those horrifying nightmares. The future, bright and shiny, stretched out endlessly before her.

She looked up at Julian, love filling her heart and mind. He glanced down and she saw the same expression on his face that she knew was on her own. He pulled her even closer to him, his eyes warm and tender on hers.

"I failed you, my love," he said. "I promised you that I would keep you safe and I did not."

She smiled mistily at him. "You didn't fail . . . You were only a trifle late—and you came in the end. All that matters now is that we are together and we have our baby and a whole future to look forward to."

"I love you, Nell," he said quietly. "You are my world, my moon, my stars, my everything. I will love you until the day I die—and beyond."

"And I you, my lord," she returned with softly glowing eyes.

"That's all well and good," retorted Charles irascibly, "but could we please get back to your house? There's going to be bloody hell to pay and I'd as lief get it over with."